Safety Harbor

Safety Harbor

Keepers of the Light

CHUCK COOPER

RESOURCE *Publications* • Eugene, Oregon

SAFETY HARBOR
Keepers of the Light

Resource Publications
An Imprint of Wipf and Stock Publishers
199 W. 8th Ave., Suite 3
Eugene, OR 97401

www.wipfandstock.com

PAPERBACK ISBN: 978-1-5326-1388-3
HARDCOVER ISBN: 978-1-5326-1390-6
EBOOK ISBN: 978-1-5326-1389-0

Manufactured in the U.S.A.   APRIL 13, 2017

Rory Cooney is a composer in Lake Zurich, Illinois. His song, *Safety Harbor*, is available at giamusic.com, and his many songs can be found on iTunes. Mr. Cooney has served as Director of Music and Liturgy at Saint Anne Catholic Community in Barrington, Illinois for 23 years.

To my beloved wife, Patty, who has shared herself with me so generously, for many years.

In the beginning when God created the universe.... God
looked . . . and it was good.

Genesis 1:1, 4

Preface

ONE OF THE MOST memorable events in my ministry took place in its earliest days.

"Mother wants to see you," said one of my parishioners, in a small parish I was serving in the Midwest. "Can you come over right away?"

Her mother was on her deathbed.

When I arrived at the house and entered the bedroom where she lay, I asked, "What can I do for you, Mother?"

"I want to know," she said, "that when I cross the Jordan River, Jesus will be waiting for me, on the other side."

I recall no quotes from any theologian or scholar that have been seared into my memory as has that dear woman's words. That plea from the depths of her spirit, in her last days, has stayed with me through all of my years.

The real depth of the spiritual life is not contained within the high echelons of religious institutions or in the public proclamations of the prominent, but in the common life of ordinary people. Here it is, that we live out our lives, with our anxieties, fears, regrets, hopes, and dreams. Here, we wrestle with the great questions of life. If we are open, it is in this living, that the *Mysterium Tremendum* comes to us in many ways and in different forms, and miracles happen.

The story told within these pages is of just such a community of people, who struggle with ambiguous relationships, who wrestle with their demons, who experience loneliness and self-doubt, who are flawed, who live with regret, unbelief, and sorrow. Yet, in spite of life's challenges, they experience joy, healing, and grace, and are capable of noble and heroic deeds.

Welcome to Safety Harbor. I think you'll like it here!

Acknowledgements

My DEEPEST APPRECIATION TO those who generously took the time read my manuscript in its varying stages of development, and who encouraged me to submit my work for publication.

I am grateful to my wife, Dr. Patty Pickett-Cooper, and to Patrick Sousa, for their kindness in editing this manuscript.

Chapter 1

THE SUMMER SUN ROSE over the hills with a surprisingly bright intensity, as if it had been on the job for several hours already. It drove the morning fog away early. The day was still cool, but warming up fast. A sweltering day was in store for the people of Safety Harbor. "Unusual for the Oregon Coast," everybody said, even in the summer. It was the third day of the heat spell.

The regulars at Joe's Diner were sauntering in, and the smell of fresh coffee greeted their nostrils with a jolt that drove away any trace of drowsiness. The sun hit their faces and they shaded their eyes, accustomed to having the morning fog still in, when they arrived.

It was excellent tourist weather and Nate Beard, the operator of The Salty Dog deep sea fishing business, was happy. He would have to eat hurriedly. The line was already forming down at the dock.

Sally Hankins went by him with three breakfast plates in her hands.

"Hey Sal! Take the day off and let's go fishin'!"

Smiling, she shook her head, slightly embarrassed.

It was the same every morning. Almost the same words even. A ritual. She poured him coffee and called out "Two eggs over easy, ham, and wheat toast!"

As with many who walked in, she didn't have to take his order. It was always the same. There was a joy among the mostly good people who assembled there, at the order and predictability of it all.

"Put a rush on that would ya?" said Nate. "There's money linin' up at the dock! I gotta get down there and get it before it gets away!"

From the view through the three large bay windows of the diner, the ocean gave off a beautiful deep hue that seemed to blend seamlessly into the blue sky. A lone kite floated effortlessly, seemingly suspended in midair, in the breeze over the waters.

Wendell Cone sat at his usual third stool from the end of the counter, sipping coffee. If his thin well-dressed frame wasn't there each morning by

6:30, people watched for him until he showed up or until they found out where he was.

Maxine had died a year ago and he still missed her company dreadfully. He woke up early every morning and left the house and some of the emptiness of her absence behind. Although it followed him everywhere, it helped to be with people.

He read *The Wave* at the counter each morning, even though it was published only once a week. His mind would still wander from time to time to memories of the past and he missed many of the details of what he read. He took his time, reading and chatting with those who approached him. The bank didn't open until 9:00 a.m. anyway. And he opened it.

Johnny Watson sauntered in, just home from Rehab. People always hoped the best for him, but had lost track of the number of times he'd gone away for help. The word around town was that his first two marriages had drowned in the sauce and his third was on life support.

Between benders one time, Joe had hired him to repaint the sign on the little cafe. When he finished, Johnny informed Joe that there had been a misspelling in the sign and he had corrected it. There had been an *e* missing, he said. It now read *Joe's Fine Dine-ing*. The hyphen should have been there all along, Johnny had said.

Joe didn't have the heart to tell him differently and paid him anyway. The past two years, he couldn't count the times tourists had come in and told him the name was spelled wrong on the sign.

"Well, now you will remember us," Joe always said. "Make sure you tell your friends when they come to town, to look for the cafe that doesn't know how to spell, but they sure do have good food and wonderful hospitality!"

It had worked. People had started taking pictures of it and sending it on to others on their cell phones. Joe's Fine Dine-ing had become a bit of an icon.

Now, because business had increased by thirty percent since the sign painting, Johnny Watson and his brother Hobe, who had held the ladder for the now infamous painting affair, got free coffee when they came in each morning. Joe had set no time limit on it, so Johnny and Hobe assumed it was a "for life" kind of thing.

Here and now, just after 6:30 in the morning, the diner was mercifully devoid of tourists and the townspeople had their meeting place back for a little while. For a few precious moments, people could just be who they are together.

Susanna Kappos always arrived at 6:43 a.m. A dark-haired Greek beauty in her thirties, she was recently widowed. When Nicholas was alive, he'd make the coffee and she always served him breakfast right at 6:43 a.m.

It had started one morning when Nick noticed that they had sat down to breakfast at that same time now for three mornings in a row. From then on, it was ritual. 6:43 a.m. No sooner—no later. If she arrived a little early at Joe's, she sat in her car until it was time. Now that he was gone, killed in a car accident, it helped her feel close to him, and at the same time, she got herself out of the house, same as Wendell.

Meanwhile, she had thrown herself into her work. With the help of an improving economy, the Argostoli Art Gallery, named after Susanna's home town on an island off Greece, had begun to thrive. Lately, she'd had to hire on some help.

Still, life felt more vacant than not for her. Nothing could fill up the hole in her heart that Nick had left. You could work hard and be around people, nice people, and still in the end you ended up going home alone. A great sadness sometimes manifested itself on her face.

She'd brought Joe some Greek coffee one time and offered to supply him with enough for a year if he would serve it in the morning, along with cheese and yogurt. She'd have that and some olives and boiled eggs for breakfast along with orange juice, just what Nick and she had eaten together every morning of their short married life.

Joe named the new Greek breakfast plate, Susanna's Special. It had proven to be a success, especially with the out-of-towners. Some of the morning locals had even departed from their usual order, at least once, just to please the beautiful young woman who seemed so unbearably sad.

Father Frank Callaghan, of Our Lady of the Harbor, was, by now, intensely engaged in conversation with Jeremy Woods, the new owner of De-light-full Bookshop, which boasted a coffee bar with free Wi-Fi. Soon, Lou Schofield, the mayor, and his wife Hope, a local teacher and artist, joined them in their booth.

Then, the Rev Meriwether Starhawk, of the Mystical Waters Spiritual Community, appeared. She had a way of doing that. She came in so quietly that hardly anyone ever saw her actually come in the place. Lately, she'd been joining Susanna at her table.

Katye Puckett, the local free-spirited professor at Coast Range Community College, and one of the few people of color in the town, came in to get an Americano-to-go. She was soon hand-signaled over by Meriwether.

"I haven't long." she said. "I've got errands to run and papers to grade."

Rev. Luther Hodges of the Always Sunny Free Will Holiness Church and the Reverend Wesley Harrington, Protestant Chaplain at Harbor View Hospital, showed up about ten after seven. Father Callaghan pulled a couple more chairs up to their table to accommodate them. It was crowded, but ecumenical.

There were more to come, including Johnny and Hobe, of course. Finally, the whole band of breakfast crew was there, minus one, by 7:30 a.m. Doc Bailey had been called to Harbor View Community Hospital for an emergency. People felt badly about their sentiments, but they hoped it was a tourist and none of their own.

Nobody ever saw Joe much. Some had never seen him. He was too busy in the back, cooking, organizing, and making sure everyone got their orders just as they wanted them. Even at other times when he'd come out to the dining room, he was a man of a few words. People paid attention when he spoke.

An enigmatic figure, people weren't quite sure of his origins. He never clarified that mystery and they were content to leave it alone. They figured there must be something personal Joe was keeping to himself. They so respected him, that, if anybody started to gossip about it, they were immediately hushed.

A line of tourists would form at the front of Joe's until about 9:00 a.m. when most of the locals would have gone home, or to work, or somewhere else. Joe could have made more money had he rushed them out for more volume; but Joe's Fine Dine-ing was about more than being a business, especially from six-thirty to nine in the morning. For a while, a little community assembled there.

For now, the quiet hum of the refrigerators and other appliances in the cafe had been overrun by the chatter of the early morning voices as people sat in twos and threes and sometimes fours. The clatter of coffee cups and the tinkling of spoons and the aroma of cooking food and human kindness went on and on in one of the few places left on the face of the earth, it seemed, where, as Joe said, "When you come inside, you are who you are, and if you have any, you leave your pretensions along with your self-importance outside."

With its white clapboard exterior, red trimmed bay windows, and simple wooden front stoop, Joe's Fine Dine-ing could well have been from another time. And perhaps it was. But it didn't know it, so it just kept on being who it was. And when the people went inside, they weren't so much from another time, as they were timeless.

Chapter 2

NATE BEARD'S FISHING BOAT, the *Far from Home,* held twenty-five passengers. Today, he had to leave seven behind. A few years ago, a competitor had gone out of business when his boat capsized with three passengers too many on board. The Coast Guard saved all but three. The offender had a couple of lawsuits hanging over his head and had lost his license. If Nate had ever been tempted to board extra passengers, there was always that unfortunate event to remember.

A couple of years ago his wife, Carrie Lynn, had divorced him and taken their two children to Vermont. Actually, it was the other way around. A friend of Carrie Lynn's from high school had come by to visit a couple of summers ago. A few months later, Carrie Lynn told Nate she was taking the kids back to Vermont to visit her parents. She never came back. He'd heard she had moved in with the guy. A few weeks later, he got divorce papers.

It was a lonely life for Nate. He missed his kids. He'd named the boat with that in mind. They came out for the summer, but those were some of his busiest days. He spent more time with them the week after Christmas than he did during the summer. If he didn't have a full boat, he would take Caitlin, nine, and Buddy, seven, on board with him. But it was a long day, and the novelty for the kids wore off fast.

The times when they didn't go along, they went to Luke and Ginny Dingell's. They had not been able to have kids and so they gave their love to other children by running a day care center. When Sally got off work at Joe's, she would go by and pick up the kids and take them home with her. It saved Nate money since she didn't charge for watching them.

He would pick them up at Sally's house. Sometimes Nate and the kids would stay for supper. Sally's husband, Keith, was away a lot in the Alaska oilfields. Sometimes, after supper, the kids would go and play with friends in the neighborhood and Sally and he would talk for a long while.

Today, the ocean was a little choppy as they ventured out, but, by the time they arrived at the fishing spot, the waters were calm. Nate went on the microphone and told the passengers that his Sonar had spotted a significant number of salmon below. They would be here for a while.

Georgia, the cook, was serving coffee on the bottom deck and taking orders for pastries. There were no fancy breakfasts since lunch was the main meal of the day and included in the price of the trip. Nate went downstairs to get some of Georgia's coffee. Her strong brew would put him over the top for the day.

When he was a kid, his dad, Walt Beard, had been in the fishing business too. He'd take Nate out with him and Nate would get deathly seasick every time. Over the years he'd mostly overcome it, but he still needed to pop a couple of motion sickness pills from time to time.

"There's the seasick fishing boat captain! Now, don't that beat all!" Johnny Watson would say every once in a while, as if he had never thought of it or said it before.

Nate had always found him irritating. They'd been in the same high school class. Back then, while they were both good athletes, Nate had worked hard for his grades. Johnny had just seemed to float along and teachers would grant him favors and extend deadlines and flex on his grades.

The day at sea was long and uneventful and when the time came, Nate was all too ready to head into shore. When he pulled his fishing boat into harbor that evening the sun was setting behind them. He could see from the landing that Harbor Days Celebration of Coast Living was in full swing, an every-summer event with something for everybody's taste.

Merchants displayed their wares out on the sidewalks. Local musicians had a chance to show off their talent. More so each year, people came from all over the country and, to some extent, the world, to see the fine Oregon Coast. Safety Harbor was a beneficiary.

Organizations and businesses that weren't already located on Safety Harbor Square By-the-Sea, set up temporary booths to promote their products and programs. Argostoli's featured both local artists and out-of-towners. There would be standing room only this evening as people gathered for the Annual Silent Auction.

Down at Harbor Village, where strips of shops lined the beach, a band was playing bluegrass music and was beginning to attract a crowd. A few dancers could be seen in front of the band.

Joe's always closed its doors at 2:00 p.m. every day. He always said that he made enough money to get along during the first part of the day. Let the other merchants, some of them struggling, have their chance. In that spirit, Joe didn't have a booth at Harbor Days. He'd been asked this year to organize the whole affair, including the parade.

Nate finished getting the boat ready for the next morning and sauntered down to the Square. Sally said she would have Caitlin and Buddy there when he came into shore. It was crowded. He didn't see her right away. Suddenly, the kids came running toward him out of the crowd and Sally was right behind them. Nate stooped down and the kids both hugged him around the neck.

He knew that he enjoyed seeing Sally too much. A moment of guilt flooded him as he realized he was looking for the married woman more than his own kids as he walked in from the boat.

Marshall Hale, the local deputy, approached the two of them, breaking the awkward and thrilling tension.

"Has anyone seen Joe? People are asking about him."

"He's around here somewhere," Sally said. "I think I saw him talking to Father Callaghan."

She left Nate and his kids with reluctance. She was hopelessly attracted to Nate, but she had made promises of her own.

Nate, Buddy, and Caitlin sauntered down the promenade over to the food court. They sat down with their hot dogs and soft drinks next to Margaret Hodges, the local state legislator and spouse of Luther Hodges. Unfortunately for her work, Margaret was an introvert. She could make a good speech, but she was personally shy. She'd been roundly criticized at Always Sunny Church for not attending more social events and for leaving right after service without staying for coffee.

There was a bit of polite but awkward conversation before Katye and Susanna joined them. Being unable to ignore a growing crowd of familiar faces, a gregarious Father Callaghan stopped by, too.

"Has anyone seen Joe?" he asked.

"We thought he was with you," said Nate. "Sally said she saw you talking to him."

"Well, I was earlier, but now he's nowhere to be found. He's supposed to be leading a Harbor Days Steering Committee meeting in fifteen minutes. He left word with Sally that he's got the answers to several questions we have not been able answer regarding the parade. We need him here!"

The Steering Committee met and decided, because of Joe's absence, to postpone the meeting. Joe didn't answer his phone or respond to email or text messages. Nobody could reach him that night.

The next morning, Sally Hankins unlocked the door of the Diner with the key set aside for such contingencies, hidden under a nearby rock. By now, Joe had always had the place open, the lights on, and some coffee brewing.

There was a rush of stark emptiness that greeted her, the kind that said "Nobody's here, but they should be." A wave of heavy chill air, both palpable and poignant, blew across her face. She shuddered. She started the coffee and turned on the stoves. It was five-thirty. Joe always opened at six o'clock. She had only a half hour to get started. Hesitantly, she climbed the stairs to Joe's living quarters. There was a note on the door in Joe's handwriting.

"Carry on," it said. An envelope attached to it was labeled, "Parade Instructions."

Chapter 3

THE WEATHER HAD RETURNED to normal with an early morning fog that kept a chill on everything until about noon. Later, the sun would come out, warming it into the sixties.

Nate was the first to arrive for breakfast. "You'll have to close the place down," he said after hearing the details.

"Well, we can at least serve coffee, and we have our daily order from the bakery."

"Yes, I suppose so," Nate agreed.

He unloaded the pastries from their boxes onto the counter. Sally already had table settings ready from closing time yesterday. She wrote out a sign and taped it to the front entrance. There would only be a continental breakfast served today.

Everyone who came through the door thought they were asking the question for the first time.

"Where's Joe? Where did he go? Do you know when he'll be back?"

"Don't know," was the answer.

It was a quiet morning. Everyone spoke in low tones or didn't speak at all. The conversation at Father Callaghan's table, which consisted of Jeremy Woods, and Mayor Lou and Hope Schofield, finally became audible to those at the table next to them. They quieted down to hear what was being said. Gradually, the whole diner was listening.

"Do we call the police?" queried Jeremy.

"I hardly think that's necessary," said Lou. "The last thing we need during Coast Days is the report of a missing person!"

"Lou!" exclaimed Hope.

"Joe left of his own accord. He has a right to his own business." Lou held his ground.

"True enough, most likely," said Father Callaghan, "but we have to face the fact that it's not like him just to up and leave!"

"We only know he's never done it since he's been here with us," said Lou.

They were reminded of just how much they didn't know about Joe, who he was, and where he had been before he had come to town, before he had bought an old empty shack, and made it into Joe's Fine Dine-ing.

"And what did he mean, 'Carry on'?" mused Jeremy.

"Sounds like maybe he was just talking to Sally about carrying on with the cafe operation," said the mayor.

"Now, how could he possibly have meant that, Lou?" asked Hope. "She doesn't have the funds or the means without operating expenses. It seems impossible."

Jeremy's hands propped up his head as he placed his elbows on the table, staring down.

"True enough, he could come back any time."

"Then again, it may be a while," said Father, quietly.

"Let's give it a day and see where we are tomorrow at this time."

The voice was that of Wendell Cone from across the room at his regular station. Everyone was surprised. He barely said a word any more.

"I agree," said Katye.

Eyebrows were raised again. Katye spoke up even less than Wendell. Lou nodded his head in agreement. "There's no sense in making drama if there isn't one already!"

"Let's meet tomorrow night if he's not back," said Susanna. "We can meet at Argostoli's. I'll have Greek coffee and some baklava."

"No one could object to that!" said Father Callaghan.

The conversation melted into painful silence. The air seemed to go out of the room as the inhabitants of Joe's Fine Dine-ing realized that Joe really was gone. Slowly, people exited the door into uncertainty.

The day went on in Safety Harbor, but with an uncharacteristic anxiety and lack of focus on the part of those who knew and loved Joe. Nate took out a full boat of tourists. Katye taught two summer classes at Harbor Community College. Johnny worked at the midway that had been set up by the water's edge. Luther led a Bible day camp on the beach. Margaret went to her local office. Lou met with city commissioners in the morning and went down to the festivities in the afternoon. Susanna went about her day, keeping an eye on the dozens of new paintings on display. Doc Bailey was called down to the waterfront for an emergency. Chief-of-Police Carmelita Biffle wrote seventeen courtesy parking tickets. As Vice President of Harbor Days, Father Callaghan called a meeting at the rectory for three in the afternoon. He invited Sally as a new member since she had the parade instructions from Joe.

Everything went on as usual, yet, to many, it felt that life as they knew it had come to a halt. Joe was gone.

Chapter 4

STEWART GRENVILLE WENT TO Portland every Tuesday for therapy. It was an ultimatum by his wife, Katye, who had set it as one of the terms for the continuation of their marriage. As a priest in the Church of Anglican Piety, because of his recent choices, staying in the church as active clergy had not been an option.

"You are a good man, Stewart," the Bishop had told him. "I hope, for your sake and others, that you get to the source of this disappointing behavior. You are grounded until all of this is sorted out."

He had come to Safety Harbor with Katye when she had taken the job at the community college.

Stewart's father had been a grocer in the small town of Smith Springs, Nebraska. His mother reared three children while her husband worked, day and night, to feed the family. It was an area deprived of culture and knowledge of the world beyond corn and bean prices and whether the Smith Springs Spartans were having a winning year.

As he grew older. he realized that their life at the Holy Spirit Baptized Church amounted to a good amount of incongruity and unintended outcomes. It was too hard to keep all the rules, riddled with pietistic hang-ups.

At the holy roller church, as people in town called it, you got married early. Normal dating wasn't allowed because kids could get in trouble if they went to dances or football games or anything out of town. This meant that the church offspring often did get in trouble, as they put it then. After all, what they could do together on a date was so limited that it left them way too much time.

As a result, nature took its course and there were many young parents in the congregation. Fortunately, there was no infant baptism, so no one was faced with a public event featuring parents who had been married for fewer than nine months, presenting a child for baptism, a scandal in that time. A considerable number of babies seemed to come early! But, since marriage was always within the congregation, it was just one big family, literally. Church secrets were family secrets and vice versa.

The sting of parental disapproval over his not going on to the religious college of their choice was soon soothed by the wonderful new world of Saint Gustavus Adolphus College. There, he could think his own thoughts and meet people for whom conversation about ideas was stimulating. Often, their discussions were lubricated by a glass of wine or a mug of beer.

Still, he felt himself to be a bit of a slug and an anomaly. Others seemed to have a kind of understanding of the way the world is, as if they knew a secret about that life he did not know. It was as if someone had taken something out of him earlier that was precious, had not given it back, and he didn't know where to find it.

As he reflected on those days, his older model Volvo made its way up over the Coast Range. Coming down out of the gentle mountains, the highway now widened into four lanes and the pent-up mountain traffic came spouting and rushing from behind as if a bottle of soda had been shaken and the cap removed.

He made his way through Newberg and the quaint little town of Dundee. He rounded the curve into Tigard where he took Highway 99 to I-5 North to Portland. Dr. Fred's office was in the Pearl District, a renovated area of old warehouses and abandoned breweries that had been converted into upscale shops, restaurants, professional offices, and condominiums.

Today, as usual, they would discuss some nuance of how out of place he felt in the world and how he could ease that pain without hurting others as he had in the past.

Chapter 5

MRS. MCCARTHY, FATHER CALLAGHAN'S housekeeper, had coffee, tea, and some biscotti ready for the Steering Committee. Father Callaghan checked off the names. Chief of Police Carmelita Biffle arrived first, then Lou, Ray Ripple, who was the grocer, Jeremy, Katye, Susanna, and finally Meriwether. Father Callaghan put a question mark behind Joe's name.

"Thank you all for coming."

Then, the priest began with a personal note. "We are all very concerned for our friend, Joe, and for his safety," he said, "but, life must go on. We must do our best to do what has to be done. In his absence, I will chair this meeting. Joe has done us a great favor by sharing his ideas about the parade."

Mayor Lou spoke up. "I have never understood what is wrong with the way we have always organized the parade."

"Lou," said Susanna, "some of us had a conversation with Joe one of the last mornings he was with us, and we agreed with his idea that it just seemed the right year to shake things up a bit. We're in a rut here in Safety Harbor."

"Well, I don't want anything crazy going on here." The mayor's voice was firm.

"Let's get to the business at hand. I say, sometimes this Steering Committee is very hard to steer!" said Father Callaghan.

Meriwether smiled. "Joe did choose some free spirits to be in this group, Frank!"

"It's not the free spirits I'm worried about!" said Father, who immediately wished that he hadn't said it.

"However, I have taken the liberty to add one more person to our group. Since Joe chose Sally to carry on and left parade instructions with her, I've asked her to join us."

Everyone nodded to Sally.

"Well," said Lou. "Let's get on with it. What's in the envelope, Sally?"

Susanna spoke up. "First, how are you, Sally?" she said. "In fact, how are we all?"

"Look," said Lou. "I don't have time for the touchy-feely stuff. I'm too busy running this city. I'm here as a courtesy. I don't see why we need to change the parade at all! It's doggone late in the day to be discussing this."

"None of us have to participate in this committee," said Katye, who had a way of keeping things on track. "I think all of us can agree that this is a volunteer group and if any of us don't want to be here, we will release anyone who wants off the committee."

"I know I'm worried," said Jeremy. "It's bad enough to have someone disappear from our little close-knit community, but to have someone like Joe go away, well, it's as if we don't know who we are any more."

"I like that!" said Lou. "The city will go on as usual, no matter who is here and who isn't here."

"Oh, I don't think that it's about that, Lou," said Meriwether. "It's a different kind of presence that Joe has among us. It's not about our civic life. It's about something deeper."

Lou dropped his eyes. "I don't understand this. I don't understand this at all."

A clumsy silence followed.

"Well," said Sally, speaking up with a quiver of timidity in her voice, "are you interested in what is in the envelope?"

There was silent assent and anticipation in the air.

They were interrupted by the tailored-suited presence of Wendell Cone.

"This is the steering committee, isn't it?" asked Wendell.

"Yes, it is," said Father Frank. "Do you want to join us?"

"Only for a moment. I don't want to interrupt your proceedings, but I thought this was important. I want you to know that fifty thousand dollars has been electronically deposited in the Joe's Fine Dining account."

The group was stunned.

"The deposit was made by some organization known as Gemma LLC and signed by a Ms. Evita DuPont, whose name is also on the account. She authorized Sally to use the funds for ongoing operations.

"Hmm," said Father.

"Does it make sense to you, Sally?" asked Meriwether. "You knew him better than most."

"I would have thought he would have chosen someone who had more skills with money than I do. I can hardly balance my checkbook! And I don't know any Evita DuPont. Not at all."

"I think we may safely conclude several things from this," said Father Frank, "that Joe's not coming back right away and he wants his work at Joe's to be carried on in his absence."

"We can't know any of that for sure," said Lou. "Who's to say this isn't some hoax? Maybe he's been taken hostage or maybe his past has caught up with him. We don't know much about him before he came here, you know."

"I hardly think that kidnappers would send money," said Susanna. "They demand money, Lou! They don't deposit it in the bank and appoint a guardian of the funds!"

Lou scowled.

"I suggest," said Katye, "that we assign the parade plans to a smaller group. There are too many of us to do this in such a short time. I think Carmelita would be the obvious choice to head it up."

"Look," said Lou. "We are just too close to this parade to make any big changes. I keep saying, although I have noticed nobody listens, I think we should just move on and do it as we always have."

Carmelita spoke up for the first time. "It would be easy to continue the parade conversation down at the station. I'd be glad to help. Marshall can handle the crowd tonight and if there's trouble I am always on call."

Sally handed off the envelope to Carmelita before Lou could object.

"May I choose the group that will work with me on this?" asked Carmelita.

Lou grimaced.

"I think the committee has total faith in your judgment, Carmelita. Of course, if we have any suggestions we can call you," said Father. "I think our work is done here for this afternoon. So, it's onward and upward until we meet tomorrow night at Argostoli's."

Chapter 6

Rocky rested his head for a moment against the garden hoe and wiped his brow with his shirtsleeve. With the direct July sun, it was a warm day to garden. He liked working with his hands. It gave him time to think. It was this easy kind of meandering flow of his mind that seeped like water into the cracks and crevices of creative possibilities that can't be accomplished when he was thinking intentionally.

Life had seemed so simple until he reached his mid-thirties. Then, the crisis hit. From then on, the world seemed to grab him by the hair and drag him along on a ride through a life that he didn't recognize and he surely hadn't planned.

He had grown up in Colorado in a good stable home. He had not been coordinated enough for competitive sports, but he'd gone out for track and kept the respect of his peers by being a recognized athlete. He was not a scholar but a good student, pulling mostly B's with a few A's and a sprinkling of C's, enough of the latter to keep him off the honor roll. His long light brown hair and blue eyes along with a good build, had made him popular.

They were Catholics in a largely Protestant town, but, in school, nobody mentioned that part of life, so mostly, it didn't matter. Religion, everybody said, was a private thing, and didn't have to do with the rest of life. It was in the same category as a car or a pickup truck preference, and maybe a category or two below that in the town where he lived!

Then one day, about three miles from his house, a school friend and all of his family had lost their lives in a car accident when two young men from a neighboring town with too much beer in them had swerved and met them head on.

None of the local churches could hold enough people for the funeral so they had services in the local school gymnasium. Four coffins lined the front of the stage. It was hard for Rocky to fathom how it could be that Tom and he had just been talking on the school bus last Friday and here, on Tuesday, his voice was silenced and he was about to be buried.

That week, Rocky went to Mass even though his parents didn't. For the first time since he'd been an altar boy, he paid attention throughout the service. Suddenly, Mass became real rather than just some rote, form, or formula. Affected deeply, when he went out into the street again, he knew somehow life would be different.

He made an appointment to see Father Crucey, who was polite but who really wanted to talk about the high school football team. He predicted a "building year" since last year most of the good players had graduated.

Rocky was disappointed. Not until he went to college did he find young people who were asking the same questions he was. The second year of his college career, the campus chaplain had offered a vocations fair but nothing struck Rocky as anything that would fit him.

"It's all right," said Chaplain Bill Reedy. "Just keep asking those questions."

No one, even Father Bill, seemed to understand that Rocky lived out of his heart. It was meaning and experience he was looking for and if they were missing, he couldn't make up his mind about anything. After graduation, he still didn't know what to do. He took a job with a small radio station as their program manager. His heart was calling him elsewhere. But, where would he go?

One of his college professors had once quoted the aphorism to him, "Go West, young man!" and he had never forgotten it. Nine months later, Rocky had saved up enough money to move to California.

Fifteen years later, with two divorces, a job loss, and financial ruin, Rocky fled the accumulated pain and landed back in his hometown. It was humiliating for him to stay with his parents, while all the good townsfolk who had praised him, now whispered about his marriage failures and his dissolute life in California.

Six months later, he made off to Oregon, where a distant cousin lived, and took a job at the State Hospital in Salem. One day, his eyes landed on a stunning brunette, a new employee with an incredible smile and laughing, dancing eyes. They were inseparable for months. Then, she went away. He tried to find her for weeks. Finally, she showed back up at work. It turned out she had a husband in Arizona and had gone back to try to reconcile. It hadn't worked out. She had asked for her old job back, and got it.

Magdalena and he gradually renewed their relationship, but it took him a while to forgive her for leaving him without a word of explanation. He never understood and he never forgot. Had he not loved her, he couldn't have gone on with her.

Now, things had finally changed it seemed. Rocky and Magdalena were a real pair. Rocky knew she overlooked so many of his imperfections and recognized them as wounds.

"My middle name is Grace," Magdalena always said, "for a reason!"

Rocky always smiled when she said that. He smiled when she said most anything.

They had often taken trips to the Oregon Coast together and the Safety Harbor area had become their favorite place. They often found themselves just south of town in an old campground called Embers. It was down a little lane off the main road that led to a group of shacks under a virtual cascade of trees that provided shade except for a few intense rays of sunlight that pierced the limbs and the leaves.

They had been delighted to find that a glassblower worked there. They became friends with Daniel over the next two years. Trust built between them and, one day, Daniel invited them to come and be a part of the little vagabond community of misfits that was starting to form under the trees. He had allowed a couple of people to pitch tents there. He also had a vacant house that he could rent to Rocky and Magdalena.

"Rocky, I think we can do this!" said Magdalena. When she said those seven words, Rock knew that it was true. So, they moved.

After they had been there a few weeks, a few more tents started appearing and three lean-to huts were being constructed.

Rocky went to see Daniel.

"How many people are we going to allow?" he asked, calling over the noise of the bellows.

Only after it came out of his mouth did he realize that he had said, "we" instead of "you." Daniel smiled. He noticed this too. He placed his most recent work in the lehr and came over to talk. His face always looked a bit gritty and carried a semi-permanent indentation from the facemask he had to use while working the furnace.

"I've been thinking, too, that this situation needs immediate attention. Word is spreading and people are coming here every day asking for shelter, just a place to be. I find it hard to turn away people, but I admit there's going to be a problem from the county pretty soon."

"Unless we have some reason for them to be here," said Rocky.

"What are you thinking?" asked Daniel.

"What if you expanded your glass blowing work and offered people jobs? I could see that we could have a whole community of glass blowers and related shops here. I could quit my job at the lumber yard and Magdalena could quit working at the library and come out here and organize things."

"That takes a good deal of money," Daniel said. "I can't take too many risks. I'm not twenty-one and flush with money, you know!"

"We have some savings," Rocky offered.

"Have you talked to Magdalena about that?"

"Truth be told this was her idea," he grinned. "All my good ideas come from her!"

"Since when have my good ideas become yours?"

Magdalena's distinct voice came from behind him. She was home from work early. It always gave him a thrill and made him blush. She came up behind him and put her arms around his waist and kissed his ear.

"There will be hurdles. Your savings won't last forever."

"What if there are some facts-on-the-ground before we go to the powers-that-be?" Rocky asked.

"Oh, Rock, I think that would just irritate people." Magdalena's voice was firm. "And we are on the edge of being illegal."

"We need to create a positive impression of this place," said Daniel.

"We could ask Father to say Mass," said Rocky.

"What's that got to do with anything?"

"That would take away the stereotype that we are "just a bunch of hippies," as the mayor of Safety Harbor has called us. If the Church blesses this project, it puts its critics in a difficult position. We could spread the word that there's a free meal offered, invite people to Mass if they want, and then ask Joe's to provide sandwiches. It would get people here. They wouldn't have to do Mass. Just come and eat. It would give people an idea of who we are. A free meal always softens people's hearts."

"You mean, like public relations?"

"Yes, you might say so. Religion and hospitality. Really, they ought to be the same thing, no?"

"Well, it's an original idea, I'll tell you that. A lot of people around here aren't religious, and some don't like Catholics if they are religious. I am not sure how it will work or if it will work at all. But I don't have a better idea. When approached, Father Callaghan surprised them and said of course he would.

"Do you worry that some are not Catholics that might participate in the Eucharist, Father?" Magdalena had asked.

He winked. "Not if you don't. Of course, don't go running to the Archdiocese, telling tales!"

The Saturday evening of the Mass, Father appeared with his traveling salvation show. As arranged, Joe's Fine Dine-ing delivery truck followed Father's car. Rocky, Magdalena, and Daniel were amazed at the crowd. People had come from everywhere, it seemed. There were far more than they were expecting. They sat on the ground. They brought chairs. Some brought blankets. The happy voices of children could be heard. A few dogs had come along for the ride.

The Mass took two and one half hours with the crowd that had gathered. Father chose Johnny Watson and Sally Hankins to assist in serving.

"They aren't even Catholics, Father!" Rocky whispered in the priest's ears.

"What is that to you if it's okay with the good Lord?" asked Father.

"I would have been happy to help!" said the Rock.

"I have other work for you to do!" Rocky heard a voice say.

Father's lips weren't moving, so who said it? No one else was close at hand. Still, the voice didn't seem to come from any one direction. It seemed inside. It seemed outside. It came from everywhere. It came from nowhere. It quieted him. He felt a strange kind of peace.

After the Mass, people were asked to sit down.

Picnic sandwiches and chips began to appear in front of people wrapped in paper that read "Joe's Fine Dine-ing." Joe's staff was now passing out meals for everyone.

Father Callaghan's voice called out over the din of voices, "Dear friends, let us bless this food before we eat!"

He repeated himself several times. Finally, Father had quieted the voices so that he could be heard. He raised a sandwich up to the sky. When it seemed that he could raise it no further he stretched and lifted it up a little higher. Then, he said the blessing.

From under the canopy of trees and wafting out over the valley as far as the crashing surf of the sea from all of the people present, there arose a surprising and resounding "Amen!"

It was at the "Amen!" that Rocky had his revelation, his epiphany. He remembered Magdalena remarking one morning, as one of the inhabitants of a tent had emerged in a long cape and cowl, that, whoever it was, looked just like a monk walking out there in the mystery of the early morning fog.

"This is a kind of monastery of the unsettled," she said.

"There can't be such a thing," said Rocky. "That's a contradiction in terms. Monks are by nature settled people."

"Not all of them. Ask the next monk or sister you see how settled they really are!" She smiled wryly.

"You act as if you know something about that!" he remarked with a grin.

"I haven't told you everything!" she said, with a sparkle in her eyes.

He had not seen it before, but he could see now, as he looked over the teeming mass of people assembled there on the grounds, how it is that we are all unsettled. It came to him in that moment that there is no permanent dwelling place, even if we have a so-called permanent address. We are all wanderers. He saw how it is that life moves on, with or without us. We meet the self of yesterday on the road of today and there is a qualitative difference. He saw how it could be that here, in this place, on these grounds, there could be a living space for those who had nowhere else to go, a place of work and prayer, adventure and meaning, as well as purpose and direction.

He looked over the crowd now and saw that there seemed to be no more sandwiches and chips and still there were at least a hundred souls to feed. He made his way to Joe.

"They don't have enough to eat!" he said.

Joe just smiled and went back to the truck. He emerged with more large boxes marked "Monastery of the Unsettled." From these boxes, he brought forth more than enough.

"You give these to those who are still waiting for something to eat," he said to Rocky.

Rocky did just that. He walked over to the crowd, sat the rough-edged crowd down in groups, and passed out as many sandwiches and chips that were needed.

That night, as Rocky made his way back to Magdalena's and his humble abode, it suddenly hit him that Joe had written the name they had just coined the community, on the boxes of sandwiches and chips.

He stood still in the darkness for a moment, stunned. How could Joe have known anything about a casual conversation Magdalena and he had about what someone was wearing when they emerged from their tent? Nonetheless, there it had been, right in front of his eyes.

Later, no one could say for sure that they had seen the Unsettlement written on the sandwich wrappers. But then, Rocky was the only one who had been close to the containers containing the sandwiches. He had given the boxes to Joe immediately after serving the people. Joe had put them back in the truck. Come to think of it, that night, he didn't see anybody but Joe inside that truck. No one could have seen anyone but Joe bringing out those sandwiches and chips.

Back then, Rocky knew what he had to do. Now, eighteen months later, over a hundred and fifty souls lived at the Unsettlement.

Chapter 7

"THAT'S OUTRAGEOUS!"

Lou was in shock. His cheeks were flushed and the pink tint worked its way up to his forehead and his receding hairline.

He was just hearing a report of last night's meeting.

Rocky and Magdalena will replace the mayor as Grand Marshals. The Monastery of the Unsettled will be given the lead place in the parade right behind the Elementary School marching band. Children from the Village of Hope Disability Center, the Pacific School for the Blind, and all current residents of the homeless shelter at Always Sunny Church will be given a prominent place in the front of the parade. Business and civic leaders serve a free meal to all parade attendees provided by Joe's Fine Dine-ing. They chose to call it Joe's Plan.

"I won't have it!" said Lou. He called out to Pinna, his assistant, "Get Frank in here!"

He turned to the women. "Somebody's got to talk some sense into you people!"

"Oh, we weren't the only ones at the meeting," said Carmelita.

"Who else? Who else?

"Sally Hankins, of course. Nate Beard, Jeremy Woods, and [*pause*] Hope Schofield," said Katye, with a Mona Lisa smile escaping the left side of her lips.

"Hope was there?"

He sank back into his chair stunned.

"We thought she might have told you where she was going last night, Mr. Mayor," said Susanna.

"She told me she was going to a meeting, but she has a plethora of meetings. I didn't even bother to ask. And Beard and Woods! Those guys are merchants! Business people! They know better than this. What will

23

this do to the city's image? I'll be the laughing stock of the Coastal Mayor's Conference!"

"Oh, it's not about any one of us, Mr. Mayor," said Carmelita quietly. "It's about the city and the community. It's about all of us, not just a part of us or a few of us. It's about everybody. It's about the people at the Monastery of the Unsettled as well as those of us who live in the city limits. That's what this community is. That's what Joe's Plan is all about and it's a good one, we think."

"Joe's Plan, eh? Where is Joe anyway? Seems he ought to have the courage to show up and present his own plan!'

Father Callaghan appeared at the door.

"To what do I owe the dubious honor of being summoned to Mayor Schofield's office?" he asked, with a mild look of amusement.

"This can't happen, Father."

"What can't happen?"

"Don't play coy with me, Frank," Lou responded.

"I have no idea what you're talking about!"

"Of course you do! You're probably behind all this!"

"That's unfair, Lou," Katye spoke up. "He hasn't seen the Plan. You know more than Father does!"

"Well, let's hear it!" said Father. "I'm anxious to know what I've been conspiring to do!"

"Essentially, it involves having some people in the parade that no one thought about, and some don't want, and it will change the presentation of the image of the city pretty drastically," said Susanna. "There are some changes, should we say, in the order of things."

Father Callaghan raised his eyebrows.

"Did Joe leave anything that explains these changes? Any reason at all?"

Carmelita handed Joe's Plan to Father.

"Let me see that!" Lou simmered.

Frank walked over to the mayor's desk, handed him the letter and bent over his shoulder to read it. After all of the suggestions that sounded more like instructions, Joe had written a small treatise. Father read it aloud.

> It is my hope that this parade will be an event beyond itself. I will be proud of this city if it has the courage to demonstrate that it is a place where the least of us are great, where all are valued, and where human dignity is respected regardless of station or status, where everyone is free to be who they are without being

censored or judged. After all, the name of our home is Safety Harbor.

No one wanted to be the first to speak up. No words seemed adequate. Even Lou was quiet. There would be no more discussion. Katye broke the ice.

"We'd better get the Unsettlement involved in this conversation to see if they're interested in participating."

Katye, Carmelita, and Father Callaghan were designated to represent the committee down at the Unsettlement. Half an hour later, they were on their way south. Katye drove. Father sat in the back. Carmelita rode shotgun. They journeyed in silence down the winding road that follows the fanciful meanderings of the coastline. The ocean was a deep blue against the sky. It was nearly noon now. The warmth of the summer sun coming through the car and the rhythm of the majestic waves, had a hypnotizing effect upon the travelers.

"I suppose we ought to call Rocky and Magdalena and let them know we're coming," said Father.

"I've already done that, Father!" said Katye. "At least Magdalena will be there."

"I should have known! You and your efficiency!"

Carmelita was nodding off in the warmth of the sun and shook herself when her cell phone rang. "Oh my! That's too bad. You'd better go tell her, Marshall, before word gets to her otherwise. I won't be back in town for a while."

"What is it, Katye?" asked Father.

"It's Keith Hankins, Sally's husband," she said. "He's been killed in an explosion up in Alaska."

"Mother o' God!" he responded. He made the sign of the cross.

"Do we need to go back?" asked Katye.

"No, we'd better take care of business on this parade. We need to stay focused, or those who are advocating for the status quo will take advantage of the situation. Marshall will go and inform Sally."

Katye turned left off the Pacific Coast Highway and drove down the long easement. Magdalena was there to meet them. She walked to the car and welcomed each of them with an embrace.

"Rock's not back yet," she said. "He had to go into Lincoln City for supplies."

There was a large tent, with open sides, erected for common meals and community meetings. They walked to one of the large tables under the tent and sat down.

Chapter 8

MARSHALL SAT IN HIS office with his feet on his desk. He'd only been in law enforcement for two years. How could he do this? Maybe he would order some lunch in the diner and then wait until everybody was gone to tell her. He rehearsed several other scenarios, but they all involved delay in notifying her. He knew he couldn't follow through with any of them. He just had to go in there and tell her.

He got in the car and drove the three blocks to the diner, pulling up next to the front entrance. For a few minutes, he sat there in a vacuous state, neither thinking nor feeling. He noticed movement to his right and turned to see Susanna pulling in beside him. Suddenly, he saw a way out. He rolled his window down and waited for Susanna to pass by the car.

"Could I talk to you a minute?"

"How may I be of assistance, Deputy?" she asked.

"It's difficult to talk about it here. Would you mind sitting in the car with me?" he asked.

She hesitated. She was reluctant to make herself vulnerable, even to an officer of the law.

"Could we discuss this over lunch in Joe's?"

"No, we can't."

The look of desperation on his young face disarmed her and she moved toward the passenger seat of the car, opened the door, and sat down, leaving the door open. She looked over at Marshall and raised her eyebrows inquisitively.

"There's no way of sugar coating this," he began. "Sally's husband has been killed."

"Keith?" There was incredulity in her voice.

"An explosion at a pipeline somewhere."

"Does she know yet?"

"No, that's what I'm here to do," he said. "I'm a bit of a wreck about it, to tell you the truth. I have to do it now before she gets the word some other way."

"I'll call her and ask her to come to my house after she's closed up. You can come over and we can tell her then."

"I don't think that's a good idea," he said. Susanna was clearly surprised that the young man disagreed with her. And so was he!

"Carmelita asked me to do it while she is gone and she might well be back in town by then."

"You are right."

"How would Joe do it?"

"He would tell her immediately, privately, and preserve her dignity at all costs," she said.

"You know what I think he'd do? I think he'd call her out back to the storage shed, away from everybody, and tell her there and then. I think he'd take her around the cafe and to his car and take her home. I think he'd have others close up for the day."

"You stay here," Susanna said. "We don't want anyone to see a uniform come in and ask her to leave the building," she said. "Rumors of all sorts will fly."

"Right."

She walked through the entrance of Joe's and stood at the counter. Sally came over.

"Hi there!" Sally greeted her cheerfully.

"I need to talk to you."

"What's up?"

"Can we go out back?"

"Can't we talk here? You see how busy it is."

"This will need some privacy."

Sally knew now that it was not good news.

They walked outside together. Marshall got out of the squad car as he saw them approaching the storage shed, joining them as they went inside.

"There's no good way to say this," Susanna said, graciously providing an opening for the young policeman to step up to the task.

"Keith has been killed in a pipeline explosion," he said.

His voice was emotionless, matter-of-fact, and yet kind. He had gotten through the hard part and had done a good job.

Sally's face fell and she collapsed against a refrigerator. Susanna went over and comforted her, placing her arm around her neck and gently steadying her with the other.

She looked up, her eyes red and filled with tears.

"How? How did it happen? Where?" she asked. "Did he suffer?"

"We don't know any of the details yet Sally. We just know it happened about thirty-six hours ago. We expect to get more word today. Marshall will take you home now. We'll get the place closed up."

Chapter 9

CARMELITA BIFFLE WAS BORN Carmelita Alessandra Sanchez in Antigua, Guatemala. When she was seven, her parents and three siblings moved to Long Beach, California. There, they joined Carmelita's mother's family, who had begun a construction business. Her father became the foreman of the company's projects.

Although a welcome change in the fortunes of the family, it was a traumatic move for them. They left behind many friends and a large extended family on her father's side. There were a number of Guatemalans close by, but Southern California was a big, strange place that seemed to waver between disinterest and hostility.

School was difficult. Racism was rampant in the elementary school among both students and faculty. By Middle School, she had learned how to survive, and by high school she had gained enough confidence to thrive, despite the prejudice.

After high school, she went to Long Beach Community College. During this time, she had decided she wanted to be in law enforcement and transferred her credits to a college in San Diego, where she enrolled in the police academy program.

There, she met Cliff Biffle, one of her professors. The attraction was strong but they kept it cool until she graduated. Within three months they were married.

Carmelita landed a job on the police force in Chula Vista.

Three years later, Cliff had an opportunity to take a position at Jefferson University in Ashland. Now, here she was again, a stranger in a strange land.

She found a place of comfort at Our Lady of the Fields Catholic Church. There, she made her first friends and joined a women's group that specialized in working with undocumented workers. They visited camps around the valley where people often lived in the shadows and needed, among other things, basic medical care.

One of her friends informed her after Mass one Sunday that there was a law enforcement position open in the little village of Table Rock. Carmelita applied. To her surprise, she was called for an interview, which turned out to be one of the strangest experiences of her life. Three members of the City Council interviewed her, two of whom, she would discover later, were facing a recall election in two weeks.

The interview was laced with verbal jabs by the interviewers at one another. One of the two male members of the interview committee asked to be excused to smoke a cigarette and never came back. Twenty minutes after her interview, she was hired as the Chief of Police. She was flabbergasted and at the same time grateful for employment.

"The last Chief lasted only about eight months," said the Chair. "It's a tough town and a tough job. You have your work cut out for you."

She wanted to talk to Cliff but she was afraid not to accept the position, so she did, telling herself that she could always back out.

Table Rock had one deputy, part time, Rodney Klein, who had been on the force now for eleven years. The next Monday Carmelita showed up for work in the building on Main Street that also housed a pharmacy and an antique store. Rodney was sitting in the chair in the Chief's Office with his feet up on the desk. He didn't get up.

"Well, well," he said. "This time they hired a woman! Will wonders never cease!"

"You're in my chair," she said without blinking an eye or saying good morning.

He looked up, obviously surprised.

"Well, it's been my chair in the absence of a Chief."

"There's a Chief of Police now. That would be me. So, get up."

Slowly, deliberately, as if he were a young boy reluctantly obeying his mother, he moved. Scowling, he retreated to his own desk in the reception area. Silence prevailed.

Eighteen months later, she fired Rodney and sixteen months after that, she was removed from her position. She later learned from Conchita after Mass one day that Rodney had been reinstated, this time as Chief.

"The safety of all the citizens of Table Rock hangs in the balance with that kid in charge," she told Cliff.

"You can't change much in a small town," said Cliff. "People don't want it. Even if they're miserable. Their misery is at least familiar."

She hated to leave Our Lady of the Fields and her many friends when, five months later, she landed the job as Chief of Police in Safety Harbor. Cliff couldn't leave Ashland. Professorships were too rare these days. So, they made a pact to keep their marriage intact, long distance.

She got an apartment in Safety Harbor while Cliff lived in their house in Ashland. He had been in town for a month now this summer and it was both good and annoying to have him around, good because she missed him and annoying because he got in the way.

Even though she was gone a lot during his visit, she let him know where she was. She had called him and told him about Keith and that they were currently at the Monastery of the Unsettled.

She couldn't tell whether he was interested or not.

Chapter 10

"THERE ARE GOING TO be a heap of changes in the big parade coming up tomorrow," Katye began.

Magdalena looked puzzled. "How would that possibly affect us here at the Unsettlement?"

"We want you all in the parade!" she said simply. She was never one to add a word to a sentence if it wasn't needed.

"What do you mean, you want us in it?" Magdalena asked.

Katye looked to Father.

"The thing is," he said, "you know Joe is gone. Disappeared."

"Yes?" She failed to connect the two events.

"Even though he is gone he left instructions for us to carry out that have been deemed by some to be, shall we say, unusual."

Carmelita nodded in agreement.

"Since Carmelita here is in charge of the parade, along with Katye, I'll turn this over to them."

It was difficult for Father to stop talking, but he did. He nodded to the Chief.

"We want to ask Rock and you to be the Grand Marshals of the parade."

"No!" Magdalena responded in disbelief.

"This was the first of Joe's instructions." Carmelita continued. "Because so many respect and love him, we want to carry this plan out on his behalf."

"Well, I'll have to talk to Rock about it," she said.

"There's more," said Father.

Katye spoke up. "We want the good people of this place to be first in line in the parade!" she said.

Magdalena was flabbergasted. "I don't know where to begin telling you how logistically impossible this is going to be," she said.

Father's eyes twinkled. "All things are possible."

"We would have to have a community gathering to talk about this. They aren't just something to be put on display, you know."

"I know Joe didn't have that in mind at all," said Father.

"I'm sure he didn't either," she responded, "but many of those who live on the harsher side of life are either invisible or two-dimensional. They need to know they are a part of things. They can't just do this and then come home and then never the twain shall meet."

"You mean the people of Safety Harbor and the Unsettlement," said Katye.

"Exactly!"

"I'm not sure we've thought that far ahead," said Father wistfully. "Yes, there will be implications, and perhaps complications."

"Some of these people go to work at regular jobs; some are infirm and are on some kind of assistance; some are unemployed and there are some who stay here all day taking care of their children and the children of others who've gone to work. Their economic status is unstable at best and to make their lives easier, they help one another out with the basics of life. We'll call a meeting at dinner time this evening when most everybody's here. I wish Rock were here. He's always good with these things and has the energy and vision to get everybody in action.

"I'm the thinker and the planner," she smiled coyly. "Rock says that things have a way of working out. Little does he know that, before he gets there he has a partner who has quietly smoothed the way ahead."

"How about the Grand Marshal business?" asked Father.

"Oh, I'm sure," Magdalena offered, "when Rock is told that Joe wants it that way that he will do it."

"There's one more thing," said Katye. "I think we should invite you to be a part of the Steering Committee. I haven't talked to the rest of the members but I'm sure that since we've endorsed Joe's Plan that they will agree that it makes sense."

There was immediate assent by Carmelita and Father Callaghan.

"It's the only thing that makes sense," said Father. "If we want to do as Magdalena says and not put people on display or patronize them, we need to ask the Monastery of the Unsettled to be a real part of this whole thing including the planning."

"I would agree with you," said Magdalena. "I will assent to coming on board if Rock and the group approve of going forward with this."

When she got back to her office, Carmelita quietly put out a BOLO on one, Joseph Vincent Magnus.

Chapter 11

By five o'clock in the afternoon, Katye had things organized. Safety Harbor-Clever School District would provide the buses to transport the people from the Unsettlement to Safety Harbor. The temporary food courts would provide dinner. The local churches would make accommodations wherever the people could make a place for a sleeping bag. Some cots and mattresses were borrowed from members. Some people opened their homes. Meriwether Starhawk's congregation met at the Country Club and she used her considerable powers of persuasion to provide the showers of the facility. Joe's Fine Dine-ing would prepare breakfast for all of them on the morning of the parade.

"Are you sure you are up to it?" Katye asked Sally when she agreed to open the Diner.

"I need something to keep me busy, to keep my mind off things," Sally answered. "It will do me good."

That evening, Magdalena called to inform Katye that the decision of the community to come to the parade was unanimous. Within an hour, the buses left the school bus barn and headed for the Unsettlement. The food court remained open after its usual closing time of 9:00 PM. As a hip-hop group performed, everyone relaxed and conversations began to cross the lines between the two communities who had joined together in the Square.

The younger people started to dance and some invited their counterparts from the Unsettlement to join them. Soon, a few older adults could be seen dancing at the edge of the crowd. No longer was it clear who came from Safety Harbor or the Unsettlement. Tourists joined in too.

The Steering Committee met, as planned, at the Argostoli Art Gallery. It was 11:30 p.m. before everyone arrived. The numbers of the group had increased to include Carmelita's ad hoc group and Magdalena. As promised, Susanna served coffee, wine, and baklava.

"Susanna, we want to thank you for your hospitality," said Father.

After an approving murmur from the group and a few who echoed Father's sentiments with a "Yes, thank you" of their own, the meeting settled and centered.

Father cleared his throat. "Friends, a lot has happened since we last met. We still have a lot to do."

"A lot is going on even as we speak!" said Meriwether. "Things downtown are still shaking!"

"I'm sure the Mayor has it all in hand!" said Father. Nate hid his smile behind one hand ineffectively.

"Sally, we are truly sorry to learn of Keith's passing," said Jeremy.

"Thanks," she said, lowering her eyes.

There was silence in the room to pay tribute to Keith. They spent the rest of their time putting the order of the parade together and made last-minute tweaks to the details of the care and comfort of their overnight guests from the Unsettlement.

"Before we leave, I think we should make sure all is well at Joe's in the morning," said Katye. "Sally, how is that coming?"

"I've got an excellent crew!" she said. "Nate is coming in. So is Georgia Wellstone. She's Nate's cook on the fishing boat."

"Ah!" everyone said, recognizing at once that with Georgia there, things would be just fine in the kitchen.

"Johnny and Hobe, too," she continued. "I wouldn't have chosen them but Joe honored them so I want to continue to do that as well.

"Katye and Liz will serve and bus tables. Jeremy will provide some of his exquisite coffee from his shop and make sure it keeps flowing. Rocky and Magdalena will round out the crew."

Just then Magdalena walked in the door. "I heard there was a meeting up here that was serving wine and baklava. I thought I couldn't miss it."

"Magdalena!" exclaimed Father, "Come in! Come in! You are very welcome here!"

The meeting was filled with excitement, anticipation, and conviviality. It broke up about 2:00 a.m.

Nate and Sally left together and for a few moments they walked side by side. Soon, both recognized that the attraction between them was too strong and they would need to part before something happened that they would both regret, or, at least, should regret.

Reluctantly, they parted ways.

Sally continued walking alone when a figure appeared ahead of her about a block away. Startled, she froze in her tracks. At once she wished she had asked Nate to walk her home. Now, the dark shadowy figure seemed to be moving on. As she took another look she was sure that it was Joe's profile.

"Joe!" she said breathlessly.

"Joe!" she called out, as the night specter disappeared out of her sight.

She sank into her bed without changing her clothes. She could not sleep. Scenes of her life with Keith kept playing back in her mind. A tear flowed down her cheek. Ironic how she didn't miss him that much when he was away and even savored her time without him. She realized her time away from him was sweet because she knew he could be coming back. Now, he would not be coming back alive.

She knew she didn't love him as a wife should love her husband, but she was fond of him and they had shared four years of their lives together. Whatever the days ahead proved to be, she knew they would be difficult. In her dreams, she saw Keith coming in the door with his arms outstretched. Her arms reached out to meet him, but he faded into nothing as she awakened.

Chapter 12

STEWART LAY AWAKE BESIDE his wife who had arrived home half an hour ago. She was sleeping so soundly that he checked to make sure she was still breathing. She was his anchor in these dark and difficult days of his life.

Sleep should come so easily, he thought. Keith's death had hit him hard. They had become friends after Katye and he had moved to Safety Harbor. It was a strange relationship. Keith was pure blue-collar working class, plain spoken, and with no pretensions. Stewart found him refreshing and welcomed a friendship with someone who had those qualities. He had a mouth on him but Stewart secretly savored that too as he was accustomed to people speaking carefully around him, unnaturally even, and when they did slip in a word of profanity or two, they would immediately say, "Sorry, Reverend."

They had met at Joe's when Keith was waiting for Sally to finish her shift. Sally had introduced them and immediately, something deep had connected within each of the men. Stewart's spirits sank lower as he thought about losing one of the few genuine friendships he had ever had. Sally had called him only a few minutes after she got word of Keith's death.

"I know he would want you to do the funeral, Stewart," Sally had said in brief phone call to him earlier in the day. "He wasn't a religious man and didn't have much time for what he called 'religious, holier-than-thou people.'"

"I'll do it!" he heard himself say. "Of course, Sally. I'll do it! It's a gift I can give him."

A sickening feeling arose from his stomach and became a lump in his throat. He was not empowered to do anything in the church right now. He would have to get permission or go ahead without permission. It never struck him as an option not to do it at all.

He got out of bed and made himself a cup of tea. He sat at the kitchen table and looked out the window. What was that movement? He got up to take a closer look. He thought he saw a shadow under the streetlights. He got up and went out the front door to have a closer look.

A dark figure walked by, a silhouette in the street light. He could have sworn it was Joe. He rushed outside.

"Joe? Joe!"

The figure disappeared into the darkness.

Chapter 13

Sometimes Father Callaghan wearied of being alone. He tried to imagine what it would be like to have a wife. As he got older, the yearnings had more power. He saw his years waning and knew that this loneliness was for life. No one in town could understand this experience. If celibacy was brought up at all, it was usually in the form of a joke. Talking to another priest didn't help much because, too often, he learned more than he wanted to know.

Tonight, in particular, was difficult. He was exhausted. Since Joe's disappearance, as he constantly offered assurance to others, he, himself, wasn't at all sure what was going on here. He tried to imagine what it would be like to have someone to meet him with open arms when he returned to the rectory, to talk over the events of the day, to have that person hold you and replace the day's troubles with tenderness and comfort. He thought that must be quite wonderful.

He reached over to the other side of the bed, pretending for a moment that someone beloved was there beside him. In his imagination, he could almost sense her presence and feel her hand reach for his.

His half-dream was interrupted by what he thought was a slight rapping on the door. It was probably a cat. He heard it again. Maybe it was somebody in need. He hoped not. He really was exhausted. The third time he was wide awake and thought that he might as well get up. He put on his robe and his slippers and opened the door. There was no one there, but he had a distinct sense that someone had been there. Down the street at a distance he could see a figure walking toward him.

"Mother o' God!" said Father Callaghan under his breath. "It's Joe!"

As he came closer, Father was sure that it was he. He stopped momentarily, smiled and waved.

The figure called out, "Good to see you, Francis!"

Then he disappeared as if into the ether.

The next thing Father Callaghan knew his alarm was ringing.

Chapter 14

A THIN LAYER OF morning mist greeted the rising sun as Sally arrived at Joe's at 5:00 a.m. Turning the key in the latch and entering the diner, she had a strong sense that someone had been there recently. She checked the back door. Everything was secure and nothing obvious was missing. She mounted the stairs to Joe's apartment. Nothing. No one. She felt both relief and disappointment.

By the time she returned downstairs, Georgia had arrived and was making herself familiar with the kitchen, all the while fussing and mumbling that it did not reach her standards. Nate was here too. Somehow, that made Sally feel more secure, more at peace.

Jeremy arrived with freshly roasted coffee. A pickup pulled up by the back entrance. Bob and Sue Abernathy had showed up with the farm fresh eggs from the Unsettlement.

"Where do you want these?" asked Bob.

"In the supply shed in the back for now," said Sally. "We'll need a runner to keep them coming into the kitchen as we need them."

This, she thought, was a good job for the Watson brothers.

"Johnny and Hobe! Could you help a minute here with these eggs?"

She was surprised at the authority in her voice. She heard it as if she were listening to someone else. Even a week ago, she had not thought of herself as being in charge of anything. Now, here she was, leading a whole operation of people.

As Nate walked by, their hands brushed each other, bringing to both a shock of erotic magnetism. It was right then and there that she admitted to herself that she was in love with Nate. It was a terrible place to be. She had just been widowed, but the sorrow for her dead husband was not as intense as her feelings for Nate. For so long she had wanted to kiss him, to hold him. Once he had taken her hand and she allowed it. It was an overpowering experience for her and she drew back immediately.

What does one do when you are committed to one person and in love with another?

"Keep busy!" she heard herself saying aloud.

"What is that you said, Sally?" asked Georgia.

"It's going to get busy!" she said, her face flushing for a moment.

A burst of energy preceded the door opening and everyone, without looking, knew that it would be Katye. The pace picked up automatically just because she was there. Father Callaghan and Mayor Lou arrived, one after the other. Hope was working with Meriwether on the bus shuttle schedule for showers. Applause greeted the Grand Marshals of the upcoming parade. Sally stole a look at Lou and noticed that the momentary pain on his face was soon replaced by his best public smile. He clapped politely.

Carmelita pulled up in the squad car with Cliff on the passenger side. Not everyone knew Cliff and she thought this was a good time and place to introduce him. Besides, bringing him down here would give him something to do. She did not always know what to do with her husband when he visited.

Susanna came through the front door and was commandeered into the kitchen to prepare her famous Mediterranean breakfast. Since Georgia had insisted that her kitchen help be competent team players, Sally recruited Carmelita, Carla, and Hope. Marshall was assigned to direct the traffic that would soon be arriving. Hobe and Johnny would be table servers outside.

Meanwhile, Jeremy and Nate were setting up tables and chairs outside that had been supplied by Always Sunny Church and the Country Club. Mayor Lou reminded everyone of the limitations on the number of people allowed in Joe's by the Fire Marshal. Even Buddy and Caitlin were assigned a task. They were busy putting silverware and napkins on the table with a bit of corrective supervision, when needed.

Ray Ripple would be shuttling groceries from his store and from the storage shed. Father Callaghan would pour coffee. Nate would keep it flowing. Cliff and Luther would keep the trash cans emptied. Katye served as Sally's assistant and was constantly on her cell phone, making arrangements for the upcoming parade this afternoon. Wendell was shining up the iconic bay windows "for this auspicious occasion" he said, and later would take receipts from all the merchants who had supplied anything for the morning's breakfast. Doc Bailey was there, on call for any emergencies that should arise. He chose to work in the kitchen until such emergency presented itself.

At the very last moment Stewart made an appearance. Katye looked pleased.

"What is there for me to do?" he asked.

"We're going to need a go-fer," said Sally. "We could use your help where it is needed, when it is needed."

"Then, that's what I'll do," he said.

Not one person was left out. Everybody was assigned somewhere. When they were all together, it was as if Joe was present, after all. For a few moments in time, no one worried about Joe's mysterious disappearance or where he was, or whether he was safe, and what he might be doing. Everything and everybody moved as one.

Chapter 15

As the buses approached Joe's and unloaded their passengers, Sally felt her heart quicken as she sensed the excitement in the air. Only a few days ago, Joe was presiding over the business. How they had taken him for granted! Had he not come to town and opened the diner, this occasion would not be happening. The people of the Unsettlement would be carrying on as if it was a normal day and the citizens of Safety Harbor would be putting on another parade, which would meld into memory with parades past.

Yes, Joe was here in some mysterious way. She could feel it. Had she not seen him among the light and shadows last night?

Meriwether arrived now, looking sharp as she drove up in her chili-red Mini Cooper Coupe she had just purchased in Portland a few days ago. It had been a busy morning as she coordinated the showers and hygiene needs at the Country Club.

Word of mouth had spread the news far and wide. People from Safety Harbor and beyond who had never been seen at Joe's before were walking in the door. Outside seating was filling up too, and Sally noticed that Johnny had gotten into pouring coffee for everyone.

The kitchen was flying with activity as Georgia cooked while barking orders. As soon as they caught on to Georgia's rhythm, Carmelita, Carla, and Hope were working as a well-oiled machine. Buddy and Caitlin were sitting in the corner of the kitchen munching on toast and drinking orange juice. Georgia had come out and commandeered Father Frank and Pastor Luther to wash dishes.

"It's good for the clergy to be humbled!" she said with a disarming smile that did not reveal whether or not she was serious about her comment.

"The Good Book says that if you want to be a big shot you have to be a servant," said Father.

"Well, that's not an exact quote," said Luther in good humor, "but it's pretty good for a Catholic!"

Clergy banter continued between them until finally there was a protest from the rest of the staff about the poor quality of their jokes.

"I've got to leave soon and get ready for Mass," said Father.

"I don't know about you Frank, but I've got my sermon ready. Did it last night!"

"After careful research, no doubt!" Father said, not to be outdone.

Sally came by and told those who had been there a while that they would need to move so that they could serve everybody. So many more had come to breakfast than they could have ever imagined. Yet no one had gone away without eating all they wanted.

After leaving the diner, they wandered and filled up the streets and continued in conversation. There, at the Square, no one could discriminate among the people of the Unsettlement and those who were citizens of, or tourists, in Safety Harbor.

Chapter 16

When Stewart told Katye that Sally had asked him to preside at Keith's funeral, she was surprised and not a little miffed.

"Sally didn't say a word to me about it!"

"Well, she wasn't asking you to do it!" Stewart said. "She was asking me!"

"Still, she knows the Bishop has benched you, that you aren't to do a thing that has to do with the church. I think he's right!"

"Why is it when you have made bad judgments that everybody thinks they have to help and everybody seems to think they know the answers and everybody claims to know better than you do! I feel totally patronized, I'm telling you! I'm tired of people deciding what's best for me, that I can't trust my feelings or my judgment, and by the way, I am condemned forever!"

As soon as he had said it, he knew that he had hurt her. "That last statement was not necessary, Katye. I'm sorry."

She became very quiet. Then, slowly, and almost in a whisper, she began.

"I don't want you to minimize what you've done, Stewart. You've betrayed me. You've betrayed your faith. Yes, you've betrayed our vows to one another. I hold you responsible. I get busy and sometimes even frenetic with activity. I know that. I enjoy people and I love the world around me and want to make it a better place."

Her voice was moving back now to a normal volume.

"You should have come to me. You should have told me how needy you were!"

"I tried, Katye. I couldn't get you to listen. I became so lonely, honey, so very lonely. Sometimes I could feel it pressing in on me like another layer of skin that was sore all over."

"This is a loneliness, dear Stewart, for which I can't take responsibility. You've had this deep within you since you were raised on the dreary

Nebraska prairie in a crazy family in an isolated town and in a sick and incestuous church. I can't make that all better for you. I wish I could, but I can't.

"You can go to some other woman's arms and she will take that loneliness away for a short time. You can replace it with the euphoria of passion, but one day the spell will break and within your heart, that same loneliness that sears the soul will invade like a hotbed of lava. But, this time it's worse because you have to live with your betrayal. You have to live with the fact that you have walked all over those who love you for the sake of a short-lived passion that passes away, and much of the time, by virtue of its own nature, ends badly

"The only reason I stay with you, Stewart, is because I know you are a good man. You feel terrible for what you have done. You have deep remorse. I know you love me. I know you need me. What I don't know is whether or not you will do it again. What I don't know is if you go back to the same kind of work, will you slip back into your old ways."

The room was filled with a seemingly eternal silence. Finally, she could stand it no longer. Katye got up from her chair and went to the kitchen.

"Would you like some tea, Stewart?" she called out.

He didn't reply, oblivious to her question, lost in thought. She was right, of course. He had always been lonely. He'd always felt himself to be the outsider. Others had told him that he was respected, a solid member of the Diocese, a trusted pastor and priest. But he didn't feel like it. He couldn't see it and he couldn't experience it. He would not feel right until every last clergy member in the Diocese accepted him and considered him their friend.

Truth was, that even if everyone considered him to be a friend or a confidante, it would not be enough. He would begin to discriminate between those who liked him most, those who liked him, and those who nodded their heads in passing. You couldn't fill up the bottomless pit within his soul.

Thoughts can get dark. Despair sets in. Judgment is clouded. You become vulnerable. Your need for closeness and comfort is magnified. You resent your spouse as she moves further away from you and seems quite okay with it.

His brooding thoughts were interrupted by Katye's voice.

"I took it by your lack of response that you didn't want tea."

He shook himself as if to cast off a spell.

"I'm sorry, Katye. I was thinking about what you said."

"What were you thinking?"

"Among other things how right you are!"

"Of course I'm right!" she smiled mischievously. "I'm always right."

"Except when you don't brake soon enough and scare the wits out of me the way you come up on the cars in front of you at a stoplight!"

Their friendly banter could always be counted on to lighten things up in a tense moment. It was one of the strengths of their relationship.

Chapter 17

BEFORE THE PARADE BEGAN, Mrs. Glover, the high school music teacher, had been recruited to lead some music down at the Square.

Father Frank had covered himself with the Archdiocese by getting the word out via the church email grapevine that there would be a Mass at seven o'clock that evening in lieu of the usual morning schedule. Whether that worked out or not, Father reasoned, was something for the angels to decide.

After the songfest, the microphone gave the ubiquitous peremptory feedback squeal as Mayor Lou approached it to address the people.

He turned to someone, anyone. "Can somebody turn this thing down?"

Hope approached him and whispered in his ear.

"Oh yes," he said in the newly adjusted microphone. "Can we get Rocky and Magdalena up here? They are the leaders of what people are calling the Unsettlement these days."

He smiled sheepishly, awkwardly. "Sort of the mayors, you might say!"

They joined him reluctantly.

"Now, on this magnificent occasion, which we don't seem to be planning, but is taking on a life of its own . . ."

"The Spirit is leading!" whispered Father Frank to Luther.

"Even Meriwether could assent to that with us!" said Luther.

"And I do!" said a voice behind them.

They looked around, surprised. "I don't agree with the Christian Good Old Boys' club too often, but I can go with you on this one!"

They were embarrassed and gave their apologies.

"This is a day for peace and unity," she said, not letting them off the hook. "We'll talk later."

Lou droned on at the microphone until Hope came up and tugged at his suit coat.

"Now I'd like to turn this over to Rocky and Magdalena," he said. "You may not know them," he said, "but I know them well."

Hope rolled her eyes at Magdalena.

"You will know them well in a short time, too! They are easy to know, easy to love, easy to respect."

There was a sustained applause as the crowd began more and more to sense the importance of this gathering.

Magdalena spoke first. "Rock and I would like to thank you for your invitation to the Safety Harbor parade! We are very excited about this day and what it may mean for the present and for the future."

She handed the microphone to Rocky. "There isn't a lot left to say except for this. Magdalena and I would like to invite all of you to the Unsettlement for a visit one of these days very soon!"

The crowd applauded.

Then Mrs. Glover led them all in "America" and "Amazing Grace."

Next on the schedule came a group from The Unsettlement in a mix of bluegrass and Dixieland jazz.

Nate took his kids up near the podium and they began to dance. Soon, there was a whole array of children from both communities dancing together, freely and joyfully. Some older adults soon joined the celebration.

Marshall and Carmelita kept close watch, especially on the children. They wanted no one in danger and no one to spoil this moment. They noticed that a ring was forming around the crowd, seemingly on its own. Those who were not dancing had joined hands in a circle to make sure no little ones got away and no one got away with one of their precious children. There they all were, young parents, people in wheelchairs, people who were rich and people who were poor, the educated and those without that opportunity, church people and people who stayed away from church as far as possible. No one could tell one from the other. It was just the human family in celebration for no other particular reason than life itself.

An outer circle formed around the smaller inner circle. By this time, they were excited and nobody needed to be prodded into dancing. Those in wheelchairs were participating with the help of someone who was dancing behind them. Soon, the whole town of Safety Harbor, the Unsettlement, and tourists, were joining in the dance.

Katye came to the microphone and called out, "Hello! Hello!" It was two or three minutes of intermittent "Hellos!" before the dancing finally stopped.

"I'm sorry to interrupt so much fun," she said, "but we have to quit dancing so we can have a parade."

There was a combination of "Yes" and moans.

Sally and Nate and the kids walked slowly up the hill to Main Street where the parade would begin.

"Did you see Joe dancing?" asked Buddy excitedly. "He was really good!"

"Yes, he was!" said Caitlin.

Sally and Nate looked at one another.

"You saw Joe?" said Nate. "Where did you see him?"

"He was standing in the inner circle of dancers right in the middle of us kids," said Caitlin! "I didn't know Joe could dance like that!"

"You saw Joe? Are you sure it was Joe?"

"I'm sure!" said Buddy and Caitlin in unison.

"He said, 'Hi Buddy! Hi Caitlin!'" Buddy smiled. "Boy! It was good to see him! I told him everybody missed him and everybody was looking for him and he said, 'I'll be back soon!'"

"But Joe," I said, "You're already here!"

"Yes I am!" he said. "That's all he said and he went back to dancing."

"Did you see him after that?" asked Sally. "Because, if you did, we need to find him and we need to tell Carmelita to take back the BOLO!"

"No, he told us he had to go and we looked and he was gone," said Buddy.

Chapter 18

THE ATTRACTION BETWEEN NATE and Sally was unmistakable to many, even to Nate's kids.

"Are you gonna marry my Daddy?" asked Buddy.

Caitlin grabbed her father's hand and held on tightly. A clumsy silence followed.

"Well, no, we're not getting married. Sally just lost her husband. We all have to be nice and kind to her," said Nate.

"Is that what you're doing Daddy? Being nice and kind?"

"Yes, he is," said Sally. "Your Dad is very kind!"

"That's not what Momma says, but I tell her she's wrong," said Buddy.

"Let's talk about something else, guys," said Nate.

Soon the kids ran ahead to join some friends they had spotted.

"We are going to have to be careful," said Nate.

"Nate, there can't be anything going on right now between us. I haven't even buried my husband!"

"I know," said Nate. "I want to respect that. I do. But, I just want to reach over and plant a kiss on you right now!"

"You think I don't?" she asked. "My marriage was over a long time ago. But still, I must respect the vows Keith and I made between us. He's not even cold in the grave yet."

"I know you're right," said Nate. "The thing is, I've loved you from the moment I saw you. I can't help it. I've tried not to. I know it's not right. I can't change my heart, Sally. I just can't."

"Nate, I just don't know if there's a future for us or not."

"I hope so," said Nate.

Sally wanted so much to say, "I do, too," but she could not. It was too soon, by far. It wasn't right.

"All I know," she said, "is that I couldn't start life again with a man who couldn't respect that my priority right now is to bury my husband. I have arrangements to make and details to see to, starting tomorrow."

"I'd like to help," said Nate.

"How would that look?"

"I know you are right," he said. "It's just difficult."

Sally's voice softened. "You think this is easy for me? We have to hold ourselves together and do what's right. We owe that to ourselves."

"Yes, and to my kids."

"Yes, and for our community. We owe it to our neighbors not to bring scandal down upon our little town. I owe it to Joe, too. I know I would disappoint him if we got into a relationship right now. We have to act with integrity, Nate. If we don't, there would be no chance at all of building a life together."

They walked together for a while in silence.

Sally broke the spell. "So, I don't think we should see each other right now or be seen together. We have to go our own ways, even more so now than ever. It hurts me to say this, but don't call me or email me, or text me, or try to communicate in any other way. We've just got to break it off, and now."

"I didn't know there was anything to break off."

"Don't play semantic games with me, Nate. You know what I mean."

"I do, Sally."

"If you love me," she said, "you'll do this."

Nate felt a thrill through his whole body. She had never mentioned that word before.

"I do love you, Sally," he said. "You know that."

"And you know how I feel about you."

"No, I don't. You've never said."

"I can't say right now for all of the reasons we have been discussing."

So, she did love him!

"I can wait for now."

Sally brushed her hand over his and then quickly walked ahead and joined another group walking up to Main Street.

Mayor Lou and Hope walked alongside Rock and Magdalena.

"Rock and I have been talking," said Magdalena. "We'd like to invite you two to ride in the Grand Marshal's car with us."

"Oh, I couldn't do that," said Lou.

"We mean that we'd like to share the car, with all four of us sharing the Grand Marshal's title."

Lou couldn't speak. He'd never had anything offered to him before, especially something that he felt strongly was rightfully his anyway! His feelings were all jumbled.

"Lou isn't good at this sort of thing, so I'll just say for the two of us that this is a very generous offer on your part and we accept!" said Hope.

"Good!" said Rock. "We don't want anything at someone else's expense and we don't want it to be either one community or the other."

"We're bound together by our common humanity," said Magdalena.

Now, Lou knew what to say. "Sounds like a good slogan for my next election campaign!"

"That's Lou's way of saying, 'Yes, thanks'!" said his wife.

"Who gets the front seat?" Mayor Lou joked.

"Lou," said Hope. "Shut up!"

"We'll get together later," Magdalena said to Hope with a half-smile. The two women hugged.

Chapter 19

SALLY LEFT THE CROWD that was moving toward Main Street and headed down to the corner of Newman and Main, where the diner stood dark and starkly empty. She was profoundly shaken by the frank and honest conversation that Nate and she had just a few moments ago. She reached for her keys and opened the door. The faint smells of breakfast were still in the air from the morning's events.

She drew in her breath sharply. Some things had been moved around since she had locked the doors on her way out. Tables and chairs had been re-arranged. In fact, there were more tables and chairs than there had been when she left. She looked out the large windows and noticed that the seating arrangement outside had been enlarged and re-arranged too. She had missed that on her way in because she had been thinking of her conversation with Nate.

She walked slowly through the diner as if she were seeing it for the first time. Her heart quickened. Joe must be home!

"Joe?" she called out. "Joe! Are you home?"

Her calls were met by silence.

She walked up to his apartment above the diner.

She knocked on the door. No answer.

She tried the door. It was locked.

"No Joe!" she said to herself aloud. It startled her. In the silence, it seemed that the voice had come from someone else.

She went back downstairs and into the kitchen. The place was immaculately clean, more so than the hurried job she had done earlier.

A note on the top of the freezer read, "Food in fridge and in storage shed." It was in the same handwriting as the note that had said, "Carry on."

She heard the front door open with its familiar loud and then softer squeak of the hinges. Maybe it really was Joe. Maybe he was home after all. She peered around the corner of the kitchen, half afraid to look.

It was Carmelita.

"I saw your car here and the lights on and thought I would come and see what was up," she said.

"You mean, you thought maybe Joe was home?"

"I was hoping so. Otherwise, I'm going to have to change my BOLO to a missing persons bulletin on him this evening."

"Well, it seems like a good idea to me."

"Let's go upstairs and see if he's taken clothes and his toothbrush and such."

"Can we do that?"

"I can do it," said the Chief of Police, "without a warrant if . . ."

"If you suspect foul play?"

"Among other things, yes."

The whole apartment was the epitome of modesty and simplicity. A light tight-weave carpet covered the floor. A couch, a coffee table, two living room chairs, and a rocker filled up the small living room accompanied by the smallest flat screen TV either of them had ever seen. A bookcase covered almost an entire wall. Carmelita went through a few of the books to see if anything might be hidden in them that would be a clue. She found nothing.

The kitchen was spotless and organized, without anything obvious that was amiss and no signs of foul play. Carmelita opened the medicine cabinet in the bathroom. The toothpaste was still there, along with his toothbrush and comb.

They circled back toward the single bedroom. Two suitcases were in the closet. They went back downstairs.

They discovered the refrigerator shelves in the diner virtually full of pre-cooked lasagna, just waiting to be reheated. Out in the storage shed, they found loaf upon loaf of garlic bread and in the freezer, an abundance of ice cream. One refrigerator was packed tight with more lasagna and the other had milk and orange juice.

"What could this be about?" Carmelita mused out loud.

Sally spoke up. "Carmelita, where did the extra tables and chairs come from, and how did they get here, and why did no one see anyone at all here doing anything?"

"My guess is, as wild and as crazy as it seems, that Joe has somehow provided this for us as the meal after the parade."

"But it won't be nearly enough," Sally said. "There are hundreds of people down there getting ready for this parade."

"You tell me what it's all about then," said Carmelita. "Do you have lasagna on your menu? Last time I checked, you didn't."

"Well, we could serve what's here until it runs out."

"Maybe it won't."

"Won't what?"

"Maybe it won't run out at all."

Chapter 20

THERE WERE A NUMBER of families in the Always Sunny Homeless Shelter who were excited that they were going to be in a parade. A few of the longtime residents at the shelter were known by the community. What surprised Luther most, though, was the people from his membership that showed up to ride the church bus, some of the ones he would least expect!

Maxine Olmay complained regularly about the people who used the shelter as dirty and unkempt. She was the first to board the bus.

Durwood Slaussenger showed up too. Luther had once described him to Father Callaghan as a real gadfly and a pain in the neck. He felt his gut tighten when he saw the old antagonist. What was he up to? He always had an agenda. What would he say? What would he do?

You never knew, but when he did it or said it, Luther would say to himself, "Of course. I should have thought of that!"

"Nice to see you, Durwood," he lied.

"I just thought I would come and see what was going on," he said.

"I'll bet you did," Luther thought to himself.

Jack and Laura Dunn came next. He could always depend upon them to provide the fresh air of sanity at Always Sunny. Emily Hooten, President of the Women for World Mission, was no surprise. Parishioners always told Luther that she did a lot of good and the harm she did ought to be ignored.

Priscilla Coover, who Luther suspected had a crush on him, boarded the bus breezily. "Good morning, dear Luther!" she said with too much familiarity and overblown cheer in her voice. Her hand reached out to touch his shoulder as she walked by his seat on the bus. He tried not to flinch.

Zeke Daniels, the church sexton, who was driving the bus, called out "All right, everybody! We're off to the parade. Sit down. Shut up. Look out the windows and wave for Always Sunny!"

"I wish I could get away with that at a Vestry meeting, Zeke!" Pastor Luther said.

"You had better not try that!" said Emily who had not perceived Luther's comments as intended humor. "That's not preacher talk!"

"By the way, thanks for the invitation," Maxine Olmay spoke up.

"Invitation?"

"I know your work when I see it! Don't feign surprise to me. There was an engraved invitation on my doorstep at 7:00 a.m. Somebody rang the doorbell, but when I got to the door, nobody was there. Instead, here was this invitation stuck in my screen door."

"Don't know anything about it!" Luther said.

"Right!" Durwood remarked, dryly.

"You, too?" asked Maxine.

"Same thing about ten after seven this morning."

Luther's head was spinning. Who would do this? He wanted to think it was someone who didn't like him who was making sure the church antagonist and his worst critics were all in one place with him. But, he couldn't imagine who that might be and, besides, who would have the time to do something like that? Everybody was so busy getting the parade together!

"So how many got invitations?" asked Emily.

"I did," said Priscilla. "I am sure I smelled your cologne on it, Luther, so don't deny it is your handiwork!"

"I did!" a half dozen people called out. Those at the homeless shelter had received the same engraved invitation as the church members.

"Who did it say it was from?" asked Luther.

"It was more like *where* it was from!" said Durwood.

"The card was from some outfit called the Isle of Gemma, LLC!" said Laura.

She had brought their invitation in her purse. She took it out of the envelope and read it out carefully. "You are cordially invited to ride the Always Sunny Church bus in the Safety Harbor Parade, Sunday, July 6."

"Gemma means "pearl" in Latin," said Zeke.

Everyone on the bus wanted to know how Zeke, of all people, would know that, but common courtesy kept them from asking, with the exception of Emily, of course, who bluntly asked, "How would a sexton and bus driver know that?"

No one said anything.

"Well, in case you wanted to know how a working man like me knows such a thing," he said, as if Emily hadn't made a comment at all, "I'm taking painting lessons from Susanna. We talk a little about everything when we are painting together. She's been teaching me a little Greek, a little Latin, a little of this and that. She says I might even become cosmopolitan soon!"

"Serves you right!" Luther thought.

"Do you paint by number, Zeke?" asked William, one of the children of the passengers from the shelter.

Everyone laughed and relief flooded the bus as a little child had quite unconsciously poured oil on a wound.

"Well, sort of, William" said Zeke.

"Zeke and I paint by number at the shelter!" said William.

"Maybe you have taught him the basics, young man, so he can go on to take lessons elsewhere!" Luther's eyes twinkled.

"Hey Zeke, we're not going to stop painting together, are we?" asked William.

"Not ever, young man."

Zeke was well beloved at the shelter. He had no one at home and often came by to fix a lock or unplug a drain. Then he'd stay and talk sometimes for an hour or two. He was especially good with the kids and was careful never to be alone with them.

"Okay, folks, we're headed out for the parade. Everybody sit down."

"And shut up!" said William.

"How impertinent, young man," said Emily.

"Thank you!" said William, smiling ear-to-ear.

Luther snickered behind his sleeve.

Chapter 21

THE ENTIRE HIGH SCHOOL parking lot was in chaos while participants waited to be told what place they would take in the parade. Katye wondered how she would ever get this started on time. Maybe she wouldn't. Maybe she shouldn't. Maybe it should start when it was ready.

She suddenly felt a warmth and relief go through her body. She relaxed. She knew Joe would approve. Maybe he was approving even now!

"Everything in its time," he had said. It was an old cliché but when he said it, it was as if it was being said for the first time.

Suddenly, behind her she heard the voice of Mrs. Saugus, the high school principal.

"Mrs. Saugus! Hi!"

"Hello yourself!"

Katye looked at her and thought that her face carried on it the time tracks of a million school days.

"I had come in to take care of a couple of matters in my office before the parade," she said. "I looked out my office window and I saw . . ."

"You saw chaos!"

"I saw an opportunity, maybe a place for me where I can help. I have some organizational skills myself."

"I'm sure you do! I could use some help here."

"I have a bullhorn that I sometimes use in the lunch room and at assemblies. I turn the volume up or down according to the situation," she smiled.

"Well, today," said Katye, "it seems we will need to use it at its loudest!"

With that, a partnership was formed. Soon Mrs. Saugus and her bullhorn were one.

"People," she called out, as if she were talking to some unruly students, "I need your attention and I need it now! Everybody in the parade needs to be quiet and listen!"

She repeated herself three times.

"You have to get their attention first," she said. "That's far from easy. The first time, you're just a droning voice. Each time, you rev up the volume just a bit. The second time, they notice someone is speaking. The third time, they deem it important. The fourth time, they really listen. You give me the order of things and I'll get these people in line!"

The "Unsettlement Band" would lead off the parade. Daniel followed with his long-suffering pickup that had seen much better days. The truck bed was filled with smiling, waving children and their parents. Behind him, he pulled a hayrack that had been arranged by Hobe, complete with bales of hay, to carry anyone else in the Unsettlement who wished to be in the parade. The children from the Village of Hope Disability Center followed in their fifteen-passenger van. A second van carried the students at the Pacific School for the Blind. Luther had arranged for those from the homeless shelter to walk with the Always Sunny church banner sign that usually stood at the driveway of the church parking lot.

Suddenly, out of the school bus garage, came the sound of a foghorn. The doors opened and a farm truck appeared, pulling a flatbed wagon. A large coffee cup, made of flowers, was mounted on the flatbed. "Joe's Fine Dine-ing" had been painted on a banner.

"They aren't on the list," said Mrs. Saugus. "What do you want to do with them?"

"They'll go next, Mrs. Saugus, right behind the homeless shelter."

"Move it right on in here!" she said to Hobe, who was driving.

There had to be music all through the parade. So, the bands were scattered throughout. The Middle School band came next.

Small business floats followed on behind the band. The nearby town of Clever sent their mayor and her husband in a new car from Clever Chevrolet. Susanna had put together a beautiful float for Argostoli's. The De-light-full Coffee Shop and Book Store came next. The Kite Shop, Ripple's Grocery, The Art Center, and many others, followed.

The Chamber float was placed right behind the high school band. And behind them all was the Grand Marshal's car with Magdalena, Rock, and Hope aboard. Everything was ready.

Now, where was the Mayor?

Chapter 22

HOPE CALLED HER HUSBAND on her cell phone. His voicemail answered.

"This is Mayor Lou and I'm not available right now. I'm out and about, no doubt, doing something good for the people of Safety Harbor. I do want to talk to you though, so leave a message for me."

"Lou, I don't know what you are doing," she said, "but we need you to get up here right now! Things are getting organized and it won't be long before the parade starts."

In fifteen minutes, Lou still hadn't shown. Hope called again. No answer. She started to be anxious.

"He's not answering his phone," she said to Katye. "It's a busy day in town. I hope he's okay."

"He's probably down at the waterfront glad-handing again and has forgotten the time," said Katye.

The truth was more concerning. Lou had collapsed. A crowd had gathered around him now. Hope heard the sound of an ambulance in the distance and hoped it wasn't about Lou.

"Somebody call Hope! Somebody call Doc Bailey! Call 911!" Voices could be heard through the crowd.

"Doc will meet the ambulance at the hospital," said Carmelita, who arrived within five minutes. "Stand back out of the way! We need your cooperation here."

The two ambulance attendants rushed to his side and took off quickly for Harbor View Hospital where they were met by nurses and Doc Bailey.

"Hello!" answered Hope, a bit loud and sounding frightened.

"Hope, this is Carmelita."

"Is this about Lou? Is he okay?"

"Hope, Lou's at the hospital and he's in good hands."

"Oh, no!" Hope answered. "I was afraid this would happen. There's so much excitement and he likes to think he's still sixteen! He hasn't slept well all weekend."

"I am sure they will want you at the hospital," said Carmelita. "Marshall will come and take you there."

Cold fear and anxiety shot through Hope. It could be a lot of things at Lou's age. Marshall escorted her inside.

"We're here to see the mayor," he said in an officious tone.

"Oh, hello, Hope," said the receptionist looking right past Marshall. "I'll see if Doc Bailey's available."

Eternity seemed to come and pass away. Hope had time to rehearse every possibility in her mind. Finally, Doc Bailey appeared.

"Hope, I believe he is going to be all right."

She sighed and shivered and then fell back in a chair.

"What's the matter with him, Doc?"

"It may be just exhaustion," he said. "I'm going to have to keep him and run a few tests. I've got to rule out a few things."

Lou was awake when Hope went into the hospital room and was fit to be tied.

"You're not going to any parade, Lou Schofield, and that's final!"

He slumped down in the bed in despair.

"Lou, quit treating this as if it were a cold," she said. "This could have been serious. Okay, if you won't listen, I'll tell you in no uncertain words. You could have dropped dead out there. Then, your people wouldn't have a mayor at all. How would you like that?"

Lou smiled faintly. "I wouldn't like that, but a few people might."

Hope's cell phone rang. It was Susanna.

"How is Lou?"

"Well, he's fine but he's not coming home any time soon.

"I'm sorry, Hope," said Susanna. "I know what it's like."

"I know you do," she replied. "I know you do."

Susanna offered no "He's going to be okay," comments. She knew that, sometimes, it was better not to say anything to those in crisis. She knew that, too often, those who couldn't think of anything to say and made something up, ended up speaking words that were most regrettable.

"I'll come up and be with you, Hope."

A tear rimmed her left eye. "That is kind of you, Susanna, but you have the parade."

"Don't worry. My staff will take care of the float. I'll come. You're going to need a ride home anyway.

"Thanks, Susanna," she said. "Thank you."

Chapter 23

"WHAT WOULD I EVER have done without her?" Katye asked herself.

She didn't realize she had been talking out loud.

"She's good at what she does, isn't she?" asked Sally.

Katye hadn't noticed her approaching.

"She was the principal when I was in high school. She's been here since anybody around can remember!" she said.

"Where are the kids?" asked Katye. "Nate said you had them!"

"Oh, they've had an offer to ride on the Joe's Fine Dine-ing wagon," she said. "They are really excited!"

"Who's driving," asked Katye. "Johnny isn't driving, is he? You never know if he's sober!"

"As a matter of fact, I am driving!" she said. "Johnny and Hobe are riding on the float!

"Of course! What a wonderful idea! After all, you are running Joe's right now. Who is more appropriate than you?" She looked down at her watch. It was two o'clock exactly.

Marshall was doing a last-minute check to see if the orange traffic cones were still standing in place to keep the side streets blocked going onto Main Street. There were always a few missing after the parade. He reported back that all looked good. Carmelita called Katye on her cell and told her that it was a go.

Katye gave Mrs. Saugus a thumbs-up and the principal blew her coach's whistle. Katye hadn't noticed a whistle before this, but there it was. That woman came equipped for all contingencies.

"Okay, people, we're going to begin now. Keep your chins up and look at the crowd. Wave and smile. This is a parade, people! This is for your town, our town, Safety Harbor, and for the Unsettlement too!"

It was as if she were giving the school cheer. This electrified the crowd, already full of anticipation, and brought a roar of response from all of the participants.

Stewart had quietly made his way down the street to watch the parade on his own. He had not found a place in which he could fit or be useful. He decided to look for a good place where he could watch the parade in privacy.

The old lighthouse! Yes! That was it! He would go to the lighthouse. This he did. He climbed the stairs to the first landing. He looked out on the little harbor town. From there he could see everything and everybody.

The parade had begun to wind its way out of the school parking lot and onto Main Street.

Chapter 24

BACK AT THE HOSPITAL, Lou, Hope, and Liz were delighted to learn that the local cable access station, KSHO, was broadcasting the parade this year. Now, here they were in a place they never expected to be, watching a parade they could not have imagined could happen in their little hometown.

It was good for Lou, thought Hope, to know that he didn't have to be in charge of everything, or appear to be, as was more often the case. The parade could go on without him, even if most of his constituents would want him there!

It wasn't long before Wendell made an appearance.

"Wendell!" exclaimed Lou. "What are you doing here?"

"I just had to come and check up on my golfing buddy to make sure he hadn't sneaked off to the country club while the nurse wasn't looking! Fact is, Lou, I can't take the hot sun on a day like this and word was that you were going to have a party in your room during the parade!"

"That's news to me!" said Lou.

"You're always the last to hear, Mayor!" said Hope, looking at him with a mischievous grin.

Georgia appeared at the door.

"I'm going to need some help from some of you!" she said. "Wendell, come along now! Liz, it's good to see you! Come and make yourself useful!"

Soon they came back with a rolling examination table laden with food that Georgia had prepared.

"This is the menu for our city dinner this evening after the parade!" she said. "We're going to try it out on you, Lou, and if it isn't poisoned, I'll serve it to everybody else!"

"Georgia, you're too kind," he deadpanned. "But, I'm not sure I can eat this. I've got tests tomorrow."

"No, not tomorrow," said the attending nurse. "We will be observing you through tomorrow. The doctor will determine what tests you need after that. If you can eat in moderation, you can go ahead. I've gotten permission from Doc Bailey."

Susanna came into the room and embraced Hope.

Father Callaghan appeared at the door. With a mocking flair of giving a blessing, he said, "Best greetings and blessings all around!"

"If you want to get Frank to make a pastoral visit, just have some food around. He can smell it for miles!" said Lou.

Father smiled good-naturedly. "Always good to see you too, Mayor!"

"I can't believe you are all here!" exclaimed Lou. "Who is left down at the parade?"

"Oh, the crowds are amazingly large," said Susanna. "Biggest we've ever seen. Word on the street is that news of our unusual parade has made it to Portland, Salem, and Eugene news media and some are streaming it on their websites."

"I wonder who managed that?" asked Lou.

"I think you are a strong suspect!"

"A good leader has to get on board with the people, Frank!" said Lou.

As they ate a delicious meal of lasagna and garlic bread, the parade began.

Susanna stood in Lou's room thinking her own thoughts. Why was this parade such a big deal, anyway? It had turned the whole town upside down and inside out. It was just a parade. The town always was a little crazy arranging it and carrying it out each year. But, this was different. There was a new kind of investment altogether. People seemed determined to make changes and to do what they had to do to make them work! In a short time, a relationship had formed between Safety Harbor and the Unsettlement. Perfect strangers rubbed shoulders with each other. Hospitality was offered. People ate together, even danced together, and now they were participating together in this new concept of a parade.

This was, in fact, Joe's Parade! It was only because of him and for him that all of this was taking place. It was a shock that he was gone, doubly so because he had disappeared so abruptly. Joe gave them a sense of direction for the community. He didn't seek an office or a position of importance in the city or try to be important. All he did was offer hospitality in his diner, cook meals, flip burgers, and share a few words of conversation. That was it.

Yet, there wasn't a person Susanna knew whose life Joe hadn't influenced. It was as if he had always been there. Now, they couldn't imagine their lives without him. She knew that the good people of Safety Harbor were carrying out all of this effort on the parade because they wanted it to be a tribute to him and what he had done for the town.

Barriers that Susanna thought would take years, even decades, to break down had come down overnight. Mayor Lou and the unofficial mayors of the Unsettlement, Rock and Magdalena, had nothing in common up to this point. Both sides had distrusted one another, each side suspecting the other of seeking to destroy the values of the other.

Tomorrow, the parade would be over and then the real work of getting back to their everyday lives would be the challenge. Meanwhile, there was much yet to come, Susanna suspected, and many miracles. She didn't know why she thought that. She just did.

Her eyes teared up and a lump came to her throat as all at once she missed Nick more than ever. She could almost feel his hand on her leg now. She flashed back to the rush she felt the first time he had done that when they had first started going out together. The early crackling excitement of attraction had matured into a more peaceful, deep, and settled, but no less exciting, love. She could almost feel him at her side now.

Unconsciously, her hand reached out for him but instead found its way to Father Callaghan's cassock. Embarrassed, she pulled her hand back quickly. If Father had noticed, he failed to mention it.

By now, the parade had reached the KSHO camera parked in front of the De-light-full Book Store and Coffee Shop.

"They're pretty good!" said Father, as he watched the Unsettlement Dixie Land Band.

"You always were a diplomat, Father," said Hope.

"He looks pretty full of lasagna to me!" said Lou.

Ever good-natured about his corpulence, Father responded by asking for another helping.

Chapter 25

THE PARADE HAD MADE its way from the school parking lot, down Maple, out onto Main Street, and was well on its way toward the city park, which was its destination. The crowds had grown thicker. Stores, restaurants, and bars strained to meet the demands for water, soft drinks, and beer.

Everyone knows how a parade should look, so who would have expected that a parade would be led off by some pretty rough-around-the-edges twenty-something musicians playing what was supposed to pass for bluegrass? Who could have even considered that a band of persons with disabilities would lead off behind them, clanging their tambourines and playing their sticks and recorders? Who could have envisioned that blind children would be waving from a bus at a crowd they could not see? It was remarkable.

Fifteen minutes into the parade, Nate wondered why things had come to a sudden stop. What he could not see along with many others in the second half of the parade line-up was that the bus had stopped in front of the De-Light-Full Book Store and Coffee Shop. The students from the School for the Blind wanted to be out with the crowd so that they could experience the parade and the staff had relented.

Each held the hand of another, as they got off the bus. With some assistance, they formed six rows of five in order to walk within the parade corridor. They proceeded somewhat tentatively at first.

A loud cheer broke out from the crowd as the students began the second half of the parade on the street among the people. Gradually, they picked up a beat from the Rhythmatics. Some began to kick their legs in the air. Another roar and rousing applause came from the crowd.

From the hospital room, could be heard loud cheers and hand claps as they watched this phenomenon on KSHO. Such commotion brought three nurses into the room.

"What is happening in here?" asked Ruth Edgefield-Martin, Lou's attending nurse. "I thought I told you that quiet and rest was in order for you, Mayor Lou!"

Then she turned and saw the spectacle unfolding in front of all of them on the television screen.

"Oh my!" she said. "There's my angel, Little Therese. See those little feet moving?"

"And that smile," said Father Callaghan. "That's a million dollars right there!"

"Oh, it's worth much more than that, Father!" she said.

A tear made its way down Father's cheek as he thought of how much this parade showed us how we could be, if only we were willing. Even the hardest of hearts had to be impressed. Even the most cynical among them had to be moved. And so, he was.

Chapter 26

THE MAYOR WASN'T A man to be alone. He preferred the voices of humans, the barking of dogs, and the sound of the tide. He was never happier than when he was generally mixing with his constituents on the streets of Safety Harbor, feeling the wind, and smelling the salt air. Now he had been sidelined at one of the most important events ever to happen in his city. He felt it deeply. Lesser men than he had arisen to higher office, but Lou was happy to live in a small town where he could be in personal touch with his people.

He had been challenged for election over the years for this office, but he had been successful in fending off all comers. There were some, perhaps growing in number, who felt that Lou had served his time and his usefulness to the city.

He believed in God, but he wasn't sure of much beyond that. His parents had taken him to a Presbyterian Church. Now, he went to church on occasion, once, maybe twice a month, at different congregations, more for his relationships with his constituents than anything else. He always put a generous check in the offering, which, he theorized, made people remember that he had been there and they would forgive him for not being there more often. He felt closer to Father Callaghan than any other clergy in town, although he had grown up to suspect the Papacy of corruption and superstition.

"All that mumbo jumbo," his father had once said after they had attended a Catholic funeral. "Up and down and up and down! Thinking that those saltines are Christ! I don't know much, but I know a cracker when I see one!"

He often called the priest "Frank" without any titles. Hope said it was disrespectful, but he had a feeling that Father enjoyed just being called by his first name once in a while by someone who didn't want anything from him.

He knew that he would have fought Joe tooth and nail on this parade business if he had been present, but since he was not, he had been ganged up on by the Steering Committee and undermined by his own wife. But, now he could see that he had been wrong. He didn't know what would come of this, but something about this parade seemed right.

Lou had always been highly aware of image, both his and the city's. He didn't see them apart from one another. He had been afraid of what people would think of this kind of a parade. But now something transformative was going on within him. He was, suddenly, very much at peace with the parade bringing out into the light those who were usually kept in the shadows, the disabled, the poor, and yes, the "dippy hippies," as Lou had once called them. Yet, at the same time, the business community was involved, the schools, the arts community, and others.

No decent mayor, Lou often said, could care for only a few of the citizens. The blind, the mentally disabled, yes the poor who had taken up residence in the Pastor Luther's shelter. They were citizens too. They were all his people. What had bothered him most was that Joe hadn't consulted him ahead of time about the changes, and for the first time he was not chairing the Steering Committee for the parade. Joe was in charge, absent or present.

"We can do this out of our love and respect for him this year," Hope had said. "We don't know what the future holds."

Now, it was as if some fated plan beyond the parade was being carried out, an inevitable event, the outcome of which was yet to be realized. He sat back in his hospital bed, watching the people around him, sad that he wasn't downtown, still, all in all, happy to have such loving friends and family around him.

Chapter 27

THE SOUND OF THE motorcycles could be heard as the town's bad boys, Jens Marsden and Roy Edgefield, descended upon Safety Harbor via Highway 101, that came through town and became Main Street. Through traffic was being diverted onto residential streets and directed out through the city limits to the other side. Jens and Roy had ignored the detour signs and now came riding into town heading directly toward a head-on collision with the parade, stopping everything in its tracks.

Daniel got out of his pick-up and went to talk reason with them. He didn't know them and he didn't know that the whole town of Safety Harbor did, in fact, know them very well.

"There's a parade going on here, guys," he began as if he didn't know they were up to no good. "If you turn around and go back to the city limits, you can see where to go to get through town."

"That so," said Jens.

"Where's your badge, buddy?" Roy challenged him.

"Look guys, we don't want any trouble, but you are holding up the parade and we'd appreciate it if you would move your bikes so we can get on with it!"

"Not gonna happen," said Jens.

It didn't take long for Daniel to realize they were in a hostile mood and he would have to back off. Nate and Jeremy and several others began to move toward the front of the parade.

Nate called Carmelita from his float. "You'd better get down here. Marsden and Edgefield have blocked the parade and there's a standoff. There's going to be trouble."

By the time Nate arrived, a crowd had gathered on the scene. He sensed, as he approached, that the situation was serious.

"Okay," Nate said, "we're all going to back off here and wait for Carmelita."

"Oh, you're bringing that woman cop into this so that she can settle a man's fight?"

"She's the law, Jens, and she'll settle this," said Nate.

"Like hell she will," Roy piped up. "Let us through or we're going to mow everybody down!"

Suddenly one of the blind students called out, "Uncle Roy, is that you?"

"No, it's not me, kid!" he sputtered. "You've mistaken me for someone else!"

"Oh yes, it is you!" the little voice continued. "I know your voice. I'm Little Therese, your niece. You know, Momma works at the hospital. Momma and I know you. Are you in the parade too?'

Silence followed.

Suddenly Jens began to laugh at Roy. "You fool!" he said. "What do you mean, 'It's not me?' What kind of a dumb answer is that? You got family in this shin-dig?"

This could have been the end of it, but Roy was humiliated and couldn't let it go.

"You stay out of this, kid. It's not any of your business!"

Suddenly Nate remembered that there was a Ruth Edgefield-Martin who worked at the hospital. She had come down to his boat with the local ambulance and attended one of his customers. Was that Therese's mother? If so, maybe she could come down and talk some sense into her brother.

Nate called the hospital.

"Ruth, this is Nate Beard. Do you have a brother named Roy?"

There was silence on the other end, broken by a long sigh.

"What's he done?" she asked.

"Well, Jens and he have just ridden their motorcycles into town. They've blocked the parade from going forward with their motorcycles and refuse to move. It's getting tense down here. It must be your daughter who recognized his voice. I figured that maybe you could come down here and at least talk some sense into Roy and maybe Jens would follow on after. Carmelita is on her way. I just thought it couldn't hurt if you were here with us to provide some back-up and support."

"I'll be down!"

"Thanks. And . . ."

"Yes?"

"Please don't tell Lou. It will just upset him and there isn't a thing he can do about it."

"Okay. Sounds good."

Ruth had never done this before so it came as a surprise to her supervisor, when she asked to leave her shift.

"Now?"

"Right now!"

"What's going on?"

"I can't say."

"You have to say. I can't let you off for no reason."

"If you have to write something down just, say it's a family emergency."

"Ruth, what's going on?"

"There's trouble down at the parade. It's my brother again and that no-good friend of his, Jens. They are holding up the whole parade. They are in a mood. I need to get down there to see if I can talk to him."

"You go."

"Thanks. I'll be back as soon as I can. Oh, and don't tell Lou. It'll just upset him."

"I understand."

But it was not to be.

Father Callaghan said, "Something's afoot. Look! The whole parade has stopped. What do you suppose is going on?"

"Well, the first time," said Susanna, "it was the kids getting out of the bus. I can't imagine that it's anything to worry about."

"Something is not right here, Susanna."

"I agree with Frank. Let's ask Ruth if she knows anything," Lou said, punching his call light. "After all, I'm paying for this gadget. They have hovered so much that I haven't needed to use it until now."

It was not Ruth who appeared at the door.

"Where's Ruth?"

"Ruth has a family situation she has to attend to," said Shirley. "She had to leave for a while."

"I hope it isn't Little Therese. She's in the parade and it's getting very hot out there!"

"No, Little Therese is okay," she said.

"What then?" Lou asked.

"Maybe it's her own business, Lou," said Wendell.

"Something is wrong," said Father Callaghan. "I can feel it. You need to tell us if it's important."

"By all means," said Lou.

"Well, the thing is, Ruth didn't want Lou to know because it will just upset him," explained Cathy Cosmo, Ruth's supervisor.

"Upset him!" said Hope. "He's the mayor. He has a right to know!"

"You are right, Hope. I know. I felt bad about keeping it a secret. Ruth's brother Roy and that Jens Marsden have stopped the parade with their motorcycles and there's a stand-off right on Main Street!"

"We have to get down there!" said Lou.

"You need to stay here and get your rest!" said the Head Nurse.

"There'll be no stopping him now," said Hope. You might as well let him get dressed. Otherwise he'll go down there in his hospital gown and we'll all be embarrassed!"

"Doc Bailey won't like this one bit," said Connie.

"You'd better figure out the paperwork on this, because I know my husband, and he's going!"

Chapter 28

FROM THE LIGHTHOUSE, STEWART could see a standoff was taking place. Carmelita's squad car had pulled up, with lights flashing. Maybe he'd leave well enough alone and let the police handle it. Sometimes, the more people who got involved, the chances for violence increased.

It didn't appear there was any use for him there. He was on leave these days so he couldn't represent himself as peacemaker by virtue of his collar. It didn't appear there was any room for him anywhere. He wished he could get himself up out of this emotional pit he was in, but he simply could not manage it.

Tomorrow, he would be traveling with Sally to the Portland airport to pick up Keith's remains. He welcomed a positive development. Anywhere. The fact that it was positive to go and pick up his friend's remains told its own sad story.

He had phoned the Bishop and asked if he could preside at Keith's funeral. The bishop was not pleased.

"We can't have you representing the Church in your present state of mind. If I were a Catholic bishop I would say you have to do penance. However, what I can say to you is that you need to go inside your own soul and find the wounded places and heal them and go out in the world and balance out what you have done. Put your world back into balance and the world will be in balance. It's a mystery but all religions call us to do that."

His last stint at St Cecilia's in the little town of Alexandria had been lonely. Its proximity to OSU in Corvallis hadn't turned out as he had hoped. Corvallis could just as well have been a thousand miles away. For some, who lived in what its citizens often called Alex, that would have been just fine.

The congregation didn't expect much out of him, but, what they did expect, they demanded: office hours, visitations, and a homily that was good and short, and if there was a choice to be made between the two, then, the brevity of the homily took priority. With only fifty members, he ran out of things to do.

The only clergy, other than Stewart, serving in Alexandria, was non-resident. She drove in on Sundays from Corvallis where she was an assistant in a larger church. She was only there on Sunday mornings and one other day during the week.

Katye was busy at the university finishing up her PhD. Sometimes he didn't see her for days. He decided he would audit a class on Archaeology in Middle East Studies at the university. After class, Professor Rita Binyon and he had carried on fascinating conversations about her stints to archeological sites around the world. These conversations graduated to a coffee shop after class. Then, they grew to two days a week. They began to take long drives in the country. One day in Eugene, they got a motel room.

Life became increasingly complicated. He lied regularly. He had to remember where he had told Katye he had been and make sure the church secretary had the same information, or misinformation. He wasn't good at this and he knew it was going to go south.

He would learn later that someone in Katye's cohort at the university had seen them together in Portland. It took her three weeks to tell her friend but she finally had to bring herself to do it. Katye was silent after her friend had told her over coffee next to the campus.

Finally, she said, "Thank you. Thank you very much." She walked out the door, forgetting to pay for her coffee.

She was furious as she walked back to the campus. Tears came to her eyes. It was as if her brain were on fire. Nothing looked familiar around her. She ran into a lamppost at an intersection and apologized. She began to chuckle at the absurdity of what she had just done and began to laugh out loud. Careening down the sidewalk, a tornado was twisting inside her soul from which there was no escape.

Back on campus, she picked up her books and laptop and drove toward home. She decided she would not confront Stewart. Not now. She might come across as the victim and she would have none of that. He would be discovered at a time he thought he was most safe. She would find a way.

It came soon enough. Stewart announced to Katye that his archeology class was taking a field trip to Portland to listen to a speaker on the Middle East at the World Affairs Council. The irony of the name of the organization was not lost on her.

She called Barney Sorenson, the President of the Congregation, and met him for coffee. In the same coffee shop at which she had been given the bad news, she revealed everything to him. Barney was of the era when people didn't talk of such things and it was difficult for him to discuss this, especially with a woman, and he told her so.

"This is so important, Barney, and we have to take care of this. We have to catch Stewart and confront him. For the good of all of us, including the two involved in this, we need this to stop right now."

"Does the professor have a husband?"

"Yes, she does."

"Anybody I know?"

"Probably not, but it's somebody a lot of people know on campus. He's the Dean of the Engineering Department."

"Oh God!" said Barney.

"We need somebody to go to that World Affairs Council meeting from the Church and confront those two on the scene."

"Oh, I dunno," said Barney. "I don't think we should put anybody in that position."

"You're right, I guess. We shouldn't have someone there that he would recognize."

Barney thought a minute.

"Sarah has a relative who's a private detective. He might do a little work for us on this. He owes her a couple of favors. She could call in one of her chits."

"Let's do it."

A week later the President of the Congregation called Stewart and told him the vestry wanted to meet with him.

"About what?"

"Oh, just some concerns we have."

"Can't it wait until the next vestry meeting?"

"No. It can't."

There was a long silence. Fear went through Stewart and he broke out in a cold sweat. His heart raced and he began to panic. Someone had found out.

"Slow down," Rita had said when he called her. "It's probably just something else and you've blown it way out of proportion."

He wanted to think she was correct, but he knew something wasn't right when he arrived in the church parking lot and saw Katye's car. When he walked into the meeting downstairs in the Fellowship Hall, every member of the Vestry was present. Katye was there too, and there was a man he didn't recognize.

As he walked in, the conversation that had been flowing, came to an abrupt end.

Smiling through a surprised face, he joked, "What is this? An intervention?"

"Yes, it is, Father," said the man he didn't know.

He was presented with video images of Rita and him at the World Affairs Council conference and of their holding hands while they walked down the street within range of a security camera; and as they returned to a hotel in downtown Portland, not emerging from their room for two hours. He was presented with the credit card receipt and a record of his checking into a room under his own name! There was video of them going into the hotel and leaving.

He was caught dead to rights. In one instant, he realized that all of the excuses, the justifications he had given himself for what he was doing, were invalidated. A dark chasm of Hell enveloped him and he realized that his life, as he had once known it, was gone and would never return. Goodness had been lost somehow, and within it, he felt a reprise of the Fall as if he were Adam himself. He, who had counseled so many couples before their marriages and led them in the vows, "until death us do part", was himself, the perpetrator of a fraud.

He could not imagine the road out or any way through this. The next few days he was trapped in a nightmare as the Bishop insisted that he come to Sunday Eucharist and confess his sins to the congregation.

Hot tears rolled down his cheeks and fell to the floor as Katye told him at their first meeting together since the fiasco that she would take him back if he would "get some help" and if he promised never to contact or to see Rita again.

"As you know, I have ways of finding out," she said. "We will not live as husband and wife, until I trust you, and I can't tell you when that will be. We're going to live in Safety Harbor where I've taken a job at the community college."

"Katye. I'll go wherever you go. I'll do whatever you ask."

They had been in Safety Harbor nearly a year now, and Katye had worked herself into the community as if she had been around forever. Stewart had not progressed well. He had kept up his promise to go to therapy, but he hadn't found a job, and he remained reclusive. It was just easier to keep a low profile and not have to explain everything, or otherwise lie to them when people innocently asked him about his past.

He had moved on beyond feeling sorry for himself. He extended his apologies to Rita and her husband. He sent a letter of regret to his former congregation. Now, his therapist was challenging him to explore his anger, so that he could figure out the source of it rather than turning it in on himself as depression.

Clearly, he had work to do.

Chapter 29

"It's too bad, isn't it?"

"What's too bad?" asked Stewart.

"Oh, that scene down there at the head of the parade. As it is right now, it's going to end badly, you know."

"I know."

"What do you think causes people to pull off senseless stunts like this?"

"Sometimes people feel left out and want to be noticed. Sometimes, they're just mean and destructive. Sometimes, I just don't know."

"Don't you think it might be because they are lost?"

"Lost? Lost. Yes, that's it. They're lost."

"When people are lost they do a lot of different things out of character. It depends upon their personalities, their backgrounds, and just how desperately lost they are."

"Yes, I think you are right, Joe," Stewart said. "I hadn't thought of it that way before."

"Many people are lost but they've been lost so long that if you told them that they were lost, they would be offended and deny it. They've found a way to compensate. The compensation itself becomes their lives. Sometimes it comes out the way Jens and Roy are acting right now."

"What's going on down there?"

"They insist on getting through the street going the opposite way on the parade route."

"Why don't they just let them through?"

"The townsfolk are right. You've got to stand up to bullies. If you let them through, they'll demand more of you, the next time. Who knows? Maybe, they'd even run over some kids or damage property. So, there's a standoff because nobody can think of another option."

"What do you think is a solution?"

"Has anyone thought of asking them to turn around and lead the parade the rest of the way?"

"Would they do that?"

"Maybe yes. Maybe no."

"That would be rewarding bad behavior, though, wouldn't it?"

"What is more important? Doing it according to the rules or showing mercy and doing what's best for all?"

"Well, when you put it that way, there's no question. It's like turning the other cheek. It's standing up to them and, at the same time, inviting them in!"

Suddenly, Stewart realized that he was talking to someone who was supposed to be missing!

"Joe!" he exclaimed. "Are you back? Are you really here?"

"For the moment, yes, for the time being."

"Well, I'm glad. I really am. We've missed you. Life hasn't been the same since you've been gone."

"Why don't you go down there and ask Jens and Roy to turn around and lead the parade?"

"But me? No one would listen to me! I'm a nobody here in this town."

"Everybody is somebody, Stewart."

"If you knew about me you might not ask me to do this."

"If we knew about one another, we would be surprised, and sometimes, not a little disappointed."

"Yes, but if you knew what I have done!" Stewart said.

"Oh, I've got a pretty good idea. I'm asking you to do this. Don't you trust me? Isn't that good enough?"

"I don't know if I can do it. I don't know what people will think. I might just embarrass Katye. She might just kick me out. I'm just one stupid move away from packing my bags."

"Well, if you go out like this, at least it'll be for something good. You will have tried your best."

"Why don't you do it, Joe? They'll listen to you!"

"Ah, but I need you to do it for me, Stewart," he said.

"Okay, I'll do it, Joe. It'll be difficult, but I'll do it for you."

"I have every confidence in you, Stewart. Every confidence."

He felt Joe's hand on his shoulder. Then he was gone.

Had he really been here? Had this really happened? Had he fallen asleep and dreamed? Was he going crazy? Still the idea seemed a good one and what did it matter? He could give it a try or find someone else to do it.

"It's you, Stewart. It's only you who can do this. This is one of the things for which you were born."

He looked around. No one was there.

He looked down at his feet as he turned to descend the steps of the lighthouse.

He picked up a business card he hadn't noticed earlier. His eyes fell on the few words on the card.

Joe

The Isle of Gemma

Chapter 30

STEWART WOUND HIS WAY down the hill from the knoll upon which the little lighthouse stood. The path was narrow and a bit steep in places. As he walked along, he reflected upon his recent conversation. Did this really happen? Maybe it wasn't Joe after all. Maybe it was just an idea he had himself. Maybe he just thought he had a conversation with him.

But, what did it matter? He had a possible solution to the madness that was taking place on the street because of a couple of bullies. It was a creative, ingenious idea. But, would they take it coming from Stewart? Maybe he should suggest it to Nate or Jeremy or maybe even Father Callaghan. They had a lot more credibility in the community.

No, it was his to suggest or not at all. After all, Joe had said something inexplicable, like, that he was born for this, or something like that. It sounded more than a little grandiose. That had to have been a dream. He must have nodded off for a minute.

He shielded his eyes from the sun as he looked ahead to see whether perhaps things had been resolved and the parade had moved on. It had not. The lights were flashing on Carmelita's squad car. She rarely used them and when she did, you knew that something mattered.

Jens and Roy had refused to turn their motorcycles off as Carmelita had requested.

"We're going," said Jens, "one way or another. Don't try to stop us. It would be a mistake."

"Do either one of you have guns on you?"

"If we do," Roy said, "it's our perfect right."

"Provided you have a permit for them," said Carmelita. "I'm going to ask each of you voluntarily to hand over any weapons you may have on you until this thing is over."

"It can be over right now," said Roy. "Just let us through."

"Have you guys been drinking?"

"No, we have not!" said Jens.

"Will you take a breathalyzer test?"

"No, we will not," said Roy.

"At least shut down those engines then, guys. Please."

By now, Little Therese was crying. With the loud engines, she was afraid her Uncle Roy was getting hurt.

Your niece is crying, Roy," said Nate. "Have a heart, man! She's afraid something has happened to you. She's worried. Do this for her."

Roy turned off his engine. Reluctantly, Jess followed. Somebody brought little Therese over and put her on Roy's lap.

"Uncle Roy, what's going on?" she asked. "Are you in trouble? Momma says you're always in trouble."

"Your momma doesn't know everything!" he mumbled.

"Just about, she does!"

Ruth had arrived on the scene now.

"Roy, have you been drinking? If you have, you put that little girl down right now! In fact, put her down anyway! Who put her on your lap in the first place?"

"I want 'em to take a breathalyzer test but neither one of 'em want to do it," said Carmelita.

"If you haven't been drinking, Roy," said his outraged sister, "then why not submit to the test? And, what in God's name are you doing here? Why are you here making such a damned fool of yourself? Don't you know you are spoiling Little Therese's day, Roy, to say nothing of all the other kids and fine people of Safety Harbor who are just out trying to have a good time?"

As she talked, she became angrier by the minute. Carmelita came up and squeezed her hand, both in solidarity and as a restraint. She didn't need this escalated any further.

There was now a stalemate. The two men had turned off their motor-cycle engines, but they still refused to move. The situation was pregnant with potential violence. Ruth removed Little Therese from Roy's lap and retreated from the scene. Arrests were imminent.

It was at this moment that Stewart walked on the scene.

"I've talked to Joe. We watched this together from the lighthouse. He told me to come down here and ask you guys to turn your vehicles around and to finish leading the parade to the park."

"Who is this?" The question was asked a dozen times or more in the crowd.

"Stewart Grenville," somebody said. "He's the weirdly reclusive husband of Katye Puckett. Just about the opposite of her, I'd say. He's unstable. He could make this situation worse."

Everyone looked at Stewart in open-mouthed silence.

Jens was the first to respond. "Oh, he did, did he? Well, just who is this Joe character?"

"It's Joe, you fool," said Roy who had been distancing himself from Jens for several minutes now. "You know, the guy who runs the diner."

"Who does this dude think he is, ordering me around?"

"He doesn't tell you, Jens. He invites you to do this; and if you want it, even though you don't deserve it, it's a place of real honor in the parade," answered Stewart.

"If he wants me to do this, why doesn't he come and tell me himself?"

"Well, nobody knows just quite where he is right now."

"The heck you say," said Jens, watching his language around Little Therese.

"He was with me a few minutes ago and some people have seen him the last few days but he doesn't seem to stay long in one place. Lately, he's been asking other people to speak for him and I guess I'm the latest."

"Give me your guns, boys. Let's do this," said Carmelita.

Slowly, Roy reached under his jacket at his waist. Both police officers had their hands on their holsters at the ready. Roy brought out a pistol and handed it over to Carmelita. She nodded her head toward his leg. Reluctantly, he pulled a Ruger from a leg band.

"Come on, Jens," pleaded Roy. "We can get ourselves out of this now. Just hand over the gun on your waist first."

First?" exclaimed Marshall. "More than one as well, eh Jens?"

He reached under his jacket and handed over his .50 caliber pistol to Marshall who now placed it on the ground with the others. Carmelita kept her hand out and open. He removed one from his lower leg, same as Roy.

"Knives?" asked Marshall. "Any knives, boys?"

"I suppose you're gonna want my pants, too!" said Jens sarcastically.

"No, but you can pull them up!" retorted the Chief of Police.

The crowd tittered and the tension broke.

"Ha, Jens! She got you!" said Roy. He broke out in a belly laugh. "Pull yer pants up, Jens! Ha! Ha! Ha! Ha!"

"That's enough, Roy!" said Ruth. "Just shut up! Things are bad enough here without you making them worse!"

Little Therese spoke up. "That's enough, Uncle Roy!"

Those who knew Roy and Jens, were aware that this could go either way. They had seen them get into it down at The Rogue Tap and knew that things could get bloody. Then, at other times, they'd leave the bar with their arms around one another, singing bawdy drinking songs. You just never knew.

"Well, I've got this little pocket knife, officer," said Jens, removing a rather large switch blade from his pocket! "Ha! Ha! Ha!" he said, sarcastically. "I guess this is supposed to be funny."

"Hand it over to the Chief," said Marshall, which he did.

"How about that semi-automatic that you've got in your backpack, Jens?" Roy doubled over laughing. He couldn't stop now and the crowd, once frightened, now laughed freely.

"I ain't got no semi-automatic!" Jens protested. "Ha! Ha! Ha! This is all so funny!"

"How about you, Roy?" asked Marshall. "Any knives or shivs?"

"Yeah, Uncle Roy!" called out Therese. "Any knives or sieves?"

The crowd laughed nervously.

"No, nothin' like that, Little Therese. I've learned my lesson."

"If you'd learned your lesson, we know that you wouldn't be carrying guns around."

"Perfectly legal," said Roy. "I ain't killed nobody."

"Not yet," said Ruth.

"I'm gonna have to take you boys in for disturbing the peace," said Carmelita.

"How about they lead the parade the last two blocks into the park as Joe suggested before you do that?" Stewart asked.

Ruth's eyes caught Carmelita's. Roy's sister's look was plaintive.

"Okay, this is ridiculous, unheard of, and all wrong on its face. But, if it will make peace and keep our parade going, go ahead," she said. "Still, the law's the law. I will arrest you after the parade!"

"Of course, you guys will have to turn your bikes around," said Stewart.

"But, we said we wouldn't turn around, Roy!" said Jens. "We'll be backing down if we do this."

"Jens, when have you ever had a chance to lead a parade? When will you ever have a chance to lead a parade again?" It was Johnny Watson. "You were a bully in school and you are still a bully. I remember when you would catch me in the back yard of the school by the fire escape and beat the bejesus out of me, just because you could."

"Johnny Watson?" thought Katye. "Johnny Watson? Where did he come from?"

"You were your own worst enemy in high school, and you still are. Here you are rebelling, but against what? Get in there and lead the parade. It's the first time and probably the last when you'll be able to lead anything. You'll probably be in jail by this time next month or next year!"

Hobe tugged on Johnny's sleeve from behind, pulling him back into the crowd.

"That's enough, John. Things are going the right direction. Don't make 'em worse."

"Johnny, I wish I could say I was sorry I beat you up, but you had such a smart mouth on you. The teachers said you were clever. I thought you were just a smart ass. I got so mad at you I just waited for the opportunity."

"You were a bully, Jens!" An unidentified voice called out in the crowd.

Carmelita sensed the tension rising again, "You can sort out ancient history later. Are you gonna do this, or not?"

"Can I ride with you, Uncle Roy?" called out Little Therese with her arms beckoning. "Will you let me ride?"

"Okay I'll do this for you, Little Therese," said Roy. "I'll do it for you. I wouldn't do it otherwise."

"And who am I gonna do it for?" asked Jens.

"Do it for Shirley!" said Johnny.

The home folks around who had lived their whole lives in Safety Harbor knew that Shirley Boley was the girl that both Johnny and Jens had competed for in their senior year of high school. There had been a bitter rivalry between them. Shirley went back and forth but ended up marrying Jens. She had left him the day that he had come home drunk and mean, one too many times.

There was an audible gasp from those watching. For a moment Jens glared at Johnny. Then a tear rolled down his cheek.

"What the hell is in the air?" he mumbled. "I must be allergic to something!"

He loved her still and he knew that he had blown it, that she would still be with him if he hadn't been so insecure, so accusatory, just so mean at times, but he just kept on being mean anyway. He couldn't hold back the tears now.

"Yeah, I can do that, Johnny. I'll do it for Shirley."

He turned his bike around and fired it up.

"Bring that niece of mine over here!" said Roy.

"She's not riding that thing alone with you Roy!" said Ruth. "I'll get on the back and hold her."

Roy fired up the engine and his sister and niece got on board behind him. Marshall had gone down to the police station and brought back two motorcycle helmets. Carmelita would not allow Little Therese and Ruth go without them.

"Whoa, people! Now, it's my turn!" said Katye. "You can't just take off and think that people are going to follow you. The parade has been stopped for an hour now, just because of this situation."

"Let me take it from here!" It was Mrs. Saugus again. "My bullhorn and I will get people in order pretty fast.

"Okay, people," she started down the parade route. "We're going to get started again!"

Every alumnus from Harbor High who heard her voice had a momentary flashback when Principal Saugus used to roam the halls, the lunchroom, and the school yard barking out orders. Those who were too young to have a memory of it would soon enough have a memory of their own. So, because they had been conditioned to do so, they automatically came to attention and waited to do what they were told.

"We're going to start just as soon as everybody's ready! I'll know every one's ready when they have zipped their lips!"

Katye followed her to the end of the line.

"Are we good to go?" she asked Mrs. Saugus.

"You tell me! You are in charge!"

"Well, the people who came up front to deal with the situation are back on their floats and in their trucks. If everybody's in place, then we will get started."

Katye called Carmelita and, within five minutes, the entire parade was in motion and headed to its destination at the city park.

Chapter 31

SHE HAD BEEN BORN, Louise Meriwether Evans, in Tarpon Springs, Florida. Her great grandmother had taught primary school there for thirty years, beginning in the 1920's, and her grandmother followed on behind her. Meriwether's mother had gone on to be a college professor at St. Steven's College, a small exclusive school in St Petersburg. She was a middle child.

Her older brother, Colonel Earl Grey Evans, went into the military directly from high school and had a successful career in the Air Force. Although he had been stationed all over Europe, he was now back home at MacDill Air Force Base in Tampa.

Her younger brother, Nigel, became chronically ill at an early age. In spite of his fragility, he had become successful in his mortgage business. He had married into one of the financially secure Greek families who had founded and settled Tarpon Springs. He still lived in the house where they grew up, although he had remodeled and added on in order to fit in better with his well-to-do in-laws. At least he hoped so. They had always been ambivalent about him.

Even as young as her eleventh year, Meriwether could feel the emotional emptiness in the house. Something was wrong.

Is this all there is to being a family? She wondered. She longed for more although she didn't know what that meant and couldn't have put it in those words at this early age. She had always found the families of other people to be more interesting. They had a lot more going on, it seemed, and there was always a lot more energy and happiness in their homes than in hers.

She wished sometimes that her Dad would yell or her mother would spend too much money on a dress or her older brother would do something that would get him in trouble or her younger brother would finally get well. Something. Anything.

She was known as a good girl, not able to bring herself to be as daring, and even outrageous, as were some of her friends. She had found herself in trouble only one time. The police stopped the car in which she was a passenger and found an open container. The officer assumed that all of them had been drinking alcohol and he had taken them all into the police station.

Although she cried real tears and declared herself forever remorseful, secretly, she enjoyed every minute of it. For a couple of hours, she had been living on the edge, at least in her world, and she felt a thrill.

How she wished that her dad would have expressed more disappointment and had been even a little hard on her. Then, she would be able to tell stories, at least one story, just like her friends told on Monday at school after a weekend of fun. But, he wasn't curious at all. He picked her up from the police station and not a word was said all the way home.

When she was a junior in high school, her father just up and left them. Just like that. He was gone. Flew the coop.

She was now old enough to realize that the dullness, even the numbness she felt in her family dynamics, or the lack of them, had been a disguise for the deep hurt in her mother's heart and her father's disinterest in her mother as a woman.

In some crazy way, she liked the fact that she could go to school and tell her friends that she was like them. Her dad was an ass after all. He was a real jerk, as one of her friends called him when she heard the story of his abandoning them.

She had taken over her Dad's recliner, which perfectly accommodated her fifteen-year-old frame in a slouch, with her legs pulled up under her. She wished that she missed her father. Sometimes, she wished that she could feel anything at all.

Predictably, his midlife romance had crashed and burned and it wasn't very many weeks before he was knocking at the door. Her mother refused him, but he was persistent. They began seeing each other again, although she would not allow him to come home.

When her father was finally allowed to come back, she told him she would not give up the recliner. To her surprise, he relented, and for a few evenings he sat on the couch. She found herself going back to her room more and more to escape his silence and the relentless and stifling boredom that, once again, seeped into the house.

The reconciliation, if it ever was one, was not successful. It was all out in the open.

One day, she came home from school and her father was gone. Not a word was said about it nor would a word ever be said about it. It was two years before the family heard from him again, and only then when he came by to sign divorce papers. He stayed a few moments, had a whiskey from his old stash, and walked off into the encroaching shadows of dusk. She watched as her mother stared out the door after him as if somehow to bring him back from some bygone era, when life was better.

Meriwether had inexplicably become popular almost overnight in her junior year of high school. She laughed more. She experienced her sexuality for the first time and she exuded it. Her grades improved and for the first time she realized she was smart.

Miss Seaton told her that she ought to write some poetry, so she tried it. Mr. Frederickson said he thought she was ready to read the classics. She tried them, too. She took up the violin, again after having laid it down for five years, and became first chair in the Community Youth Orchestra. Her grades improved to the point that she was on the Honor Roll. She was the queen bee at lunch and drew a crowd at her locker in the hallway.

She was deliriously happy. Her extroversion was obviously off the charts. It was as if she had awakened from a coma. Now, life was real. She was real. It was only when she went home and was alone again, that the old darkness came upon her; the dread of becoming emotionally frozen over, living trapped inside herself, as if someone had put a padlock on her life.

She looked in the mirror one day and saw a disturbing emptiness. What was missing? What was needed to fill up the void in her eyes and in her soul?

It was God that would do the trick, her next boyfriend told her. She needed to be forgiven of her sins and Jesus would do that for her if she simply asked. She went to a church service with him, a large auditorium, really, that held about five thousand people.

The pastor wore jeans and a muscle shirt and sat perched on a stool as if he were at the bar. Almost everyone hung on his every word. They didn't want to miss anything. Maybe he would say one thing that they needed, that would make them happier, that would get them more money, out of debt, happy in their marriage and in their jobs. Maybe they would hear the magic formula for finding romance or a successful career or recovering a faltering marriage.

She was in love and she wanted to fit into her boyfriend's world. So, at the end of the service, she raised her hand to be saved. She went forward at the altar call and Denny went with her for support. So far as she knew, she was saved now, as they put it.

When they got back out to the car, Denny said, "Now, we can do it!"

"What?" she asked. "I just got saved, Denny! Can't you give me a minute?"

He wouldn't. He didn't. He pounced on her with all the force of an attack dog and began to tear off her clothes violently.

"Stop!" she said. "I mean it!"

"Can't you see that since we're both saved it's okay now? We can, you know . . ."

"No, we can't!" she protested.

"The Bible says I can't be close to people who don't believe, but you're a believer now so what's to prevent us from yoking up?"

"Last I knew I had to be willing, and I'm not!"

"I'm the man here and you are the woman. You are supposed to meet my needs!"

"I'm not your wife!" she said, angry now and a little frightened. "And even if I were your wife . . ."

"You will be, soon enough."

"No, I won't! If that was ever going to happen, it won't happen now!"

She reached for the release to open the door and get out of the car, but Denny had locked it from his side.

"Denny, let me out right now!"

"You have to kiss me first! Then, I'll let you out!"

"Absolutely not!" she said.

Immediately, when she realized there was no chance that she was going to get away unless she did something he wanted, she gave him a lover's kiss. All the while, her stomach was turning and churning with revulsion and her heart was beating in fear.

"Now!" she said breathlessly, pulling away. "Let me go. You said you would, and you're saved so you can't lie."

"When you say it that way," he said.

He allowed her to unlock the door, but while she was leaving the car, he pulled on her blouse and tore it off, leaving her exposed.

"Here!" he said. "Take this blanket, and cover yourself up! Try to have a little modesty. No wonder guys go after you!"

She walked through the empty parking lot. She didn't know whether or not he might change his mind and come after her. He did not. He started his car and drove off the opposite way. She shivered in the late October night and made her way home. She walked in the back door and tiptoed quietly to her room.

The next morning the phone rang. A voice on the other end said, "This is Pastor Paul Swearingen. My son would like to apologize to you for his ungentlemanly actions last night. I know you will forgive him. I've prayed with him and God has forgiven him. If God forgives, so must we. I have also forgiven you for leading him on until he lost control of himself. I ask that we keep this among ourselves. It would only be embarrassing for both of you kids if this got out and it would hurt our church."

Denny was, it seems, the pastor's son. He hadn't mentioned that. So, that was the end of church for her.

When she went to college, she changed her name to Meriwether Louise. All those years of dullness and dreariness she was "Louise." It is a nice name, but it wasn't a good name for her. It was time for a change now, a new start.

She needed to leave everything behind and so she did, at least geographically. She went clear across the country to Occidental College in Los Angeles, and, before she knew it, she was first chair in the Pasadena Philharmonic Orchestra, one of the few paid positions available.

When she finished college, she decided to take a break before graduate school. The orchestral position was not enough to survive. When no job readily came along, a friend suggested she try to sell real estate, as the market was hot. She was dubious to doubtful, but took the test anyway. To her surprise, she passed with flying colors. She discovered she was good at it and made a lot of money.

Three years came and passed quickly. Awards and recognition kept coming her way. She often received standing ovations for her work in the orchestra. She had a platonic male friend named Charles. He was attentive and kind.

"This is not all there is," she said one day aloud in the middle of orchestra practice. "Definitely, this is not all there is."

She thought that she thought it, but she had said it, too.

People turned and stared, curiously. She knew by the way they looked at her that there was something not right with her. She began to laugh out loud. When she heard herself, she laughed at her laughter. Those around her began to titter expecting that they would soon know what the laughter was about. But, their response turned to uncomfortable silence and sideward glances as the laughter persisted and she began to double up and laugh so hard that tears came to her eyes.

She laughed uproariously, as if she had just heard or seen something hilariously funny. She couldn't sit any longer. She walked around the room in peals of laughter that stopped and started again and then she laughed herself out the door. She got in her car and laughed all the way home. She was chuckling when she went in the door.

Two weeks later, she got her last check in the mail, with a note from the conductor that her services would not be needed.

"It is often when we feel the most unbalanced, when we look the most unbalanced, that we are about to make a breakthrough," her therapist had once told her.

She stayed in bed for three days. By the end of it, she was hungry and dehydrated. Slowly, over the next forty-eight hours, she came back to life. Then, for a while, she lived on her savings, taking in museums and art galleries in Pasadena as a restoration for her soul.

Somehow, she knew that the scene with the orchestra was a cataclysmic break from the past. Life would never be the same again, even though she did not know what the future would be like.

It was at the end of that week of cocooning that she came to a startling realization. She had no real friends. Truthfully, she had no life. When she was in trouble, she had a million people to call upon, but not one of them could she trust. There had been no man to whom she had ever felt close or committed.

Good God! She was turning into her parents! Life was flat. Her world was small and shallow.

On the last night of her nervous breakdown, she dreamed of Santa Fe. When she awakened, that is where she felt compelled to go. Once again, she picked up and left town, leaving behind, she thought, all of the pain and disappointments and the distinct inability to enjoy her own accomplishments. When she left, there was no one to whom she really wanted to, or needed to tell that she was leaving and that she wouldn't be back.

She experienced her epiphany in Santa Fe. She had never seen so much color in her life. Never had the sunlight shone more brilliantly. Euphoria filled her as she walked the streets replete with art shops, museums, and Indian crafts. The home of Georgia O'Keeffe was just a few miles away. Her soul was warming from the light and waking up to the dance of color and contrast.

She graduated from the Albuquerque School of Law. She married two husbands, one for seven years and one for three. She became a successful lawyer. She joined the Santa Fe Symphony. After ten years, she had accumulated enough money to buy an art gallery on the Santa Fe Historic Plaza.

One summer evening, at an outdoor concert on the plaza, she met a handsome young musician who afterward invited her to join him for a glass of wine outside a small cafe on the plaza. She readily agreed. It turned out Esteban was an adventurer, a traveler, a romantic swashbuckler, a man of the world; and yet, he carried with him a sense of innocence, marked by child-like curiosity and wonder.

Meriwether was hopelessly attracted to Esteban right away, and she would fall in love with this man, who was in awe of everything. He was good company and a good conversationalist. He was respectful, and he proclaimed his undying love for her. They traveled all over the world.

During her thirty-ninth year, she woke up in Jerusalem, in a French guesthouse called Notre Dame, located outside the walls of the Old City near the Jaffa Gate. She had opened her eyes for seven mornings in the Holy City, but this particular morning, she really awakened. The Jerusalem morning sun wore a Santa Fe brilliance.

Esteban's note said he had gone off to meet with a couple of friends he had made. He would catch an early breakfast while she slept late.

She dressed and went down to The Allegro Bistro for something to eat. She surprised herself by going to the chapel for daily Mass. She had not been to church since that the night she gotten saved and assaulted in the same night. The priest spoke in French, and she found to her delight that she understood about two-thirds of it all.

Having decided spontaneously not to wait for Esteban to return, she put on her backpack and headed off to the Old City. She walked for the better part of the day through the Jewish, Muslim, Armenian and Christian quarters, stopping to rest occasionally out of the hot sun, buying a dozen bottles of water and consuming them all, looking at the wares displayed, all the while fending off the advances of men. She discovered some delightful hole-in-the-wall falafel cafe for lunch.

Esteban had texted her about noon, lost in wonder in the Shrine of the Book where the Dead Sea Scrolls were on display. They agreed to meet later that evening for dinner at the Notre Dame Center.

It was about three o'clock in the afternoon, when she stopped at the Armenian Tavern on the old Patriarchate Road, for a beer, and afternoon snack. The atmosphere immediately changed from the hardened bustle and clamor of the streets of the Old City to one of peace and restfulness.

Even though the place was full, voices were low and subdued and there was a palpable sense of lightness and joy in the air. It was a welcome change, and a relief.

"May I help you, Meriwether?"

She looked up to see the kindly looking countenance of a man looking down upon her. She was drawn to his face, and for a moment, she stared at him before looking away, embarrassed. Yet, she could not keep her eyes off him, looking back again.

"What do you recommend to a semi-lost tourist in Jerusalem this time of the day?" she asked.

"How hungry are you?" he asked.

"Famished," she said. "And tired."

He brought her a Mediterranean Meza platter with olives, dates, figs, cheeses, pita bread, dips, and hummus.

"A veritable feast, my lady. May I recommend Shepherds' Beer?"

"I'll take your recommendation on that, too," she said. "So far so good, sir!"

"Shepherds' specializes in a Blonde Pilsner," he said.

She noticed his name tag read simply, *Joe*.

"Good. Let's have that then, Joe."

She watched as he walked away. He radiated peace in this haven away from the chaotic cacophony of Jerusalem's streets.

Returning with her beer, Joe asked her, "What is your soul needing and are you finding it?"

What a strange thing for a waiter to say and what an eccentric way to say it!

"I'm not sure I've thought about it that way, Joe," she said. "Esteban wanted to come and I'm here with him. I had never thought of coming here but now I'm glad I did."

"Most people come here for their souls whether they know it or not," said Joe. "Sometimes they think they are here on business, or to tour the holy sites, or to go to the Dead Sea. There are countless things to do and to see here."

"We're largely here because of my boyfriend's curiosity, I think," she said.

"Maybe you came here for the beer!" His eyes twinkled.

"Maybe I did!" she smiled back.

"May I sit down?" he asked.

She readily agreed, surprised that he had the freedom to do so.

"I'm thinking that you came because you wanted to, you needed to, that you needed to see something, that you wanted to meet someone who would keep you from wondering, if, after all of your accomplishments, that's all there is to life."

"How did you know?" she asked.

"Many people walk around wondering that without ever letting in that longing and wondering. They cover it up with their work, their braggadocio, or the appearance of a happy family life."

"Not my family life, Joe!" she said. "What a childhood I had, or didn't have!"

"I know," he said. "I can see it in your eyes. The eye is the window to the soul. Your eyes have layers of pain in them. You must go deeper, Meriwether," he said. "You must go deep within and find the person you really are. Only then will you know why you are in this world and what you are to do."

He excused himself and walked away. She found herself not wanting him to leave. She hoped he would be back. At least he would have to come back to leave a ticket.

Later, a man approached her, who carried himself with the air of the owner.

"Is there anything more you would like?" he asked.

"No thank you. I'll take my ticket. I'd like to see Joe before I leave. I want to thank him for the good service."

"Joe?" he asked. "We don't have anyone by that name who works here!"

"Are you sure?"

"Absolutely!"

"But, I know I talked to a man named Joe who served my food!"

The man looked at her with pity in his eyes. She knew it was of no use to pursue it.

Since coming to Safety Harbor, she had never told anyone that she had met Joe before on the other side of the world; and Joe didn't show any signs of recognizing her, when their eyes met for the first time in this little town. Sometimes, she doubted the veracity of that experience.

What was it all anyway? Was it only a dream, a fantasy?

She had decided the less said about it, the better. Still, it was that conversation, real or imagined, at the Armenian Tavern in the Holy City, that had turned her life completely around.

When they arrived back in Santa Fe, she recognized that Esteban would always be a solitary wanderer, who occasionally welcomed companionship on the road, and she let him go. For two more years, she ran her art gallery. She made day trips to the home of Georgia O'Keeffe every three months, where she imbibed the clear air, the dancing energy, and the profound collective memory of the place where the artist had lived and worked for so many years.

She knew this much. Christianity was not going to do it for her. The message, if it had ever been anything, had been ruined long ago by those who used it in order to obtain power and status. Her experience in the church parking lot said it all. The church had stripped her of her dignity and had tried to take her by force. She would have none of it.

But, she wouldn't allow her memories of the church to rob her of her soul either, of her spiritual nature or her vocation, the very reason she had been called into this world. Nobody could do that. No one.

She applied for seminary at Holy Unity Seminary in Albuquerque where she wrote her PhD on *Mysticism and the New Science*. She was ordained as an Interfaith minister in the New Universal Church. She changed her last name to Starhawk, after one of her heroes.

She was shaken from her reverie of memory by Mrs. Saugus.

"Wake up, Meriwether! We're going to get started up again!"

The heat was oppressive. She reached for her bottle of water. It was nearly empty. And how was it, she asked herself, way back there in Jerusalem, years ago now, that Joe had known her name?

Chapter 32

HOPE PUSHED LOU DOWN the hallway in a wheelchair while Wendell went to get his car to take her husband downtown. Word had arrived earlier that the crisis with Roy and Jens had been resolved, but Lou wanted to go anyway. He had the makings of a speech written for this occasion which he had committed to paper some days ago. It was home, but he remembered the main points. Now that he had made his escape, he was determined to deliver it.

"Let's get a move on, Hopey! I've got to get there in time to address my constituency!"

She grimaced and bit her tongue. This was the stuff he lived and breathed and she couldn't stifle it. She thought it would be far better for him if he didn't go, but then again, it probably would be more stressful for him not to be there.

"I want this damned hospital bracelet covered up too! I can't give any room for my political enemies to take advantage of the situation. They'd like nothing better than to get a close-up of that bracelet and use it to their advantage in the next campaign!"

Hope's and Susanna's eyes met and rolled in tandem. Wendell drove up in his Tesla. Lou stood up and Father Callaghan opened the passenger side front door for the Mayor.

"Here you go, Mr. Mayor," said Father, with an exaggerated bow.

"We can all go in the Tesla," said Wendell. "There's plenty of room."

"No, no, no!" said Lou. "I need time to go over my speech. I'm going to need the rest of you to ride in a different car, even you, Hopey. Sorry."

Susanna drove the rest of them to the park.

Downtown, Jens and Roy had begun to move forward, under the watchful eye of Carmelita. Allowing this to happen went against all of her instincts as an officer of the law. Under normal circumstances, she would have arrested them for disturbing the peace. She had plenty of reason. Their rap sheets would back her up.

She was sure Lou and the City of Safety Harbor would want a written narrative of this incident so that she could explain herself. She wasn't sure she had a good one. What would she say? Joe suggested it? So far as she knew, Joe was still missing!

Well, all would be clear later. She wanted to think that with all of her heart. Right now, she had a parade to get to the finish line. It was only two blocks, but it might as well be two miles. She had no idea how stable Roy and Jens were or what they might do. Was this really a responsible decision? She honestly did not know. In most circumstances, she would say absolutely not. But in no place that she had served before had there been anybody like Joe.

Just by his presence, and now by his absence, he influenced people to act out of character, to do and to say what they usually would not do or say, to surprise themselves and others. Attitudes and worldviews that went unquestioned, suddenly, were shown up as wanting, in the light of just a word he might say, a nod of his head, or a look in his eye.

They were moving now, slowly, with Little Therese and Ruth on Roy's motorcycle. Jens followed behind.

"A little child shall lead them'!" Father Frank would say later when he heard how the parade came into the park.

A cloud of dust appeared to be moving on its own in the distance, coming from the hospital. A contingent of three cars could occasionally be seen through the swirling mass. In the Tesla was Mayor Lou and Wendell, followed by Hope, Susanna, and Father Frank in Susanna's BMW. The third car was a hospital vehicle, equipped with an EMT and a nurse. Doc Bailey was taking no chances.

They entered the park through the rear entrance and made their way to the gazebo in the center of the ten acres of lush grass and leafy Ash, Cypress, and Weeping Willow trees. In the corner of the park, a remnant of an old thick orchard of large filberts from another time stood like an ancient fortress.

It was as if it all had been choreographed. The Mayor's car pulled up at the gazebo at the same time that Roy arrived with Little Therese and her mother on the back of his motorcycle. Jens pulled up beside them.

The mayor got out of the Tesla slowly, accompanied by the attendant nurse, and made his way to a seat in the front row on the gazebo. Hope got out of Susanna's car and climbed the steps to sit by her husband. The parade came into view and processed past the gazebo. Hope and Lou waved at each float, each band, and every marcher that went by them.

"This is your city, Mr. Mayor!" said Hope, smiling, tugging at Lou's sleeve and giving him a peck on the cheek.

"Rock and Magdalena!" said Lou. In the midst of all that had been happening he had simply forgotten about that whole business. "Get them up here when they arrive! This is a joint effort between the two communities. We want them up front. We want them to have some credit."

The parade had nearly doubled in length from what was normal. Within a few minutes, the procession itself was all into the park and settled while the parade watchers followed, walking to the park behind them. It took another twenty minutes for the whole crowd to assemble.

Katye was about to introduce the mayor, when Little Therese asked her if she could say a few words about him. Her first thought was to let her down, gently. And yet, Little Therese had been the hero in this parade. She had proven herself to be more mature than her own uncle. She had mellowed him out and had made him into a human being. She had this strange and illogical thought that she ought to allow her to speak. Maybe her words could be in lieu of Lou's introduction. What could it hurt? Lou didn't need an introduction anyway after all these years!

The little girl's eyes shone, when Katye gave the go-ahead. She betrayed no signs of fear or resistance. She was young, but she was smart, a bit of an old soul, some said. She couldn't see, but she perceived a lot more than some people ever would who had two good eyes.

"I like that," she said. "Uncle Roy, you come with me."

Roy looked over at Jens who nodded as if to say, "I won't give you a hard time about this later."

He searched out the eyes of the Chief of Police too, since she had informed him that Jens and he would be placed under arrest forthwith.

"It's okay, Roy. Go ahead," she said.

"Pick me up, Uncle Roy, so I can see everybody!" said the little girl.

"But, Little Therese, you can't see!" said Roy.

Not to be fazed, Little Therese said, "Oh, I can see, Uncle Roy. If you lift me up I can tell how far back the crowd goes. I know that as far back as I can hear, there are people."

They went up to the microphone.

"Don't be afraid, now, Little Therese," said her mother.

"Oh, I'm not afraid, Momma. My Uncle Roy's arms are big and strong."

A tear ran down Roy's right cheek. Little Therese turned and wiped it off his face with her sleeve.

"Hi everybody!" she called out in the microphone.

The chatter continued.

From the back of the crowd, Mrs. Saugus's voice could be heard through her bullhorn.

"Listen up people. We're starting now. Give the front stage the attention and respect they deserve!"

Roy tapped on the microphone as if Mrs. Saugus's direct orders were his cue.

"Go ahead, Little Therese!" he said.

"Ladies and gentleman!"

The voice of an eight-year-old girl, sounding forever like a woman-child, got everybody's attention. The crowd went silent. Katye suddenly realized nobody knew what this little child would say.

"Some of you may wonder what a kid like me is doing up here. It's a surprise to me, too, but Katye gave me permission to do this. And, as we all know, Katye is a formidable woman!"

"Formidable?" Katye was stunned. "Where did an eight-year-old get that kind of language?"

"At least that's what I heard the Mayor say! I did get that word right didn't I, Uncle Roy?"

An audible chuckle spread through the crowd.

"Yeah, did she get it right, Roy?" called out Jens.

Carmelita gave him a stern look. "You're on shaky ground, Jens. I wouldn't push it."

"That's who I'm here to introduce today. I don't know him well. My Mom says that Mayor Schofield is a well-meaning person who does good work, but his mistakes are always whoppers!"

The crowd's response had grown from a chuckle to a hearty laugh.

"I go to school where people can't see as you do, so we have to find other ways to see what you see with your eyes. Sometimes, I feel faces and I can tell a lot about them. So, I would like to ask Mayor Schofield to come up so that I can see his face with my hands."

The crowd went so silent that everyone there could hear the wind blowing, the birds chirping, even the trees growing. Hope helped Mayor Lou to the podium. Roy stood across from him while Therese placed her hand on his face and felt every crevice and curve down to his neck.

Then she said, "Mayor Lou is a good man! I like him. I can tell he worries a lot. Mayor, you have some smile marks but not as many. You need to smile more! But, you have a nice face so I think you must be a nice man!"

"Although," she added, "not as nice as my Uncle Roy!"

The irony was so obvious that there was a knowing laugh from the crowd. Here was Safety Harbor's ultimate citizen standing next to one of the town bullies; and they were in this moment brought together by a child, moreover, one who could not see.

"But anyway, this is my Uncle Roy." She touched his face. "And this is Mayor Lou. My Uncle Roy talks too much already, my mom says, so, it's Mayor Lou's turn!"

She gave a little wave to the crowd. The applause lasted for five minutes. Lou had been sitting down for the duration. Then, with Hope's assistance, he returned to the podium.

Lou began to speak very quietly, almost inaudibly, close to the microphone.

"As you know, I had a close call earlier. Doc Bailey says I'm probably all right but he wants to run a few tests. They let me out today because, well, I'd have come anyway! They couldn't stop me, so they gave me permission! A lot has happened over the last few days. Much of it, frankly, I resisted at first. But then, as things began to develop, I began to see how, as unusual as Joe's Plan was, maybe there was something to it after all."

"What's Joe's Plan, Mayor Lou?" It was Little Therese again.

"It's kind of a way of doing things," said Lou. "You wouldn't think it would work well, because people just aren't that good at heart. They won't let things like Joe's Plan go forward. People are selfish. They look after themselves and their own. After that, they couldn't care.

"Yet, it does work. It can work. We proved it today. We came together even for a little while in unlikely ways with unlikely people. Let's face it. Most of us didn't know each other. We passed each other like ships in the night."

He put his hand on Rocky's arm and drew Magdalena up on the other side with his arm around her.

"These kids, these young people, this splendid couple, are doing a great job putting together a community for folks that we simply aren't equipped to welcome on a permanent basis. They participated in our parade, a parade for all of us, and I think now that regardless of our geographical division and other inequities, that we can be two parts of one community."

Lou's voice gradually increased in volume and strength.

"I had thought we ought to keep doing things the same way. I thought we shouldn't mess with things that seemed to be working the way they always did. I was wrong. I stood corrected by some people who had eyes to see things I couldn't see and to have a vision I didn't have. I was afraid if I associated myself with the plan and it failed that you would all blame me. And, well, you see, I like being mayor.

"The idea of asking the ones who many of us don't often even think about to lead the parade, and the ones with more status to move to the back positions, went down badly with me, at first. I would have fought it more if it hadn't been Joe's idea. We all think the world of Joe, although some of us who are more practical, think that he's too idealistic, for his own good and ours. But this time, I thought, 'Let's do it'!"

Hope came up behind him.

Someone spoke up from the crowd. "Revisionist history, Mayor. You had no choice. Even your wife was against you! Good thing you have Hope to keep you honest!"

He smiled. "Okay, okay, so I lost! But we all won. It's been a great day! I have a feeling more will come from this than we know!"

"Anyway folks . . ."

His voice trailed off. Suddenly, Lou looked tired.

"Come on, Lou, we're going back to the hospital," Hope said.

The attendant brought a wheelchair. The nurse and attendant from the hospital helped to load the mayor into the ambulance.

"No lights, no siren!" Lou barked out orders. "We don't want to panic people. I'm just a little tired."

As the ambulance drove through the crowd, people lined up on each side of the road and applauded Lou until the ambulance drove out of the park. Lou could not be seen but a stubborn hand could be seen, raised to the window and waving.

Magdalena came to the microphone.

"We all pray Lou is okay. We'd like to give tribute to him and the credit he deserves for being so flexible. We know he loves this city as we love our little place we call the Unsettlement! And we pray for Joe, wherever he is. This day would not have been possible without him. It was he who got us together, even though he wasn't here with us."

Father Frank, ever accustomed to making announcements, came forward.

"We don't want this to end. Well, it isn't. We're all due down at Joe's for a delicious lasagna dinner. Then, remember all you Catholics. Mass at seven o'clock sharp tonight!"

Later, people would say that nobody knew how the lasagna dinner could have possibly come off, even though it did. There were hundreds of people. No one was turned away. Miraculously, they did not run out of food.

That night, Our Lady of the Harbor was filled and overflowing with people who had come to Mass. Father had received special dispensation from the Archbishop for non-Catholics to receive Communion. Magdalena and Rocky were altar servers. Luther assisted. Father hadn't received permission for his Protestant colleague to assist, but prayed that Archbishop Malarkey wouldn't choose to show up. It was better to ask forgiveness than permission when you know the answer to the latter will most certainly be "No!"

During the homily, Father was brief but powerful.

"Joe has given us the opportunity to be the kind of human beings we can be every day. A little child can lead us and can say the wisest things to us! Those who are the worst troublemakers among us can become humble leaders, if they will. The weak and the infirm can make all of us strong. The first can go last and not be crushed or discredited. The last can go first and can lead us in ways we never imagined. We can transcend boundaries that are only in our minds. Our home can be a mansion or a tent. No matter. We are all human beings. We are all God's children.

"What is more, we are called to service, to serve one another. I've never seen this town so happy as we have been today. And yet what have we been doing? We've put others before ourselves. We've pitched in and made things happen and not worried about who got the credit. I saw all the smiles on your faces all day."

"Yeah! And Joe was there!" piped up Buddy.

Father couldn't think of a good transitional sentence to get beyond this awkward moment. He thought of his own experience, in the night, when he was sure he saw Joe as the elusive specter that walked the streets outside the rectory.

"He sure was. Boy, was he dancing up a storm!" said Caitlin.

Nate put his finger to his mouth to shush them.

"I am sure he was," said Father Frank. "He is always among us and sometimes he seems closer than other times."

He would just let people take that any way they wanted.

Chapter 33

THE NEXT MORNING, STEWART came by to drive Sally to Portland for the sad task of picking up Keith's body.

"I really appreciate this, Stewart."

"I'm glad to do it, Sally, but I wish it wasn't necessary."

"So do I."

"Do you know where we go?"

"I'm told that we go to the freight office."

"The freight office. So, he was shipped along with packages and pets."

He startled himself. He didn't know whether he had spoken that last thought or not. He must not have. He hoped not. She didn't reply if he did.

"I think it's one of those buildings alongside the parking lots before you get to the actual airport."

She got out her notice that Carmelita had given her. She read the address again.

"What did you think of yesterday?" he asked.

"Oh, I thought it was wonderful. You did a great job of problem solving with those bullies. I don't know how that would have come out if you hadn't intervened."

"Oh, thanks," he said. "I had a little help."

"What do you mean?"

"I had a visit from Joe. I was in the lighthouse when he came. I had retreated from everybody because, well, I'm just so out of it these days. I just wanted to watch from afar."

"He came to you in the lighthouse?"

"I know you'll think I'm crazy."

"No, I don't, Stewart. Just night before last, I thought I saw him walking down the street."

"I don't know what it means, Sally. He's missing, but there are those of us who have seen him."

"Maybe more like we've experienced him?"

"Yes, well that's true. Actually, come to think of it he was always behind me when he was talking but I swear I saw him. It must have been in my own mind."

"Well, I did see him, but it was kind of as if he were in a different dimension. Yet, he was walking down the street at the same time."

"I know."

"I'm glad you know what I mean. It means I'm not crazy."

"Or we're crazy together."

On the way into Portland, they stopped at the Ice Cream King, that stood as an island to itself, with no other shops and no town in sight. It was one of the few decent byways on the route to Portland. It was early for ice cream. They bought some coffee to feel better about using the rest rooms and moved on toward the airport.

When they continued their journey, Sally asked, "Have you found a job yet, Stewart?"

His face flushed. "No, I'm embarrassed to say I have not."

"What are you looking for?" she asked.

"Well, at first I was picky, but now I'll take just about anything."

"I'm wondering if you'd like to wait tables at Joe's. It's nothing like you're used to, I'm sure, but it would be an income. I know there's a vacancy. Joe is open to my recommendations."

"I'd like that, Sally! Thanks! It would be a privilege to work at Joe's!"

"Welcome aboard then!" she said, looking over at him and smiling.

He was relieved, somehow, that his future was more certain. Who would have thought that he would have considered working in a diner? It would have been beneath him. But now, somehow it was not the same at Joe's. It was almost like taking a high office in the church, except better.

Stewart and Sally spotted an airport van marked *Air Freight*. They decided to follow it to the long rows of metal storage structures. They pulled up behind the van and stopped. They were fortunate. He had come to meet them. He unlocked the overhead door and pulled it up. They walked down a long corridor of boxes and containers. There, in the midst of all the freight, was a box, indicating that, within, there were human remains.

Both Stewart and Sally were shocked. Keith's body wasn't set apart or given any dignity. It just lay among the boxes as if it were nothing special.

Stewart found himself putting his arm around Sally. She drew in her breath and didn't let it out for so long that Stewart began to be concerned she would faint. He wasn't feeling so well himself.

"When is the funeral home coming?" he asked.

"I told them to be here about eleven o'clock."

"They should be here right now."

Ever the punctual one, at least when he was sober, Stanley Bates, of Bates Compassionate Funeral Services, drove up to the storage shed and parked behind Stewart's car at eleven o'clock. His heavy mane of white hair blowing in the wind emerged from the hearse.

Sally nearly fainted again as she saw the funeral car. She bent over sobbing. Stewart held onto her to keep her from falling to the ground. Quietly and deliberately, Mr. Bates and his assistant went about their business, loading the remains into the hearse.

When it was finished, Bates came to her and said in a low and slightly saccharine voice, "Mrs. Hankins, we're going to take Keith back home to Safety Harbor now. Sometime today or tomorrow, you may come in and choose a casket and we can talk about other arrangements."

"That'll be fine, Mr. Bates. Thank you."

Chapter 34

Carmelita awakened with a start. The events of yesterday were still fresh in her memory, but it was a new day now, and the old nagging issue of Joe's disappearance was on the front burner. She had to assume that Joe did not go missing voluntarily. If he did, well, he did. But, if he didn't, it would be a terrible failure of her office, to say nothing of her own sense of fairness and justice, not to begin a search, in earnest, for their dear friend.

She wandered out of the bedroom in her robe. Cliff had made coffee. He poured a cup as she entered the room, and handed it to her. She took it and before drinking the first crisp taste, she breathed in its aroma. The day was beginning. What was left of dregs of sleep was chased away by the piping hot elixir that somehow gave promise of a new day, sometimes even a good day.

"Did you sleep okay, dear?" asked Cliff.

"I slept the sleep of exhaustion."

"I can't imagine how you got through all of it."

"We have to start a serious search for Joe today," she said.

"But what basis do you have for that? You don't have any evidence that he left without consent."

"I don't have evidence that he left voluntarily either. If this is a case of foul play, I'd never forgive myself for not pursuing this, with all deliberation, Cliff."

She gave him a morning kiss and headed to the shower. No sooner had she turned the water on, when Cliff called to her that her cell phone was ringing.

"Will you answer that, Cliff?" she called.

She allowed the water to begin to fall on her back, and then, slowly work its way up her neck to her hair. She stood directly under the stream and was engulfed in the comfort of its wet warmth. It was amazing what coffee and a good shower could do!

"Nate is on the phone for you. He says it's urgent."

Her shower was over, prematurely. She stepped out and Cliff handed her the towel that had been hanging on the rack by the shower.

"Dry off my back, will you?" she asked.

The sensation of the rough surface of the towel on her skin, caused her, for a fleeting moment, to consider inviting Cliff back to bed. Not this time. She wrapped the towel around her head and then, picked up the phone.

"Yes, Nate. Good morning."

"Carmelita, I think we might have a situation down here."

"Are you at the harbor?"

"Yes."

"What is it?"

"Well, it might be a clue about Joe."

"Don't hold back, for heaven's sake, Nate. What is it?"

"One of my crew came by this morning and said that he noticed that Joe's boat was gone out of its slip."

Why hadn't they thought of that before?

"Nate, I'll be right down," she said.

Hurriedly, she dressed and combed her hair out. No makeup today! That would have to be good enough for now. She gave Cliff a peck on the cheek and squeezed his hand.

"Where are you going, honey?" he asked.

"Down to the harbor," she said. "Joe's boat is not where it's supposed to be. In fact, it isn't there at all."

She started her car. The tires threw a little gravel. She moved quickly through the back residential streets, slowing down at stop signs. Some came to their doors or peered out of windows wondering where the Chief was going so fast, and why she was going there. It took only take a few minutes for a crowd to form at the harbor.

Nate met her at his fishing boat. They walked down to Joe's slip.

"It sure is gone, Nate. Does anyone know when it was last seen?"

"Well," he said, "nobody knows when the boat went missing, or if it has anything to do with Joe's disappearance."

"You can add two and two together, can't you?" asked Georgia Wellstone, who was with Nate. They had planned on going out to sea today.

"Well, we can, Georgia, but that's not police work. We've got to have evidence."

"But, don't you have to start out with some kind of theory?"

"After you have a number of the pieces together, you can see how they fit and try to envision the rest of the pieces. We simply aren't there yet. This is one of the pieces though."

"All you know is that his boat is missing. You don't know why. You don't know where he's gone."

"How right you are," Carmelita said.

"What do you want to do about this, Chief?" asked Nate.

"We know that all of this is completely out of character for the man we know. I'm going to get Marshall down here and tape this up as a crime scene. It may not be one. But, it may."

Chapter 35

HOPE AWAKENED AFTER TWO hours of sleep, and forced herself out of bed. In a few minutes, the smells of coffee brewing and bacon cooking, stirred her daughter and moved her from between the sheets, into the kitchen. Both moved silently and fixed breakfast together as they had done for years when Liz was home.

"He's going to be all right, Mother."

"I know he is, Liz. I know in my head. There's just something deep inside that's so afraid. I don't think I could bear to lose him. I don't know what I'd do."

"He needs you to be strong for him now."

"I know he does. That's why I try to do my collapsing at home. The parade was a boost for everybody yesterday and for a few precious moments we could set our troubles aside. All of us."

"Well, not quite. Carmelita had her hands full with the village bullies."

"Yes, she did," said Hope. "But I'm not sure that wasn't a real life-changing experience for those two guys. I wouldn't be surprised if they straightened themselves out a bit now."

"Daddy's changed too, Mother. He lost a bit of his crotchetiness. I was surprised when he went along with things and by the end of the day you'd have thought the whole thing was his idea!"

"That's what makes him a good leader, Liz."

"You mean a politician?" Liz joked.

"No, I mean a leader. He takes on a lot of peoples' ideas. He gives credit where credit is due, and then moves on and owns them for himself."

"He's got you hoodwinked, Mother!'

"He's had me hoodwinked for years. Otherwise, you wouldn't be around!" she smiled. "He's a good man, your father."

"Pray God, he's got many good years left, too."

"I hope so. I saw some real changes in him this weekend. Maybe he can be a little more at peace in his later years."

"He'll never give up that mayor job, Mother. It's his life. It's his identity. If somebody beats him out, that'll be the day I worry about him."

"I'm going to try to ease him out in the next few years, Liz."

She heard herself saying this, realizing that she was talking of a future, a long future together with her husband. She teared up. One rolled down her cheek. Liz reached over and staunched its flow with her thumb without saying a word.

"Let's go see him!"

They found Lou's room empty when they arrived. Hope's stomach turned completely over when she saw the unoccupied bed.

"Lou's been undergoing tests for a couple of hours now," said the nurse.

"I thought he couldn't get any tests until he had done some preparation!"

"Mrs. Schofield, you'll have to ask Doc Bailey about that. I can't share any more with you than I have."

"Could you call him, page him?" asked Hope.

"I can try," said the nurse, clearly miffed. "He's very busy with his patients, you know."

"I'll have you know that she is the mayor's wife!" said Liz, the tension raising in her voice.

"Liz! I don't want any special consideration!" Hope said.

When the nurse had gone to page Doc Bailey, Liz whispered to her mother, "You have to use whatever influence you have, Mother! Clearly, she didn't want to help you. It doesn't hurt her to find the doctor. He can make the choice whether he has the time to see you right now."

When she returned, the nurse said, "He wants to see you. He is in his office down the hallway and to the left."

"We know where it is!" said Liz. "We've known Doc Bailey for years. He brought me into the world so I guess we know where his office is!"

"Liz, that's enough!"

Hope now realized that Liz was worried, too, and it was coming out sideways.

They found Doc talking on the telephone. He waved them on in as he finished up his call.

He turned to face them.

"Sit down, friends."

He was quiet for a moment.

"We've found a small spot, probably a lesion on his left lung. We don't know if it's anything yet. We'll have a van coming by from the hospital in Lincoln City to do a PET scan. We're lucky they can come by this afternoon.

Liz asked, "Has he been told yet, Doc?"

"Yes, we've let him know. Right now, his heart health is getting a good going over with the stress test and an EKG. We're putting him through the mill today. No food so that we can do tests on the stomach and colon tomorrow."

"Poor Lou," said Hope. "Poor, poor man!"

"Daddy is strong, Mother."

"I know. I know. At least he puts on a brave front."

"He should be through with today's tests in about an hour. If you want to wait in his room, he'll be back about noon."

"Just in time for lunch, if he could have any!" exclaimed Liz, smiling.

Chapter 36

LUTHER WAS FUMING AS he sat down for breakfast.

"I'll tell you, Margaret, I've had it! There we were, in one of the most unique moments in Safety Harbor's history, and I was stuck in that bus with that damnable Maxine and Durwood yesterday, to say nothing of Emily Hooten, who is the biggest hypocrite God ever made a mistake creating. As if that weren't enough, I had to put up with that Alice Coover, who makes my skin crawl, with all of her fawning on me!"

Margaret smiled. "She likes you, Luther. She has good taste in men!"

Luther's eyes flashed. "Don't give me that! I'll have none of it!"

"You know I'm kidding, honey!"

He was silent. This was not good news. A quiet Luther was more concerning than one who spewed out his frustration from time to time.

"It's not a bit funny. This is my life. I'm trapped in a time warp here in this church, Margaret. Nothing has changed here since 1942 and then for the worse because they got a ten-million-dollar endowment and they guard it as if it were their own. They won't even fix their own damned roof, let alone think of using any of it for helping the needy."

"What about the homeless shelter? That's something."

"You know that Jack and Laura support that or it would not be happening. If Maxine could close that thing down, she would do it in a minute. She may very well manage it one day.

"Such a metaphor that bus was, Margaret. There I was, confined in those walls of my portable prison with *those people*. I have a feeling this parade is going to make a big change in our town, but it won't matter at all at Always Sunny. Everything will go on the same as always, as if nothing happened. No wonder people are so unimpressed with so many of us who make a big deal out of our faith!!"

I know, Luther. I meet so many people at the Capitol, and some of the least becoming are the religious people."

"I'll tell you, Margaret, it's not that they're people who oppose change or fail to see the needs out there in the world. They're just indifferent. Oh, they talk a good game all right. They give in the special offerings for the needy all around the world, but then, they go to their coffee klatches and continue to run down the poor and the needy, calling them lazy; and they include me in their gossip for good measure. All the while, they are smiling, slurping, and gossiping, they claim to be looking after the good of the very people they demoralize and demonize and demean. I could have been some help yesterday when Roy and Jens started making trouble. No, I was too busy babysitting the needs of my congregation, as usual!"

"What do you mean, dear?"

"In the middle of that crisis, Maxine was ready to get off the bus and Durwood with her. They were going to confiscate the bullhorn from Mrs. Saugus and announce their rummage sale next week."

Coffee spewed through Margaret's lips as laughter exploded from her lungs.

"Think it's funny, do you?" Luther asked with a faint smile on his lips. "You can laugh. You can get out of here! You can go to your legislative office in Salem! It's about nothing but their own interests and their own little insular world. It's a club, I'll tell you! It's a club, and they think I'm their employee, the director in charge of their amusement! I'm ready to quit. I want to go in today and call a meeting and tell them all to go to hell while I pack and go somewhere else."

"That's probably not a good idea," Margaret said, still trying to gain control of her laugher, from the image of Maxine, trying to wrestle the bullhorn from Mrs. Saugus.

The phone rang. It was Carmelita. They were going to organize a search party to look for Joe. They were asking clergy and community leaders to come together to get the project organized.

"There, you see. You can get beyond your people."

"Yes. Too bad it has to be because Joe's missing. Carmelita wants you there too as the local state legislator if you can, to handle any press that gets involved. You're good with them, she says."

Luther helped her take the dishes to the sink. Together, they got in the car to go to the police station to begin the search for Joe.

Chapter 37

JOHNNY WATSON AWAKENED, FEELING good. He had the impression that he was re-entering the mainstream of life in Safety Harbor, indeed, if he had ever been there, before this. After all, he considered himself to have been a key person in getting Jens and Roy to turn around and go the other way. Heck, he had helped save the parade. He had saved the day!

Hobe had said to him just last night, "Don't get too cocky, Johnny. You've got a reputation to overcome. You've got a lot of trust to rebuild."

"Yeah, but people really like me, Hobe! They always have. I've just tried their patience."

"I know. They like you. You've got a heap of good will in this town. God knows why, but it's the only reason you've gotten away with so much over the years. I've let you off the hook, too. Johnny, you've got to break off that love affair with alcohol."

Hobe was right, of course. The evidence was clear this morning. It was the first day Johnny could remember that he hadn't awakened bleary eyed from drinking himself to sleep. He'd been so worn out from the parade that he fell asleep on Hobe and Georgia's couch without even turning on the television. This morning, the caffeine went right to his blood, rather than having to fight a battle with the remaining alcohol running through his veins. He was wide-awake.

"I think I'll walk into town."

"Joe's isn't open, you know."

"I know. I guess I'll just walk around and see what's new."

Hobe and Georgette's house was about two miles inland from Safety Harbor. He reached the road to town from the long driveway and stuck out his thumb. Durwood drove by, looked him in the eye with mild contempt, and drove on. Johnny didn't even mind. He didn't even remember seeing Durwood yesterday at the parade. Maybe he'd missed it altogether. He was too happy to let the old sourpuss ruin his day.

Ray Ripple was coming back from Portland with supplies and stopped immediately. Johnny opened the door, climbing in amidst the mountains of supplies in Ray's van.

"Why don't you get a bigger vehicle to haul all these groceries, Ray?" Johnny asked.

"Why, I'd have a big payment and I couldn't go to Portland as often!" he said, smiling.

"I know how you love to do that!"

Ray's ex-wife lived in Portland. Anybody in town could tell you about the end of the days of that marriage. Ray chose to ignore his remarks.

"Where you goin', Johnny?"

"I just thought I'd go into town."

"Probably not much happening after yesterday, besides regular business, I'd say. And tourist traffic."

They rounded the corner, descending into Safety Harbor. To their right was the park.

"Nobody'd ever know anything happened there yesterday," said Ray.

"Ain't it the truth?"

Down two blocks toward the harbor, vehicles were gathering at the police station.

"Whoa! What is that?" asked Johnny.

"I hope it's not bad news. I hope they haven't found Joe washed up on the shore, somewhere."

"Let's go down and see what's goin' on, Ray!"

Ray made a hard right turn down Descent Street, pulling alongside the police station. Several other cars followed behind them. They walked in and found most of the old Steering Committee and the parade organizers, including Mrs. Saugus, standing around in the small lobby. Rock and Magdalena were there, along with Bob and Sue Abernathy, from the Unsettlement.

The growing crowd made it close quarters in the small police station. Johnny wasn't surprised to see all of them together. He figured something must be up about Joe. He was shocked, though, when he saw Roy and Jens there. Nate wouldn't look Johnny in the eye. He still felt contempt for him, after all of these years. Some of it he understood and some of it, he couldn't explain. He just didn't like him.

Carmelita began speaking.

"Good morning, all. We're here today because we're going to start a search party for Joe. We're going to hold the meeting next door in the old city bus barn where there's room for everyone. We have coffee and refreshments."

The small crowd shuffled out the door and into the empty building. There was a noticeable murmur of approval from them as they saw the tables filled with coffee from the De-light-full Book and Coffee Shop and pastries from the bakery.

"Help yourselves. We'll be starting in eight minutes," she called out, looking at her watch.

In precisely eight minutes, Marshall blew his police whistle to the startled surprise of everyone in the room and to the consternation of Carmelita. Some days she felt like smacking that kid but he was so well meaning that she let things go.

"As you know," she began, "we are here to form a search party for Joe, who has been put on a missing persons list as Joseph Vincent Magnus. This search will take place on three fronts. The Coast Guard will search on land and sea with helicopters and boats. I've also called the Washington State Police in case Joe is over the Oregon state line. They will be following through on the ground on their side of the state boundary. The third is the one in which everybody in Safety Harbor can get involved. We need you to cover the streets of this city, the back alleys, the out-of-the-way places, and the coast, from one end of the beach, to the other. Deputy Hale will be doing a house-to-house search throughout the city, at least on the first day.

"What we need now, is for all of you to make contacts all over town, and recruit them to be back here by noon, exactly. Use your cell phones, email, text; do what you need to do, in order to get people here. We want to do this job as thoroughly as possible. You are all very key to the success of this endeavor.

"Look for anything suspicious. It could be clothes, shoes, watch, wallet, or anything that might look like it belongs to Joe. If you find something call me or text me immediately and we will be there on the spot."

By late morning, tension and a strange excitement was beginning to fill the old city bus barn, as an increasingly large number of people showed up on the scene, some to gawk, but mostly, in order to be a part of an intense search for their friend.

Chapter 38

LUTHER KNEW HIS PEOPLE. He held his nose, called his office, asking his administrative assistant to call Maxine and Durwood. The search party would be in need of some sandwiches, hot dishes and soft drinks. These people knew how to do that.

"Activate the prayer chain," said Luther. "Tell them this time it's not only time to pray, but to get busy, too. Anybody who can come down to the barn and help look for Joe, so much the better. But Always Sunny could, at least, support the search party with sustenance.

"And call Zeke. Tell him we may very well need him to transport people around town. See if he will bring the church bus down to the police station."

At 11:45 a.m., Katye came forward to the podium.

"We'll have teams of twelve people going out to search. I've appointed the leaders. Their names are on the white board in the police station lobby. I have maps for you to follow so you know where your territory to search is. Don't be afraid to go beyond it though. A second pair of eyes is always better."

Rock and Magdalena joined Katye at the podium.

"We are going to get as many of our people up here as can come," Rock said.

"Always Sunny bus can help with that," said Pastor Luther.

"Our Lady of the Harbor will open its sanctuary to anyone, regardless of faith or no faith, creed or no creed," Father said. "It will be a place of prayer or meditation, or just for getting away for a few moments, if you need it."

Carmelita said, "I've asked Roy and Jens to ride the back roads here and check into some of the heavier underbrush and small trails."

Johnny wondered why those two weren't looking out through bars. He had gone to the clink overnight for a lot less.

"As you may know," she said, as if she had heard Johnny's thoughts, "Roy and Jens are on a short leash since yesterday. I've told them that I would ask for community service rather than jail for their menacing and malicious mischief yesterday. They are starting their community service today, and any other time we may need them, until Joe is found."

They both waved. "We're sorry, good people," said Jens.

We really are!" said Roy, who, it seemed, had been humbled by the presence of his little niece yesterday, in the parade.

Johnny was feeling stressed. He wanted to stand out. He wanted attention, to be thought of as a good guy, courageous even. What could he do that was special, that would get him noticed like yesterday? Nothing presented itself.

Back at Always Sunny, Zeke fired up the bus in the back of the church parking lot and headed down to the Unsettlement. Katye had persuaded the community college to release students from class. Later, cell phone records would prove that more calls were made in Safety Harbor that day than any day in history, as people contacted neighbors and friends, even into Portland, Eugene, and as far away as Medford and Bend.

Carmelita was concerned when, from her office window, she saw the traffic pouring into Safety Harbor. Word had spread like wildfire and people wanted to help. It was clear they were going to need more law enforcement. She called Newport, Florence, and Lincoln City. Not one could spare personnel. The two of them would not suffice. She would have to deputize a few people.

She called Marshall.

"Get me Johnny Watson and Nate Beard. We just don't have enough law enforcement. There are people pouring into town and we are going to have to have some crowd control here."

Katye came in just then with the overall three-day plan for Safety Harbor's part of the search party.

"It looks good, Katye," said Carmelita. "By the way, have you heard from Stewart and Sally? When do you expect them back in town?"

"Stewart called a few minutes ago and said they were on their way back, but that they would probably stop for lunch on the road, somewhere. Not many places to stop between there and here."

"There's always the casino!"

"Yes, there's that!"

Chapter 39

STANLEY BATES DID, IN fact, take the exit off the road back to Safety Harbor, and drove toward the casino. Stewart and Sally looked at each other. Sally nodded and Stewart followed behind the hearse.

"Have you ever been in here?" asked Stewart.

"Keith took me in a couple of times. I really don't like it."

Stewart pulled up beside the hearse in the parking lot, shut down the engine, and turned to her.

"Keith was a dear friend of mine, you know."

"I know he was," Sally said.

She reached out and squeezed his hand.

"Thank you," she said quietly. "Thank you for doing this. It means more than you could know. I don't know what I would have done."

Soon inside the casino, Stewart could feel his lungs tightening up as his allergy to cigarette smoke took over. He moved away from as much of it as possible, but he was resigned that it was going to bother him until they left this place.

They went through the buffet. The conversation was stilted. For as long as she had been in town, Sally had never met Mr. Bates.

As if reading her thoughts, he said with a faint smile on his face, "Not many people know the mortician in town. I'm the one to be avoided until you need me and then you'd rather not see me again!"

"Not true, Mr. Bates," said Sally, although it was.

"I don't know anybody much at all," said Stewart. "I've only been in town for a year or so. My wife, Katye, is the real person-about-town. Everybody knows her."

"Oh, you mean Katye Puckett?" asked Penny, Mr. Bates's assistant, speaking her first words since they had met her.

"That's the one!" said Sally. "Quite a bundle of energy!"

"A gadfly, some may say," Stewart said, smiling faintly.

"We can meet at the office whenever you are ready," said Mr. Bates, bringing up finances in his less-than-nuanced way.

"Stewart will join me tomorrow morning in your office," said Sally.

"About ten o'clock then?"

"Yes, that will do."

When they had finished eating, the three of them went to the parking lot and waited for Mr. Bates to come out. After ten minutes, he had not yet appeared.

Finally, Sally went over to the driver's side where Penny was seated.

"Do you think he's okay?"

"Oh yes, he's fine. We usually have to wait on him a bit. He usually spends a half an hour at the slots. I should have told you!"

Sally was shocked.

"You mean he does this when he's on the job?"

"Yes, he is always glad to go to Portland so he can stop here on the way back."

"So, here my husband's body lies cold in this hearse, and he's in dueling with the one-armed bandit?"

"Yes, and he's probably had several more drinks."

"What? He's not driving my husband home if he's drunk."

"He'll need me to drive. That's why he likes me to come along, I think."

Sally's hands tightened into fists at her side and she shook her head, the latter of which was a real sign that she was approaching rage.

"I'm going to give him fifteen minutes and then we're going in there!"

"I wouldn't give him that long," said Penny.

"Well! Let's go, then!" she said.

She marched over to Stewart's side of the car where he had been waiting.

"Stewart, we're going in!"

"What's going on?"

"Nothing that can't be cured by a good slap upside the head! Our so-called funeral director is inside drinking and gambling!"

He exited the car and they walked briskly toward the casino.

Once inside, Sally said, "Penny, you go this way! I'll go that way!" She had turned into a hunter-warrior. "Stewart, you stay here in case he walks by."

It was ten minutes before Sally and Penny returned. Sally was holding Mr. Bates by the scruff of the neck.

"Our esteemed funeral director is ready to go now!"

Penny helped Bates into the passenger's seat. They took the entrance leading back to Highway 99W. The hearse went on ahead of Sally and Stewart, a bit faster than made Stewart comfortable.

"She's burning up rubber. I'm going to let her go ahead without trying to follow her if that's okay."

"It's okay by me. I don't want to see that slouched over shaggy mane in front of me anyway."

Stewart slowed to a comfortable fifty miles an hour. Almost instantly, a car passed them as Sally described it later, like a bat out of hell. They were shocked at its speed. Suddenly, it turned off at a ninety-degree angle. They both gasped as they watched a crazed driver cross the median into oncoming traffic. Defying the law of physics, the car kept going straight down the road ahead of them while the front was pointed ninety degrees in a different direction, skidding sideways, and all the while, the wheels were still turning forward.

They both stared ahead, not being able to believe their eyes, certain that they were going to be involved in a fatal crash with the car up ahead. The car continued its bizarre path about three miles down the road. Then, it turned around and moved down the road, pulling off at the nearest turnout.

"Shall we stop?"

"I don't know," Steward said. "He might be dangerous."

"It seems that the car is dangerous. Maybe he's hurt."

"Something's wrong, that's for sure."

Stewart pulled over ahead of the car so they had a better chance at escaping if this turned out to be a bad idea. When he approached the car the driver's side window lowered. It was unusually dark inside and the driver could not be seen clearly.

"Are you okay?" Stewart asked him. "Do you need help?"

The driver did not answer and made no effort at a conversation.

"Let's go," said Stewart, uneasily. "This is creepy."

Both shaken, they got back in the car.

Almost immediately, the car passed them again, and once again, turned ninety degrees to the left and kept going straight ahead.

Suddenly, the road narrowed into two lanes as they entered the Van Duzer Corridor. In the face of the crazed driver, who was taking up both lanes, oncoming traffic had to pull over to the side of the road, some careening precariously to a drop-off, others straight into the trees on the side of the road. Desperately, some drivers began to cross over into the westbound lane.

"Pull over, Stewart!" screamed Sally. "We're going to be killed!"

There was no shoulder. He had no choice but to drive wide-eyed down the road, watching the extraordinary scene ahead of them and at the same time trying to avoid oncoming traffic. The car disappeared over the crest of the hill. By the time they started down the steep incline leading out of the

Van Duzer Corridor, it was nowhere to be seen. Stewart drove cautiously and Sally looked to her right. to see if it might have crashed into the trees.

"He could have gotten off at the rest stop we just passed," said Sally.

"I'm not going to check it out, if it's okay with you!"

"Fine with me!"

They drove silently, the rest of the way to Safety Harbor.

Chapter 40

In the end, Carmelita deputized Nate Beard, Johnny Watson, and Frances Saugus, the latter at her own insistence. Jens and Roy would work out their community service doing her bidding, but she could not bring herself to deputize them under the circumstances. With their record, it probably wasn't legal. In addition, she brought on Jens's ex-wife, Shirley, to work temporarily in the office. Jens had recommended her, since she used to work as dispatcher for the Sheriff's office in Lincoln city.

"There can't be any trouble between you two guys when you are working together."

"Oh, I think there's no more blood to be spilled on that account, Chief," said Jens.

"Good!" said Carmelita. "Let's make sure of it!"

Nate was dismayed down to his bones when he heard the announcement that Johnny was going to be a deputy. The two nodded to one another. The three stood up in front of the crowd that had gathered, while Carmelita swore them in as her deputies. She shook hands with each of them and handed them a badge. Everyone clapped and cheered.

When it quieted down, a voice called out, "Gosh, I miss Joe somethin' awful and I only just met him once!"

It was Little Therese. As with her, a lot of the townsfolk didn't know Joe very well, if at all; but they were always surprised at his common touch and his humility, when they finally came face to face with him.

Their first thought was often, "Really? This is Joe? Really? This is the guy that everybody is raving about?"

He could have been anybody's uncle. Had he not been introduced, Joe would have passed them by, unnoticed and unrecognized. But, in the end, just meeting Joe once had changed them in a qualitative way that they couldn't explain.

Father Frank's spiritual director, Sister Mary Margaret, had once asked him, "What is it that you admire about him so much?"

"I don't know, exactly," Father had said.

"From what you've told me, could it be that he seems just completely human and without any pretense?"

"Yes, I think that's it! He is so fully human that one can see the spark of the divine in him!"

"Well, that's pretty solid theology, wouldn't you say?"

"Yes, you are right about that, Sister. I've become so cynical over the years, although I try to hide it. I despair of human nature, including my own. Just about the time I think I've got some character flaw under control, it flares up again.

"And as for my people, well, there's the Confessional. Lay people have no idea how it is that listening to confessions can make a priest cynical. You know that people aren't confessing what's really bothering them. They confess some little thing, or maybe two, or even three things that are barely recognizable as sins, if at all.

"They reason that if they throw off part of the baggage maybe the bigger stuff won't be so heavy to bear. Maybe they can sneak into heaven with half a load of sins. And since there are so many who no longer think they're going to Hell any more, or even Purgatory, they really don't worry about walking away with the big stuff still intact."

"Father, you do have a heavy load of cynicism and maybe more than a small load of sins to cast off yourself."

"I don't doubt that, Sister. Every day my cassock seems heavy, sometimes as heavy as armor, as I realize my unworthiness for the task to which I have been called. Oh, I put on a good Irish priest act, but inside, there is a lot going on that nobody knows."

"I know that, Frank. You're more transparent than you think. Your humanity shows through time and time again. And it's not that holy man persona that people love. It's the humanity that shows through. It gives them hope that if Father can be human, it's okay for them to be human too."

"Oh, if they only knew how human I am."

He wanted so badly to talk about the anguish of his celibacy, of the loneliness of being intentionally unmarried, of the many times he had gone back to the rectory after a meeting of people who would all eventually go home to someone that night, while he would go home alone, to an empty bed.

His thoughts were interrupted when he heard his name being called from the microphone to come up front and offer a blessing to the search parties.

Chapter 41

BACK HOME FROM PORTLAND, Stewart slipped through the crowd and made his way to the lighthouse. He watched from his perch as people made their way out of the city bus barn. Some were going up Descent Street to Main, to look in the alleyways and byways of the village. Others were headed up in the hills and through the woods and valleys and streams to the east of town, while still others made their way up the seacoast. Katye sent the last search teams north to search from Lincoln City as far as the Washington state line.

In the distance, the sound of a loud engine was approaching. Everyone on Main Street looked back up the hill where the road into Safety Harbor wound down past the city park and into town.

The car that Stewart and Sally had seen in the Van Duzer Corridor was barreling down the road at full speed with the front end of the vehicle pointed toward Portland and the rear pointed west toward the sea.

"Get off the road!" screamed Jens. "This idiot is dangerous!"

"How's he doin' that?" asked Jeremy.

"Mother 'o God!" gasped Frank and made the sign of the cross.

A few cars appeared to be nicked and bumped as the strange specter passed through Main Street, skidding and touching the ground, and then raising up off the street, one or two wheels at a time. Carmelita and Johnny Watson were in the squad car coming to the crest of the rise that brought them to Main Street just as the car passed by.

"Let's us go get him, Roy!" said Jens.

As Johnny and Carmelita rode out of town, now well behind Jens and Roy, she placed the light on top the car and they barreled off down the road, south, toward the Unsettlement. They sped along for the next twenty miles until they arrived in Yachats, where Roy and Jens were parked in the parking lot at LeRoy's Blue Whale Restaurant.

"Never saw that car again, Chief," said Roy.

When the four of them returned to Safety Harbor, the search parties had been out for some time. Carmelita drove down to the police station. Roy and Jens followed.

"Strangest thing I ever saw, Chief," said Johnny as they approached the station.

"I'm not even sure what I saw, Johnny."

Back in town, the search had gone on for several hours. It was about two o'clock in the afternoon and Stewart had fallen asleep on the landing of the ascending spiral staircase of the lighthouse. He dreamed of the car that he had seen, twice now, in one day. A wise old woman stood by him as they watched the phantasm drive through a strange town that looked like a ghost town right out of the Old West.

"What is this car, Mother?" he asked the wise woman.

"It is the shadow of darkness that sweeps over the land wherever it goes. It is known as the Car of Darkness and Doom."

Suddenly, he felt himself falling as if into deep, dark space. He was grasping on to the old woman's hand in desperation. He awakened to find himself clinging to the lighthouse staircase, his torso dangling precariously off the stairs and into space. He had begun to fall from his perch on the landing halfway up the lighthouse staircase. Only unforgiving concrete would stop him thirty feet below.

Desperately, he tried to pull himself up. His arms were just not strong enough to lift his body weight. He was in trouble and he knew it.

"Oh, God!"

He didn't know whether it was a prayer or an exclamation of terror. His hands became clammy with fear, causing even more slippage, decreasing the chances of his survival by the second. The fall would almost certainly kill him. He watched, almost detached, as his hands seemed to move in slow motion, gradually losing their grip on the metal stair railings. Then he looked down. His legs and feet were moving chaotically, in some crazy dance of death.

"Reach up!" a voice called out. He couldn't see anybody.

"I can't reach up!" Stewart cried out. "I can't even hold on!"

"Reach up!" The voice called out again.

"If I reach up, I'll have to let go!"

"Reach up!"

He was losing his grip fast now. He was seconds from death.

"Look up!" the voice said.

Through the fog of fear in front of his eyes he thought he could see Joe with his hand reached down to him.

"Can't you come down a bit?" Stewart said.

"Let go and reach up."

Stewart knew there was no other way out. He let go of the railing with the only hand that was still gripping the railing. For a moment, he was grasping nothing. He could not quite reach Joe's hand on his own. Then he felt a firm, warm, strong hand grasp his, pulling him up. His legs dangled and argued as if they were their own persons, as Stewart felt his body being lifted up to safety. Strangely enough, he did not struggle or strain as he was lifted up. Once he had reached up to Joe's hand and Joe grasped it, he was immediately on the staircase. He sat, stunned and exhausted. He looked around. Joe was standing above him three or four stairs.

"Everybody's out looking for you, Joe!" he said. "We'd better stop this search and let them know you are back here in Safety Harbor!"

"Let them go. They will have to find me on their own. Don't tell anybody that I've been here."

Then he was gone.

Stewart looked out the window of the lighthouse and saw that he was in the old ghost town where the Car of Doom had gone sideways down the street.

"My God, I'm still dreaming!" he thought. "Is it a dream within a dream?"

He woke himself up with his own question. He was still seated firmly on the landing of the staircase. He shook himself.

"Joe?" he called out.

"We're still lookin' for him!" A voice came from below. "We haven't found him yet."

He smiled to himself. He was a dreamer! Maybe that would be his new career. A dreamer. Yes, a dreamer. There must be a position for Dreamer-in-Residence. It had a nice ring to it.

Chapter 42

SALLY HAD NOT BEEN able to stay away from the search. She had gone home after the exhausting ride. She was restless, and she was disturbed that she wasn't as sad about Keith's death as she wanted to be. She had cried at the airport, but that was more out of shock than grief. Maybe the feeling would come. But, the deeper part of her knew that her love for Keith had died long ago.

When she married him, she still had a nagging nodule of doubt growing on her heart. The doubt slowly turned to certainty over the years of their marriage, that this thing should never have happened.

He had spent so much of his time away in the oil fields, and it seemed to her that, during his long spells away, not much had changed since she was single. She was still alone, after all. He didn't want her to work, but, out of desperation, she had taken a job at Joe's anyway when he was away, just to get out of the house and talk to somebody.

Now, it appeared she was going to be in charge of Joe's as long as it stayed open, if it reopened at all. Nobody knew, at this point, what would happen.

For a minute, she panicked as she realized that she would either be completely out of a job or in charge of the whole thing and she couldn't imagine at the moment which one would be worse. Maybe they really would find Joe alive and well. Maybe this would be a glitch in time and soon they'd all be back to the old rhythms in Safety Harbor.

She wondered where Nate's kids were while he was out with the search party. Boy! It didn't take long for her mind to wander from Keith to Nate! She didn't have to wonder long. As she walked out of her house and past the elementary school, she noticed that the play yard was full of children who were obviously being watched while their parents looked for Joe.

Caitlin and Buddy waved at her as she passed by, and she waved back!

"She's gonna be my other Mom!" Buddy called out to his friends.

She blushed and hurried on down toward the police station.

Only Hobe and Georgette Watson were in the building to watch over valuables and inform any latecomers of what group they should join in the search.

"Hi Sally! We're sure sorry about Keith, honey!"

"Thanks, Georgette," said Sally. "We just brought him home today from the airport. Stewart was kind enough to take me into town and be supportive."

"Stewart? I haven't heard of him!"

"Oh, he's Katye's husband. He's pretty quiet. Keith and he were best friends. Everybody called them the odd couple, my blue-collared Keith and the clergyman with the white collar."

"Help yourself to some of Jeremy's coffee!"

"Thanks, Georgette. I will."

When she returned from across the room, she said, "I'm going out on the search."

"This late, honey?"

"Well, you never know. One person may make a difference."

"That's so. I'll call Katye and see where she wants you."

Rock and Magdalena said they could use another person. Georgia called and found that they were located north beyond the park where the cliffs began and the large rock formations jutted up out of the sea. They were on top of the cliffs, amid the brush, that could well hide a body.

Sally made her way to the familiar woods where Keith and she had spent time exploring when he finally moved down to Safety Harbor with her.

As she approached, Magdalena called out, "Welcome, Sally! Just take a place on the edge of the search party near the woods!"

"Thanks! I will!" Sally called out.

A rush went through her and her cheeks flushed, as she realized that she would be walking next to Nate. There he was, standing out in the crowd, as if not another soul was present.

"You are, by far, the most beautiful woman I have ever laid eyes on!"

She pretended not to hear. He had said that to her the first time he met her. She had hoped no one else heard him say it then and she hoped no one heard him say it now. Still, she loved hearing it.

Chapter 43

JOHNNY AND CARMELITA DROVE toward the elementary school for a welfare check on the children of the search party members.

"I'd sure like to know who owns the sideways car. I'd feel better if I could meet them. I am not sure who is safe and who isn't in this town right now."

"Katye's been calling it the Car of Doom, Chief. She said something about it being Stewart's idea. I don't know how he came up with that."

"Oh?"

"You know, you lead an exciting life, Chief."

"You could say that," she said. "Sometimes it could be less exciting and I wouldn't complain."

"You wouldn't think there'd be so much going on in a small town like this, would ya?"

"I think, since we live in a small town, we're just more aware of everything."

"And everybody's business too, Chief!"

"True enough, Johnny. True enough."

They drove past the elementary school.

"Let's just stop and see what's to see here."

"Okay, Chief!"

Carmelita parked the car and they both got out and approached the schoolyard where about forty kids seemed to be everywhere it was possible to be.

"Who's in charge here?" asked Carmelita of the closest adult available.

          ↬

Chuck and Dottie Springfield had closed their clothing business for the day and had agreed to head up the childcare project during the search.

"It's quite wonderful, really," said Dottie. "We have about ten kids from the Unsettlement who have joined us, in addition to those from Safety

Harbor. Marc and Cathy Albright are helping us. They are from the Unsettlement, too. In addition, some young people from the community college have come to help us out."

"Well, the reason that I came by is that, we may well have a visitor in town and we have some concerns."

"Give us a description," said Chuck. "We'll see to it that they don't get near the kids. I've got some mace in my car."

"Well, that's the thing," said Johnny, speaking up. "We really don't know what the guy looks like. We only got a look at his car. Stewart and Sally saw him on the way home from Portland today and said they laid eyes on him directly, but when they talked about how to describe him, they said there wasn't one distinguishing mark about him that stood out."

"Besides all that, the car . . ."

Carmelita cut him off quickly. She didn't know how Johnny was going to say it.

"The car came through town today and despite our efforts not to believe our eyes, it was moving forward but pointed ninety degrees the other way," Carmelita said.

"You mean it was going south, and . . .?" asked Marc.

"Yes, it was going south while the front of the car was pointed toward the Coast Range and the rear end was pointed toward the harbor."

Johnny spoke up. "Them tires wuz just skiddin' along. Sometimes they wuz on the ground, and sometimes, the car wuz in the air. It was a sight, I tell ya! We chased the car down the Coast Highway, but no dice. It disappeared. We went as far as Yachats, and turned around, and came back home."

"If it had just come and gone, it would go down in the newspaper as one of the weird events in Safety Harbor, but with that car being back in town, well, we just don't know what they want," said Carmelita.

"Some nerve they have, takin' the Chief on a long chase, getting away, and then coming back to town!"

"We just wanted to make sure the children are safe, that's all," said Carmelita.

"Everybody is okay here. But, we'll keep an eye out," said Dottie.

Chapter 44

THAT NIGHT, AFTER A beer and sandwich at Our Lady's, Meriwether, Magdalena, and Susanna met at Susanna's apartment over the art gallery. They had coffee and the usual baklava. After chatting for a couple of hours, Susanna said, "Morning comes in about four hours. Shall we call it a night?"

"I don't think we have any choice," said Meriwether.

Meriwether and Magdalena walked together for most of six blocks, reflecting on the wonders of the last few days.

"Just think. A few days ago, I didn't know any of you," said Magdalena. "Now, it seems as if I have known you for a long time. I've never seen anything like it. Joe has brought such an unlikely crew together and he isn't even here! I hope we can find him! He was so good to us at the Unsettlement."

"Everybody admires him. I've never heard a bad word said."

"You know, there's always been something about Joe that's been . . ."

"Unusual?

"That's one way of saying it!"

"I've never told anyone here about this, but I've met Joe before!"

Magdalena was incredulous. "You have?" Her jaw dropped.

"Where?"

"In Jerusalem."

"Jerusalem?"

"Yes, in Jerusalem."

"I know of a Jerusalem in Arizona. Is that the one you mean?"

"No. Jerusalem."

"That Jerusalem?"

"Yes, that Jerusalem."

"Where? When?"

"I was traveling there with my boyfriend. He had gone out for the day and left me behind. I decided to go to the Church of the Holy Sepulcher, and, after a long day, I stopped along the way for something to eat. He was the waiter."

"No!" Magdalena was incredulous.

"Well, he was for a while anyway."

"What do you mean?"

"I had experienced a splendid lunch with good conversation from the waiter and excellent service. When the manager came by and I wanted to thank Joe for his service, he said they had nobody working there by the name of Joe!"

"Let me guess. You haven't told anyone for fear they would think you were crazy."

"Precisely."

"Magdalena, do you think he's real?"

"What do you mean?"

"Is Joe a man like other men? Is he human in the way we are human? He seems so common and down-to-earth and yet something is different. Just take the parade yesterday. Look how Roy and Jens were changed, just like that. Joe isn't here, but the whole parade was about him, and what he has taught us. If not for Joe's influence I'm sure those two would have been arrested immediately and would have spent at least the night in jail, maybe even gone to prison with their criminal history! And look at Little Therese. How many of us even knew her before yesterday? And there she was, a little girl who cannot see, up there giving a speech. What has happened to our town? I don't recognize it from three days ago!"

"So, what did you say to Joe the first time you saw him in town after seeing him in Jerusalem?"

"He's never acknowledged that he met me before."

"Maybe it was his doppelganger."

"I don't think so. Everything was the same. His mannerisms. The way he turned his head. And he has these little tattoos on the back of his hands in the shape of a cross."

They were nearing the Country Club now and Magdalena turned to go up the sidewalk.

"Tell Rocky thank you for loaning you out!"

"Oh, Rock and I don't own each other."

"You know what I mean."

"I'll tell him you said 'Hi'!"

She walked briskly up the path. The security man let her in. She found their small overnight suite, pulled off her clothes, slid into bed, and snuggled up close to Rocky's lanky frame.

Chapter 45

Roy and Jens pulled into the parking lot of The Rogue Tap around 10:30 that night.

"We prob'ly shouldn't be doin' this, Roy!"

"Doin' what?"

"We prob'ly shouldn't be at the bar."

"Why?"

"We're deputies."

"Not really."

"As good as . . ."

"We can't do no drinkin' though."

"No serious drinkin'. Nope."

"No drinkin' et-awl, Roy!"

"Jens, are you tryin' to ruin my life?"

"No, but maybe you are! We got a chance, Roy! We got a chance here, to turn things around for us."

"We'll have a couple and then be off. I promise."

"If our friendship were based on the promises you kept, I'd be in another state!"

"It'll be okay," said Roy.

"I don't think I'm goin' in."

"Of course you're goin' in!"

"For a few minutes, yes. All right. Just a few minutes, then."

⌒

They approached the door. Someone they did not know was standing there.

"Good evening, boys," said the man.

"Do I know you?" asked Roy, more as a statement than a question.

"No, probably not. You've seen me and I know you, but you've probably forgotten."

"Prob'ly so," said Jens. "Does it matter? We just want a drink."

"Or two," said Roy.

"Come in!" said the man, with an overdramatic welcoming gesture.

He accompanied them into the bar.

"Give these two gentlemen a drink on me!"

"Oh, that's not necessary!" said Jens.

"Don't knock it!" said Roy. "Sure, we'll take it."

"You fellas did good work today!"

"Oh, were you around?"

"Yes, I pretty much saw everything that went on today."

"You a local?"

"Sort of, you might say. I'm here and there."

"Well, you were here today!" said Jens.

"Yes, I was."

"Yeah, we became deputies today!" said Roy. "We're lookin' for this ol' fella who's gone missing."

"Old, is he?"

"Yeah, well, he's kind of in his fifties or somewhere around there."

"Kind of like my age, then."

There was a twinkle in the stranger's eye.

"Yeah, come to think of it! He was your age."

"Or maybe we should say, 'is' your age, Roy!"

"True enough. True enough. But they say it don't look good."

"Who says that?"

"That young fellow. You know, the deputy."

"You mean the real deputy?"

"Yeah, the deputy's name is Marshall. Don't thet beat all?" Roy slapped his leg and laughed at his own joke.

"And Johnny, too."

"That's Johnny Watson?"

"Yeah, you know him?"

"He did some work for me one time."

"I hope he did some good for you. He don't care much for work."

"I'd say that's true."

"Say! What's your name? Did you say your name?"

"I didn't say," said the man. "No, I didn't."

"Well, what is it?"

"A lot of people have called me a lot of names over the years, believe me!"

"Yeah, me too," said Roy. He drained his beer and asked for another one.

"I'm just buying one drink for you fellows."

"Oh, that's okay. I can get the next one," said Roy.

There was no answer. They looked around and the man was gone.

"Wait! Where'd he go? He was just here."

"Yup. But he's gone now."

"How many drinks have I had?"

"Just one."

"Maybe I'd better quit for tonight. I have to be a deputy tomorrow."

"That's not like you, Roy!"

"Well, I got Little Therese out there lookin' up to me and I've got people depending on me tomorrow."

"Holy mackerel!" said Jens. "I can't remember the last time we left this place without being hammered."

"Well, maybe it's time we started."

"Maybe it is. I'm jus' sayin'."

"Yah, you're always just sayin' something!"

"Let's go then."

As they left the bar, they did not notice the Car of Doom, stopped, just a block away from the parking lot.

Chapter 46

WHEN LOU AWAKENED, HE realized he was in an ambulance and it was speeding down the road. He felt a pain in his lower left arm. He looked up and saw that a needle had been placed in it, and fluid was going into his veins from a plastic bag placed above his stretcher. Above him was Ruth from the hospital and another attendant he didn't recognize.

"What happened?" he asked.

"Hope and Liz found you passed out in your bed and called me in to have a look at you," said Ruth.

"Have I had a heart attack?"

"We don't know, Mr. Schofield," said the attendant.

"Don't know? I think you know. There are two answers for that question. One is 'No' and the other one is 'I don't know.' The last one means 'Yes, probably'!"

Ruth turned to the male attendant.

"Well, the mayor is definitely awake and I think we can say that he is himself," she chuckled.

"Mr. Schofield," said the male attendant. "I can tell you that your heart did not stop. We were able to wake you up without trying to revive you."

"So, I was out cold, eh?"

"You were, Mr. Schofield. Yes, you were."

"Where am I going?"

"We're taking you in to Good Shepherd Hospital in Portland."

"I'm feeling very tired right now."

"Try to go back to sleep Mr. Schofield," said Bernie. "We're right here and if there are any changes, we've got some things to do for that."

Before he could finish, Lou was out.

The next time he awakened, he was in a hospital bed at Good Shepherd. Hope, Liz, and Father Callaghan were standing over him.

"What's happened? What's going on? What's the priest doing here? I'm not ready to kick the bucket yet!"

"Not yet, you old goat!" said Father. "Looks like you're going to be with us for a while, for better or for worse."

Hope came over to the head of the bed and placed her hand on his shoulder.

"You had a blockage of one of the arteries in your heart, honey. Serious at the time, but they've managed to do a procedure on you to keep it open. The doctor will be in soon to explain everything to you."

"So, I can go home then?"

"Not yet, Daddy," said Liz. "You're going to be staying another day or two, and while you're here, they're going to be taking a closer look at those spots on your lungs."

"Oh, for heaven's sake! How many more tests do they need to figure this out? They just take these tests, one on top the other, to get into your wallet."

"We want to get to the truth, Daddy. If there's something more, we want to take care of it. We want you around for a while."

"What time is it?"

"It's about two o'clock in the morning!"

"What morning?"

"It's Tuesday, Daddy."

"So they looked for Joe yesterday. Did they find anything?"

"No, nothing Lou. No sign at all," said Father Callaghan.

"Well, I want to be there! I'm sick and tired of missing out on one of the most important things we've had to do as a city! God knows, most of the town council is worthless, when it comes to something like this. I'm sure they're too busy making money off this tragedy to worry much about poor Joe."

"In all fairness, Mr. Mayor," said Father, "three of the five have been quite diligent, quite helpful in all of this."

"And I'll bet I can tell you which ones!" he said.

Father Callaghan was about to respond when he noticed that the mayor had suddenly fallen asleep. The little company of visitors quietly exited the room.

All three had come to Portland together and so they headed back to Safety Harbor together in the rectory car. Before leaving town, they stopped at a local all-night restaurant for an early breakfast. By the time they were descending the hill into town, the sun was coming up behind them in the east. As they passed the police station, they noticed that Carmelita's car was there.

"Let's stop in and see how things are going. I see lights on in Carmelita's office."

"You think so, Liz? She might be getting some much-needed sleep."

"You know better, Mom. You know our Carmelita and she's not likely to sleep much if at all at a time like this. Maybe we could be some help. Let's go see."

"I think it can't hurt. If she's sleeping, well then, we'll back out quietly," said Father Callaghan.

Carmelita was not sleeping.

"How's our mayor?" she asked before they'd had a chance to get in the door.

"He's hanging in there, Carmey," said Hope.

"So, he's going to be okay, then?"

"He still has to get the final word on those spots on his lungs, but Doc Bailey hasn't gotten his morose face on, yet."

"Yes, Doc is closed-mouthed," said Father. "But, he can't hide it on his face."

"Is it okay to call him? I need some permission for some latitude around some enforcement issues."

"It's early yet, but I would think after eight o'clock the hospital couldn't say much."

"By eight o'clock," said Father, "they'll have him in the lab doing tests. You don't know when you'll catch him then. We all know Lou and we all know he isn't sleeping right now. He's wide awake. He's fussing and worrying. Being in touch and needing his help would be a real tonic. I'd say call now!"

Without hesitation Carmelita called.

"Mayor?"

"Yes, this is Carmelita. Can I put you on speaker phone?"

"Sure thing. Is everything okay? Is there some emergency? Are Hope and Liz all right?"

"Yes, they're fine. They're here with me right now. Everything is as it was yesterday, Lou," she said. "Except that we have a lot more people coming in from out of town to help with the search. We already know that there will be some people here up to no good, so I've appointed some people to help me."

"Who?"

She told him.

"Good!" he said with just a hint of dubiousness in his voice. "That Mrs. Saugus is a treasure, isn't she?"

"Yes, Mayor, she's a wonder, a treasure, and a lot of other things too!

"Here's the thing, Mayor. I need your permission to suspend giving out parking tickets today. It's good for public relations; and besides that, we wouldn't want to insult some of the people who've come to look for Joe by giving them even a courtesy ticket."

"It makes sense, Carmey," said the Mayor. "I'd say go ahead. Are you going to provide free parking then?"

"No, we wouldn't advertise free parking. We won't turn down money if people want to put it in the meter! We just wouldn't give out tickets for parking violations at the meters. True enough, some vehicles may have to be towed if they're in the way. But, we just think it best if we do this today and tomorrow as well."

"The search goes through tomorrow, right?"

"Yes."

"Lou, honey," Hope spoke up. "You're going to be busy there at the hospital. You may not always be available for consultation. Who do you want to speak for you, in case you're not available while you're there? One of the city councilors?"

"No, none of them. A couple of them, if they got any authority at all, wouldn't want to give it up. Let them go out and participate in the search."

"Who would you want, Mr. Mayor?" asked Carmelita.

"I say let Rock and Magdalena fill in for me."

"Remember, they aren't citizens of our fair city," said Father.

"By God, they are citizens of these United States and the great State of Oregon. I trust them to make good decisions. They're leaders."

"But they do not have any local elected authority, Mr. Mayor."

"Authority, poppycock! Rock and Magdalena can serve as my advisors. I am appointing them, right now. Hopey, have a letter written by my assistant and have her use my seal, making them my official advisors who can act in my absence."

"Okay, I will, Lou. I'll get in touch with them and make sure they know."

"You might ask them first, Daddy," said Liz.

"Well, of course you ask them. But, when the mayor asks, you aren't supposed to say 'No.'"

"That's the way it will be then, Mayor," said the Chief. "Thanks for giving me the latitude."

"You bet. And, if anything else comes up today, talk to Rock and Magdalena."

"You sound tired, honey. Try to get some rest."

"Ha! In this place? They'll be in here momentarily to do something or other."

"In the meantime, do what you can to catch a few winks!" said Father.

"Okay Frank. I'll do it. I've gotta go now. Someone is here, just as I predicted."

He hung up the phone unceremoniously without a good-bye, as was often his custom.

"Quite amazing indeed," said Father. "Lou's attitude about almost everything has changed in the last few days. It is a miracle that he wants Rock and Magdalena to be involved to this degree, although we know it's not legal and we can't really do it. Obviously, since Lou didn't appoint anyone from the Council, that'll be up to them."

"It certainly is," said Hope. "But, maybe Joe won't be gone long enough for a replacement to be necessary. I'm very tired now and I'm going to get some sleep. I'll join the search party about noon."

"I think that's a good idea," said Carmelita.

They got back in Father's car and as they turned right onto Main Street, in front of them was Joe's Fine Dine-ing.

"It's so sad to see that place now," said Hope. "Just a few days ago, we were here having breakfast and coffee and good conversation, unware that things would change so abruptly."

"Yes, sad it is. Sad indeed," said Father.

Chapter 47

WENDELL CONE HADN'T SLEPT for nearly the whole night. He stirred, exhausted, and yet sleepless, as if he'd had a good dose of a steroid for his occasional gout attacks. He especially missed his wife right now. With Joe missing, somehow, her absence seemed more pronounced. At least he knew where Irene was, out there in the cemetery, ensconced in that coffin, upon which he had spared no expense. They didn't know where Joe was, but there was a good chance, Wendell knew, and so did everybody else, that Joe was dead.

A wave of sorrow and disbelief overwhelmed him, as it hadn't in several weeks. He'd never see Irene again. He'd never talk to her, never kiss her good morning, never drink any of her good coffee. He'd never see her smile again and he'd never feel her tender touch that had never grown old. She was out there, cold in the grave.

He wished at times like these that he were there with her, as cold and dead as she was. You didn't talk to people about this sort of thing in the daylight. You couldn't say, "I wish I were dead," or people would get all upset and call you suicidal and send you to the hospital or set up some kind of spy network to keep track of you.

No, if he were suicidal, he would be dead. He would have done the deed. But it's not out of the question to wish that you were also dead with the one you love, whatever that means.

He held out hope, much of the time, that, as Father said, she too would rise in the resurrection of the dead and at the same time, even now, she was in Paradise. Not long from now, he would join her, both in that graveyard and in Paradise. But, sometimes he didn't believe it. He just flat didn't believe that he could be both dead and alive at the same time.

And oh, the nights were long sometimes. This one was especially long. Yes, it was. And he found himself wishing that they were out looking for Irene, and Joe was out there in that grave instead. He hated himself for it, but he wished it. At least maybe they'd find Joe. He didn't have to look for Irene. Everybody knew where she was.

Even now, he thought he could smell her coffee being brewed in the kitchen. It's funny how the mind could play tricks on you. Even your senses were fooled. He turned one more time on his side to see if maybe a few moments of sleep would come. Maybe he would doze in that sweet way that comes when we know that morning is almost here but there are a few moments left when we can rest. If the body is relaxed enough, one's sense of well-being is delicious.

He was almost there when the aroma of the coffee penetrated his nostrils again. He found himself frustrated that he couldn't get his mind to quit doing acrobatics on him. He couldn't even get these few minutes of fleeting sleep.

He sat on the side of the bed, then mustered the energy to place his feet on the floor. Putting on his robe and walking in his stocking feet out to the kitchen, he was amazed to see the coffee maker had been on and coffee was ready to serve. That automatic timer must be out of kilter again.

He went back to the dresser and put on his glasses. Going out to the kitchen again, he saw a man standing in the corner. Yet, he wasn't so much standing as, it seemed, he was appearing as some sort of hologram.

Good God! It was Joe!

"Hello, Wendell. I've made you some coffee after your long restless night. I know you are grieving. I wish I could tell you that it was going to get better right away. But, it doesn't. Not at first. It will get better some times and then it will get worse again. That's the way it is when somebody dies."

"Are you dead, Joe?"

"Well, they're afraid I am, but I am here talking to you, am I not?'

"Well, I might ask if you are alive as I am alive, then what are you doing in my kitchen!"

"You have a point there, dear Wendell. Please forgive my precocity. I let myself in and I can let myself out now."

"Oh no! Stay for coffee! I could use the company! Say, shouldn't you go and tell the folks at the police station that you are home? Hundreds are assembling out there to find you. It seems that everyone is looking for you."

"Ah, you must not tell them that you have seen me, my dear man. They are doing so well together. If they weren't looking for me, what would they be doing? They'd all be out there on their own, doing their own thing, ignoring one another, finding reasons to fight with one another, getting greedy and jealous and wanting what the other has. When they're out there looking for something they have all lost, they are so much more themselves."

"You have a point, Joe. At least I think you do. But, I'm going to feel foolish looking for you when you are already here."

"Well, I'm not here in the way that they want me to be."

"Will you ever be coming back in that way?"

"There are still many things for you to understand, but it isn't time yet. There are still some things that need to take place, that need to happen in this good little town, before there can be a full understanding of my absence and my presence."

Wendell was in tears. Joe brought him a steaming cup of coffee, just in the way that Irene had done it, two sugars, and a drop of cream.

"Thank you, Joe."

"You are most welcome, my dear man."

Wendell realized that it must be a dream. Without a word, he walked back to the bedroom. No, he wasn't dreaming. He wasn't out of his body. He couldn't look down from where he was and see himself sleeping on the bed. He was having a real experience.

He went back out to the kitchen. His cup of coffee sat, steaming on the table. The coffee maker registered six cups left. But Joe was gone.

He sat and drank his coffee while wondering what all of this meant. He got up to get a refill. In the sink was another cup. It had a bit of coffee left in the bottom, and stains running down the side. Joe had not only been here. Joe was real! He had helped himself to a cup!

"I love you, Irene," he said through tears. "Oh, I do love you so."

Deep from within his heart he heard her sweet voice so clear and crisp and gentle, "And I love you too, my darling Wendell. I will love you forever."

Chapter 48

THERE HAD BEEN A time when Safety Harbor was young, new, and sparkling. In those early days, the settlers found Indian graves, some of which were accidentally uncovered when some homes of the earliest white people were built inland, from the sea. There was no small fuss about it in town and, to his credit, the first mayor, Rufus Lange, decreed that those lands should not be touched and the bones reburied where they were. The city maintained it, but it was never clear who owned it.

Bartholomew Grundy, the earliest land investor in town, claimed that it was his and deeded it to the city. Although nobody was really sure Bartholomew legally owned it, the city accepted it as a gift anyway. A small museum was built in the 1950's, after the Women's Book and Bible Society of Always Sunny Free Will Holiness Church had done some research and found that the land next to the cemetery had been an old substation for the Alsea Indians.

In the 1970's the Tribal Council went to the mayor, Wendell Cone, and asked that the museum be given over into their care. Wendell was a conservative fellow and had to be persuaded, enlightened, as some of the young people of the area told him. Some activists from Portland came and demonstrated in front of the mayor's office. They did not impress Wendell but the face-to-face meeting he had with the great granddaughter of Ida Case Ingalls, the first white person to be born in the area, made all the difference. Wendell agreed to the request of the descendants of the Alsea and Siletz Indians to take possession of it with the affirmation of the City Council. From that time on, the museum area had grown and changed.

A gift shop was built to sell the wares of the indigenous peoples. The store and the museum hosted a good number of tourists; but the largely white population of the town and the indigenous people who came from the reservation to work and to sell their wares. remained a people apart. After the shop closed in the evening, the First Nations people went back to the reservation. Sometimes they would go into Ripples for a few items, but they appeared as shadows, more than as real people, to most of the citizens of Safety Harbor, noticed only in passing, or not at all.

In the eighties, there was a move to put a casino on the south edge of Safety Harbor but Lincoln City won out and Safety Harbor remained a small village of 1152 people. They benefited from traffic from the casino, but were largely protected from the outside world penetrating their culture and changing much of what was charming and essential about the city.

Lou had been elected mayor in 1992. He campaigned on the platform of making Safety Harbor a safer and more functional place to live. With each election cycle, Lou won by bigger margins until he was considered a fixture. He not only knew how to get elected, but he knew how to be mayor. He understood his people and they returned him to office, again and again. He was one of them and they knew he did his best to keep their little town stable and, if not gaining in population and economic strength, at least not going backward.

This also went for his neighbors who came to work in Safety Harbor from the Siletz Indian Tribe. He always treated them as equals and with great respect. He came to their defense when somebody made a disparaging remark and went after those who did.

It was in 2008 that Ruby Malone, head of the Tribal Council, came to visit Lou, showing him documentation that in the reservation allotments in 1891 and 1892, some Siletz Indians were awarded property off the reservation. She further brought him documents indicating that the land near the graves had once been deeded to her great-great uncle.

"Your Honor," she said, "there is no record that this land was ever sold to any white person. I'm asking that the ownership of this property be reviewed in order to find out its authentic history."

The Siletz records indicated a half-acre of land, from the ocean about up to the middle of the village square, had been owned by Ruby's relative under the Revised Homestead Act. Lou asked Ruby for some time, and, within six months, he had persuaded the City Council to deed the half-acre, including the museum, store, and cemetery, to Ruby and her kin. From that time on, Ruby and he had been fast friends.

That relationship was why she was on Lou's cell phone at eight thirty in the morning on the second day of the search for Joe.

"Mr. Lou Schofield!" she responded when he answered with his usual nasal "Halloo!"

"Yes, Ruby! How are you?"

"Not well. Not good. Not at all."

"Whatsa matter, Ruby? Is someone sick?"

"No, but someone's missing and you didn't tell us!"

"Oh, you mean Joe? Everything's happened so quickly, Ruby, and then there was the parade on top of it."

"I'd like to come by the office, Lou!"

"Well, you could do that, Ruby, but I won't be there!"

"Why not?"

"Well, I'm in the hospital over in Portland!"

"What for, Mr. Mayor?"

The tone of her voice turned from frustration to concern as she demanded answers.

"It's a long story. I collapsed on the day of the parade and I've had a little heart surgery since I got here, and I've got a couple of spots on my lungs, which is prob'ly nothin', Ruby. But we've got to find out. So here I am."

"Well, Mr. Mayor, I am sorry to hear that. We will spread the word over to the City of Siletz and the Grand Ronde Reservation."

"Thank you, Ruby."

"Thoughtless of me, Mr. Mayor. I am bothering you at this early hour and you are at the hospital! I shouldn't be calling you with anything at all! You need to get rest!"

"Frankly, Ruby, I'm bored. And it takes my mind off things too, because, honestly, don't tell anybody, but I'm a little worried."

"Well, let us take your worries, Lou. Get well. That's all we want so you can come back to us. I want to know how we go about volunteering to help with the search for Joe. Do they need more people?"

"I'd say get in touch with Carmelita."

Lou tried to hold himself back from getting out of bed and dancing a jig, as it was the first time there had been any hint of a closer relationship between the citizens of Safety Harbor and the Confederated Tribes.

"Wow!" he said under his breath.

"What did you say, Mr. Mayor?"

"I said 'Now', Ruby!"

"Now, what?"

"Well, now, I'd say that this is a good way to go about it. Just call Carmelita."

"Will do, Mr. Mayor. Now you get better."

Lou hung up the phone and couldn't help but break into a smile.

"Wow!" he said, out loud this time. "Wow!"

Suddenly, and without warning, a swift, deep sadness swept over him and then, settled into him, deeply. Is life cruel, or is God cruel, or both? He wondered. Why was it, just when he could have been in the middle of things in his city, that he was sidelined? He would ask Father Frank about that when he got all of this all cleared up and got back home. But, then, Frank would probably weasel out of the question with some tortured and circuitous Jesuitical response that seemed perfectly logical at the time.

"Mr. Schofield, it's time for you to go to the lab!" his nurse called out while coming into his room.

With that, Lou reentered the labyrinth of hospital-world; and Ruby and her people joined the search for Joe.

Chapter 49

SALLY HAD SLEPT FITFULLY. She had persistent dreams of Keith and Nate. When she awakened, tears were streaming down her cheeks and dampened the sheets around her.

Sally wiped away her tears, put on her slippers, and slid her feet along the wood floor, making her way to the kitchen. She got out the coffee grinder and made a pot of coffee. She was going to see that despicable undertaker to arrange Keith's funeral and to pay him, so that he could gamble her hard-earned money away. She wasn't hungry, but she knew she should eat. She made a breakfast of wheat toast, yogurt, and two boiled eggs and forced it down.

She checked her email. There was a message from Katye that they would start the search at 8:00 a.m. There was another from Caitlin telling her that Buddy and her daddy were thinking of her. She wondered if Nate had instigated the call. Right now, she had to get it together and get over to the funeral home. She showered, dressed, applied her makeup lightly, and headed out of the house.

She took a right turn on her way to Main Street, and went by Always Sunny. She saw Luther heading out of the rectory. He looked preoccupied and maybe even angry. What she did not know was, that the Finance Committee had decided that a good way of making money during the search for Joe would be to rent out parking spaces to the volunteers at twenty dollars a pop. As an added blessing, the youth group would wash their cars for five dollars. Luther had been outraged and humiliated. Everyone in town, with the exception of only a few businesses, had closed to join the search. Their parking spaces were provided free for those who came to search for Joe.

As he walked down the church sidewalk, toward the street, Sally stopped her car.

"Would you like a ride, Luther?"

"No thanks. I need to walk."

"I can get you there a whole lot sooner."

"Well, okay. You have a point. I'll be glad to accept your ride, Sally."

She noticed he was sweating profusely. It was going to be a warm day but the morning was still cool from the fog hanging over Safety Harbor. "Are you okay? Are you ill?"

"No, just upset, Sally."

"Wanna talk about it?"

"No, not now."

"Okay, then. Are you sure you feel like going out today?"

"Yes."

His answer was terse enough that she sought no more information.

"Look at all the cars in town. More than the usual tourist crowd."

"Sally, I haven't had a chance to tell you how sorry I am about Keith."

"Thank you. I'm on my way right now to make arrangements."

"Oh, I'm sorry, Sally. I know it's hard. But, it must be done."

"Yes, it must."

They reached the corner to turn left on Descent Street where the elevation began to slope toward the sea. A right turn, past the police station, and then to the city bus barn. Sally had to find her way carefully through the near mob assembled out front.

"Thanks, Sally!" Luther looked over at her and smiled. "I appreciate it."

"Don't give it a thought. Glad to help."

She turned left at the end of the row of cars, made her own path in the gravel and low growing weeds around the parking lot back up Descent Street. Then, she turned right toward the funeral home. The sound of an engine that came from behind her was, somehow, eerily familiar. A chill spread throughout her body. She looked in her rear-view mirror. It was that car again. It was moving in its uncanny way, as the hood pointed toward the east and the rear end pointed toward the sea.

Suddenly, it sped up and rode her bumper. Panicked, she floored it and it backed off. She sighed a sigh of relief. The next moment it was riding her bumper again. This time, she held her ground and this time, the specter did not back off. It was only another few blocks to the funeral home. She white-knuckled it to the driveway. Mercifully, the car continued on past her and south toward Clever.

Stewart was waiting for her, standing outside his car. From his viewpoint, the car could be seen on Main Street.

"My God, Sally!" he said. "Are you all right?"

"Not really."

He was surprised when she came over to him and embraced him, bursting into tears. She sobbed on his shoulder until he became a bit uncomfortable. She released him slowly and backed away.

"I'm sorry, Stewart. I've just got so much . . ."

"You've got so much going right now. More than any one person should have to experience."

"Yes, and this damnable monstrosity of a car just put the topping on it."

He offered her his arm as they walked together toward the funeral home. Mr. Bates greeted them with a dignity and propriety that belied the drunken mess he had been just yesterday.

She did her best to hide her repulsion. She had to be strong. It was time to put Keith to rest.

Chapter 50

SALLY HAD BEEN REARED on Vashon Island, a community of about ten thousand, one of several prominent islands in the Puget Sound, in the State of Washington. Her parents, Harry and Louise Persinger, were of sturdy working stock ancestry. Sally was born in Indiana, but had virtually no memory of it, since they moved from Indiana to Vashon when she was three.

After doing some menial work, as he could find it, Harry landed a traveling sales job with a wholesale auto parts company. It took him all over the tristate area. Louise worked for a mortgage brokerage as the office manager.

The oldest of three children and the only girl, Sally enjoyed her status in the early years and took advantage of the ability to boss her twin brothers around, who were five years younger.

Although she wasn't exactly popular in school, teachers described her to her parents as a well-liked student. She adjusted easily and found her niche in playing golf. [Later Wendell and she would become fast friends as competitors on the course between Safety Harbor and Clever.] She sang in the choir, joined the yearbook staff, and got asked to the prom.

The call came on a Friday night in late October, when Sally was a junior in high school. Harry had been expected home some hours ago. He always tried to take the ferry over to the island before the heavy going home traffic. Sally remembered specifically that it was 7:04 p.m. One of the local cops came to the door and told them that Harry had been involved in a traffic accident on the road between Yakima and Seattle. By then, Sally could drive, and her mother and she packed up the boys and headed for the Hunt Memorial Medical Center in Seattle.

It was touch-and-go for Harry for three days. On the fourth morning, the phone rang in their motel room. Fearful that it was bad news, Sally answered. The voice on the other end said the doctor wanted to see them right away.

As it turned out, it was good news. Her father would live, after all, but there were extenuating circumstances. He had suffered a stroke right after the accident, before he was even pulled from the wreckage. There would be extensive rehabilitation. In the meantime, he couldn't work.

While they were overjoyed that he had come home, Sally's mother, Louise, was acutely aware that life carried some big changes for them in the immediate future. Not more than six months ago, they had bought a small bungalow on Fisher Creek. Now it would be a challenge to keep it.

The biggest changes came for Sally. There would be no way around it. She would have to quit school and go to work if the family was to stay together. Even though friends said they would stay in touch, it was not long before they stopped coming by Ponder's Country Store where she worked at the cash register and stocked shelves.

The next two years were lonely. Her heart was full of pain and sadness at the tremendous loss of her high school experience. She knew she could never get it back again. Still, her reward was to come home and to see her father improving and there was a satisfaction in knowing that she was keeping the mortgage paid and the family in the house.

Meanwhile, the twins were growing, and, by the time the three years of Harry's rehabilitation had finished, they were entering high school. Harry went back to work, but his daughter's life had stopped three years before, and she had no idea how to get it started again.

One day, a ruggedly handsome man stopped by the store. She was lonely, vulnerable, and open to a relationship if it could get her off the island. Three months later, they were married by a Justice of the Peace. They headed for Alaska. Keith would work at Prudhoe Bay while Sally stayed in Fairbanks. She found herself depressed, as she realized that, once again, she was alone and at a dead end.

The time came when she realized that she was worse off than she had been before she married Keith. At the age of twenty, her options had become severely limited with no education and an absentee husband.

On one of Keith's trips home, she informed him that she couldn't stay in Alaska anymore and that she had to get back to where life was more familiar. He objected to her going back to the lower forty-eight and told her so in no uncertain terms. Keith went back to the oil fields with their six-month-old marriage under severe strain.

This time, in his absence, Sally met a wild woman named Sinder-Ella Bottomley who moved into the apartment across the hall. She had been married and divorced three times, she told Sally, and was now living with her boyfriend while managing all of the above history without a scintilla of guilt. Sinder-Ella had seen the world, not so much geographically as she had experienced it deeply and widely wherever she had been. She had known Sally only three days when she gave her some advice. It was simple.

"Get out of Dodge, Sally. I don't mean to say that we don't want you for a neighbor, but you clearly don't belong here. Why are you letting some man push you around?"

They were in Gil and Sinder's apartment. Gil was quietly playing his guitar across the room and raised his eyebrows, slightly, at the last question.

"If Gil ever told me what to do, I'd tell him to go to you-know-where! He fixes his own supper and mine too and cleans up the dishes as well. There's a price to pay to sleep with this woman! That's so, Gil! Right?"

"Yep, that's so," he almost whispered. "That's so, fer shur!"

"So, don't let no man tell you what to do! I tell ya, a woman's gotta stick up for herself, cuz there's always some cowboy hangin' around to take advantage!"

Sally looked toward Gil who kept his eyes lowered all the while picking at something that resembled a mangled version of *The Red River Valley*.

"Now go, I tell ya, and tell your man later, when you've safely arrived at your destination. Where ya goin'? Do ya know?"

"I have thought about going back and staying with my parents for a while."

"Oh God, honey. Only do that if you have to. They'll treat you like you never left. In fact, it'll be worse. They'll say that you should have taken their advice and not married this man. Oh, they may not say it directly, but you'll never hear the end of it. Get out of there as soon as you can. And if you have to go there, don't call ahead. They'll tell you 'No' for sure. But if you go there, they'll have to take you in."

Sally left Fairbanks a week later.

Her reception was as Sinder-Ella had prophesied.

Her mother was surprised and her father said, "Come on in out of the rain, honey, and sit a spell," as if she had just come back from running an errand.

Sinder had been right. There were out-of-the-side-of-the-mouth comments about Keith and quick marriages, and "thank God there are no babies."

She got a job at Ponders again and slept in her old room. She didn't call Keith for another week. He didn't take it well. Most days, it was as if she had never gone away from Vashon. She had to do something else, something more.

One day, a man came into the store after filling up his car with gas at the pumps outside. He bought a loaf of bread and a bottle of wine. He did not sit down, but stood at one of the tables nearby, and opened his loaf of bread and the wine that he had just purchased.

"Have you got some glasses or cups?" he asked. "I'd like to share with anyone who would like a piece of bread and a sip of wine."

There were only three people in the store, but they gladly came over to the table to share bread and wine with this stranger. Normally, it would seem pretty weird, Sally remembered, but it seemed the thing to do in that moment. Word spread outside and others came to join the table.

She remembered now, how he had taken the loaf, and raised it up for all to see. He poured the glasses of wine into the paper cups she had provided and then parceled out generous pieces of bread to all. Two children came in just after he had finished dividing and distributing the loaf so the stranger broke two pieces from his own portion and gave it to them.

He raised his glass.

"To life!"

"To life!" they all said.

Sally remembered how it seemed that the whole room was filled with a kind of glow. There, on that day, they enjoyed the generosity of this stranger. How long it lasted, Sally didn't know. She only knew that time seemed to stand still, and, all around, enchantment seemed to have fallen upon them.

"I must go, dear friends. I do call you friends, since we have shared the sustenance of wheat and grape. We will all remember this moment in our hearts, and we will live in one another's hearts. I bid you farewell."

With that, he was off. No one seemed to have seen him go, but they did hear his car starting. He left behind a business card that simply said, *Joe.*

She went out the front door to ask him why that's all his business card said, but he was leaving already. When he saw her, he rolled down his window, gave her a pleasant smile and called back to her, "Come down to Safety Harbor, when the time is right, and help us."

All kinds of people came through that store from men trying to pick her up to pickpockets and people who tried to sneak food and other items out of the store without paying. But, most people were good. Most people were not memorable. This man was both.

She put the business card in her pocket. She forgot about it until she was undressing for bed. She took the card and buried it in her underwear drawer.

Sally spent the next three years getting her GED and her AA from the local community college. Her self-esteem and confidence improved greatly. The twins were graduating from high school and had gotten scholarships to fine colleges back east. Her parents were all aglow about this and Sally was proud of them too. Still, she wished that they would stop her sometime and just thank her for the sacrifices she had made, to keep them in their house and to get them back on track with their lives. It was not to be.

One day, as Sally got dressed, the little card made its way out from under her underclothes. Suddenly, the memory returned to the surface of the stranger that came by the store and shared bread and wine. She could see him now, driving away and calling out that she should come down and help him. But, for the life of her, she couldn't remember the name of the town. She fingered the card and felt raised letters on the back of it. Odd. She hadn't noticed that before. She turned over the card. Safety Harbor.

"That's it! Safety Harbor!" she said out loud. "Time to put the Sinder-Ella method to work, once and for all!"

She did an Internet check and found Safety Harbor, Florida and Safety Harbor, Oregon. She decided to go to the nearest one first to see if she could find Joe. She'd call Keith when she got there.

Chapter 51

WHEN MAGDALENA HEARD ABOUT the experience of Stewart and Sally, immediately, she knew what it was. The second morning of the search, she had sneaked away from the city bus barn and went up the street to Oak and Main where she had heard it was now parked.

She sucked in her breath as she saw it. She approached it slowly. Memories exploded as a volcano in her brain.

She looked in through the tinted glass of the passenger door from her view on the sidewalk. Fifteen years ago, when she had seen this car, it had Illinois plates. How could she know for sure that it was the same car? After all, if she were asked to describe it, she couldn't tell anyone. And still, she knew. It was in the Chicago, Illinois suburb of Cicero near where she lived with her parents that she had last seen it. She was thirteen.

Her twenty-year-old sister and her friends were going into Chicago to see a show. Magdalena had pestered them until they relented and let her go along.

On the way home, they had taken a backroad that went through Cicero.

"Hey!" said Heather, one of Margaret's friends, "Don't they say that this town is owned by some organized crime family?"

"Yeah, I think that was the case a few years ago. Now, not so much."

"Maybe yes. Maybe no," said Heather.

They were driving down Laramie Street when they noticed squad cars right next to the Cicero Bowling Alley.

"Something is going on here!" said Margaret.

"Let's keep going!" said Magdalena.

"Let's not!" said Heather. "Let's stop."

"Stay in the car!" said Magdalena, demonstrated more maturity than the twenty-somethings.

"You stay in the car!" said Margaret. "We're going to lock you in the car and go see what the commotion is about!"

This, they did. Soon, they were out of her sight, lost in the growing crowd of people around her. She felt very much alone and frightened. A car pulled up beside her. The driver rolled down the window. She kept her eyes averted and fled to the opposite side of the car behind the steering wheel.

She could not keep away from the car any more. It seemed to draw her nearer. She went back to her seat on the passenger side.

Slowly, she looked up at the driver. The eyes were piercing and compelling. She remembered that much. There wasn't much else at all about the rest of the face to notice. The nose, mouth, cheeks, and chin could have been the face of a mannequin.

She could feel the stranger calling her to get out of the car, even though he wasn't saying a word. She opened the door and stepped out on the street. The back door of the car slid open. She was climbing into the vehicle when she felt arms around her pulling her out and away. She turned and saw that a kind-looking man was pulling her from the car.

"Don't go in there!"

He held her hand tightly as he walked up to the front door and looked in at the driver.

"Have you found me, my enemy? Yes, you have. But, I have found you, too, about to commit a foul deed. You cannot have this young woman. You cannot have her life. You cannot steal her future. Now, move out of here and go back to the place from whence you came."

The man walked to the intersection and faced the car, watching it leave. He picked her up in his arms. She turned and hugged him. He held her close. She was strangely comforted. She did not want to leave his arms.

The car moved on and away. The stranger let her down as soon as it was safe and held her hand, leading her back to the family car.

"You'll be safe, now. Get in and lock the car."

She did as she was instructed, then looked around to thank him. He was gone.

When her sisters returned, they awoke her from a sound sleep.

"What was going on out there?" she asked.

"It's a crime scene, actually."

"Yes, actually," said the two women from the back seat in concert, still feeling their martinis.

"What kind of crime scene?"

"It was the mob!" said Heather breathlessly. "A hit, they call it!"

"You mean the mob out there?"

"No, silly. Not the crowd. The Mob. The *M-O-B*. The Mob."

"I think I know what that is."

"Anyway, they went right into the bowling alley and shot him right where he was. But, somebody was there with a gun of his own and shot the shooter! It's all very exciting!"

"What have you been doing while we were gone, Magdalena?"

"Sleeping, obviously," said Margaret.

"Oh, something happened before I fell asleep."

When she told them, they laughed.

"Wow, Magdalena! You have great dreams!"

She shook herself awake from her memories and back to the present.

Now, looking back on that day, she knew. The kind stranger had been Joe! How could she not have realized this before? There had always been something about his voice that had been familiar, ever since she met him.

She turned and walked back toward the city bus barn. Suddenly, she heard someone sobbing. She turned to look. There was no one there. Then she realized that it was she who was crying uncontrollably. She stopped, leaning against a light pole, until her shaking subsided and the tears stopped flowing.

Now the friend, the man who had saved her, was in need of rescuing, if it wasn't too late.

When she went in the city bus barn, her face showed signs of a recent cry. Rock caught her eye and went to her. He asked no questions, but shielded his friend, wife, and lover from curious eyes and well-meaning inquiries as to her well-being.

Chapter 52

THE SECOND DAY OF the search, the number of people looking for Joe doubled. By the time Sally reached the bus barn to help, the search had been going on for three hours. She was virtually destroyed from her conversation with Stanley Bates. His glib pomposity and his pseudo-dignified persona was remarkably incongruent with his drunken display the day before. She could hardly stand him, and yet, this is the man she must talk to about her husband's funeral.

Hobe and Georgette assigned her to the same search party north of town in some rough terrain along the coast, with abrupt drop-offs and trails that led into obscure areas. Those in the party had to be in good shape to manage it. Eventually, Sally found her comrades, Susanna and Magdalena, amid the crowd. The way became too difficult for some to manage, so they wanted to turn back. Rock was concerned that if they were already too weak to go forward, they may very well not make it back to the bus barn.

He called Carmelita.

"It seems I remember that Always Sunny has a bus. I haven't seen it in use. Do you think if we asked nicely we might be able to transport some of these people back to town?"

"You are right!" said Carmelita. "Let me call Luther and see if we can get it."

When she reached him, he gladly assented and called Zeke.

"I don't know. Durwood said it couldn't be used!"

"Durwood Schmurwood! I don't care what he said. There are some people who need our help. If we can't help them, why are we around anyway?"

"I don't want to lose my job!"

"You won't lose your job. I may, but you won't! Go and get those people. Here's Carmelita's number. She'll tell you where they are. I'll deal with the fallout when I get home today from the search."

Stewart had gone on down to the lighthouse after helping Sally at the funeral home. He needed to decompress from the conversation with Bates. He had seen a lot in his time, but he had never seen the likes of the old funeral director. The lighthouse, for him, was becoming a haven and an oracle of insight. The effect of the place had a kind of mysterious emptiness to it and yet the emptiness was not a cold or void. Stewart felt comfortable here. He felt at home, even more at home than he felt with Katye, sometimes. He felt close to Something that was not the God of *The Book of The Prayers of Anglican Piety.*

He knew he had to call the Bishop to inform him that, despite the Bishop's objections, he would be speaking at Keith's memorial service. He thought the chances were about fifty-fifty the Bishop would approve, since it was more or less a secular service.

But, when he called from his perch on the steps of the lighthouse the Bishop said, "No, Stewart. You are never not a priest and no matter that it isn't exactly a religious service. People know you're a priest and would think of you as one when you led it."

"I'm just doing this as his friend, Bishop. Honestly, I'd be doing this if I weren't a priest."

"And you wouldn't be in Safety Harbor at this moment if you were the kind of priest you should have been. You'd be somewhere serving a parish."

"But, I am not. Right now, I am in Safety Harbor and that is where I am supposed to be right now. This is my friend and I want to have the privilege of burying him, by God!"

"Let's put it this way, Stewart. You can lead the memorial service. But don't come back to me asking for a parish anytime within the next hundred years, because you're not going to have one!"

"So, it's a choice between honoring the life of my friend and comforting his widow or keeping my credentials as a priest, in hopes that, someday, should you choose, on a good day, when you are feeling generous, you will make me a real priest, again."

"Now, you're going too far, Stewart. You've shown me that you have so much more work to do."

"Maybe not as much work as you might think, Bishop."

He knew he should say no more. He paused for a minute and looked out over the scene below of the little town of Safety Harbor. There was Harbor Square not far away and Main Street, with the coffee shop and bookstore nestled in among the other shops and galleries. Still closer to the sea and not far from the Square, was the Indian Cemetery and Museum. The Rogue Tap was just up the alley from Main Street in the middle of town. To the right and up the hill was Harbor High and just beyond, at a little higher elevation,

Harbor Hospital could be seen. Hidden from view up Main Street, if you turned right instead of left toward the high school, you would find Argostoli's Gallery. Down below and to the left just off Pacific Coast Highway, were the City of Safety Harbor offices, the police station, and the city bus barn. In the upper left hand part of the scene was the park and beyond it the Country Club and Golf Course. Just before Main Street became Pacific Coast Highway again, was Joe's Fine Dine-ing. He could see all of this and more.

"Stewart? Stewart? Are you there?"

Suddenly, he knew that this little town was his. He would always be here, at least for a long time. It was his home and he wanted it to be, rather than adopting some strange city the Bishop said was his, when it really wasn't.

He knew that staying here had many implications for himself and others. He knew it meant the end of his career, as he had known it. He felt surprisingly good about it. He felt free. He felt sane. He took in a large deep breath of ocean air.

"Stewart, are you there? Can you hear me?"

"No, Bishop, I can't hear you anymore."

Chapter 53

THE SECOND DAY OF the search brought no new discoveries. Hope for Joe's rescue, or even finding his remains, was slipping away. From her own experience, Carmelita knew that the last day of the search, the number of out-of-town volunteers would not be nearly so numerous. People lose interest.

That afternoon, Doc Bailey entered Lou's hospital room. He cleared his throat and coughed, quietly. Lou stirred, but turned over, still into a deep sleep.

"Mayor, I need to talk to you!" He raised his voice considerably.

"Oh hi, Doc. I just drifted off to sleep a couple of minutes ago."

"The nurse tells me you've been sleeping for hours. That needle biopsy on your lungs causes some stress on the body, even when you're anesthetized."

"Oh, I hardly remember that. Maybe I don't remember it at all, come to think of it!"

"You did have several tests that proved to be inconclusive. So, they decided to go ahead and do a biopsy where those spots are showing up."

"For cancer?"

"Yes, Lou, for cancer. There won't be any conclusive results on this for several days, so I think you are going home in the morning!"

"Are Hope and Liz in town?"

"Yes, I think they are at the hospital guest house now."

"Let's get hold of them, Doc! How can I call them?"

"I think they'll be by soon. It's about dinnertime. My guess is that they're dining at one of those nice restaurants on 23rd Street."

"Without me!" Lou wailed dramatically throwing his hands into the air.

"Not for long, Lou. You will go home in the morning. I can all but promise."

"When will I know the results, Doc?"

"Usually, they're back in about three days."

"Okay then, so I'll know by the weekend or Monday."

"I'd say that's about right."

"Do you think I have cancer?"

"I don't know that, Lou. The biopsy is testing for that."

Their conversation was interrupted by his nurse.

"Mr. Schofield, have you ordered dinner?"

"No, I haven't, nurse! I just woke up! And, when I do call down and order something, they say, 'No, Mr. Schofield, you can't have this. No, Mr. Schofield you can't have that.' Why don't they just send me up something I can have and get it over with!"

"You'll have to forgive him. He's just awakened from some tests."

"Oh, I know. I've read his chart. And I've also read about how he's a bit contrary but soft in the middle."

"Yeah, I'm a marshmallow; but listen, I am, as a matter of fact, getting rather tired of getting either measly or mushy food from down below or wherever it comes from."

"Well, Mr. Schofield, you won't need to worry about it after tomorrow morning. Chart says you're going home."

"Good! Good!"

"I'll let you rest now, Lou. We'll see you back in Safety Harbor!" said Doc.

"You betcha, you will! Now, I gotta call Hopey and Liz and give 'em the good news!

"Good night, Lou!"

"Good night, Doc!"

Chapter 54

FRANCIS CALLAGHAN WAS STIFF and sore in places he hadn't heard from in a long time. The two days of searching had been hard on him. His extra thirty-five pounds didn't help and he wasn't getting any younger. He went to bed early.

He had been asleep for some hours when the phone rang. He heard it, but knew that Mrs. McCarthy would get it and he went on back to sleep. But, there was a knock on the door. Mrs. McCarthy cracked the door open and said, "Father, a woman named Ruth is on the phone. She says it's urgent."

He stirred himself awake.

"Father Frank here."

"Father, I am so sorry to call you this late."

"What time is it?"

"It's eleven thirty."

He glanced at the clock on the wall.

"Of course it is," he said. "And what can I do for you?"

"Father, it's Little Therese. She's just awakened from a bad dream."

"I'm not sure I can help you with that, dear woman."

"Father, I've been talking to Little Therese for an hour and she won't have it any other way than to talk to you. I hate to ask you, but could you come over?"

"Ruth, I really can't. But you could come by the rectory. Mrs. McCarthy will make us some coffee, I am sure."

"I can hear your eyes rolling, Mrs. McCarthy!"

"What did you say, Father?"

"Oh nothing, Ruth. Never mind. I was just asking Mrs. McCarthy to make coffee."

He could hear her steps down the hallway. Five. Ten. Fifteen. Seventeen. After this many years, he knew how far it was from the kitchen to his bedroom. Eighteen steps. He was right. She had been eavesdropping.

It was a quarter past midnight when Little Therese and Ruth arrived.

"Come in, Ruth. Hello, Little Therese."

"Hello, Father!"

"Come into the parlor. Mrs. McCarthy has made coffee and put out cookies. There's some punch for you, young lady!"

She giggled. "Thanks!"

"I hear you are having bad dreams."

"I didn't have bad dreams, Father. I had Joe dreams. Maybe a little scary but mostly not."

"What did you dream about Joe, Little Therese?"

"I dreamed he was in trouble."

"Trouble? What sort of trouble?"

"It seemed he was out on the water and couldn't get back. He said, 'Tell my friends that I've had to go away for a while and help some other friends of mine. I'm not sure when I'll be back, but they mustn't worry or fret.'"

"And you said?"

"And I said, 'Joe, we're all out looking for you'!"

"And he said?"

"He said, 'Tell them to keep looking. We'll all get back together in Safety Harbor.' And then he said somethin' real funny?"

"Funny? What was that?"

"He said, 'Tell them to come toward the light to find me.'"

"And you said?"

"And I said, "What light, Joe?"

"And he said?"

"He said, 'Look for the light and you will find me.'"

"He said that."

"Yes, he did. It's a funny thing, Father. Usually my dreams are just sound, 'cause I'm blind, but, in these two dreams I actually saw. I saw Joe and I saw the light. Both times."

"Amazing! What was the second dream about?"

"Well, I saw a boat, Father. I know it was a boat. I've never seen a boat, but I knew in my dream it was a boat."

"What about the boat? Was it just there or was it going places? Did it have anybody on it?"

"Well, I saw these sails on the boat but they were pretty tattered and torn. I heard Joe's voice this time and he said. 'Sail on, little boat, through the rough waters. Soon enough you shall see land.' I want to go home and dream again, Father. I liked seeing!"

"Little Therese, you see more than most of us. You are a gift to us."

They sat quietly for a few moments in the dim light of the rectory parlor.

Suddenly, little Therese started singing,

Silent night. Holy night.
All is calm. All is bright.
Round yon virgin mother and child.
Holy infant, so tender and mild.
Sleep in heavenly peace.
Sleep in heavenly peace.

They sat for a few more moments, stunned from hearing such a beautiful carol on a hot summer night from the lips of a little child, with a voice as pure as the blue sky. They stood. Father gave them a blessing and escorted them to the door.

"Good night, Little Therese. Sweet dreams," he said. "Sleep in heavenly peace, now, dear one."

He gave Ruth a warm look and a firm, but tender, handshake.

"You have a wonderful daughter. She belongs to God. She belongs to all of us."

The priest went back to his room but could not sleep. He dressed quietly and sneaked out the door so as to avoid the all-seeing eyes of Mrs. McCarthy. He walked down the path from the rectory, following it down the hill to Main Street to the center of a town, now quiet in slumber.

There was motion down by the dock. He could only see a dark figure moving back and forth on a boat. As he got closer, he could tell it was the *Far from Home* and Nate was there working on it.

"What are you doing out here so late, Nate?"

"I'm getting the boat ready for tomorrow."

"You going out on the water for the search?"

"I have just felt uneasy, like we're not even coming close to finding Joe, because he's not where we've been looking. I am not sure at all that he is a victim of some crime, a kidnapping, or that he's a hostage somewhere. I noticed yesterday, that his boat is missing from the slip where he usually anchors."

"Do you think he's out there somewhere?"

"I think it's more than likely that he is."

"But, the Coast Guard has been out for the last two days. The Governor has given us three helicopters. If they have missed him, what makes you think that you can find him? They are the professionals, Nate. I know you mean well, and your boat is hardy, but please reconsider. At least don't go out too far."

"Not any farther than I have to go."

"That is small comfort."

Father reached out his hand.

"Blessings on you, my boy. You are brave. It's a courageous thing to do."

"It's what I can do, Father."

"Yes, you can. You certainly can."

Chapter 55

"MOVE IT, HOPEY! FLOOR it!"

"I'll do no such thing, Lou! I'm going way over the speed limit now and if I get a ticket, it will be your fault! Now, get some rest before we get home!"

He reclined and within three minutes he was deeply asleep.

"Daddy will want to stop right away at the police station and see Carmelita. He won't want to go home first. Let's use the rest stop in the Van Duzer Corridor."

"Makes sense, Liz," said Hope.

Half an hour later, they pulled off the road. Liz counted six vehicles in the parking lot. As she came out of the rest room, she noticed a car parked well off the driveway in the woods. Something seemed odd. She couldn't name it, but it just did. Her mother had not come out yet. She started to go over to the car to see if everything was all right. Fifty feet from the car, she stopped in her tracks as she realized that good judgment had to overrule curiosity here. A woman alone does not approach an unknown vehicle anywhere for any reason.

As she turned around to go back to the car, she heard the engine start. Her pace quickened toward where their car was parked. The car passed her on the right. She noticed the sprinklers had been on, not long ago. The ground was slightly wet and even mushy in places beneath her feet. But, the car left no tracks, no imprint upon the grass at all. She watched it undulate through the field, onto the driveway, and then toward the road. Just before the driveway narrowed, the car made a complete three hundred and sixty degree turn.

As the steering wheel side of the car came into view, she saw the faint outline of the driver. Even through the darkened window, she could see the piercing eyes. The rest of the face seemed to glow in the light of the eyes that projected from the driver, but not so much as to make out any detail.

Liz shook her head. It had been a long few days. She must be more tired than she knew. When she looked up again, the car was gone. She must have been hallucinating. She was exhausted. She saw her mother coming out of the rest room. Hope hadn't seen a thing. Daddy was still asleep in the car. She decided not to tell anyone and vowed to get a good night's sleep tonight.

Soon, they were coming up and around the hill where, at the crest, you could see the entire town of Safety Harbor.

"Wake up your dad," said Hope. "He'll want to see this!"

"Golly goobers!" exclaimed Lou. "It's good to see home again! I hope you tell me when it's time to quit, Hopey!"

"Tell you when to quit what?"

"Quit being mayor!"

"Oh, I'll tell you, honey, but I'd bet the family farm that you won't listen!"

"You're probably right, but you know I always come around to your way of thinking."

Hope looked at Liz in the rear-view mirror and rolled her eyes. Lou did not notice. His nose was pressed to the window like their Cocker Spaniel.

"Stop at the police station! Look at all the cars! And look at all those people. Let's go find out how the search is going!"

As Safety Harbor's first family walked in, the people assembled in the city bus barn began clapping. Carmelita came out of the police station and made her way next door. Lou shook her hand profusely.

"How is it going, Carmey?"

"How are you, Mr. Mayor?"

"Well, they don't tell me as much as I want to know, but then, they don't know all of it yet, either. I've had some tests and I'll know in a few days. How many do we have out in the field, Chief?"

"Not as many as yesterday, Lou. We are looking on land, from the air, and on the sea. That's all we can do!"

"Yes," he said. "Yes, it is. Where can I be useful, Carmelita?"

"Honestly, Mayor, I think if you just went around the search area and greeted people, it would boost their morale. It's a hard day today. We haven't seen anything that would indicate Joe is anywhere around here, and we are running out of time. It would be comforting and a boost to their morale if our citizens knew you were back among us.

"That's what he does best, Carmelita!" said Liz.

"I'll be the chauffeur!" said Hope protectively.

"Hopey is always so supportive!" Lou said.

"When I get you through this, buddy, you are on your own!" she said affectionately.

"Mayor, we've got some coffee in here from Jeremy's shop!" said Georgette. "We've got some pastries from the bakery too!"

"Careful, Daddy!" said Liz. "You've already had breakfast at the hospital."

"If that's what you call it!"

Chapter 56

NATE WAS BUSY RECRUITING his crew. He needed people in good health, alert, and with stamina. In addition, they needed to be team players. Carmelita urged him to take Johnny Watson. The crowd of searchers had thinned out and not all of her assistants would be needed.

"You know, of course, that there's bad blood between the two of us," he said.

"Surely, you can let that go for one day for the good of finding Joe."

"Well, okay," he had said. "I'll do it for Joe and for you."

Rocky came to Nate's mind first. He didn't know him well, but what he saw, he liked. He was intrigued with what Magdalena and he were trying to do at the Unsettlement and wanted to know more about it. He was strong, young, and healthy. In the city bus barn that morning, he had asked Rock if he would come along. He consulted with Magdalena.

"Yes, I'll go," he said. "Thanks for asking!"

"Do you have any other ideas for a crew from the Unsettlement?" asked Nate.

"You know, a guy who's often overlooked is Daniel Lineberry. He owns the property where the Unsettlement is located. He's always been here in the crowd, but mostly overlooked. I know he'd be happy to come along if you asked him."

"Can you do it?"

"I'll call him right now!"

Nate spotted Carla Chavez, the mail carrier, across the room.

"This is my day off and I'd be happy to go to sea. I want to help. I'm a first-class sailor, if I say so myself!"

"Let's go!" he said.

Jeremy overheard the conversation and said that he was interested. Nate took him up on it.

"Take Father Callaghan," a voice said to him.

He ignored it. Father was out of shape.

Again, the voice. "Take Frank Callaghan. You're going to need him!"

"I wouldn't miss it," Frank said.

Nate tried to turn away from the voice, but it was in his head and this was of no use at all.

"Take Meriwether, too."

Meriwether? He knew nothing about her.

Nate was a simple man. He saw things in a practical and concrete way. He had no idea why he had gone against his better judgment and listened to voices inside his head. Maybe he was losing his mind. The past few days had been more intense than he had experienced since more than two years ago, when he was in the middle of the throes of his divorce. He could be delusional from lack of good, uninterrupted sleep. Most certainly, he would not tell anyone about it.

They were just about to leave the dock, when Mrs. Saugus showed up and announced she was coming along. Nate could not refuse his old high school principal. Georgia would come along as the cook. No one could do without her.

Nate had his crew. They set sail at half past eight.

Chapter 57

LUTHER DROVE THE SEARCH party in the Always Sunny bus up the coast to Seal Rock. Susanna took attendance. Twenty-seven souls were counted.

An hour and a half into the search, Magdalena found herself alone. She had, inadvertently, wandered away from the group. She felt a bit of panic, but soon calmed herself. Just ahead was what looked like an access road to the beach. She could hear what appeared to be the soft purr of an engine coming down the beach from what must be Pacific Coast Highway.

When she saw the car approaching, her heart sank into her stomach and then popped up into her mouth. All of the old feelings from the Cicero experience came back. It was the same car. She knew it. How could it be? Yet it was one of those rare times in life when there was not a scintilla of doubt about her memory or her experience.

She stood in shock, unable to move, mesmerized. The car pulled up and, just as if no time had passed, it stopped in front of her and the back door slid open. There was only utter darkness inside the vehicle. She felt a strong pull toward the open door.

Just then she felt a strong tug on her shoulder. It was Susanna.

"Magdalena, what are you doing?"

"I don't know."

"Do you know these people?"

"No and yes, Susanna but the simple answer is 'No.'"

"Whatever that means, get back from that car. Don't go any further."

Susanna grabbed her hand and pulled her back.

"We need to get away from here and we need to call Carmelita right now!"

Before they could move, the back door slid shut and the car moved forward. It left the road and moved over onto an open green space. It made a clockwise circle and then a counterclockwise circle before coming back to the road. Then, it headed back toward the Coast Highway.

"This isn't the only time I have seen this monstrous thing."

"What are you saying?"

"It's a long story. I'll tell you later. Let's not waste any more precious time. This is the last day of the search."

Chapter 58

"LISTEN UP, EVERYBODY!" SAID Nate. "You need to know that we're going to go farther out than I would normally take this baby when we have tourists on it. If anyone feels uncomfortable with that, let me know."

"Back out now, if you need to," said Mrs. Saugus. "Otherwise, it is full steam ahead!"

Nate grimaced. Mrs. Saugus never could take a back seat. If push comes to shove here, he would have to let her know who was in charge. But he wasn't going to die in that ditch. Not yet anyway.

No one spoke up.

"I have a little Celtic fisherman's prayer for all of us," said Father.

Everyone bowed their heads.

> *Big Sea, Little Boat,*
> *Dear God, be good to us;*
> *The sea is so wide,*
> *And our boat is so small.*

There was silence, as if, for the first time, the crew recognized the magnitude of their task.

"What do you want us all to do?" asked Mrs. Saugus, ready to play Lieutenant if she couldn't be General.

"Rock is going to be the First Mate. If you are unsure of something, check with Rock. He's my main man. Between the two of us, we will give you assignments. They may vary depending upon what we find.

Mrs. Saugus looked disappointed.

"If either he or I need to get something out to all of you, Mrs. Saugus will give the general information or instruction. She's my information officer."

Now, she looked pleased.

"Let me introduce Georgia to you. She is the chief cook, honestly, the only cook!"

Everyone clapped.

"If you think for a moment Georgia limits herself to being cook, you have badly underestimated her! If she catches you violating the rules, she'll let you know. Don't smoke anything, and I do mean anything, or she'll cast your pipe, your stogie or whatever it might be you have lighted up, overboard, and you'll be lucky if you don't go with it!"

The crowd laughed as Georgia flexed her biceps in front of them.

"All kidding aside, she's known as Momma Bear on this boat and she doesn't suffer fools!"

Georgia nodded.

"Hey Nate, where do you want me?" a voice asked.

It was Wendell. Nate hadn't seen him slip on board.

"Where did you come from, Wendell?"

"Mrs. Saugus asked me to come along. She thought I would be needed!"

Of course, it would be Mrs. Saugus. That made sense.

"Welcome aboard, Wendell."

"I checked to see if he gets sea sick before I asked him along," said Mrs. Saugus.

"Well, even the captain . . ."

Mrs. Saugus placed her hand on Johnny's shoulder and said in a loud whisper, "Not today, Johnny. Not today."

Chapter 60

JENS RUBBED HIS EYES, squinted, blinked, and then blinked again. He thought he saw smoke. He cranked up his bike and drove over the hill into town. It was Joe's!

He drove through town at breakneck speed, yelling, "Fire! Fire! Fire down at Joe's!"

He went into the grocery store to tell Ray Ripple, who was the volunteer fire chief. Ray wasn't there.

Shirley had just received the news about the fire as Marshall entered the station.

"There's a fire at Joe's!"

"Call the chief! Then, call the mayor!" he said.

"I tried to call Ray Ripple, but he's out of touch. His cell phone is probably in a dead zone."

"Where's Ripple?" asked the mayor when he learned of it from Carmelita. "Get him down to the fire station right away. Who's left on land to help put this damnable thing out?"

"Everybody's got their assignments right now."

"Well, everybody better leave their assignments and get that fire out! Somebody's got to be in charge down there. Decide who it is and get with it!"

The mayor was back home and back in charge.

Carmelita drafted Jens and Luther to go down to the fire station.

"How do you get in the damned door?" asked Jens.

"There's usually a key somewhere under a mat or over a door or something."

In fact, the door was unlocked.

"Now that we're in, where is the key to the truck?" asked Jens.

"Maybe it's in the ignition," suggested Luther.

"I wouldn't think so!"

It was. They started up the ancient truck which, at first, rebelled, and finally gave way to Jens's insistence.

"Clutch is sticky!" he said, as he struggled to get the truck to move ahead. "The gas gauge is on empty!"

"The next thing is to find out if that fire hydrant works!" said Jens.

"Of course it works!" said Lou, who was standing within hearing range and was surprised to see one of Safety Harbor's marginal citizens driving the fire truck.

"Good!" said Jens. "No offense intended."

The mayor lied. "None taken."

"Who's supposed to be doing this, Luther?"

"From what I understand," said Lou, "it's Nate, Johnny, Georgia, Carla, and Frank, and they are all at sea."

"Frank? The priest?"

"He's the chaplain."

"Oh," Jens grunted. "So he's hanging around praying for us while we do the work, eh? That's why I've never liked priests, one of the reasons anyway."

"Get to work, Jens. We don't have time for such talk. Joe's is burning, for God's sake!" The mayor was getting impatient and cranky.

While Jens struggled with the fire hydrant, Luther went around the back of the building in order to assess the damage and the progress of the fire. From what he could see, it looked as if the fire had started upstairs.

"A funny place for a fire to start in a café," he said to himself. "You'd think it'd come from the kitchen somewhere, or the electric box."

Sally came around the back and joined Luther. She was devastated. She covered her mouth when she saw the actual flames shooting up out of the building.

"Oh gosh! I hope I didn't leave anything on in the kitchen."

"It looks as if it was started upstairs," said Luther. "What's up there?"

"Mostly, Joe's apartment. There's a room across the hall that Joe keeps locked all the time. There's a safe in there."

"This side is Joe's apartment?"

"Yes."

"It looks like it must have started in there."

"I don't know how. There's nothing up there but Joe's living room, dining room and a bathroom. He takes all his meals downstairs. Gosh, I hope they are going to get this out before the whole thing burns down!"

Carmelita had requested help from the fire department in Lincoln City, but they were a good hour away. The coast road, with its circuitous ways and hairpin curves, took longer. Clever sent its hook and ladder. Clyde Beamer, Joe's cantankerous neighbor, had brought out his garden hose and was doing his best to reach the fire upstairs. Even so, compared to the growing fire, it was a feeble, albeit sincere, effort.

Sally was about to open the door downstairs to see if there was any damage so far.

"Don't do that!" Lou said. "It'll create a back draft and make the fire worse! It'll spread like wildfire. Hell! It'll *be* wildfire!"

"Daddy! Watch your language!" said Liz.

Soon, but not soon enough, in Lou's opinion, the stream of water was flowing up and onto the roof.

No one noticed just then, but under the shade of the trees up the hill in the park, the Car of Doom was parked. It purred and slowly whirled clockwise, just above the ground. The Assistant had parked in a place where he could view the fire that was his creation.

Chapter 59

CARLA COULD FEEL THE vibration of the engines below deck and could hear their muffled labor as they took the *Far from Home* out to sea. Georgia and she had become friends over the years. She knew and liked most of her postal customers, but Georgia was exceptional. If she was far enough ahead on her route, she took her break at Georgia's house on days she wasn't out to sea.

The little house was always cozy. The coffee, it seemed, no matter what time of the day she dropped by, was always fresh; and whatever treat Georgia had prepared was never disappointing.

There is a friendship that transcends all natural and imagined barriers and scoffs at pride and prejudice. Such was the companionship of Carla and Georgia.

Carla was thirty-eight and Georgia was sixty-seven. Carla was from Arizona, a second-generation immigrant from Mexico. Georgia's great grandparents were slaves in Tennessee. She was a widow with two children and six grandchildren. One of her daughters and four of her grandchildren lived here in Safety Harbor. Carla was not married although she had been engaged twice.

Down in the galley, as if they were sitting in her home, Georgia brought out the coffee and cookies she had made and stored up for times such as this.

"I'll bet your daughter and your grandchildren aren't too excited about you being out here today."

"They tell me I'm too old to be going out on this boat any day of the week! Norma Jean wants me to retire and come and take care of her kids while she works, but I'm not getting into that trap. I want to have grandkids, not foster children. I want to spoil my grandchildren. I had to make Norma Jean and Augusta behave, and that was challenge enough. Those days are over.

"Sometimes, Carla, I think my independent streak comes from my great grandparents. I have often gone to sleep at night in tears thinking of them living in such squalor. The pigs they took care of got better care than they did, and they were certainly as caged in as the livestock in their care.

"My great grandma got tuberculosis and the Ol' Massa, as they called him, had to calculate whether it would be better for him to get her to a doctor or let her die. Whichever would cost him less and bring him greater profit was what he would always do with his slaves. He got her well because she was young then, and he figured that she had enough years of productivity left to make it worth it. That's the only reason he did it.

"One year, he considered giving her away as a wedding present to his rich nephew and his new wife but Great Grandpa begged and pleaded and promised to work more and harder if he didn't do it. So, he gave somebody else's wife away to the new couple instead. They say Grandpa never got over the guilt. Every day he would see the man whose wife had been taken and how it nearly killed him. He died early, Great Grandma always insisted, because of his sorrow for the other man and his wife. He felt guilty, and he felt relieved at the same time, and he just couldn't take it, they said.

"That's why I get out and about and am nobody's slave, not even my children's or my grandchildren's. They have their lives and they don't have any idea how lucky they are to have them. Nobody tells them what to do or where to go. Nobody keeps them in chains or puts punishment necklaces on them for disrespecting their hostage-takers or for trying to escape, as they called it. Can you imagine that? 'Escape', they called it!

"So I'm going to keep going, until, one day, I just fall over or die in my sleep. Why should I stop living? Is there some age you are just supposed to quit and wait to die? I never read that anywhere. Still, people will tell you that every day in their own way.

"'Slow down!' they say. 'You're not getting any younger!'

"Oh, and here's the one I love. 'Stop and smell the roses!' they say. "I ask you, do you ever see them stop and smell the roses! Carla dear, they haven't seen a rose in years, let alone stopped and sniffed around on one!

"Oh my, but I've gone on! You should stop me sometime when I'm in the middle of such a long speech!"

"Wouldn't think of it, Georgia! We can say anything to each other!"

"Well, not anything. There are things and feelings and such that are best left unsaid if they're not really important. It only takes a little knife to leave an open wound. It only takes a little word to do it, too."

Carla reached for another cookie.

"You really shouldn't be feeding me this stuff, at least this time of the morning!"

"Well, in about an hour and a half you would be stopping by for your morning coffee and treat, so it's just a little early."

"How far are we going out today? Do you know?"

"Nate never goes beyond twenty-five miles, but today he's going to stretch it and go out to about thirty-five or forty, he said."

"So, we're not looking for anyone alive, are we?"

"Probably not, but you never know. People have been found clinging to parts of the boat and by sheer determination and will, kept themselves alive. The chances aren't good. Exhaustion and the cold water are pretty vicious enemies."

"I understand the Coast Guard has been making a thorough search here the last couple of days!"

"Yes, they have. I think our chances are slim to none that we will even find a corpse. Sharks are ever present and lots of sea life will feast on human flesh."

Carla put her hands up to her mouth, sick.

"Oh, I'm sorry, darlin'. I just live with this every day and could tell you many tragic stories and precious few of them have a happy outcome."

Up on deck, Nate had placed his crew on the boat at the stern, starboard, port, and the bow of the boat, in order to keep watchful eyes looking in all directions. Rocky was up in the wheelhouse. Carla and Georgia were below deck, while those above looked out over the big picture.

Mrs. Saugus had brought along all of the field glasses owned by the outdoor school program at the High School. There were three more than was needed.

"Just in case," she had said. "Just in case."

Nate planned to move in spirals out in ever widening circles until he had gone to a forty-mile perimeter. Then he would come back the same way. Their job was nothing more than to keep their eyes peeled. If they should see an object, they would call out, "Man in the water!" Even if it turned out to be a piece of sea garbage, they would assume it was a human being until it was determined that it was not. If somebody fell overboard, the rest of them were to throw anything that floated over the edge of the boat.

The members of the little crew continued on their journey of hope.

Chapter 60

A LARGE BEAM HAD fallen and what was left of the back half of the top story of the diner collapsed onto the first floor. Miraculously, the front part of the building where the safe was located, stayed intact. Most of the flames had been extinguished by the time the Lincoln City fire department arrived. They helped to put out the hot spots left in the debris.

Sally was beside herself. Had she been negligent? Had she left something on? Was it her fault? She walked through the hot smoldering ruins on the bottom floor.

"Come on out of there, Sally!" called out Hope. "You are going to get hurt!"

"For God's sake, Sally!" called out the mayor. "Get out of there. Half of the second story could fall any minute."

She shook herself and heeded the voices calling out to her to come back and away from the charred ruins.

The growing crowd of onlookers by now had been allowed across the street to get a closer look at what was remained of Joe's. Almost everyone had an opinion of how it got started.

Luther and Margaret, whose lives rarely brought them together in the daytime, were standing together.

"I hope Joe had insurance," said Margaret.

"Surely he did. He was a very responsible fellow."

"Yes, he is," Margaret said. He noticed she had changed the tense of the verb. "Oh, ye of little faith, Luther."

"I fear I've given all of my faith away," he said.

"It's true. Anytime the grim reaper can come and whack us down!" said Jens, who had been overhearing the conversation. "My grandmother used to say that. Grandpa said that she was disappointed when something turned out all right!"

The mayor did not allow such thoughts to enter his mind. At such a time as this he had to stay alert and focused.

The Car of Doom had departed its post near the diner, moving up Main Street without much notice. Somewhere out of sight, and moving toward the Unsettlement, it turned around and came back, almost as if in a victory lap. It stopped in front of Joe's with the engine exuding its low purr, as if surveying its accomplishment. The arsonist had returned, once more, to the scene of the crime.

Roy returned to the lighthouse after several hours of fighting a losing battle against the fire.

"We think it must be a total loss," he said. "The back half of the building is gone. The front half still has some parts of it that haven't been burned. They think it might be arson."

"Of course. things can happen sometimes without anybody doing anything, especially with a building that age," observed Stewart.

"Where's the boat right now?" asked Little Therese.

"It's sailing to the northwest," answered her Uncle Roy.

"It's going in the right direction then. It's going toward the light."

Chapter 61

ROCKY WAS GOING CRAZY in the wheelhouse. The steering mechanism of the *Far from Home* simply was not responding to his efforts. It was as if some force had taken hold of the boat and would not give it up. The vessel was sailing inexorably out to sea, with no indication that it was going to give way to human efforts to adjust its course.

Father Frank made the sign of the cross. Others began to pray in their own way. Fear crept in the boat and stayed there. The *Far from Home* had become a vessel over which they had no control. They were heading to a destination they had not planned for and of which they knew nothing.

"There's a storm ahead!" called out Johnny.

Nate had been so busy he had not noticed. Now, he saw the clouds headed toward them, dark and thick with rain and angry with wind. The waves increased. The little crew of seekers reached the edge of the storm quickly. They felt the first cold pelts of rain and shivered as the wind increased. No one was speaking. No one was moving.

Nate called out, "Everybody get below deck except for Rock, Jeremy, and Daniel! "Do it now! Johnny, you're in charge, below!"

"I want to stay up here too!" yelled Carla above the wind. "I can handle this as good as any man. Maybe better."

Nate nodded. "Okay."

It was neither a simple nor an easy task to get below. Georgia went first and then stood on the stairs, reaching out to the next person in line, steadying them as they struggled to escape the onslaught of the terrible wind, doing their best not to be taken away by it, before they could find safety below. She counted each of them from the list she had made of everybody who had come on the search.

"Is everybody here, Johnny?" she asked.

"Wendell's not here!" he said. "I don't remember helping him down the stairs! I don't!"

"Somebody has to go up and look for him."

"I'll go," said Mrs. Saugus. "I'll go."

Johnny started to say, "Oh no, you won't!" but he knew she would go anyway. There was something left over from childhood that would not allow him to tell his old high school principal she couldn't do something. Georgia, Johnny, Meriwether, and Father, held their breath as they watched Mrs. Saugus make her way slowly, and some thought a little unsteadily, up the stairs.

"God go with you!" said Father Frank, making the sign of the cross.

"God can damned well stay down here out of my way!"

They were stunned. Johnny started to laugh.

She looked back. "So far, God isn't doing so well helping us out. Looks as if we're going to have to take this into our own hands!"

"We're rooting for you down here!" said Meriwether. By then, her frame had disappeared.

"I hope she's all right," said Johnny. "I could have gone, but she wouldn't have stayed down here, and she wouldn't have let me help her if I'd gone along."

"You are right, Johnny," said Meriwether. "Then, there would have been two of you in danger, instead of one."

Johnny wished he had a drink.

Nate and Rock were in the wheelhouse, desperately trying to keep the vessel afloat while it was tossed on the waves. Still, there was nothing to do because the boat's direction and speed had been taken out of their hands. The storm was increasing in intensity every moment.

It was Jeremy who noticed Mrs. Saugus struggling to come across the deck.

"What is she doing up here?" he asked.

"Whatever she wants!" said Carla. "What she wants is the question!"

"Let's go get her before she goes overboard!"

"Yes, let's."

But she reached them before they could get very far.

"We can't find Wendell!" she called out.

"What did you say?" The wind was howling ever louder now.

"I said Wendell's not down with us. Is he up here with you?"

"I don't know!" said Jeremy. "I don't think so!"

It was a tortuous search. Wendell was nowhere to be found.

"Let Nate know!" Mrs. Saugus called out through her megaphone.

"We will!"

Carla moved her slight frame easily up the stairs to the wheelhouse.

"Throw a couple of life preservers overboard, just in case."

"Do we have enough to do that?"

"I've got thirty of them. Throw off five. There's not much chance he's alive if he's in that water, but throw some over anyway."

They all knew that, in this storm, Wendell's chances were slim to none. For the next half hour, they looked in every possible corner of the *Far from Home*. They were sickened and frightened.

Mrs. Saugus returned downstairs.

"We can't find Wendell."

"Mother o' God!" exclaimed Father Frank, making the sign of the cross.

Meriwether went to a far corner and sat down in one of the booths, praying in silence. No one spoke. The howl of the wind and the pelting of the rain could be heard below.

The boat was now taking on water. The waves were tossing the *Far from Home* to and fro, and those aboard began to think of their loved ones and the possible impending arrival of death at sea, for each one of them. One of them may very well have been swallowed up in the depths already.

Nothing was visible to the lost souls at sea but the grey of clouds and fog. Nothing invaded their senses but the driving rain and cold fear.

"So this is what the valley of the shadow of death looks like," said Father, mumbling to himself and Meriwether who sat nearby. "Damned if it isn't overrated!"

"What? What did you say about death, Father?" asked Johnny.

"Oh nothing, really."

"I didn't know priests lied!" smiled Meriwether.

"Pastoral lies are permitted!" he answered. "One must spend only a few hours in purgatory, for such an offense."

"How many hours have you racked up?"

"I don't want to think about it!"

In the midst of the storm, they laughed.

Chapter 62

WENDELL HAD GONE OVERBOARD, when an especially strong gust of wind had come across the *Far from Home* and a wave had washed up over the deck. Between the push of the wind and the pull of the wave, he was helpless against the forces of nature. No one had noticed. All of the crew were either desperately making their way against the storm, across the deck to the stairs that led below, or fighting to keep the vessel afloat.

The wave carried him, surprisingly gently, down into the depths of the sea. No longer did he feel the chaos of the storm, but only the peaceful calm that lay deep under water beneath the wind and the waves.

He gasped for air but only took in water. He panicked. Then, the waves tossed him to the surface again and he was able to cough up enough water to take in air. For a moment, he was above the sea and began to hope against hope that someone had seen him and he might be rescued.

He tried to raise his hand above his head and wave, calling out, "Help!" But, the scream only bounced back against the terrible sound of the ocean's foamy anger and the wind's furious ranting tantrum. Then, he was under water again. He struggled fiercely to get to the surface once more, but his efforts were of no avail. He was but a mere matchstick against the prevailing forces of nature.

"God!" he tried to call out. But, when he opened his mouth, water rushed into his mouth and down into his lungs again. He was tossed to the surface once more, but, by now, he was too weak to call out, too exhausted even to breathe, and soon enough, buried again within the ocean's depths.

This was the moment for Wendell, in this catastrophe, when he once again came in touch with the fact that the sea was the original home of human ancestors. Before we had lungs. Before we had legs to walk.

The fish came to him and he understood them when they said, "We were your brothers and sisters before the dry land mammals were. Before you knew the roads and pathways of the earth, your mind carried within it the map of the ocean. We are glad you are back, brother. You are welcome to pass through here."

The struggle ended. It was over. His eyes began to see beyond the water, now. He looked up and there, bathed in the beauty of her youth, was his beloved Irene.

"Hello, Darling!" She reached out her hand. "My dear man, my husband, come closer to me. I've come for you! You are going home now!"

"I'm ready to go home with you, Irene! I've not changed our bedroom a bit since you left. Your pillow is still there beside mine. I go to sleep every night looking at your picture on the bed stand. I've kept the dishes out of the sink and cleaned up in case you walked in the door. Every picture is in place. I've watered your plants. Oh, I did lose one. I am sorry. I just couldn't keep it going! Golly! You're going to surprise everyone back in Safety Harbor when we get back to town!"

"Oh no, dear husband, you are going home, we are going home, to our real home. Our house in Safety Harbor was just a porch, just the entry to the love we will share together in the place where we are going, Beloved. Come, you don't have to stay here any longer. Take my hand and come with me!"

"Who's that behind you, Irene?"

She looked behind her and then turned around to him and smiled.

"Why, it looks like it's Joe!"

"Joe! We've been looking all over for you! Where have you been? I was on the boat looking for you. How did I get here?"

"Your brothers and sisters, the fish of the sea, delivered your soul to us, dear Wendell!"

"Gosh, Joe! It's good to see you again! I'll sure be glad to drink your coffee once we get home. There's just no place for coffee like the diner. I guess we ought to call it a cuppa Joe eh?"

All three laughed.

"Come on, good friend. Let's go!"

And with that, Wendell's soul was lifted out of the water, up and up and through and out of the atmosphere in a stream of light, soaring past worlds and worlds, past suns and over galaxies, through the cosmos, to the edge of the misty beginnings of creation, where the angels stood at the gates between time and eternity and welcomed him to that place where everything began and to which every living thing returns with ecstatic joy, to a reunion with the All That Is.

An observer from this planet might have interpreted what he or she saw that day as two white birds flying up out of the storm, upward, ever upward, until they could no longer be seen. Wendell and Irene disappeared, away from the curious weakness of human vision, into an existence of astonishing beauty, such as eyes have never seen, where choirs sing the endless anthems of the spheres, and where all that is created and all that is eternal carry on forever, together in the whirling and ecstatic dance of heaven.

Chapter 63

THERE HAD BEEN NO sign of Joe on land. Every inch of ground within a seventy-five-mile radius had been covered.

There had been accidents. People took sick. The little ER at Harbor View Hospital had been overrun with people who had general illnesses and normal mishaps. Sometimes, people had injured themselves through attempted acts of heroism that could be said to be acts of foolishness and downright stupidity.

Sometimes, there had just been too many people and some had been in the way, more than anything. But, Joe didn't turn anyone away when he was here, so, Katye thought that they couldn't turn anyone away, either. Searching for Joe was an experience in itself.

Criminals, of course, had taken this as an opportunity to ply their trade. They are everywhere, even amidst the noblest of deeds and efforts. They came to see what they could see and to take what they could manage. They all came, rich and poor, good and otherwise. Katye had even seen people on crutches and in wheelchairs making the door-to-door house calls around town. For some, it was a real struggle. She admired that. It moved her.

It had been amazing to see the teens, who followed the leadership of some of the twenty and thirty somethings, picking up trash, after they had been out on the search all day without anyone asking them. People did what they found to do.

Yet, it had been a failure. Katye knew that they could call off the search right now. But, this last day she had begun to think not so much of finding Joe. It wasn't going to happen. Not on land. Not in Safety Harbor. Not around here. She was thinking of those who had come just for today. They needed the chance to be searchers, too. They deserved the experience of saying that they had looked for Joe. They would have mementos of their experiences. They would take selfies and send them to family and friends. From what she had heard, the search here in Safety Harbor had traveled on social media around the world.

When the mayor finally got around to his mail he would discover hundreds of letters and cards from well-wishers. When he checked his email, he would be overwhelmed. Safety Harbor was truly on the map, now.

Katye did not know how to describe what she felt. It could not be expressed by one emotion. There was sadness but not despair, disappointment but not defeat, fatigue but not surrender. There was nothing to do but to take this search through its last day.

Those who had come to help put out the fire at Joe's had assembled around the crime scene tape that had been set out by the police department. Luther stood surveying the damage with tears in his eyes. He held Sally's hand as she began to sob quietly. Magdalena stood alongside Hobe and Georgia who had come up to survey the damage. Ray Ripple had come late to the scene, thinking that, had he been there, maybe they could have saved the place with his training.

Susanna and Magdalena were there and Jens shyly made his way up beside them. Chuck and Dottie Springfield joined them along with Bob and Sue Abernathy from the Unsettlement.

"Lou's coming," said Magdalena.

They turned their heads. Magdalena thought that perhaps she had not seen anyone who seemed so desolate and lost as Lou did in that moment. She could not help herself. She went and joined him, locking her arm in his as they came up Descent Street, across Main, and then to the front lawn of Joe's.

"Hopey and Liz are on their way," he said quietly.

Some shook his hand. Others opened their arms and embraced him. They began to circle around what remained of the cafe. They made their way carefully around the south side, carefully avoiding stepping onto the property of Clyde Beamer. Surprisingly, he joined them when he saw them through the window of his kitchen. They were all quiet. There was nothing left. Burned-out kitchen appliances stood, as if alone. Wiring lay strewn around the ashes and debris. Metal from some of the dining chairs and the odd object such as a cupboard had gone strangely untouched by the fire. The stairs were half burned away.

One room upstairs remained intact.

"What is in there?" asked Lou, as Hope and Liz joined the group.

"Joe never sent me in there," said Sally. "But, I have seen him go in and use the safe. The room that is gone upstairs, of course, was his living quarters. I've been in there. Very simple."

They made their way around to what used to be the side entrance of the building on the north. Sally noticed that the key that had been hidden, known only to a few, now lay on the ground. Without comment, she picked it up and put it in her purse. They came around full circle and stood there, not wanting to leave, lost for words.

"Speak up, Luther!" he said to himself. "It's your turn now."

"I think," he cleared his throat, "I think that we ought to pray each in his or her own words, each in his or her own way for those who are . . ."

". . . lost at sea," said Magdalena.

The word penetrated to the soul, those who heard it. Lost. Yes, their friends and lovers were lost.

Silence followed.

Then in a voice, at first, tremulous, but slowly building up more strength and finally reaching its full volume, the Mayor began to sing the only hymn he knew by heart.

> Eternal Father, strong to save,
> Whose arm hath bound the restless wave
> Who bidd'st the mighty ocean deep
> Its own appointed limits keep;
> Oh, hear us when we cry to Thee
> for those in peril on the sea.

Some began to sob softly. Without exception, all were teary-eyed. Katye had joined them by now. Sally reached out to her and pulled her next to them. There was nothing more to do now except to hold each other close. And this they did. Time stood still and time flew. They stood in silence.

Finally, Lou broke the spell.

"I'll go see what is going on with the search. I'll let you know."

"I'm going to see what's going on with Stewart in the lighthouse," said Katye.

Susanna invited Magdalena and Sally over to the gallery for coffee.

Luther walked back toward Always Sunny. He had never felt lonelier than in this moment. None of his parishioners had been involved in this whole business. Not one. He felt anger well up within him as he saw the parking lot full of the vehicles of those who had come to help in the search and had paid the church to park. Nobody had thought to join in the search with the exception of Zeke who drove the bus that he wasn't supposed to drive. It wasn't that they decided not to help. It had just not occurred to them. They were too busy with the church and Luther would hear about that later.

The more he got connected to the larger community, the less connected he felt to his flock. He could make a choice to join the church in their unconscious isolation, or he could become a part of real life, it seemed. He had not known when he started out on his vocation, idealistic, sure of himself, clear eyed, innocent and naive, that he would have to make such gut-wrenching and lonely decisions. He could fulfill his vocation to serve or he could allow himself to be formed in the image of those he currently served. He couldn't do both. The crunch was coming and he knew it.

Chapter 64

WILLIE BOWERS WAS THE latest in a long line of succession of drivers for the Car of Doom. The vehicle of evil had appeared in many forms throughout the ages and had borne many names. Its mission: to kill, to destroy, and to keep the world in darkness.

Once you were chosen as a driver, a letter was delivered to you personally [in our time, it would be an email or a text] summoning you to a particular place, unobtrusive, and out of the way. Nothing fancy or obvious. Many times, it was a parking lot. In another era, it may have been a livery stable. You might be handed the reigns to a horse and covered buggy and told to keep moving.

One must agree to terms. They were simple. You belonged forever to the Bread from Stone Agency. As the driver, you would never see your family or your friends again. Some drivers hadn't made been able to manage it. Should you choose to break your contract, you departed at your own risk. Whether they stayed or whether they chose to go, they were never seen or heard from again.

The driver was simply known as The Assistant. Within the contract, in small print, were agreements that only the most discerning of readers would notice. Each novice Assistant would be told that they were immune to death as long as they were driving the Car of Doom on assignment. The latter had proven to be false as there was not one that had not lost his or her life while on duty. They were all dead. In fact, it was often an early death.

The interior of the car, and all of its versions in the past, was simply empty, vacant of all form and shape, a darkness within an abyss. It was sheer nothingness, non-being and annihilation. The Assistant must grow accustomed to this. Going into this darkness completed the process of the complete loss of all identity. Being The Assistant was all that mattered. It crossed Willie's mind, as he signed the contract, that this contraption could well be called Hell on Wheels.

Two kinds of people made the best assistants. Sometimes, the head-hunters from Bread from Stone would go to church, find those who appeared to be the most pious among them, and make them an offer. At other times, they would be waiting outside prisons when criminals who had done their time were being released.

The headhunters knew that both the criminal and the intensely outwardly pious religious person often had the same weaknesses. The criminal would readily admit that he or she believed he was better and smarter than everyone else while the religious person would feign humility, and, at the same time, with varying degrees of success and failure, cover over their obvious pride with a veneer of glib and insincere self-deprecation.

Willie was ideal, they thought, because he was a little bit of both. He wore a persona of feigned goodness. He used this mask to develop relationships, as he called them, with the naive and the innocent. He had seduced women and walked away without a thought. He had borrowed money and never paid it back. He got other people to clean up his messes and they thanked him for the privilege. He made appointments and never showed up. He had landed jobs with nonprofits because he seemed, well, he seemed to radiate goodness and self-confidence. He was an expert, he said, at handling money and could see through the most sophisticated disguise of an embezzler. For some of his crimes, he had gone to prison. Never one to waste time or opportunity, while he was an inmate, he had written a book about how he had found God.

It was at one of his book promotion appearances where Bread from Stone discovered him. They took him to dinner at a fine restaurant. They made him an offer that he could not refuse and they knew it. What he had managed to keep on the QT to his admirers was, that he had violated his probation by going out of the country. But, Bread from Stone had ways of knowing things. What he had not told the people that night, at his book promotion, was, that he was going to be locked up tomorrow for eight more years for his violation. He was willing to do almost anything to avoid that.

His job description consisted of following goodness wherever he may find it, and to destroy it. He jumped at the chance. He had been doing this all of his life. Now, he could lose his identity as well. This was an obvious answer to all of his problems.

And there was this matter in Safety Harbor, which the CEO wanted handled. There, in that little seaside village, he was told, lives a man who threatens everything that Bread from Stone has organized to accomplish. His name is Joe. Take him out. He would be good at that. This was Willie's assignment. Currently, he was in Safety Harbor to carry out this mission.

But, while he waited, he would drive his vehicle around to see where he could create calamity and chaos, and bring fear into the hearts of men and women.

Chapter 65

WILLIE SAT IN THE funeral home parking lot. He watched as Old Man Bates came out the front door of the mortuary. The Assistant could sense vulnerability in his walk. He would be easy prey.

Bates got into his car, and slowly drove out onto Pacific Coast Highway. Willie noted that he turned south toward the Unsettlement. He followed Bates at a distance. Bates drove slowly and deliberately, maddeningly so, and piled up traffic behind him. Fifteen minutes later, Bates turned into the parking lot of a convenience store. Willie pulled over and waited.

An hour and a half later, Bates emerged from the store and got into his car. Suddenly, it occurred to Willie what he had been doing. He'd been playing video poker.

Willie couldn't help his excitement at seeing his prey. He followed Bates again down the coast highway until he reached Lucky Dog Casino in Coos Bay. He watched him pull up and slowly make his way to the front door.

Willie laughed as he noticed how Bates's dignified posture and upright gait had changed into that of a seriously bent over old man. His hair had been transformed from perfectly coiffed to a disheveled mess. Once white to a fault, it now seemed to take on a soiled, slightly yellowish hue.

"Dissipated. Wasted. Old man, you are wasted."

It was a long wait. Three hours later, Bates came out of the casino, obviously intoxicated and, no doubt, with his wallet considerably lighter than when he went inside. He stopped to rest at one of the light poles, and, for a moment, sagged against it before he picked up once more and continued his lurching, drunken pilgrimage. Willie waited as Bates went from car to car looking at it closely to see if it was his. Half an hour later he had found it and was standing against it, breathless.

It was at this moment that Willie pounced. Driving up next to him, he stopped and opened the back-passenger door on the left.

"Taxi?"

"You're right. I need a ride home. Can you give me one?"

Bates could only see the bright and shining eyes of the driver. Willie nodded.

Chapter 66

THE *FAR FROM HOME* was sailing at breakneck speed now, as if the little vessel had a mind of her own, knew her destiny, and was traveling there with dispatch. The storm had increased in velocity and intensity, tossing their barque, as a thimble on the sea. All but Nate and Rock were below deck now, torn between sorrow and fear, knowing that Wendell had gone overboard and deathly afraid that, at any moment they would meet a similar end.

Father Frank felt his own heart seize up. A memory came to him from several years ago when he heard Mrs. McCarthy singing to herself, as she cleaned and picked up around the rectory.

"How is it that you stay so cheerful, Mrs. McCarthy?" he had asked.

"Oh, I just keep singing," she said.

A song that Joe had taught them came back to mind. The choirmaster at Our Lady had even made a musical arrangement of it. He had learned it by heart, simply through hearing it rehearsed time and time again by the choir.

The words immediately calmed him and filled him with peace.

Sweet vision, Bless my eyes!
Land upon the western skies!
Constant stars, I bid you rise
Over Safety Harbor.

"Folks," he called out. "Folks! Folks! Folks!"

Finally, he broke through the curtain of terror and got their attention.

"I want us to sing the song Joe taught us about our beloved Safety Harbor."

Meriwether joined him. Then Johnny Watson broke forth. Everyone was shocked at his voice. No one knew he could sing. His voice was a rich and mellow one. And Georgia too! Who knew? Others joined until finally almost everyone was singing.

Yours the calm and peace I claim
When I face the waves and rain,
When the sea road calls my name
Out from Safety Harbor

Through the fearsome, foaming gale
When no spirit fills my sail,
I shall see tho' sight may fail,
Lights of Safety Harbor

Where from the windows of the tower
Bright the beacon burns.
Faithful friends at ev'ry hour
Watch for my return.

Heart's haven, mem'ry's shore
call me through the tempest's roar
where the pilgrim sails no more
home to Safety Harbor.

They sang until they were hoarse, until finally, they felt the boat land with a scraping *thud.* They were high-centered on some rocky shoal. The storm was still raging against the shore. The place was made visible by a piercing, yet friendly, light that shone through the heavy clouds and the blinding rain.

Nate descended from the wheel room to below deck.

"We've crash landed!" he said. "But, we don't know where. And, as you can hear, the storm is still going at a pretty good clip. I'm going to ask you all to stay below deck until we see what's going on."

After a few minutes, he returned.

"We're pretty much stuck here. We're hung up on the rocks. We're all going to need to get off this boat really quick. Don't panic, but don't delay either."

Chapter 67

AT FOUR O'CLOCK IN the afternoon, on the last day of the search, volunteers came wandering into the bus barn. Some had given up early. Everyone was tired. Some were exhausted to the bone.

Reporters were eager to interview those who returned. Through these three days, reporters had found tall precipices upon which to stand for effect, featuring stunning backgrounds of the rocks and the sea, and cozy settings of what they called a charming, eccentric village, in order to file their reports.

"The crux of this story," said Sally Martini, in her report to KHX News in Portland, "is not so much that a person is missing. It's the fact that this simple man who ran a diner seems to mean so much to the town. He wasn't rich. He wasn't famous. He was even a bit shy, people say. Yet, the whole of the citizenry has turned out, it seems, in order to find him, to say nothing of the week-enders from Portland and other places in the state, who have come pouring in here in droves from all around the Northwest and beyond.

"And even though it's ended in failure tonight after looking for him for three days, the whole project has been just remarkable, a veritable icon of the extent to which people are willing to go for the simple love and affection they have for one another."

By five o'clock, approximately two hundred and fifty people were in the city bus barn. The crowd overflowed into the parking lot around the police station. Food and drink was completely consumed. Sally, Magdalena, and Susanna made their way down from the gallery to mingle with the crowd. When they arrived, Katye motioned them to the front of the bus barn.

"Is there anything in Joe's little warehouse behind the diner that this crowd could eat?"

"Nothing," said Sally. "Nothing that wouldn't need a lot of preparing and there's no kitchen to prepare it in, even if we had the time."

"If Joe were here," Katye said, "he would know how to make something out of very little or nothing."

"But, he's not here," said Susanna.

"If only Joe were here," said Magdalena, "things would be much different indeed. And it's funny I would say that, because I met him only once, but I feel as if I know him. Somehow, it's as if he's here, even when he's not."

"Sort of gives you chills, doesn't it?" asked Sally.

"I'd rather say it's odd, mysterious, maybe even slightly . . ."

"Magical?" asked Susanna. "We had some strange things happen in our little town of Argostoli, when I grew up there. I am a believer in things happening that we can't explain."

Sally made her way up to the diner to look at the ruins.

There was a sign that had been placed on the door of the old storage shed.

"Come and dine," it said.

"Odd," Sally said to herself.

She opened the door of the shed. In front of her were stacks of ready-made boxed lunches of sandwiches and chips. There were hundreds of them, stacked to the ceiling. They were labeled, "Joe's Fine Dine-ing." She opened the refrigerators and found them filled with soft drinks and water.

Excitedly, she called Katye. Soon, those who were still in the bus barn were in the back yard of Joe's burned-out diner.

"This hits the spot!" said Buddy, noisily eating his sack of chips.

Everyone laughed at the child's unmasked exuberance.

No one dared ask the origin of this miraculous meal of sandwiches and chips. They all knew, but no one said a word. And, for long hours afterward, the fellowship of those who were seeking for Joe went well into the night.

Chapter 68

STANLEY BATES AWAKENED FROM his drunken stupor. He opened his eyes, but he could see only empty darkness in front of him. Where was he and how did he get here?

Every time he sobered up from one of his benders, he thought of the money he had taken from those who were building up savings in their funeral fund and this was no exception. It started one day when he was short of cash for lunch. He had a deposit he hadn't taken into the bank yet and he borrowed ten dollars. He meant to put it back but he never did. He transferred funds. He used the debit card on the account. It snowballed on him and, before he knew it, he owed the fund well over a thousand dollars. He would take a little more, he told himself, and win the funds back. One day he would win big and his worries would be over; but he never did. Now, he had no idea how much he had stolen.

Here, in the Car of Doom, it was so dark that he wasn't sure he hadn't gone blind. He reached up to touch his face and he could feel nothing. He tried to touch one hand with another. Nothing. He reached out to touch his legs. Nothing. He tried to move them. There was nothing to move. Was this what it was like to be dead? You were there but you weren't there?

"Where am I?" he called out. "Is anyone there?" he screamed.

"No, no one is there because there isn't a here!" a mocking voice answered. "You aren't anyone and neither am I. You aren't anywhere!"

"Am I dead?" Bates cried out.

"You are neither dead nor alive, Bates!"

The Voice knew his name!

"You and I simply are no more. Our identity is erased. We are nothing. We are no one. There is only this darkness. Only this emptiness."

"Who are you?" Bates called out.

The Voice laughed uproariously.

"What did I just say? I am no one, I am nothing, same as you. I was Willie. Willie Bowers. Now, I am nothing."

"What do you want with me?"

"Nothing. Nothing at all. Don't you get it? There is nothing. You are nothing. So, nothing is required."

"I want to get back to my home, my work, back to Safety Harbor."

"Oh, we're heading back to Safety Harbor right now."

"Well, can't you drop me off then at the funeral home on the way in?"

"Well, I would but there is nothing, or I should say, no one, to drop off."

"I don't believe you."

"Oh, belief means nothing. Oh, there I go saying that word again. Nothing!"

By now, Bates was clearly irritated. He decided that he must be having drunken delusions. He'd just go back to sleep. Sleep would not come.

As if to have read his thoughts Willie said, "Oh, don't try to sleep. There is no sleep in this state. Fact is, you are neither awake nor asleep. You can never get away from being nothing."

"Is this Hell?"

"You might wish it were," said Willie.

"Why did you want me?"

"Oh, I didn't want you. You wanted me. You asked me for a ride."

His memory was foggy, but Bates dimly remembered a car pulling up beside him and the back door had opened in front of him. He had fallen. That's the last thing he remembered.

"No, I didn't. I remember now. I fell down. Blacked out. You must have picked me up and put me in the car."

"Oh, okay, you've got me there, but really I didn't. A very nice fellow came along and assisted you in getting into my accommodations."

"Who are you?" Bates asked again.

"I'm known as The Assistant."

"Assistant to what? Assistant to whom?"

"It's a job that's been around a long time, forever, some say. I pick up wasted souls like you and put them out of their misery."

"Well, you haven't succeeded. I'm still miserable."

"You've been miserable a long time, Bates. I didn't make you miserable. And, as for your still feeling miserable, well, you see, this becoming nothing takes a little time. I've picked up people and sometimes they've been in the car for two or three days. One was around for two weeks! I'll be talking right along to them and then all at once they don't answer."

"Where have they gone?"

"Nowhere! You still don't get it! Nowhere! They are nothing. It's as if they never had been born!"

"That's a damned lie!" shouted Bates. "You're wrong. I'm not nothing. I'm someone. I'm Bates. Stanley Bates. Stanley Ewing Bates."

He continued his argument.

"So, how come it is that *you're* still here? How come you don't just disappear from this damnable car you're driving?"

"Oh, I'm needed!"

"For what? Who needs you?"

"I work for a large concern, my man. Bread from Stone, they call it. They've got a whole fleet of these cars. We drive around all over the planet. That's one of the benefits. Great travel. You get to see the world. Nobody sees The Man, they say. He stays back in his office. He issues orders and Corporate sends out assignments to all of us Assistants. We stay busy, yes, I'd say very busy. I haven't had a vacation in forever."

By now they were parked outside his own funeral home. Bates was screaming, as if into the very Abyss.

"By now, Stanley, you shouldn't be able to feel your feet any more. Can you feel your feet?"

It had been a long time since he felt solid, but he could still feel himself present, until now. He realized that The Assistant was right. He could no longer even have the illusion that he had feet. He screamed in agony at the thought.

"Yes, I thought it would be about now. You are right on schedule, Mr. Bates," he mocked.

Chapter 69

THE STORM CONTINUED ITS relentless assault. It was dark, except for the glow that pierced through the clouds, providing an unearthly hue over the island that lighted their way, as they exited the boat. Their feet touched land. The whole area was rocky and the cliffs were steep. That much they could tell. After managing the dangerous rocky shore for an hour, they found an area that was flat and sheltered against the cliff. Exhausted, they sat down. For what seemed to be a long time, they didn't speak. Some dozed off. Others prayed.

"I thought I heard a voice," said Johnny, breaking the silence.

"I didn't hear anything," Carla replied.

"Listen! Can you hear it?"

"I think it's just the sound of the storm."

"No, I don't think so. I'm going to walk toward it."

"Not alone, Johnny!" said Nate. "I'm coming with you."

"I'll go!" said Carla.

"Okay. Come on!"

Carla counted fifty steps.

"It's close now."

"It does sound like somebody groaning."

"Here it is. We're here!" said Nate who had run ahead about a stone's throw.

It was a cave. A rock was blocking the entrance except for about two feet at the top.

"You look in, Johnny. I'll have to hold you up so that you can see in over the rock."

Johnny put one foot in Nate's outstretched hand and boosted himself up to peer into the cave. He turned his flashlight into the darkness.

"My Lord!"

"What is it?" asked Carla.

"It's Joe!" We've found Joe!"

Nate's jaw dropped.

"Joe! Are you sure? How can you tell?"

"He's got on his "Joe's Fine Dine-ing" shirt on!"

"You'd better look again!" said Nate. "Maybe you were imagining things!"

"No, I'm sure I wasn't, but I'll look again."

"Boost me up, Nate," said Carla. "I'll take a look."

Nate helped her up as before and Carla looked in on the scene. Nate, not to be left out, had to have his turn.

As he looked in the cave, his eyes filled with tears. "Yes, it's Joe. It's really Joe! But he's in real trouble. He's hurt. We've got to get him out of there."

Carla and Johnny went back to tell the others. Nate stayed at the cave.

"Mother o' God!" exclaimed Father, when he heard the news.

She expected them all to be glad, but instead, among some, there was confusion and disbelief.

"Are you sure you didn't hit your head on something, Johnny?" asked Georgia. "Are you sober?"

"Would I kid you, especially at a time like this?"

"No, we're sure you're sincere, Johnny, but, you have to admit that it seems very unlikely, especially here, wherever we are."

"Come and see for yourself."

Carla led them through the storm to the cave.

"There!" she said. "Joe is right in there. Nate is standing near the cave."

Rock needed no help. He scurried up and looked into the cave.

"Yes. It's our Joe! Now, we've got to get him out of there!"

"What can we do?" asked Carla. "That stone seems to have slid down over the opening."

"Yeah, he probably crawled in there when he was injured. Then the storm came along. This is a terrific wind and these rocks seem way too unstable along here. He just got trapped in the landslide."

"How are we going to get that stone out of the way?" asked Carla.

"We've got to find a way. We've come all this way to find him. We can't leave him there," said Johnny.

"No, we can't," said Rock. "We'll figure a way."

"The rest of us will go back and see if we can settle in for the night. We won't be able to do anything until this storm is over and we have some light. Any of us could slip and fall on the rocks. We'll go back to the boat and get some equipment from there, first thing in the morning. Meanwhile, Carla, you and Rock stay here and guard the place."

The storm continued relentlessly. They were often awakened from the deadening trance of exhaustion by the howling wind and the pelting of rain against the rocks. They huddled together, for shelter and warmth.

Chapter 70

WHEN THE REFUGEES FROM the *Far from Home* awakened, there was none of the usual yawning, stretching, and gradually coming to awareness. It was as if they were all awakened together, instantly. Their clothes had dried while they were wearing them. There was no sign of the storm from last night. The pungent sweet smell of flowers pervaded the air.

"Does anybody know what time it is?" Nate called out.

"Where is the sun?" Mrs. Saugus said, her eyes toward the sky.

"It must be hiding behind the cliffs," said Meriwether.

"No," said Mrs. Saugus "if that were the case, we'd be in the shadows."

"This is different," said Jeremy. "There is light with no sun; we don't know whether it's morning or high noon or the middle of the afternoon because nobody's time piece works. It feels like a bright and early morning, but we don't know that because, well, there's no way of knowing!"

"Maybe it's like this all the time here!" said Carla.

"Maybe Johnny is right," said Georgia. "Maybe we are all in heaven!"

"If that's true, where is God and Jesus and the Holy Ghost and Mary, and all that sort of stuff?" asked Johnny.

Mrs. Saugus turned and stared at the high cliffs behind them.

"They don't look like anything I've seen before," she said.

"Look over there!" said Carla. "It looks like there are steps carved right into the cliffs."

Mrs. Saugus still had her field glasses around her neck. She raised them to her eyes.

"Yes, those are steps all right, but they don't go to the top. They just seem to disappear."

"You mean, they just quit?" asked Johnny.

"I'd say they go inside."

"Inside the cliff?" asked Nate.

"Yes. There's something there, an opening of some kind that shows up just as the steps end."

"Right now, we've got to get back and see how we can rescue Joe," said Nate. "Let's all go up there and take a look so that we can figure out what we need to do to get that stone away from the entrance."

When they got to the cave where Joe was, they found Carla and Rock staring into the cave.

"What happened? How did you move that stone?" asked Nate. "That's impossible!"

"We didn't," said Johnny. "The only thing we can figure is that the windstorm moved it. But that's unlikely. We just don't know. It was there and then it wasn't.

Rock was the first inside the cave.

"He's still breathing!"

"Glory be!" said Father.

The whole group clapped and laughed and cheered.

Carla, who had once been a paramedic, rushed into the cave. She checked his vitals. He had a terrible fever. He was deeply wounded in his side and had some severe bruises on his head. His hands and his feet were bloody. It was clear that he had been attacked.

"Joe's critical," she said.

"We'll need a gurney," said Johnny. "C'mon, Jeremy. Let's get to the boat."

When they returned, they lifted him lovingly, carefully, and tenderly, onto a makeshift gurney that they had brought from the boat. The processional slowly made its way over rock and crevice, over the rise and fall of the shoreline, until they came back to the open flat space where most of them had slept. Father took off his cassock and gently laid it under Joe's head. Others spread some of their clothes, to make him comfortable. Before this offering was over, each person had given something to Joe.

"Oh, how dear he is to us," said Georgia. Then she began to sing to him. Some of them sang the last few lines of the song with her.

Precious Lord, take my hand.
Lead me on. Help me stand.
I am tired. I am weak. I am worn.
Through the storm, through the night
Lead me on to the light.
Take my hand, precious Lord,
Lead me home.

There wasn't a dry eye in the little assembly as they finished. For a moment, there was silence, then a stirring. Joe was waking up! Those who had been standing at a respectful distance now hurried forward to see Joe and maybe to hear what he had to say.

"Oh my! Oh my! You are all here!" he said.

He sat up slowly while they all gazed in amazement.

"Francis and Johnny, Rocky, Georgia, Carla, Daniel, Meriwether. And Mrs. Saugus! There you are!"

She smiled shyly.

"Rocky, where is your Magdalena?"

"She's back home, Joe," he said, his voice trembling.

"Daniel, here you are. Without you, there would be no Unsettlement."

"Jeremy, nobody knows what you do because you do it so quietly and privately. But, I know how you look after the poor, how you take care of the needy when nobody's watching."

He looked around. "Where is Nate?"

"Right here, Joe. All of us have given you a piece of our clothing for a bed."

"Oh, I thank you all for your love and generosity."

"Where are we, Joe? How do we get back?" asked Father.

"Oh, Safety Harbor isn't far from here, not very far at all. It's just a short excursion through the veil. Don't try to get on the island. proper. We are on the shore of the Isle of Gemma and you can't go any farther. Don't try to take the steps upward because, if you do, they'll end and you can't get in through the entrance gate. It's not meant for you."

"So we have to go home," said Johnny.

"Well, I'd say that the best strategy is to go back to Safety Harbor," said Joe. "That's where you're most needed, especially right now."

"You say, through the veil, Joe?" asked Meriwether. "What do you mean?"

"You'll see what I mean soon enough. I recommend that we take my boat back since your boat is, no doubt, wrecked because of the storm. Maybe you can make some changes and turn my little sailing boat into an outboard motor boat. It'll take some doing, but I know you can manage it."

"Well, Joe," said Nate, "we'd better get busy and get you out of here to a hospital."

"I would say you are right, dear Nate," said Joe. "Now, I'm very tired and think I will rest again. My friends, let us begin the journey and all will be made plain to you."

He reclined upon the bed, made of their gifts of clothes.

Johnny came over to him, knelt down and said, "You're not just a man, are you? You're more than that!"

Joe looked up at him, smiled faintly, and, with a twinkle in his eyes, he said, "You say so!"

Then he slept.

Chapter 71

RUTH, LITTLE THERESE, ROY, and Jens had wanted to carry on their nightly vigil for Joe in the lighthouse with Stewart. But, they decided on Pilsner Hill when Carmelita reminded them it was illegal to go into the officially abandoned lighthouse without a permit. At minimum, she didn't want an eight-year-old child up there. She had, reluctantly, given Stewart permission.

The next morning, Ruth rolled over and looked at her watch. Ten thirty! She looked around. Where was everybody? Then she saw them, Roy, Jens and Little Therese at a nearby picnic table. She walked over to them.

"We thought we'd let you sleep," said Jens. "Little Therese says you were up in the night."

"Yes, Little Therese wakened me, and insisted she could hear someone up on the lighthouse making a lot of noise. We walked over to the edge of the Point where I could see. Surely enough, there it was, a bright new lamp, shining for all it was worth. It was as if it had been there all the time."

"Is the light still there, Momma?"

"Where? What light?" Roy asked.

"Yes, there is. There's a light."

"Who put it there?"

"How would I know, Roy?"

"You're supposed to know everything, Sis!"

"But I don't, Roy. It's time you grew up. I don't know everything. Nobody knows everything. Sometimes, I don't think I know anything."

"Okay, Sis. I'm sorry."

"It's a light from somewhere else. It's a light from where Joe is," said Little Therese.

"I wished I lived in your world, Little Therese. It sounds like a good place."

"Oh, it is, Jens. It is. It really is. It's a wonderful place. It's more real than where you live. I know you don't believe me. I know you don't think I know what I am talking about, that I'm a child, and I live in my imagination. You'll see, Jens. You'll see soon enough."

Chastised by the child, Jens was very quiet until he said, "I'm sorry, Little Therese. I don't mean to make you feel bad."

"I'm sorry Jens," said Ruth. "She's so precocious sometimes I don't know what to do with her."

"Sometimes," said Little Therese, "I don't know what to do with myself either."

Ruth blushed. They all had a good laugh.

Then, while Ruth and Little Therese resumed their vigil near the edge of Pilsner Point, Roy and Jens hopped on their bikes, and went back on duty.

Chapter 72

ABOUT TWO O'CLOCK IN the afternoon, a small van arrived and parked behind Joe's diner. A Hispanic man with a slight build, got out of the van and walked around the burned ruins, circling it first one way, and then another. He walked through the debris and ashes, and stepped off the length and the width of the foundation.

A woman with a small child, a boy of two or three, got out of the van and watched from afar. By now, Shirley had noticed them from the window in the coffee room of the police station. She called Carmelita.

"There's somebody parked up at the diner. A man has been walking around the building. Now there's a woman with him and a kid. They're just standing there."

"I'll go up and see, Shirley. Thanks."

The Chief of Police parked behind Joe's near the van and approached the stranger.

Before she could say anything, he said, "I am Miguel and I have good news for you. I have come to rebuild Joe's."

"That's good news indeed! Who sent you?"

He handed her his business card. It read *Miguel: The Isle of Gemma, LLC.*

"This fire was not started by any human being," said Miguel. "The one in the Car of Darkness and Doom has made the trouble. He was sent here to prevent the light from coming, to prevent Joe's work, to keep your people from listening to Joe's message and following it. He knows a great light is coming here and he will stop at nothing. I only have three days to do this! Then I have to go!"

She sucked in her breath. "Three days? Who can rebuild something like this in three days?"

"It is possible!" the man smiled. "I will need to get started soon."

"Tell you what. I will go talk to the Mayor."

He nodded, but was otherwise silent. The young woman and her child remained at a distance. Carmelita went to greet them before she left. The woman nodded and smiled bashfully. The little boy respectfully extended his hand to her. She took it in hers, bent over and kissed it. He laughed in delight.

Chapter 73

THE ASSISTANT WAS GETTING agitated.

"Bates, why are you still here?"

Bates was relieved that he wasn't gone. In this deep darkness, he certainly could not see his hand in front of his face, or even if he had a hand to put in front of his face. Maybe he had no body at all. Maybe he was all ready nothing. But then, if that were so, how could he speculate about it?

"Where are we?" he asked.

"Does it matter? Does it really matter? You're not going anywhere. Okay, so I'll tell you. Right now, we're in front of Always Sunny. Say, by the way, don't you have a funeral coming up, Stanley? Looks like you're not going to make it. Looks like you're not going to make it even to your own funeral!"

The Assistant laughed in such a way that Bates thought he could hear it echoing down the hallways of Hell.

Now, he realized a new development in his gradual demise. He could no longer hear himself speaking. He was gradually degrading into nothingness.

"How could you lower yourself to do such a job as this?"

"It's my job, Stanley. It's what I do to stay alive!"

"If you call that living!"

"Wow! Aren't we getting clever?"

"I'm sorry for my sins!" Bates blurted out. "I'm sorry for all the money I took from people and gambled it away! I'm sorry for those left behind in their loss. I'm sorry for sending Edith to an early grave from my dissolute life. I'm sorry for taking advantage of lonely widows as part of my funeral follow-up plan!"

"Why, Stanley! You old fox! Follow-up plan, eh? I didn't know you had it in you, Stanley! Well, I do suppose that generous mane of hair you have could turn some of the ladies' heads. Keep going, Stan the Man! Think of this as your last confession, from which there is no redemption!"

His shrieking laughter bounced off every corner of the car and penetrated down into Bates's very soul.

"You are something else, Stanley! I don't think I have taken such a pitiful soul as you for a ride in a long-long time."

"You probably say that to every unfortunate slob that you trap into this hellhole."

The Assistant was silent. Now, Bates was tormented in another way. As long as he was talking to the Assistant, he knew he was still there. In the silence, he didn't even know if he existed.

So, he spoke again although he could no longer hear himself.

"I confess to Almighty God . . ."

"Not in here, Stanley. No God in here, I'm afraid. No confession either."

Suddenly, a little verse from the Psalms, that Bates's aunt used to quote, that had scared him half to death as a child, came to him. He fairly screamed it out.

"I can never escape your Spirit! I can never get away from your presence. If I go up to heaven, you are there; if I go down to the grave, you are there."

The Assistant was quiet. All that could be heard was the purring of the Car of Doom, as it made its way, Bates knew not where.

Chapter 74

CARMELITA WENT DIRECTLY TO the Mayor's office.

"He's not here!" said Pinna, Lou's assistant.

"Do you know where he is?"

"He went home right away after getting a call from Doc Bailey."

"I hope the news wasn't bad."

"I don't think it was good, Chief."

"I have something quite urgent to talk to him about. Do you think it would be okay to go by the house?"

"I've known the mayor through all of his terms here," she said. "If it's important to you, he'll want to know about it."

"I'll go then. Should I call ahead?"

"Why don't you let me make that phone call for you!"

Pinna came back in a few minutes.

"It's okay. They're expecting you."

Liz came to the door. She greeted Carmelita warmly.

"Is your Dad in?"

"He is, but he's supposed to be resting. Mom and he are in the bedroom with the door closed."

"Is everything okay?"

"No, Carmey, everything isn't okay. Dad is going to have to have some radiation on those spots on his lungs and maybe even some chemo."

"Oh, I am sorry to hear that."

"I think Doc Bailey was pretty sure of it, but he didn't want to get Dad worried if it wasn't necessary."

"Can he get it done locally?"

"I doubt it. He'll probably have to go to Portland."

"I've got some people up at Joe's. It's a man, and I assume his wife and his little son. He claims he's come to rebuild the diner!"

"He what?"

"And that he has three days to do it. I don't know how he thinks he's going to do it and with what. He doesn't take no for an answer."

"Do you think he's disturbed?"

"He doesn't seem hooked into reality. I thought if I could get Lou to talk to him that he could talk some sense into the poor guy."

"Let me go and see if he wants to come out and if Mom will let him! Oh, and do come in! I am sorry to have kept you standing in the doorway. It's not a good time here."

"No worries, Liz."

Carmelita made her way into the handsome, but unpretentious house, and sat down on the couch. She looked around and noticed that Hope had a nice touch with a combination of the beautiful and the personal. A portrait of Liz hung above the fireplace and, on the mantle, were a number of figurines and small family photos. One corner was filled with memorabilia of Lou's campaigns and swearing-in ceremonies over the years. A Monet print was hanging on the wall she was facing, with a Chagall in the corner, and a Van Gogh on the opposite wall. Fresh flowers were on the coffee table in front of her, and in the space, next to the entrance to the kitchen, was Liz's Steinway.

After a few minutes, the mayor came padding out in his slippers. He smiled broadly.

"Hello, Carmey!" He opened his arms and gave her a generous hug.

"Liz has told me you're going to need some treatment."

"Yes, I'd like to keep that between us, though, if that's okay with you."

"Sit down, Daddy!" said Liz. "Your police chief has a situation. She needs your help!"

After the Schofields had heard about the stranger who was accompanied by a woman and child, Carmey, Lou, Hope, and Liz all went together in the squad car driven by Carmelita, up to the corner where Joe's had once stood.

Chapter 75

"I DON'T THINK THERE is any night here!" said Mrs. Saugus.

"How do you know that?" asked Jeremy.

"I haven't seen the sun come up over the land yet. I haven't seen a sun anywhere."

"Does anybody know what time it is?" asked Father Callaghan.

Everybody's watches proved to be inoperable.

"Well, when did your watch stop?" asked Jeremy no one in particular.

"It looks like about four o'clock yesterday," said Mrs. Saugus. "That must have been when we crashed on the island."

"How do you know it was yesterday?" asked Jeremy.

"We've lost track of time," said Nate. "That's for sure."

"Maybe there isn't time here," said Mrs. Saugus.

Meriwether, Carla, and Georgia were tending to Joe. His fever seemed to have gotten worse and they had commandeered all of the aspirin that everybody had on them. First aid kits had been harvested from both vessels. The worry was Joe's wounds, especially the deep one in his side.

Nate, Daniel, and Rock had left the little crowd on the flat surface on the shore that they now called home and had gone to survey the damage on the *Far from Home*. They decided that Joe was right. His boat was the only one that was seaworthy. It would be best to try to convert his sailboat into one with a motor from the *Far from Home*. The vessels had come to shore about a hundred yards apart from each other, so there would be no small amount of work transporting materials, to say nothing of the task itself. They came back to the gathering site to let everyone know their conclusions.

"There's no manual for this," said Nate. "Our phones are dead, so we can't get on the Internet for this either. We're completely cut off, for whatever reason."

"We'll just have to figure this out for ourselves," said Rock, grimly.

"There isn't anything else to do. Everybody else is depending on us," said Nate.

"I wish Doc Bailey were here," said Carla. "I wish we could contact him and get some help with doctoring this dear man. Here we are without anyone with medical expertise except for me and I've done all I can. There's really nothing that we can do at this point. We have no treatment for him except a few aspirin for his fever, and should he, God forbid, stop breathing, I'm trained to attempt resuscitation."

Joe stirred and they immediately turned their attention to him. He looked at them and smiled. His eyes shone brightly. They had not noticed before how full of love Joe's eyes were, how they seemed to be absent of guile. There wasn't a care-worn mark upon his face.

"Hello, Joe! We're here, looking after you!" said Georgia.

"Anything you need, Joe?" asked Meriwether.

He said nothing. His smile did not go away. She thought she noted a small movement of his head signaling that he did not.

"We brought some stuff from the *Far from Home* for us to eat," said Nate.

"I know how to take your sailboat and make a motorboat of it, Joe, just as you asked us to do," said Johnny.

Nate grimaced. Johnny had not said a word about his ability until now. He hated to admit it, but if Johnny could do what he said he could do, his coming along on this trip was a good thing, after all. Truth be told, with all Nate knew about boats, he knew nothing about the task at hand. He knew how to sail them, but that was it. They may not have even hoped to make it home without Johnny being here.

"We've brought some supplies out of your stock, Joe," said Carla, "and we're going to have a bite to eat before we get started on this project. Would you like to eat with us?"

"I will not eat with you again until heaven and earth are one," he said.

Joe asked to be sat up from his gurney. He reached out his hands and received the bread in them. He raised his hands, and said the blessing. Then, he broke a piece of bread from the loaf and gave it to each one of them as they passed in front of him. Johnny was at the head of the line and he bowed deeply before receiving the bread. The others followed suit.

"Bread, fish, and veggies," said Georgia. "That's all there is, and since Joe has blest it, we know there will be enough for everybody."

They ate until they were filled. They implored him to eat with them but he declined politely.

"I think we all ought to go to the stream and get ourselves some water," said Meriwether.

"Well, that seems like a good idea although I'm surprised I'm not that thirsty!" said Jeremy.

"No one here is going to get dehydrated!" said Carla with her EMT authority in her voice. "Everybody must drink."

She hurried on ahead of them, showing off her agility and prowess, as she fairly skipped over the rocks and rough terrain. When they arrived, she was waiting for them.

"Come and drink!" she called out as they came into view.

They stood by a small waterfall and were able to cup their hands and capture the water.

"This water is delicious!" said Father.

"You are right, Father!" said Daniel. "There's almost a sweetness to it!"

"Oh it is! It's very sweet indeed!" said Meriwether.

"To what shall we raise a glass, Rock?" asked Father.

"To the light!" said Rock! "To the light!"

"To the light!" they all called out as they raised the cupped palms of their hands.

"May God bless our efforts to get home to Safety Harbor and those we love!" said Nate.

"May those who wait for us not be anxious!" said Rock.

"May we not be anxious," said Jeremy.

Ever the practical one, Mrs. Saugus reminded them, "Somebody ought to come back here with some canteens and get some water for the trip home."

Chapter 76

A<small>FTER THEY HAD REMOVED</small> the engine from the *Far from Home* that Johnny chose to use for Joe's boat, there wasn't a lot to do except for small errands whenever Johnny would say, "Get me that wrench," or "Hand me that screwdriver."

Suddenly, Rock announced to the group, "I'm going exploring! I can't help with this project since I haven't the slightest idea what I'm doing!"

"You can't go alone, Rock," said Father Frank.

"You think I ought to go with him to make sure he stays out of trouble?" asked Nate, with a wry smile.

"Good idea!" said Father. "Mrs. Saugus will keep us in line while you are gone!"

"We're going for a walk, then, guys!" said Nate. "We'll be back before dark!" said Rock.

"Dark? In this place? That could be a while!" said Johnny.

The explorers made their way inland, from what they had begun to call the *Joe Boat*, toward the cliffs in the distance. There was no trail. They made their own path, doing their best to use the *Joe Boat* as a frame of reference, traveling straight to the bottom of the cliffs. When they arrived, they made a mark on a rock with a unique formation to orient them to the way back.

They walked what seemed to be some distance along the cliffs when Rock said, "We're climbing, Nate! Yes, we're definitely going higher and we're turning a corner too, going around to another side of this land mass."

They walked upward until they reached a kind of knoll where they spotted their first vegetation.

"There's some grass up here!" said Nate. "Let's sit down and take a break!"

"How long have we been gone?"

"I don't know, maybe an hour, maybe two. I don't think they'll be near done with that project. I think we can look around awhile."

They stared down at the view from the knoll where the land descended gently to the sea.

"Gosh, it's beautiful here!"

"I think it's the light," said Nate. "Everything is brighter and the contrasts are greater. Detail is incredibly clear. The colors are amazing. Those rocks are just beautiful going down to the ocean."

"Is that a path?"

"Where?"

Rock pointed to what appeared to be a narrow thread parallel with a little stream gurgling down the hill.

"Maybe we could use it on our way back."

"Yeah, well, maybe. Let's explore a little further, come back to the knoll, and we can decide then. I am concerned about getting back. I don't want to get lost," said Nate.

"You won't get lost with me!" said Rock.

Nate noticed now that Rock's eyes were wild and burning now, like a mad man's.

"We will never come back here, Nate! This is our only time! Let's see what we can see," Rock said, almost plaintively.

"Well, maybe you are right. We don't even know if we are going to get off this island. Let's see of it what we can. Our fate here could be mighty grim in a few days if our plan doesn't work. Nobody is looking for us, or at least nobody is finding us. I haven't seen or heard a plane or a drone or a helicopter or anything. I'm not sure they can find us. I think maybe we are where they cannot come."

They moved on upward until what seemed like a natural path curved left, close to the cliffs. Still higher they climbed.

"By now, the air should be getting thin!" said Rock. "Are you having any trouble breathing?

"No."

"Me neither."

"Let's go a little farther and then we can turn around and go home."

"Okay, but not much farther. It isn't that far to the top!" said Nate.

"No, it isn't, is it?" Rock turned and smiled. Nate was alarmed at the determined look in his eyes.

"You're going to go up there?"

"I'm gonna try. You can stay here if you want."

"You know, Joe told us not to go up the ascending stairs back where we landed. He said it wasn't for us to go there."

"Well, Joe isn't here, is he?"

"I'm getting concerned about you, Rock!"

"I haven't been this free in a long time, Nate! I'm going higher!"

"I'll go with you so that you don't kill yourself! Look up there! You are going to go up, literally, against a rock wall that dead ends and goes straight up from there. There's nowhere to go when you get there, and then, how are you going to get down?"

Nate was right. The natural path ended about two-thirds of the way to the top. There they stopped.

"Looks like there's a cave about half way up the cliffs from here," said Nate.

"I didn't see it!"

"That's because you're mad. You've been so focused on climbing that you haven't noticed where you are!"

"You think we can get up there?"

"I don't know and, even if we can, I'm not sure we should. How would we get back down? There are limits, Rock. It looks as if we can only go so far here; and we have people waiting for us, depending on us, to get back and get them and us off this island!"

"You're right! Of course, you're right! Let's go back. But first, let me go around the corner and see if I can see if there's any more access upward."

"Okay, Rock, but I'm gonna stay right here and wait on you."

Rocky gave a quick wave and he was off. The path had become narrower as it ascended and the drop off became more pronounced with each step forward. One false step and Rock was gone. Nate shuddered.

He waited on an outcropping of rock as far away from the drop off as he could. His adventures were on the sea, not on the heights.

What was it about the air here, so clear and crisp? He wondered. Had he fallen asleep? Was he dreaming? He could not tell. What he knew was that the most beautiful music he had ever heard was wafting through the air. The lyrics were in no language and every language, it seemed. He could understand them but if he had to tell you what he had heard and what they were, he could not do so. There was one voice. There were a thousand voices. To the song, there was no beginning and no ending.

He looked up from the outcropping toward the cave. The glorious and sweet sounds seemed to be coming from there. It would have been impossible for so many voices, so many songs, so much volume and beauty to be coming from such a place. He guessed the cave must be serving as a kind of conduit for something going on up on the land, above the cliffs.

He was disturbed, whether from his waking or his sleeping he could not tell, by the rather desperate sounding voice of Rock.

"Nate! Help!"

"I hear you, Rock! I'm coming!"

"Hurry! I can't see!"

Nate climbed further up the outcropping that Rock had used for a path. He would not have come here on his own. As he turned the corner he noted that there was an immediate drop-off to the left and a sheer cliff to his right. Rock had attempted to climb the cliff. What had possessed him to do this, Nate did not know. He had to be possessed. Yes! That was it. The higher they climbed and the brighter the light, the more euphoric Rock had become.

Nate could see that his foothold was steady at the moment, but he clearly had nowhere to go. The cliff was now sheer and as smooth as glass. He could only come down! He wanted to ask Rock how he could get himself into such a spot as this, but, he was too concerned about keeping his own footing and considering the slim possibilities of rescuing his friend.

"The light got too bright Nate! I climbed too high. Now, I'm blind. Too much light. More light than my eyes could take."

"Let's get you down from there!"

"You're going to have to help me. I can't see a thing."

Slowly Nate guided him down rock by rock, step by step, over the precipice, to each foothold that Nate hoped would hold them.

"Now, your next step is going to be the path. You can't step back at all or you are going to drop off the cliff and take me with you. When you step down, hug the side of the cliff and I will help you around the corner to where it is safer."

A light breeze from the sea began to blow against the cliffs. One small gust could make the difference as to whether the two men fell into oblivion, or not. Nate realized that he was going to have to get on the other side of Rock in order to guide him along the path.

"I'm going to have to get around you, Rock, if I'm going to get you home."

"I can't help you with that, Nate."

At that moment, he heard a voice. "Whether we live or die, we are the Lord's."

He heard the sweetest music that he had ever heard, and all fear left him.

"Can you hear the music, Rock?"

"No, I can't. I must not only be blind but deaf too."

"Whether we live or die, we are the Lord's, Rock."

"What did you say?"

"It isn't going to matter whether we make it down from here or not. Either way we are in God's hands."

"Oh, okay. If you say so."

"Say it, Rock. Say it. 'Whether we live or die, we are the Lord's.'"

As they began the mantra, Nate began to move slowly around Rock and miraculously made it to the other side.

"Keep saying it, Rock. Keep saying it. 'Whether we live or die, we are the Lord's.'"

As they moved toward the cave and the outcropping where Nate had sat, either dreaming or awake, suddenly Rock said, "Now I can hear music. It must be a choir of angels. It's so beautiful."

Their path had become safer now and Nate now held Rock's hand a little more loosely.

"That's the music I was telling you about, Rock. It's coming from that cave. It's coming from above, on land, I think."

"I got too close, Nate. I just got too close."

"Too close to what?"

"I don't know, but the light became so bright I could not see. It was like looking directly at a thousand million suns. I couldn't look away because there was nowhere to go. So, I just stood there in a kind of stupor, thinking that most certainly I would die soon. If you hadn't heard me . . ."

"We'd better get back, Rock."

"You're going to have to lead me."

They made it down to the grassy knoll that had served as a kind of rest area for them on their upward climb. They sat down for a few moments of rest.

"Rock, I see a path directly down to the sea by a little stream. It's going to be easier to get down that way since I have to lead you down. There's grass growing near the water and it looks like a better way to go!"

"I can't say much to agree or disagree, my friend. I am totally dependent upon your eyes and your judgment."

They began their descent.

Chapter 77

THE SCHOFIELD FAMILY STOOD with Carmelita and Miguel on the street corner across from the ruins of the diner.

"I only have three days to do this, Mr. Mayor," Miguel said.

"You can't rebuild this little joint in three days! That's ridiculous! It would take the rest of the summer, minimum!"

"I have to do it, Mr. Mayor!"

"You have to do it? Who told you that you have to do it?"

"I've got my orders."

"Who gave you your orders? Nobody in Safety Harbor! I'm sure of that!"

"No. No one in Safety Harbor. My orders are not from your world but from the Isle of Gemma."

"There's no island named Gemma around here. Is that the name of a construction company?"

Miguel smiled faintly.

"You might say so!"

"Don't speak to me in riddles, sir!"

Carmelita spoke to Miguel on her own quietly in Spanish.

"Carmelita tells me that she thinks she knows who I am and that I should tell you who I am!"

"Who are you?"

"I am Miguel."

"I know that! You've already told me that"

"I think you say Michael. Michael the Archangel. I am here to help you overcome the darkness. The way I am doing this is by rebuilding the diner."

"What do you mean, the darkness?"

"He means the Chariot of Darkness, Lou, the Car of Doom. It's been plaguing our town now and stalking our people for days. There is something evil about that car, I tell you. Something sinister. It wants something or someone, maybe even more than one of us."

"You're talkin' nonsense now, Carmelita. Just pull the driver over next time you see him and give him thirty seconds to get out of town!"

"It's not that easy, Lou. This is a dangerous situation and I don't think it's going to be solved by the normal police work. It's, well, it's a spiritual problem."

"The City of Safety Harbor is not established to solve spiritual problems, Carmelita. You and I are public servants. We leave our religion at home or in the church or up to the clergy, but we don't go around doing exorcisms or crazy things like that!"

"I didn't say we did, Mr. Mayor, or that we should. This is Michael from the Isle of Gemma, who has come to fulfill a divine task. Maybe he can do it. Maybe he can't. But, it's not up to us to judge or to get in the way."

Up to now, Hope and Liz had stood by in silence. Carmelita nodded to them.

"Lou, honey, I'm worried about you getting involved in this because of your health. You're going to have to go and get some treatments in a few days, and it's absolutely necessary that you get your rest. You're going to be exhausted afterward."

"Mom's right, Daddy. We shouldn't get involved. Let it go. What will happen will happen, and it's better you don't know anything about it."

"But, I do, I do. I can't pretend that. It's too late for that."

"You can say, 'I don't know anything about the details, because you don't!" said Hope. "You don't know how he proposes to go about it, how he plans on getting materials and labor. You don't give out the permits. You aren't the mayor in order to tell him what to do and what not to do.

"What will Carmelita do? She's the law around here. She can't let just anything happen."

"She won't, but you want to know nothing about how she chooses to handle it." said Liz.

"You mean, I need 'plausible deniability'?"

"That's what we mean," said Hope. "You should have figured that out already. Read between the lines of what I am saying, Lou! You're the politician!"

"Harrumph!"

Lou started toward his office.

"Lou? Honey?"

"What?"

"Let's go home now. You need your rest."

"Momma's right, Daddy!"

He acceded to their increasingly insistent pleas reluctantly. Carmelita watched as they crossed the street together, down the hill, several blocks beyond the mayor's office, where they lived within sight of the rolling waves of the glorious water of the endlessly pulsing sea.

Chapter 78

SALLY WAS AT LUKE and Ginny's. They had decided that the three of them should tell Buddy and Caitlin that Nate and his crew were all going to be out on the sea looking for Joe a little longer than they had anticipated.

"Why did they decide to stay out longer?"

"They must have decided to go farther out to sea" said Sally.

"Do they have enough food?" Caitlin asked.

"You know Georgia!" said Sally. "She always has enough food and to spare."

"When will they be back? Can I talk to him?"

"No, not right now. He's out of range," said Luke.

"Then how do you know where they are? How do you know my Dad is all right? How do you know?" asked Buddy.

"You don't know, do you?" said Caitlin.

The adults all looked at each other. Sally gave each of them a nod as if to say, "We have to tell them."

Ginny drew in her breath and began.

"We don't know where they are right now, kids. We know that your Dad is the best fishing boat captain in the Northwest. He wouldn't take any chances. We have confidence that everybody will be okay."

Buddy began to tear up. Caitlin put her arm around him protectively.

"We've just got to be strong, Buddy. We've got to be brave. You know how hard it is to leave Mom to come and see Dad, but when we get here, we're glad we came."

"Yeah, I know, sister," his voice quivered, and he sniffled.

Suddenly he sat up straight. "We can do it. I know we can. I know my Mom and Dad will be back."

"You mean Daddy will be back," said Caitlin. "Mom is back with Grandpa and Grandma."

Buddy began to cry again.

"I wish Momma was here!"

As she heard his wails, Sally felt a shock of realization throughout her entire body. No one had told Carrie Lynn. She nodded for Ginny to accompany her outside.

"We're gonna have to notify their mother!"

"I think that's a job for Carmelita, don't you?"

"Well, I do, but the first thing the kids are going to want to do is call their mother. It's only natural. And she is the other one with custody. We have no legal right to be their guardians."

"Yes, you are right. We'll have to do something. Tell you what, I'll go in and put them off and you get hold of Carmelita."

It was at that moment that Carmelita's name came up on her cell phone.

"Here she is as we speak! I'll be in when I'm through with this phone call."

"I can't come down, Carmey," she said. "We're in the middle of telling Nate's kids, well, in so many words, that he's missing."

"That's tough."

"Yes, it is tough. The big problem we face next is how and when to call Carrie Lynn. If Nate's absent, and nobody knows where he is, then, nobody here is legally responsible for them. They're fine, but the other parent has the right to know. Still, I don't want to meddle in their affairs."

"And you want me to do it, I'll bet."

"Luke and Ginny and I thought you would be the obvious choice."

"Tell you what. We'll do a quid pro quo. You come down to the diner and I'll call Vermont."

"Okay, but what do you need at the diner?"

"Your opinion. Your judgment."

"Mine? Nobody wants mine!"

"I do, in this case."

Within fifteen minutes, Sally had arrived on the scene. By now, Carmelita had been joined by Ruth and Little Therese. The little mystic had told her mother that they were needed there.

"This is Miguel," said Carmelita. "He's come to rebuild the diner."

Sally looked at Miguel and then back at Carmelita.

"Okaaayy!" she said, drawing the word out to emphasize her incredulity.

The woman and her child sat nearby on the picnic bench in the back yard of the diner.

"Who are the woman and child with you?" asked Sally.

"She is Sophia, the beginning and end of all wisdom," said Miguel, with a slight smile. "The child is her offspring, the second Adam, the father of the future of all redeemed humanity."

He smiled, this time broadly. "But, for purposes of this visit, if asked, she is my sister Ana, and her child, Eashoa. We call him Eshy!"

As they continued the conversation, the Car of Doom came into view on Main Street. It turned up the unimproved Newman Street on the other side of the diner and stopped near to where the mother sat with her child. Those who saw Miguel at that moment thought that they literally could see light blazing from his eyes as he slowly, determinedly, walked toward the vehicle, without hesitation, and stopped on the passenger side of the car.

"Let Bates go!" he called out. "Let him go! You can't have any of these people! You're not going to get the one you really want! Your day is coming very soon!"

Slowly, the car started up again and drove away.

When he came back to the group, he looked as if he had grown in stature by a foot and the force of his personality was somehow greater than before.

"Senora," he said to Carmelita, "I can get rid of the Car of Doom for you, but I will have to rebuild the diner first."

"It makes sense, Momma," said Little Therese, "if you know how to think about it, if you don't think in a straight line!"

"Come here, Little Therese!" Miguel said. "May I pick you up?"

He looked over at Ruth and she nodded.

"Of course!"

He picked her up gently and held her on one arm.

"Have I ever told you what a treasure you are, Little Therese?"

"No," she said. "But you can if you'd like!"

"You have been sent to this place as a prophet."

She turned her blind eyes directly toward him and smiled.

As he held her, he spoke once more to Carmelita.

"I must rebuild the diner, Senora. That is my assignment. I have my orders from a much higher place. If I may build, without hindrance, then, I will be finished in three days. It must be the next three days. They are momentous days, in heaven and on earth!"

Ruth asked, "Sir, do you know where Joe is? Do you know where Nate and the rest of our beloved people are?"

"I am only here to rebuild the diner."

"So, you are not going to answer our questions!"

"Senora Ruth, I will ask you a question. 'If I told you one way or the other, would you believe me'?"

"He knows, Momma! I'll bet he knows!"

Miguel called Carmelita aside. When they both returned, she said, "He wants to show us something."

Sally said, "I'm texting Magdalena and Susanna. They need to be down here, pronto."

Miguel, clearly in charge now, led them to the back of the diner.

"Do you see that room up there?"

With that, Miguel raised his hand above his head and the entire second story that had remained standing came down. As he performed this feat, it seemed that he had become even larger in their eyes. He pulled back some of the debris and uncovered a safe.

"Allow me to show you something," he said. "In order to see it, you must look away. You must not look upon it directly. I will tell you when you must turn around and look toward the east."

He stooped down as they watched, and began to work the combination lock. In only a few seconds he turned and nodded to Carmelita.

"He wants us to turn around now and face the east! Don't look back for any reason."

Suddenly, a great light came from behind them and illuminated everything around them, even though the sun was bright and high in the sky. All of them would agree later, when the story was told to others, that it was as if they could see through things, rather than just see them, and yet, at the same time, they could see them as they really are. Even the old shed shined like a palace. Each board and beam shone through as alive and with an identity of its own, filling its place in an old utility building that could now be a palace.

"Look at the trees!" said Ruth. "Oh! My dear Little Therese! I wish you could see the trees! Every leaf is shining, singing, vibrating in beauty!"

"I see them, Momma! I see them! With this light, you can see everything, even though you cannot see!"

The sky was no longer blue, but was filled with doorways and entries into the great mysteries. Angels stood at each entrance, either to guard or welcome. Except for the voice of the Eshy, who was pointing toward the heavens and chattering excitedly, there was silence. Carmelita knelt and made the sign of the cross.

Suddenly, the light disappeared as quickly as it had come and they heard the safe close. When normal vision was restored they found themselves in a prostrate position on the grass.

"Get up and turn around now!" said Miguel. "Come closer so that I may tell you what you have experienced.

"The light that you have seen has come from a stone from the Isle of Gemma. Joe has kept the shining stone from Gemma in the safe until now, for this very moment, in Safety Harbor. The human eye on earth, in time and space, is not made for this light. If you had looked directly at the stone, you would have lost your sight or you would have died.

"Why, in God's name, did Joe ever bring this stone with him and how did he ever get it here?" asked Katye.

"I can tell you that he brought it here because Safety Harbor has been chosen for a new divine initiative in the world."

By this time, they had all sat down on the ground behind the diner.

"You have been chosen as a place to determine whether or not the time might be coming soon when all people are ready to receive the light that is to come into the world."

"That's why Joe came here?"

"Yes, that's why he came."

"So, he didn't come here to go into business," said Susanna.

"Yes he came here on business of a sort. The parade was all about determining if you are ready! He wanted to see if you all could bury your egos, become your true selves, and make something work that was completely counter to the way you thought and the way you lived, even for a day."

"And, if we did?"

"Then you passed a lot of the test."

"A lot of it? What's left?" asked Magdalena.

"There are a few details to be worked out yet. Joe was quite sure you were all going to get through the parade successfully. After his time with you, he felt that Safety Harbor may well be ready to be one of the gates of light in the world."

"What do you mean, 'gates of light'?" asked Susanna.

"Safety Harbor will be a pilgrimage place that people come to, not as a shrine or a temple, but, as a place where they receive power and wisdom to become their true and best selves. They will be happy and at peace, not because of what they do here or what they buy here, but, because this is a gate of light."

"A gate of light to what?" asked Sally.

"To where?" asked Susanna.

Miguel laughed.

"So many questions! A gate of light is what you call a thin place between heaven and earth, where time and eternity meet, where the glory of the Holy One may be experienced in more fullness on the earth than ever before. Safety Harbor will be a vision of the future, of what it will be like when the life of heaven comes in fullness to all of the earth. You will find out more when Joe returns. He will give you the full picture."

"You mean, he's coming back?" asked Sally.

"Yes, but he will not be back as he was when he went away from you."

"Many of us have thought that we have seen Joe at different times the last few days," said Sally. "He came to us in the night. Others saw him dancing. It was uncanny. How could he be here and someplace else at the same time?"

"You are all creatures limited by time and space and can only be in one place at once, so it is difficult for you to comprehend this," said Miguel.

"So, the light in the lighthouse. Is that from Gemma?" asked Magdalena.

"Yes, it is. I, myself, installed that light just recently in the night hours.

"Now, I must rebuild the diner right away, in part, because we must contain the light that is in the safe that can no longer be hidden effectively there any longer. It is simply too much light for the safe to contain."

"How are you going to do that?" asked Magdalena.

"I have my instructions."

"Another part of Joe's Plan, eh?" said Magdalena.

Miguel nodded toward her and smiled.

"You might say so!"

"So what you're saying is that we have three days to get this done or our city is in danger?"

"Yes, Safety Harbor can choose to be a blessing, or it can continue to be oppressed by The Assistant and his bosses from Bread from Stone. It all depends upon the diner being rebuilt."

"Well then, we have to do it!" said Carmelita.

Chapter 79

BATES KNEW HE COULD not last much longer. Even now, it seemed, his soul had become weak and he felt as if he was twinkling off, and then on again, like some Christmas tree light in its last season. For a moment, he would be in the Car of Doom, tormented, and then he would not be at all. Each time he came back, it was a shock, and he wished that he could just go into oblivion and be done with it. But, that was not the way it happened. It was exhausting to be in and out of nothingness. But, the torment came again and again in a seemingly endless cycle.

He now really did want to be nothing. His life had been a misery even at its best. He saw now that he was a miserly, lonely, self-indulgent predator who had put on an air of dignity, when, all the while, his soul was rotten to the core. He even grew tired of himself. He could not imagine how much others wearied of him.

He had no friends. He couldn't go anyplace where people knew him, without their putting distance between them and him. They were afraid. He knew that. They were afraid they might catch death. After all, he was in contact with it almost every day. For some, he had prepared the bodies of their loved ones, their children, their wives, their husbands, their friends. He was the last to see their faces before he shut their eyelids and applied makeup and folded their hands in repose.

But, on top of all that, Bates was just an unappealing man. Even in his role as funeral director, you had the feeling that you wouldn't want to leave him alone with your wife or your sister.

"You still back there, Bates? Hah! By now, you ought to be bobbing in and out! I'll talk to ya anyway in case you're there. My old nemesis, Miguel, is in town and that means we're about to have a showdown. He always brings that woman and her kid along. I never caught onto that one. Seems they'd be in the way more than anything! So, it's pretty close to high noon, Bates!"

The Assistant let out his eerily echoing roar of laughter.

"Maybe I ought to go through town again, and put the fear of God into them, but then, it's kinda the opposite from that, ain't it, Bates?"

"No! No! Don't torment these people anymore! Kill me. Take me! I'm the one who is worthy to die! But leave these good people alone! Many of them don't even know I've taken their money and their funeral savings and gambled it away long ago. They will suffer enough when they know that! Leave them alone!"

Bates shouted until he had no voice left. He didn't know whether anyone could hear him. He knew he could not hear himself; and by now he didn't know whether he was speaking or whether these were just desperate thoughts.

"You sure did make a mess of things, Batesy!"

So, The Assistant could hear him. Or maybe he couldn't. Maybe Bates could hear The Assistant but The Assistant couldn't hear him. Maybe he really was already in oblivion and the only thing left of him was his denial. What pain! What torment! What anguish this was!

"We're gonna cruise through town again, Batesy, and see if we can see what's going on. Bates, tell you what. Let's go down and see what's shakin' at the police station. I kinda like that Carmelita. She's hot! Bet you didn't try anything with her, did you, Bates? No, she'd have knocked your block off before you had a chance to run! Oh! There's Miguel right now! He's coming out of Carmelita's office. Ha! Old Mikey sees us and he's gonna come over here! By Jiminy, he's gonna! He's gonna! Hoo boy! This ought to be very interesting!"

Miguel rapped hard on the window. The dark glass slid down the driver's door, revealing the plastic looking face of The Assistant.

"Get out of here! I've all ready told you that you don't belong here in Safety Harbor! Fact is, you don't belong anywhere on this earth. Go to hell!"

"Oh, I've got a portable Hell in my back seat! And Batesy is there. But then, you know that."

"Let him go, bastard son of the Devil! You know the plans we have for this town and you are not going to spoil them!"

"Oh, Mikey! Some of these people are going to disappoint you. They're going to let you down. There was plenty of darkness here before I came around."

"Shadows maybe, but not darkness. No, you brought that with you and you're the one scaring people! We're not going to tolerate it. You have to leave and you have to give up Bates!"

"I will not! I will not! I will not!"

The car window slid back up into its place and the Car of Doom took off at great speed, throwing rocks across the uneven graveled ground between the Mayor's office and the police station.

"That's it!" said Carmelita. "Go after him, Marshall. Put your light on, and your siren too! Pursue him as far as our jurisdiction goes. We'll notify the highway patrol. This can't go on any longer!"

Marshall pursued him down Pacific Coast Highway until he lost him somewhere around Devil's Churn.

Chapter 80

LATE THAT AFTERNOON, SALLY was surprised to find Miguel at her door.

"Eshy, Ana, and I would like to visit you in your home tonight."

She remained calm on the outside, even as she felt a kind of shock go through her entire being. An angel would be visiting her house, accompanied by the Virgin Mary, and her child! It sounded absurd, even crazy.

"Of course, you are welcome."

"My visit is of a highly private and confidential nature. We will arrive at eight o'clock. Will that time work for you?"

Later, Sally was in her kitchen, preparing dinner. The evening shadows penetrated the little cottage and lengthened across the room. She felt a melancholy infiltrate the kitchen, the sort of exquisite sadness that comes with the end of the beauty of a day, when the light fades into golden and purple hues.

She missed Nate and was terrified for him. Her husband was dead and his body was waiting up at the funeral home, his memorial service delayed because of the crises going on in town, including a missing funeral director. Buddy and Caitlin knew by now that their Dad was missing. What a crazy set of facts she was living with and what a chaotic mix of emotions she felt!

Ten minutes later, Sally heard a car pull up. Looking out the window of her living room, she saw a beautiful woman, mature in years, well dressed, and obviously too sophisticated for Safety Harbor, walking toward her house, accompanied by Susanna. She noticed her well-coiffed hair was of no color that she could determine, but was oddly shining in a way she had never seen before. The thought rushed through her that maybe she was seeing a halo for the first time.

She met them at the door.

"Sally, this is Evita du Pont," said Susanna. "She's a client of mine from San Juan Bautista, California and has come up for the weekend in hopes of selling some of her paintings. She is a dear friend of Miguel's and he has asked that she be at the dinner tonight."

Sally immediately felt inferior to this sophisticated woman. How could she invite her into her modest house? She began to regret her agreeing to host this dinner. Her best dishes and table furnishings were probably what this woman's servants used! Well, she was hosting Michael the Archangel, Maria Sophia, and her son! When you thought of it that way, she thought, a sophisticated mortal shouldn't bother her!

"Welcome to my house! Come in!"

"I thank you for your hospitality!" said the new guest in town.

They had just been seated in Sally's tiny living room, when the doorbell rang. It was Miguel and the woman and child.

"Good evening!" he said.

"Good evening, Miguel!" said Sally, thinking that her brave moment had passed.

"Good evening!" She smiled and extended her hand to the woman, who in turn took her hand in hers, saying nothing.

The child put out his hand to Evita in such a way that she almost laughed at the dignity upon the face of someone so young.

"Miguel," said Evita, "We are wondering if Susanna may stay for dinner or if you wanted this meeting to be just among the five of us."

"Susanna may stay," he said. "She has been called here. She is a part of Safety Harbor's future."

"Good! Then she will stay!"

They moved into the dining room and were seated. Miguel blessed the meal. Afterward he cleared his throat and everyone knew that he was about to state the reason for their gathering.

He began.

"My friends, Joe's has been an initiative by the Island of Gemma to determine whether or not the city of Safety Harbor could become a Gate of Light.

"The world is not ready for heaven and earth to become one yet, in order that the light may come into every corner. This planet is still a dark place and it cannot be transformed until men and women everywhere get right inside, and with each other, and want the light more than they want the darkness.

"But, the Holy One and the hosts of heaven are not willing to wait forever until the last soul has abandoned the old ways of greed, war, and dividing the world into good and bad people. The last contest for good and evil may well come soon. The time may be short and the need is urgent. God wants to dwell with God's people. God longs for them as a lover longs for the one who is absent.

"So, a scheme was hatched for the light to inhabit small places in the world where people might seem ready to receive it. Joe was sent here to be among you for a while to see if the good people of Safety Harbor might be viable candidates."

"You mean, Joe . . ."

"Yes, Sally, Joe is a part of this celestial experiment. He is the one who finds people who are ready."

"In a diner? By running a diner?" Sally was aghast.

"What would you want it to be?"

"Well, I don't know, but a diner somehow seems so . . ."

"Mundane? Pedestrian?"

"Yes!"

"Well, it's the place where many of the good citizens of Safety Harbor meet regularly or, at least, show up once in a while, don't they? And when they come, what do they receive?"

"Friendship," said Susanna, "and good food!"

"And the service is great, too, right?" Sally smiled.

"Since going there more after my husband died, I've found that I've grown to trust people, to love some of them, really. I would risk my life for my friends there!" said Susanna

"Do you know where Joe is?" asked Sally.

"Joe had to leave you for a while."

"Why? Where did he go?"

"There was an assault by the dark forces against the Isle of Gemma. He was called back to help in the battle. When Joe returns, he will explain everything to you."

"What about our loved ones? Are they okay?"

"They have met with many tests and trials on the sea, and all but one will return to you."

Sally's heart sank. Which one was not coming back? Her heart was filled with fear that it may be Nate, and then with shame at her selfishness that she hoped it might be someone else among her friends.

"When?" asked Susanna.

"I don't know the times for all of this to come to pass. I only know that I must rebuild Joe's in three days. Sally, you have been designated as the new manager of Joe's and Susanna you are the official Keeper of the Light!"

At once they were overcome and cried tears of awe and joy.

Miguel waited until they had time to regain control over their emotions. The woman looked at them and smiled. The boy had begun to cry, too, out of sympathy.

"Oh, little one, do not cry!" said Evita. "We are not sad. We are all happy! You be happy too!"

With that, she beamed a big smile at him. His face lighted up in delight.

When the room became silent, Evita turned said to them, "Miguel has asked me to invest some operating money into the new Joe's and I have agreed to contribute whatever is needed for the project. We have worked together before. I have financed the gathering places at other Gates of Light across the country and yes, around the world."

"You mean you planned on being in town because you knew you would be needed?"

"Well, yes. Sometimes people never meet me. I prefer to work behind the scenes. It is a real joy to be a part of this one and to get to know those who have been chosen for this wonderful work of heaven on earth."

"Wow! Just wow!" said Sally.

"Every City of Light must also be beautiful," said Miguel. "The light shines upon everything, even the darkest corners of the city, and exposes everything. Susanna, as Keeper of the Light, you will head up a group of people in charge of beauty, not just outward beauty, but the inward beauty of the soul.

"I also need Katye to be my foreperson for construction of the diner. I will visit with Stewart and her later tonight."

"Stewart has been in the lighthouse for days, waiting for Joe and now for all of our loved ones," said Sally.

"Yes, he waits and prays as some are called to do.

"We will need all of your help beginning in the morning. There will be much to do. Be patient and persevere with us. You must keep all of these things and ponder them in your hearts. You cannot tell anyone else. It is a fragile moment in which eternity is entering time. As creatures of time, humans must continue to live with only a faint awareness of the eternal presence among them. They can only experience things in time. That is the way with you as well. That you know more about how we are involved than others, makes it even more incumbent upon you to keep to yourselves all that you have learned here and all that you have experienced with us."

"Miguel, what about the Car of Doom, or, as some say, the Chariot of Darkness?" asked Sally.

"Avoid it. Ultimately, nothing about it can hurt you, or can cause you harm. Only if you give it attention or give in to the efforts to get you inside, will you perish."

Chapter 81

THIS TIME, BATES THOUGHT he was a goner, for sure. The Assistant was obviously upset and agitated and Bates didn't know whether he could take it out on him by hastening his demise or not. He didn't know if he could do such a thing.

"I thought I had taken care of that damnable diner for good, and now I see building materials lined up and some earth moving equipment, enough to make a skyscraper! I wonder what these Gemma people are up to now? Looks like they're going to try to rebuild that thing, Bates. That can only mean one thing. They're trying to drive us out of this area, Stanley. Yep! They're gonna do their best to drive us out, I'll tell you! And you know what that means to me? This is maybe the biggest job ever assigned to any assistant by Bread from Stone. If I mess it up, I'm toast."

He snapped his fingers three times and raised his voice.

"I'm gone, good ol' Stanley Bates!" he screamed. "I'm gone, same as you. And that can't happen. We're going to have to do something tonight. We're going to have to make sure that doesn't happen. I'd say it's planned for tomorrow since they seem to start everything on a Friday. Seems odd, doesn't it, that they start things on the weekend. They're in a different time zone, I hear, and on another calendar. Odd. Downright odd."

At once he raced the engine, let out the clutch and the car lurched forward, burning rubber, and headed north toward Safety Harbor.

"I don't know where we're goin', Stanley. But, I need to think. I think best when I'm driving. I think best of all when I'm driving very fast. So, hang on for your life, Bates! Oh, that's right you can't hang on, can you?"

His laugh echoed through the caverns of hell.

Chapter 82

THE PATH WAS NARROW. Nate could not guide Rock down alongside him. Instead, he must walk ahead of him and let him know details of any obstacles or unusual hooks or small curves in the pathway. Rock had developed an uncanny sense of what was around him intuitively, from his years of rock climbing, but it was not enough for him to come down on his own.

"This is hard on me, Nate. I've always been a pretty self-sufficient guy!"

"This is no time for pride, my friend. We have to do what we have to do to make it. There are others waiting for us down there to get them home."

"You really think we will make it back to Safety Harbor?"

"I really do. I think we will make it."

"I wonder what Joe was doing out here."

"I don't know."

"I hope Johnny has got the boat ready when we get back down this path."

"Look out! We are going to need to walk a little slower. There is a drop-off on both sides. To the left, it's about thirty feet and maybe even a little farther down on the right. We are about a football field from the water."

"I miss Magdalena!"

Nate wanted so much to say that he missed Sally, but he could not. He chose to remain silent.

"How long you been divorced, Nate?"

"Carrie Lynn left two summers ago to visit her parents and never came back."

"I'm sorry."

"Well, I'm not any more. The only thing that bothers me is the kids. Lucky I've got them for the summer. Trouble is, I'm so busy all the time since it's my best time of year for making money and I'm away from them so much. That's why I named the boat the *Far from Home*."

Suddenly, the path became even more difficult to navigate.

"Look out, Rock! The path narrows right here. Literally, put one foot in front of the other!"

Five minutes later, it widened again and they could resume conversation.

"I wondered about that name, Nate."

"What name?" Nate had been focused on getting them through the last five minutes alive.

"I mean the name of your boat."

"Oh yeah! I bought it one of the last few days before Carrie Lynn went back to Vermont and never came back.

"Buddy had named it *Captain Blackbeard*, but when they left and didn't come home, I decided to name it what I was feeling at the time about my children."

"Oh, that makes so much sense, Nate. And little did you know that your craft would be on this kind of a journey, so far from home that we really have no idea where we are."

"I have an idea, Rock, that we are somewhere not many people go in their lifetime."

Momentarily, Rock slipped and lost his footing, sliding nearly out of reach. Nate managed to bring him back up the precariously slippery side of the cliff. The shore was near now and they could hear the lapping of the water against the rocks just below them. Suddenly, way before Nate had anticipated it, they came to a flat surface that slowly slanted down to the sea. Nate marveled at the water.

"It's crystal clear, Rock."

"I wish I could see it."

"I wish you could, too."

"I just wanted to get closer to the light, Nate. I was taken over by the euphoria of the seeing the light."

"Look there, Rock! Oh, I'm sorry . . ."

"S'okay."

"It looks as if there's a place for a boat to land, right there."

"I'll bet this is where Joe intended to land, but he somehow got knocked off course."

"I'll bet you're right. Maybe he came through the same storm we did."

"Most likely, I'd say."

Chapter 83

RUTH, LITTLE THERESE, ROY, and Jens spent the night on Pilsner Hill in a yurt that the mayor had offered them from the city inventory. They were awakened by the sounds of engines, the screeching of brakes, of voices calling out, "Come back! Come back! Just a little bit more! There! Good enough."

Roy pulled himself up out of his morning haze. Boy, it sure wasn't as hard to get up these days when he didn't have a hangover! He rubbed his eyes and looked in the direction of all the noise. Dumpsters had been put in place in strategic areas where loaders could deposit the debris from the fire. The remainder of the walls were, even this very minute, coming down.

Roy could not resist a scene such as this. This was his kind of work. Just put him on a loader or a tractor or some earth removal equipment and he was at one with the world. He had to get down there to see if there was a job opening! He hadn't worked in quite a while and the unemployment benefit was running out. Oh, heck! He'd work for free! He didn't care. He pulled on his shoes and headed down the hill, through the park, across the street to the site of the diner.

The equipment and the uniforms of the workers were branded Gemma LLC. He wondered who these people could be. He hadn't heard of such a company or a place, or a name brand, and he'd driven a lot of trucks for a lot of companies.

Katye motioned him.

"What's goin' on here!"

"We're rebuilding the diner!"

"We are? Ya think I could help out here?"

"I think you can."

"I'd love to drive one of those front-end loaders."

"We're missing a hand on moving some of those materials out of the trucks. You ever drive a fork lift!"

He smiled broadly. "I was born on a forklift!"

She flashed him a smile. He didn't think a woman as beautiful as Katye had ever smiled at him before. It gave him a real pick-up for his day, and he moved on in the direction she had pointed out to him.

Soon, man and machine were one.

Chapter 84

As it turned out, Carrie Lynn could not come out to Safety Harbor in Nate's absence, nor could she bring the kids back home to Vermont. She was somewhere, off in Europe, with her old high school sweetheart, probably in the South of France, Carrie's mother thought, but didn't know for sure. She didn't answer her cell phone.

Luke and Ginny came down to the construction site with the kids to tell Sally the news. Buddy and Caitlin rushed toward Sally when they saw her, grabbing her around the legs and hugging her tight.

"Oh! Oh! Oh!" Sally pretended to complain. "You are too strong, Buddy! Caitlin, you squeeze too hard!"

They laughed delightedly at seeing her.

"Do you know when Daddy's comin' home?" Buddy asked.

"He'll be along soon!" said Caitlin.

"We don't know, Buddy," said Sally. "But, until then, you have a lot of people to love you and to take care of you. You are not alone!"

"I know that!" said Buddy. Still he continued to hold on to her hand tightly.

"Have you met Little Therese?" Sally asked. "You two really ought to meet her. See? She's right over there!"

"Whatsa matter with her?"

"Nothing's the matter with her, Buddy. What do you mean?"

"I mean, whatsa matter with her eyes?"

"She doesn't see, Buddy. She can't see out of her eyes like you and I can."

"Why not?"

"Don't know. We never asked her."

"Why not?"

"It's very personal."

"What's personal mean?"

"That means something so close to you that it's nobody else's business unless they decide to tell you."

"Oh."

"So, don't ask, Buddy!" said Caitlin. "You'll embarrass us all."

Sally had noticed how, in the six weeks since she had been here, she had gone through one of those uncanny changes that kids go through at her age, when, all at once, they lose their baby faces and start showing signs of what they might look like as an adult. Her attitude had changed too. She expected puberty would come on soon, if it hadn't all ready.

Ruth, Jens, and Little Therese had come down the hill to the construction site not long after Roy had stolen away from them.

"I was hoping Buddy and Caitlin might be able to meet Little Therese!" said Sally to Ruth.

Like so many in a small town, they knew who the other was, but did not know each other well.

"Sure!" said Ruth.

"Why are you blind, Little Therese?"

"Buddy!" said Caitlin.

"Buddy, no!" said Sally.

"It's all right, Buddy!" said Little Therese. "Everybody wants to know, anyway. I was born blind, Buddy. My eyes just didn't get made just right. Some people think I didn't get enough oxeeejin, but nobody knows for sure."

"How do you see, then?"

"I don't know how to tell you, 'cause I don't see the way you see. I guess maybe the best way to put it is, that you can see what is happening right now, and I can sometimes see things that might happen or will happen."

"So what's going to happen?"

"What do you mean?"

"Are they gonna find my Dad?"

"No, they're not!"

Buddy began to wail. Caitlin drew her breath in. All the adults were flummoxed.

"Calm down, Buddy!" said Caitlin.

"Nobody will find your Dad, but he will find you. He will find us."

"What do you mean?"

"That's just it. I don't know what I mean. I just know what I said."

Luke and Ginny offered to take the three kids to the school playground near their home. Ruth readily agreed. Little Therese lived in a grownup world so much of the time and she worried that her little girl would get too isolated from her peers and not know how to be with them later.

Ruth and Sally watched as Buddy and Caitlin put Little Therese in between them and held her hands, one on each side. Still, little Therese seemed to be walking just a half step ahead of them.

"Who is leading whom?" asked Luther as he walked up and stood with them.

"It's hard to say!" said Sally, smiling. "It's hard to say, isn't it?"

She looked at Ruth. A tear was making its way down her face.

Chapter 85

NATE WAS ALMOST SURE he knew the way back to the boat from here. They hoped that they would find Joe's vessel outfitted and ready to navigate the waters. They were able to walk upon what seemed to be either a path or a natural path-like formation along the sea. It was wide enough for them to travel side by side. To their right, was the ocean and, to their left, in the distance, were the steeply ascending cliffs that made their way upward until their end was obscured by the light.

The only sounds were the wind and the splashing of the waves up against the rocks. Nate realized, as he viewed the wide expanse beside him, that, not once had they seen any creatures at all. As if his thought gave birth to the wrongness of his observation, he saw, in the distance, what appeared to be, creaturely movement.

"There's something coming toward us, Rock."

"What?"

"Don't know. I can't tell yet. It's moving right along so I'd say it will be here soon."

They stood still in anticipation of its arrival.

"It's a dog, Rock!"

"A dog? What's a dog doing out here?"

Nate watched as a canine, its size somewhere between a collie and a beagle with a long-haired coat of light shining brown hair, came bounding up.

"Is he friendly?"

"Can't tell yet. Looks like it, though."

"We're soon to find out."

The dog greeted them both excitedly as if they were long lost friends, jumping up so hard that he almost knocked both of them over into the water. They laughed as he squealed with delight at seeing them. He licked them both fiercely. Then, at once, he turned to leave.

"He's leaving just as soon as he got here!"

"Really? Where's he going?"

"If I don't know where we are, how would I know where he's going?"

"You're right," said Rock, chuckling wryly.

The dog went down about fifty paces and then looked back at them. He walked a few more feet and then turned to look at them, this time sitting down as if to wait for them.

"I think he wants us to follow him, Rock. We have to walk this way, anyway. Maybe we can be traveling companions for a while."

"Sure does beat having just you around!"

"I wish I could disagree!"

They moved on ahead and, as they did, the dog got up and began to move ahead of them, allowing them to catch up until they were close enough to see once again the long, bushy almost foxlike tail that seemed to be in perpetual motion.

"We've been walking a long time, Nate."

"Have we? I guess I haven't noticed."

"Well, at least we've come a long way and I should feel tired by now but I don't."

"That's true. I'm not tired at all. The brightness of the light, it would seem, ought to make us feel overly warm, but I'm just comfortable."

"That dog still up there?"

"Looks like he's sat down now, waiting for us to catch up. We're just even with that opening in the cliff that I thought was parallel to Joe's boat, but it isn't here. I must have misjudged it. He's moving on. It's almost as if he wanted me to see that fact."

"Must be further ahead."

"Either that, or we're totally lost."

"We don't have much choice. He seems like he's the only one who knows where he is and where he's going."

"Boy! I've been lost before but never before have I not known my approximate place in the world. I don't know where we are at all. We could be a million miles from Safety Harbor. My God, Rock! Now we've come to another of those caves upon the cliffs with steps and an opening and still I see no sign of our friends."

"Where's the dog?"

"He's sitting down again, as if to wait for us."

This time, the dog allowed them to catch up, and he came, and nuzzled each of them, allowing them to stroke his smooth and ample coat.

"What do you suppose his name is?"

"I don't know. I can't see him."

"How would that help?"

"Sometimes, a name just strikes you when you see a dog."

"I have a feeling he has a name already."

"You are right. He seems familiar with these parts. He's somebody's dog."

He turned to move on again, looking back to see if they were following.

"We have our marching orders."

"Okay then, let's go!"

It was at the fourth cave-gate parallel that Joe's boat came into view.

"We're there, Rock! We're almost there! I can see figures in the distance!"

"You sure it's our people?"

"Pretty sure!"

"Well, if it isn't, we have some new problems on our hands."

"Someone's running toward us, so they must recognize us."

He saw, as she grew nearer, that it was Carla.

She stopped to say hello to the dog, bending over and petting him.

"Who are you?" he heard her say.

Quickly, she moved on to Nate and Rock, putting her arms around their necks, hugging them fiercely.

"We thought we'd never see you again!" she said, tears running down her cheeks.

"We sorta got lost!" said Rock.

"We'll tell you more about it later," said Nate. "How are our friends? How is Joe? Is the boat ready?"

"Rock, what's wrong with your eyes? From the looks of things, you're having a hard time seeing where you're going."

"Blinded by the light when I got too close. It's a long story in the telling. Let's just get back so we can all be together again."

"Everybody is okay. Joe is still with us but, he's very sick. He's in and out of consciousness, and yes, we think we've got the boat ready to go."

Suddenly, they heard the amplified voice of Mrs. Saugus. "Hello, boys. We're right over here!"

"My God!" Nate chuckled. "I had almost forgotten about that blasted bullhorn!"

By now, the dog had fallen back to walking beside them.

"Who's the dog? Where did you get him?"

"He just came running toward us and then turned around and came back with us to here. He led us, I am sure, because I was way off base as to where we were and we may never have gotten here without him."

As they approached the boat, more people came to greet them.

"Mother o' God!" exclaimed Father Frank, making the sign of the cross. "We are so relieved to see you boys!"

"Johnny, I'm even glad to see you!" said Nate.

He extended his hand to Nate and he took it and shook it firmly.

"I am glad to see you, too!" Their eyes met in such a way that it seemed to everyone around them to be somewhere between a truce and a reconciliation.

Jeremy, Meriwether and Daniel greeted them warmly. Mrs. Saugus stood back smiling broadly. The dog, too, joined in the reunion, jumping up to give everyone a sloppy lick.

"Rock has lost his sight on the way," said Nate. "We don't know what's happened, but we think it has something to do with some overexposure to the light."

"Oh my!" said Father Frank.

Carla came over to look at his eyes more closely.

"Do you mind?" she asked.

"Mind what?"

"If I have a closer look."

"No, but I don't know what you'll be able to see."

"I don't, either."

After a moment, she said, "It's odd. I don't see anything unusual. No scarring, no redness or irritation. It's as if they just stopped working, but still have all the equipment intact."

"Enough of me," said Rock. "How's Joe?

"Georgia is with him right now."

"Let's go see him!"

"He's very ill," said Georgia. "His wound is very deep and, although the hemorrhage has been staunched, it hasn't been stopped completely, so he's very weak."

They could see that a small infirmary had been created at the center of the boat that was surrounded by the fiberglass panels and seating that had been built into the boat to protect passengers from the weather.

Joe was now placed upon a hospital-like bed that was from Nate's fishing boat, provided for sick passengers. His head was held up by two pillows and he was covered with a quilt.

Nate approached him quietly.

"Hello, Nate," said Joe faintly.

"Hello, Joe! I'm so glad to see you are still with us!"

"I'm glad to see you two are still with us! Where's Rock?"

"He's back here. He lost his sight on our little side excursion."

"Have him come closer."

As much as was possible, everyone drew close to hear what Joe had to say.

"Rock, my friend!"

"Joe, my friend!" Rock's blind eyes cried profuse tears.

"Come here and take my hand, dear boy!"

Meriwether guided him closer. Rock took the outstretched hand in his. Joe's grip was so weak and yet, so strong. His hand was so rough, and yet, somehow, his skin was so smooth. For a moment, Joe's hand faltered, then, regained its hold.

"Will I be blind forever, Joe?"

"You will be healed in time, my son. In time, you will be healed."

"Thank you, Joe! Thank you!"

With that, Joe's arm fell to his side. He seemed weaker, now.

"I see that Ebenezer accompanied you!" Joe's eyes were barely open, yet they could see the twinkle in them.

"Ebenezer? Is that the name of the dog?" asked Rock.

"Yes. Ebenezer."

"Does he belong to you?"

"He belongs to no one, but he will accompany us and he will be with you for a while."

"Ebenezer? That's a long name!" said Daniel. "Maybe we can call him Ben!"

Joe chuckled faintly and said, "I always have. Come here, Ben. Come here, dear boy."

The dog approached him gently, climbed carefully upon the bed, stood on all fours, looked into his eyes, and licked his face tenderly. Joe reached up and patted him. The dog climbed down and made his place, firmly, by Joe's wounded side.

Chapter 86

SALLY SLEPT SOUNDLY AFTER all of yesterday's exhausting activities. She did not know why she still held out hope for Nate and his crew. The Coast Guard had returned from their search with nothing to show for it and they weren't going out again. That could mean only one thing. The whole party was presumed dead. She knew that, and so did everyone else.

Why did everyone carry on? How could they in the face of this tragedy? In its latest edition, *The Wave* had just published the photos of those who were missing. It was hard for the whole town to see them, frozen in time. Buddy and Caitlin had seen the photos and asked why their Dad was in the newspaper.

Maybe everyone was in shock. Maybe, when the first bodies show up on the shore, they would all awaken to what had happened, whatever had happened.

This morning, as she arrived at the construction site, she was taken aback at what she saw. There were now four walls erected and the crew was installing insulation. This was moving fast.

Magdalena and Susanna had arrived at the construction site before Sally, and when she came, they greeted her warmly. By now, they were close as sisters.

Miguel was standing near a small tent off to the side. He beckoned.

"Come. Join me in the tent."

They were stupefied at what they saw. A beautifully formed stone, that they recognized as coming from the cliffs down by Clever, had been placed in the middle of the tent. It was aglow with a radiant, unearthly light. It evoked different hues all around it on the walls of the tent. The sides of it seemed to reflect the whole spectrum of color at the same time.

Slowly, almost reverently, they came forward and stood across from Miguel on the other side of the stone.

"This is the Stone of Illumination. It was cut from the very stone of your cliffs and transported here by our workers in the night. It has been cut open and hollowed out; and the pure Stone of Gemma, that was in the safe, has been buried deep within the stone hewn from your planet. This was necessary, since human eyes could not see it without losing their sight.

The women were stunned to silence. After a pause to allow them to absorb what he had just said, he continued.

"This stone is the container of spiritual light itself and will be healing for the souls of those who come to Joe's Diner. The Luminous Stone, as you may call it, is the fusion of heaven and earth, a heavenly presence within an earthly vessel, a metaphor of the human being.

"It is more than we can take in, Miguel," said Susanna quietly.

The others nodded in silent assent.

"You are Keepers of the Stone of Illumination. Its properties most surely will stir the hearts of wicked and greedy people to gain it for themselves, imagining that, by possessing it, they may gain great wealth and fame. But, it will bring them and the world great harm if they do this. Holy things in the hands of evil men stir up the forces of the cosmos and can sometimes bring great natural and spiritual tragedies upon the face of the planet."

"But, how can we three women protect this Luminous Stone?"

"Not through natural power or force, but by the spiritual authority and power given to you. It is within your own hearts. You are already strong in spirit, but you will become even stronger as you become protectors of the Stone. Give it the due reverence as light from heaven, but do not worship it. It only points beyond itself to a place, so to speak, of greater light, where all will be gathered in the light of God.

"Stay with the stone for a while, so that you may absorb into your minds all that I have said and, so that you may open your hearts to the great light that is shining here and soon will shine for all to see when they come into the environs of Safety Harbor, a new Gate of Light to the New Creation."

Miguel left them alone with the precious Luminous Stone over which they were stewards.

"Miguel!" called out Sally. "Is this about Joe and our friends at all? Is this connected? Will we see . . .?"

"You will see me again!" It was Joe's voice. She looked behind her right shoulder, as the voice seemed to be coming from there, but there was no one.

"You will see your loved ones again."

She looked to see if the other women had heard this, too. From their expressions, they had not.

Chapter 87

WITH HER SHARP EYE, Carmelita had noticed that the Car of Doom was parked just past Joe's on Newman Street, hidden behind one of the construction trucks. She called Carmelita.

In a matter of seconds, the Chief was on the road. She pulled in just in front of the Car of Doom, angling the squad car across the narrow road to block any fast getaways. This ensured a confrontation of some kind.

She took in a large breath and slowly exhaled. She moved slowly, but deliberately, toward the driver's window, rapping firmly on the glass. No response. Again. No response.

She could feel the tension rising inside her. There was going to be resistance, she could tell that. The Assistant panicked. Fear ran up his spine. Claustrophobia, hit him like a brick. He started to roll the window down just a bit. Maybe he could just talk to her a minute and she would go away.

"Get out of the car, driver!"

He rolled the window up quickly. This was not the way to go. He clicked an icon on the dashboard computer, raising the suspension about six inches farther up in the air. Slowly, the car began to turn clockwise, gaining momentum as it made a three hundred and sixty degree turn, then counter clockwise and clockwise again. The car whirled silently as if it were a creature. With each completion of clockwise and then counter clockwise, the car sped up and was soon spinning furiously in the counterclockwise direction.

The Assistant felt the old arrogance and power come back into him with each revolution. Something about this action stirred up dark power. It was an ingenious invention. It shocked people. It mesmerized them, disarmed them, even; and, at the same time, just a few revolutions of the Car of Doom could change the power quotient in a situation without a word being spoken and without an action being taken.

"That'll show 'em Bates!"

He didn't know whether Bates was still in the car or whether he had by now passed on into oblivion. He didn't care. It was someone to talk to who couldn't talk back just like his ex-wives and the others upon whom he had committed dark and evil acts.

"That ought to put the fear of God into them." He hesitated. "So to speak!"

He roared at this own joke and the car continued to pick up speed.

Carmelita stepped back immediately when the whirling movement began. The car began to stir up gravel and dust from the newly-graveled Newman Street. Rocks flew, some a distance of five hundred feet or more. Some began to project like missiles onto the construction site. Work stopped immediately as people ran for cover. Pandemonium began to take hold.

"Take cover, everyone!" Lou called out as if he were directing something, even when it was already taking place spontaneously. He had not been able to stay away and was now back on the scene.

Carmelita had her hand on her holster. The faster the car spun, the more darkness descended upon the place as a tremendous cloud of dust rose up to cover the sun. With this darkness, a sense of foreboding overtook those who saw and experienced it. It was as if the center of an awful evil was revealed to them. It was so close to them that they could feel it. It projected the odor of fear and the hostility of violence. Carmelita took her hand off her holster and made the sign of the cross.

"Madre de Dios," she said.

"Take me to the woman and the child," Little Therese insisted. She had just returned from her playtime with Buddy and Caitlin.

"Take me to them."

"You can't go out there!" said Ruth. "We're not going to allow you to be exposed to the flying rocks and whatever else is going on."

"Take me to them, Uncle Roy!"

Roy looked at Ruth with questioning eyes. She gave him the nod to go forward. He picked up Little Therese, sheltered her with his arms and bent down over her, running toward the woman and child who were standing under the tree that bordered the road. Unlike everyone else who was in panic, they did not flinch.

When Roy and Little Therese reached them, she said, "Thanks, Uncle Roy! You can go now. I'll be safe with them!"

"I'm not leaving you here by yourself!"

"I'm not alone. I'm with Ana and Eshy!"

Roy backed off about ten feet and kept watch over his niece. None of the rocks seemed to be touching any of the three of them as they stood there together.

There were varying reports as to the details of what happened that day, but there are the facts upon which no one disagrees. The little girl walked over to the boy. They smiled at one another and then gave one another a warm embrace, as if they knew each other. Then, they joined hands and raised their arms together.

Immediately, the Car of Doom stopped spinning. It halted with such abruptness that The Assistant was knocked unconscious. For the space of a moment, there was absolute quiet.

Not everyone had seen what had happened. Few in fact, had seen it. Most were in hiding. But those who did, said that so instantly did the car stop that it rocked on its wheels from one side to the other. Some thought that it might fall over on one of its sides, but finally, after several close calls, it righted itself.

Only now did Roy notice that Miguel was standing by Carmelita as she approached the Car of Doom. She rapped on the window.

"Safety Harbor police! Open up!"

There was no response. There were no door handles to be found. Opening the door from the outside was impossible.

Inside, The Assistant was just awakening. He rubbed his head.

"Ohh!" he moaned. "What happened, Bates?"

He shook himself and realized now that he had a terrific headache. Looking through his one-way tinted windows he saw Carmelita standing outside the door. Now he remembered. He had put the vehicle into what he called full torque spin, that usually solved any problems he might be having with interfering or overly curious locals. It hadn't worked this time.

"Ohh!" he moaned again, rubbing his head.

Carmelita had seen the car begin to move ever so slightly as The Assistant awakened. She knocked again, this time more sharply.

"Safety Harbor police! Open up! Get out of the car!"

He saw that she had her hand poised at the top of her holster. If he obeyed Carmelita's orders, he would have to show his face to the world, and this he did not want to do. Revealing himself would cause him to lose his power, perhaps even his life.

Then, as if it were an inspiration from Hell itself, a plan, a strategy, came to him in a flash. It was a solution of his own and it was also something that could make him famous. It could earn him the title of First Among Assistants.

Each year that he drove, he found himself filled with more lust for power, more thirst for fame, and glory. He became more competitive among his peers to take more souls into oblivion. Like a drug, at first, each soul he captured gave him a sense of exhilaration. Predictably, with each passing taking of the hostage, the returns became less and less. So, he craved ever more deeply to send the unfortunate on into the darkness. He had developed an addiction for souls.

He began to rev up the engine. Carmelita drew her weapon.

"Stop! Shut down your engine! Roll down the window and show me your hands!"

The Assistant laughed with such glee that the peels of his delight echoed down and back again from Hell itself.

Roy suddenly realized what the Car of Doom was planning.

"Jens!" he called out. "C'mon!"

Jens was across the yard near the construction site. Both of their motorcycles were parked nearby. Roy was the first to get his started. Jens followed soon after.

The engine of the Car of Doom became increasingly louder until it seemed as if there were many engines roaring at the same time, as if an airplane was overhead, flying low, shrieking with ever greater intensity. Now, everyone knew what Roy and Jens had sensed earlier. The car was coming for them all.

Above the noise, Roy called out to Jens, but his voice was swallowed up in the danger that lurked.

Suddenly, the roar of the engine increased in volume and intensity, as if it were not coming from the car at all, but from every direction. Gravel began to fly as the back wheels began to spin. Carmelita thought about shooting out the tires, but couldn't take the chance that one of the bullets wouldn't ricochet and kill some innocent person.

Worst fears were realized as the car was now pointed directly toward the construction site. Roy and Jens sprang into action. With a nod toward one another they revved up their engines and moved closer to what they knew was going to be the intended path of the car.

Clearly, The Assistant's plan was to crash into the new construction, and while he was at it, to take as many souls as he could with him.

Jens gave the signal and both began their efforts to foil the Assistant's plan. It was as if their actions had been choreographed. The car began careening toward Joe's. So many had their eyes on the scene before them, that they had not noticed Roy and Jens until now.

They watched in horror as the two men drove their powerful motorcycles right in front of the car just before it could reach the area of the yard where people who had not been able to flee the scene, hunched down together.

Just as they reached the moment of impact, Roy looked up and saw the woman and child with Little Therese at the side of the boy.

"This is for you, Little Therese!" he called out.

The impact was ugly. The Car of Doom was stopped in its tracks, as all three moving vehicles came together in a promiscuous, scraping union of metal. The motorcycles were bent and shredded beyond recognition and the two men were forced by the impact onto the windshield.

The Assistant was flummoxed. A chill ran up his spine. He might be in over his head. The faces of the two men stared in at him through the darkened windshield. The look of surprise was frozen upon their faces and he couldn't tell whether they were living or dead.

He had to get out of here. He backed up suddenly. The men fell back and to the ground.

"Stop!" he heard Carmelita say. This time she did fire her weapon, sensing him at a disadvantage. But, he was moving too quickly now and he knew she couldn't touch him. He made his way back onto the side road and turned right onto Highway 101 toward Tillamook.

The two men lay silently upon the ground. The impact had either wounded them badly or they were already dead. Carmelita called Shirley in the office, to get an ambulance. Two injured, possibly dead.

Someone had the presence of mind to call 911. Ruth rushed over, and bent down to examine them. It was hard for her to maintain her professionalism as she saw her brother there, on the ground.

She checked for pulses in both men. Jens had a faint heart beat but she could find no pulse for Roy. Tears filled her eyes.

By now, the sea of onlookers was growing larger, and pressing against the scene of the conflagration.

"Folks, you must move back!" said Carmelita. "This is a dangerous situation here, and we have to have the freedom to work!"

The traffic had slowed down through town. Marshall had gone up to the intersection to direct traffic and to hustle the people on out of town. Ruth continued to perform CPR on her brother. Some kind soul in the crowd pulled her away gently and took her place.

After what seemed forever, the volunteer ambulance from Harbor General arrived. Triage determined that Roy was the most critical and he went in the ambulance first. Jens would have to wait for the Clever paramedics.

"I'm going with him," said Ruth who by now had returned to the scene. The attendants nodded and she climbed in the back with her brother.

They administered the paddles three times. Still there was still no response. Ruth screamed.

"Ma'am," said the attendant, "you're not helping your brother any and you're ruining my concentration. Please center yourself or we'll have to stop and let you out and that's just time delayed in getting him the help he needs."

"I know. I know. I'm sorry."

By the time they reached the hospital, Roy was still not breathing and she had almost given up. She got out of the ambulance quickly so that they could get Roy into the hospital as soon as possible. The ambulance loaned by Clever for the search for Joe, was pulling in right behind them with Jens.

Doc Bailey met them at the door.

"We'll do our best. Ruth!" he said.

"I know you will! Go! Go!" she said urgently.

She hoped that she hadn't sounded rude. Out of the corner of her eye, Ruth thought she saw the woman and her child. She looked again and they were gone if indeed, they were ever there.

Roy was revived, but now lay in a coma. Doc was afraid that he would have some brain swelling, due to what he called significant trauma inflicted upon his skull. The outcome was still tenuous. As for Jens, he had several cracked ribs, but otherwise, no apparent injuries.

"Go home and get some rest," Doc Bailey told Ruth.

"Easy for you to say, Doc!"

"Yes, it is! That's why I say it!"

Chapter 88

"YOU'RE GOING TO CONTINUE then, even after this terrible scene?" Carmelita asked Miguel.

"We have to, Senora. Future events depend upon it."

It was in this moment that Carmelita recognized, more than intellectually, that she was in the presence of a heavenly being, as were Abraham and Sarah of old, Jacob and Rachel, and Isaiah, and yes, the Blessed Mother.

She fell to her knees, making the sign of the cross.

"Stand up on your feet. My identity must not be revealed to everyone. Otherwise, my work cannot be accomplished. What we do now, we do so that the light may overcome the darkness, so that heaven and earth may be moved and the hearts of all may come to the truth."

"Forgive me, Miguel," she said.

"If there were anything to forgive, I could not forgive it," he said. "Angels are not in the forgiving business."

"I have felt so overwhelmed in these days that my faith and trust have faded."

"You are having a human experience," he told her. "Faith and trust are tentative connections between the human soul and its eternal home. You must not think it your own doing when your faith wavers. Everything will be worked out in its own good time. Now, you have work to do and so do I. These next few hours will bring great changes. We must prepare for them."

As for The Assistant, he did not go far out of town.

"What am I doing, Stanley? I've got to get back there. Something big is about to happen. I just know it. I can feel it. If we don't stop it, it's going to set our whole program back a good hundred years! I don't want to be, I can't be, responsible for that. I could end up like you!"

He parked across from Pilsner House and just on top the rise before going into town.

"I have a feeling it's almost show time, Bates!"

Chapter 89

THE LUMINOUS STONE HAD been moved into the diner.

Miguel's assistant, Rafael, had gathered Katye, Magdalena, Sally, and Susanna, asking them to put their hardhats on, although they noticed he did not do the same. He then took them through the new diner, nearly finished, except for some the finer interior work and painting the outside. They were pleased to see that it was the same floor plan as the original Joe's, although it was generally brighter from the light radiating from the Luminous Stone.

He took them upstairs. Joe's old room was now the office. A large portrait of Joe hung behind the manager's desk.

"So, Joe's not coming back," Sally said as half question, half statement.

"Joe is coming back," said Rafael.

"What is the meaning of these gates of light? Why are they needed?" asked Susanna.

"Remember the old story of Noah? Up until then, God had tried to persuade all of humanity to return to lives of love and peace and rightness of living. Instead, people kept getting more and more wicked, tempting God, with their outrageous behavior, debauched living, killing, maiming, stealing, all the while, becoming less and less human.

"The world was destroyed by a flood and God decided to start over with just one family. God turned to just one people, in order to redeem all of humanity through them."

"Ah!" said Magdalena. "So, we are sort of starting all over again with these gates of light?"

"Not entirely. Maybe, you could call it an added step. Since the Creation, the dream of God has always been to unite heaven and earth once more. However, increasingly so, it looks as if the world is not going to be ready anytime soon."

"So, these gates of light are like little Noah's Arks in the world, then?" asked Katye.

"You have it! You have it exactly, Sally!"

"Where is Joe? Do you know?" asked Katye.

"Not even I know exactly where he is, nor does Miguel. We do not know when he is coming back either, although the orders from Gemma have been to get the diner ready right away. What is important for you to know is that whatever happens and how, because of Joe, none of you will ever be the same again. Your lives have changed in ways you cannot yet realize."

"That is true," said Katye. "That was true even before he left and especially now that he is gone!"

"Think of Roy and Jens!" said Susanna. "Just a few days ago, they were big bullying troublemakers in town. Now, they've both just become the town's heroes!"

Rafael smiled. "You will see even greater things happen in the future because Joe has come among you. Come. We must keep moving on as our time here is short."

From that moment on, all of them realized that Rafael and Miguel and all of the workers from Gemma were not of this world.

Chapter 90

"COME," SAID RAFAEL. "I am going to take you now to Pilsner House!"

"Pilsner House!" said Sally aloud. "I've never been there."

"Oh, I've seen it and it's beautiful," said Susanna. "There have been some art shows up there that I've attended and I've displayed some of the work of the locals a couple of times."

"I'm with you, Sally. I've never seen it," said Katye.

They walked behind Rafael in single file up the path through the park and onto the grounds of Pilsner House.

"Tomorrow, there will be a great banquet here," said Rafael.

"Everybody has an invitation. What's the occasion?"

"We do not know, Katye," said Rafael. "We angels don't know half of what you think we know. We only know that there will be food both from your land and ours."

"You actually mean fruit and vegetables from Gemma?" asked Magdalena.

"Well, we don't have such categories," said Rafael. "But yes, if you insist. Yes."

"Wow!" said Katye. "Will the people know it?"

"Only those whose eyes are open will see."

"Wow!" said Katye again. "So, they really want everybody! This must be a special occasion. Maybe Gemma's going to announce something!"

"We don't know ourselves," said Rafael. "They tell us very little. We only know that Gemma is always well coordinated. They don't miss a detail."

"Maybe they think you would spill the beans!"

"Well, that may be true, Magdalena. We angels are here to announce things, so that's probably why they do keep things from us. Once we know something, what else could we do?"

He led them in through the back door, an entrance to a large kitchen where workers were preparing food with such pungent and delicious aromas that their mouths literally watered.

"This will be a veritable feast!" said Susanna.

"We are bringing in some of the best wines from your vineyards all around the area," said Rafael.

"So, some of the wineries are being visited today by angels and they don't have a clue!" Magdalena laughed.

"Well, they'd have to be pretty sharp to notice!" Rafael smiled faintly. "I do think the farmer's markets all around have been pretty well decimated by our heavenly shoppers! Your Ray Ripple has been very busy, hauling things from Portland the last two days. His job security has never been better now!"

"May we see the rest of the house?" asked Sally.

"Of course."

He led them through several rooms with narrow doors on each side that Sally recognized as workers' corridors. Finally, after one last bend in the hallway, they were led out into the library. They all took in an audible quick breath. This was no room with a few books and expensive furniture that some chose to call a library. This was a full and functional operation with bookshelves to the ceiling, without one obvious remaining space for another addition to the collection.

He escorted them from there, out into a large and spacious living room that looked as if it was designed as much for large gatherings and dancing as it was for small areas where groups could gather in intimate conversation. Wallpaper decorated the walls all the way to the high ceiling.

Over the fireplace mantle was a photo of the Pilsners in their earlier years. Individual portraits of children were on each side. One daughter looked particularly strong and precocious.

"Now, on to the most important part of our visit."

Rafael led them to a large banquet hall that was clearly meant for very large gatherings.

"Mr. and Mrs. Pilsner held two parties for the employees of their businesses every year, one in the summer, and one at Christmas. He designed this room with them in mind."

"And look!" He led them to large sliding glass doors along one wall.

"When all of these doors are open, this entire side of the house is open onto the patio. More tables can be placed out there."

They looked out upon a large and expansive raised concrete platform that looked toward Pilsner Point. They walked out onto the patio.

"All of this, including the patio, is where the citizens of Safety Harbor, the Unsettlement, and beyond, will dine tomorrow. We will have designated picnic spots out on the grassy lawn out to the fence that divides the house property from the rest of the park. You are welcome to stay for a while. If you will excuse me I have a few visitations to make!"

For a few moments, the women sat on a picnic table taking in the glory of Pilsner House, imagining what it must have been like for the Pilsner family to live here and anticipating how it would be when the whole city was gathered for a great celebratory banquet.

Chapter 91

Roy's room at Harbor General was dim and solemn. Around his bed stood Little Therese and Ruth. Jens had joined them since being discharged from the emergency department. Little Therese was in prayer, with her hand in Uncle Roy's, and her lips moving silently. Ruth's head drooped, as sleep came in small packages, waking just enough to realize where she was before going back into her exhaustion-induced state.

"Oh, who turned the light on?" she moaned.

Jens stirred slightly, his eyes halfway open. Slowly, the bright light brought Little Therese and Jens to a waking state. Little Therese turned her head toward it the light.

"There's light Momma. I can see light."

"What?" Ruth jerked awake. "What is it? Who is it?"

The cloudy figure at the door suddenly became clearer.

"Doctor? Are you a doctor?" she asked.

"I am Rafael. I have come to give you a message. Because of the faith and prayers of Little Therese, Roy will not die, but will live."

"Oh joy! Joy! Joy!" Little Therese jumped from her chair and began to dance around the room with such grace that no one could have perceived from her movements that she could not see.

A slight smile came to Rafael's face.

"You must live with such joy as this little child has."

Jens, by now, had regained consciousness, and was staring, wide-eyed.

"Jens, because you did not value your life above others, you will live anew. Your life has changed. It is changing. It will change. Do not go back to your old ways. You will be tempted, but always look toward the light."

"What light?" he asked.

"The light, Jens. You will know it when you see it."

"Oh, okay. If you say so."

Once again, a faint smile came to Rafael's lips.

"I say so!"

As Rafael went over to Roy's bedside, Little Therese moved as if to get out of his way. But he said, "Stay with me, child."

He reached out and touched her on the top of her head affectionately. Then, with the other hand, he touched Roy on the forehead.

"You will be well," he said.

Suddenly, Little Therese could not feel his hand on her head.

"Is he gone, Momma? Is he gone?"

"Yes, he's gone, but I didn't see him go. Did you, Jens?"

"Was he here? Was he really here or are we in a dream?" asked Jens.

"He was here," said Little Therese. "I felt his presence."

"Did he say Roy was going to get well?"

"Yes, he did, Jens," said Ruth.

"I heard him say it, too," said Little Therese. "I sure wish Uncle Roy would wake up. Since he's going to be better, it might as well be right now!"

"I'd say I agree with you, Little Therese."

"He had some pretty good words for you too, Jens."

"Yes, he did but you'll have to tell me what he said. I was so stunned, I don't remember a thing he said."

"He said you're a hero, Jens!" said Little Therese. "He said good things are coming but don't get a big head about it and mess it up!"

"Well, Little Therese, that's not an exact quote, but it's close enough for now. I think Jens will remember it all later," said Ruth

"The light is still here," said Little Therese.

"Yes, it is," said Ruth. "It surely is!"

Roy stirred ever so slightly. Immediately, they watched closely to see whether he was coming to consciousness. But there was only quiet following the stirring. The vigil continued.

"Momma, I think we should go back out to the Point and wait for Joe tonight."

"What about your Uncle Roy? He needs us here."

"But, the angel said he was going to be fine."

"Adults aren't at all as sure of what they have seen and heard, Little Therese."

"We're just worried about your uncle, Little Therese."

"He'll be fine, Momma, but the angel didn't say anything about Joe."

"No, he didn't. You are right."

"So, Joe needs us to be waiting for him, watching for him."

"Haven't you almost given up, Little Therese?" asked Jens.

Ruth threw him a dark and piercing glance.

"No, I haven't. You haven't either, have you, Momma?"

"We can never give up hope, Little Therese."

"Tell you what," said Jens. "Why don't you go on down to the Point with your mother and I'll wait here for your Uncle Roy to wake up."

"That won't work. He will want to see Momma when he wakes up, not you!"

Jens smiled. "Well, that may be true, but I can't take you down there by myself. It's not right."

"Why don't we see if my friends Buddy and Caitlin can go down there with me? Maybe Sally could go too and Luke and Ginny. Then you and Momma could stay here with Uncle Roy."

"Oh, that's a lot to ask, Little Therese."

"No, it's not. Not if they all want to be there."

A few phone calls later, it was all arranged. Sally would come and pick up Little Therese right after dinner, and Luke and Ginny would be there at the Point, waiting for them with Buddy and Caitlin."

Chapter 92

"I DO LOVE IT here!' said Johnny. "So much light! I've never seen so much light!"

"I think for some of us who have had our share of darkness, this light is especially exquisite," said Jeremy. "I've had too much darkness in my life."

The group was generally surprised to hear Jeremy say this. He was usually quite guarded with his privacy.

"It reminds me of my morning reading, recently, "said Father, 'The light shines into the darkness and the darkness has not overcome it.'"

"Where do you find that," asked Daniel.

"Oh, it's in the Gospel of John somewhere," said Johnny.

"You are right, Johnny," said Father.

"The Christian religion isn't the first to talk about this," said Meriwether. "You know the Magi, the so-called wise men? They were probably priests of a Persian religion started by Zoroaster. His followers said that below the earth was a realm of chaos and darkness."

"You mean, like hell?" asked Johnny.

"Yes, like hell! And above the earth is what is called the realm of endless lights."

"Like heaven?"

"Yes, Johnny. You are correct," said Meriwether. "Sort of."

"Ah! Plenty of time to talk this over when we get home, sailors!" said Nate. "Right now, we've got to launch. Everyone aboard! Let's take roll. I don't want to leave anyone behind. We can't come back after you!"

Suddenly, all the talk was over. All the waiting had come to an end and they were going to, just as Joe had said, "Launch out into the deep."

One by one, Mrs. Saugus called out the names of all of those present and they responded as many had in high school. At the end of her list, was Wendell Cone.

"Wendell Cone!" she called out.

There was a moment of solemn silence.

"May eternal rest be his," said Father. "May light always shine upon him."

"I'm sure it is," said Carla. "God rest his soul. I'm sure his face is aglow with light. Maybe he's right here on Gemma somewhere, or on some other holy island of light."

Nate started the engine and he boat launched with an abrupt jerk. Immediately, the little boat began to sail as if on a predetermined route. "It's just as before!" said Nate. "We have absolutely nothing to say about where we go."

The boat continued to pick up speed as it went.

"Hold on, everybody!" said Carla. "If you fall off, we can't stop and pick you up!"

Nate noticed how the bright light overtook the hue of the sky and the ocean, offering up to them an appearance of liquid gold. He was mesmerized, and reflected upon how the boat seemed to be skimming over a churning sea of amber. He was saddened that Rock could not see such beauty.

Everyone was involved in their own thoughts. All of them knew just how serious this was, how uncertain their lives all were at this moment, and that they had been given the awe-filled task of bringing their wounded friend home. There was a growing awareness among them that some great Power, some Benevolent Presence, was both leading them, and supporting them, on this journey.

Johnny Watson broke the silence when he suddenly called out, "Praise for the light!"

It was so unusual for him to speak in this way, that people's heads immediately turned and all eyes fastened on him. His hands were raised as if in ecstasy.

Meriwether went and stood by him, placing her arm around him, steadying him, and at the same time, offering him emotional support, in case he might be embarrassed.

"Yes! Praise be!" she responded quietly.

The boat picked up more speed. The amber-colored ocean waves began to splash into the boat. Rocky and Georgia held on ever more tightly to Joe. Father Callaghan began to white knuckle it as he sat on one of the undercover tourist benches beside Joe's sick bed.

This is a transformative journey!" called out Meriwether. "I'm with Johnny. Praise for the light!

"Praise for Joe who brought us to the light!" said Rocky.

"Yes, he did," said Meriwether. "Yes, he did. Indeed, he did."

The boat had reached its maximum speed. It continued on what seemed to be a straight course. The engine, at this point, seemed irrelevant to the speed of the vessel. Some other energy was moving it along on its watery path.

Father led out in a few lines of their pilgrim song.

> *Through the fierce and stormy gale*
> *When no spirit fills my sail*
> *I shall see, though light may fail,*
> *Lights of Safety Harbor.*

"I want you all to know that I'm damned sorry for all the sins I've done!" said Johnny, in a loud voice.

"Why, Johnny, you're no bigger a sinner than the rest of us!" said Father Callaghan.

"Some of us might say you aren't a sinner at all!" said Meriwether.

"Oh, he's a sinner, all right," called out Georgia, followed by her familiar belly laugh.

"Yeah, Jeremy, when you were remodeling your book shop, you left a twenty-dollar bill on the counter and I took it and kept it for myself."

"You did?"

"I did!"

"Well, I'll be!"

"And I shorted you on lumber, Daniel, when you were remodeling your shop!"

Daniel's face turned red.

He went on, admitting to Mrs. Saugus of the times he had cheated in school. He told everyone of the many times that he had driven with a suspended license and how he had carried on with one of the bartenders at The Rogue Tap.

"Don't you think you have punished yourself enough, now?" asked Father Frank. Confession isn't self-shaming, Johnny. It's just admitting that you did what you did, to whom you did it, and to God, saying you're sorry, turning your back on those old ways, and getting on with things."

"I suppose you are right, Father. I am ashamed. Fact is, I'm often full of shame. And now that I've gotten to know all of you on this journey, I'm even more ashamed of what I've done to you and to others. I just want to be one of you instead of using you and taking advantage of you."

"I can't say whether or not others present have or will forgive you, but I can say this: If they don't, they won't be forgiven, either."

"You're one of us, Johnny!" said Nate.

"Thanks, Nate! Coming from you, that means a lot!"

"You're forgiven, Johnny, of all sins confessed and those unremembered," said Father.

"And I forgive you, Johnny, for your bad spelling!" called out Joe, who had awakened and had overheard the conversation.

At once, they rushed to his side. His fever had temporarily broken and he was in good spirits.

They talked for a few minutes, while he was able.

How long will it be before we reach Safety Harbor?" asked Carla.

"Not long," he said.

Then, he smiled and went to sleep.

Chapter 93

STEWART HAD AWAKENED EARLY. Katye was up and gone. He assumed she had gone home to prepare some breakfast and bring it back to the lighthouse.

"A lot of things are happening to your soul here in the lighthouse eh, Stewart?"

He did not turn around. The voice was all too familiar and had visited him before.

"I think I've been in a tower all of my life, Joe. I have stayed above the fray, waiting for more ideal conditions, waiting until I fit in better, waiting until someone invited me to the parade, so to speak."

"That's good insight, Stewart. In this case, being in the tower has done you some good!"

"Are you coming home, Joe?"

He felt the hand rest on his right shoulder again.

"I'll be home soon, but I'll need your help!"

"My help!"

"There you go again! Yes, your help. I will need your help, along with the life and vitality of others to carry on my work here in Safety Harbor."

"But, I thought you were coming back, Joe!"

"I am. You will be there when I return and you will understand it then. It is too early for you to comprehend it now. Carry on, dear son. You are needed in this tower. Don't leave now."

"I won't, Joe."

Then, he was gone.

Stewart didn't know if these visits were real or not, but he had given up on trying to ascertain the answer to that question. In the end, what did it matter? Nobody was there to question his sanity or the authenticity of Joe's appearances. If they were delusions, they were most helpful, and who needed to know?

Stewart took note that the radiant light from the northwest seemed to shine brighter than ever. It was still early morning. Nearly all of Safety Harbor still slumbered and slept.

Chapter 94

No one on the boat could quite say when it happened. One instant, they were traveling in the reflective radiant light of the island shores they had just departed, and in the next moment, it was as if a veil had been thrown over their vision. The boat suddenly slowed and the little engine suddenly labored to carry its load along in the water.

While all the rest were noticing that they could not see as well as they had moments ago, suddenly, Rock was aware that his vision had been restored.

"I can see again!" he shouted. "My eyesight is back! Oh, how can it be? I thought it would never happen!"

He went around to each person, looked them directly and intently, and hugged them.

"Boy, it's good to see you!" he could be heard saying.

People answered, "You too, Rock! You too!"

"Well, that is a sign, then," said Father Frank.

"What sign?" asked Jeremy.

"We are back in time. Don't you remember what Joe said earlier, Rock would be healed in time?"

"You are right!" said Carla. "We did hear him say that!"

Father Frank looked back and could see no trace, in their wake, of the golden dimension in which they had just traveled. There was not a sign that they had ever been anywhere but in this boat and within time and space. He wondered. Could it have all been a dream?

Instinctively, Nate glanced down at his watch. It was Sunday morning. It was three minutes after six. He pulled his hand-held GPS out of his pocket. It was working again. They were about fifty-three miles off the shore of Safety Harbor! Not far at all!

Chapter 95

The Assistant had parked the Car of Doom overnight behind the large billboard just outside the city limits sign. This way, he reasoned, he was both out of sight and out of the jurisdiction of those who had been on the lookout for him.

As if they knew he had just awakened, the Bread from Stone headquarters came up on his cell phone.

"Uh-huh. What've you got?

"Joe's back in time and he's on his way back to Safety Harbor," said the voice on the other end.

"No!"

"Yes!"

"What'll we do"

"We've got to throw up the shield."

"What shield?"

"What do we specialize in?"

"We're good at instilling a paralyzing darkness and chaos within the soul that causes human beings to make mistakes and misjudgments that can end up being crippling to their spirits or even cause them to end their lives."

"Right. Joe is on the boat with the others from Safety Harbor. If we can disorient them enough, we can get them to lose their way in the water, and, if we're lucky, they will decide to end it all or it will end for them. Do your damnedest."

Chapter 96

CARMELITA WAS DREAMING THAT she was walking on the edge of a high cliff. The static from the radio sounded, within the dream, like rocks that were giving way, collapsing the path in front of her. She awakened with a start, now realizing that she had never made it home, that she had been sleeping here in the office since last night.

"This is Nick, from the *Joe Boat*, calling the Safety Harbor Police Department."

Startled, she jumped out of her chair and over to the two-way radio. Her voice was trembling and her hands were shaking. She skipped protocol.

"Nate!"

"Carmelita?"

"For heaven's sake, where are you?"

"We are now about fifty miles from home."

"My God! Where have you been?"

"It's a long story, Chief."

"Is everyone okay?"

"We have lost Wendell. We don't have the *Far from Home* anymore. It crashed against the shoals of the island where we landed. We're lucky to be alive. We're coming in on Joe's boat."

"All of that effort, and Wendell's death for nothing. But, at least you're still alive!"

"No, not for nothing. We found Joe!

"Are you still there, Chief?"

"Yes, but I thought I heard you say that you found Joe."

"Yes, that's what you heard. We found Joe."

"I'm afraid to ask. Is he alive?"

"He's alive. He's been hurt bad, and he's going to need medical attention right away. Right now, we can't even be sure he'll be alive by the time we reach land. In this small boat, we can't be sure that we'll make it either."

"You'll make it. We'll see to that. We'll call the Coast Guard first thing!"

"I'm going to have to get some help in here, Nate. Stay with me while I make some calls."

She notified the Coast Guard in North Bend. Helicopters would begin scouring the area within two hours. She got back on with Nate and told him the news.

"At least they're on their way! Chief, you've got to make sure that people don't start out in their private boats looking for us"

"We'll do it, and we'll clear the area for you. We have had enough tragedy on the water!"

She called Marshall and ordered him into the office. She asked Shirley to come in as well.

What next? She would call the mayor, of course.

Hope answered the phone.

"Oh, my Lord, that's good news! I'm going to wake Lou up, right now!"

She handed the phone to Lou, who was still in bed.

"Haalloo?"

"Mayor, the lost is found! Nate has been in touch with us. They are off shore now and on their way home!"

"The hell you say!"

"Lou!" Carmelita heard feigned scorn in Hope's voice.

"I think maybe you ought to come down here and we ought to organize some kind of coordinating office together, in order to handle the exiles' arrival on shore."

"Be there in twenty minutes."

"It would be best to have the coordinating office here," Shirley said Carmelita, after she had hung up with Lou. "Lou could have the bus barn all to himself and set up as much of his equipment as needed. We have the walk-through between the buildings that will help us keep in touch."

"I think that's a good idea, Shirley. You make him think it's his idea!"

"He'll convince himself of that!"

Chapter 98

THE NIGHT-WATCHERS ON PILSNER Hill were stirring when Carmelita called Sally with the good news.

"Daddy's home?" asked Buddy, excitedly.

"Not yet," said Sally.

"But, he's okay??"

"Yes, your Daddy's okay. They are still some distance out on the ocean yet, and will need help getting here.

"They'll be okay, Buddy," said Caitlin.

"Yes, they will," said Little Therese, "but first they will have to go through a great darkness."

"Yur always talkin' funny like that," said Buddy. "Why don't you talk like we do?"

"Most of the time, I do," said Little Therese. "But, sometimes I get what Momma calls my *inklings* and I just have to say things."

"You sure are funny, Little Therese!" said Buddy.

"What do you mean, they'll have to go through the dark?"

"I don't know."

"Well, how do you expect us to know if you don't know?"

"I don't."

By now, Little Therese was getting teary.

"That's enough, Buddy," said Sally. "Let's be glad your Dad is okay. We'll get him home."

Chapter 99

RUTH WAS AWAKENED BY the sounds of Roy stirring.

"Dear brother, are you awake?"

"Oh!" he moaned. "Who's getting me up this early? I have a terrible headache! Must be a hangover!"

Ruth began to laugh and then to cry with relief.

"You weren't drinking, Roy. You were, you are, our hero. You, along with Jens.

"Jens is a hero? That's hard to believe!"

"That's enough for now, Roy," said Doc, who had arrived on the scene. "We're going to take you down right away and get a CT scan on you."

Two attendants came in and took Roy right away to the inner belly of the hospital.

"Yes, Doc. Is everything okay?"

"Well, it will be, it may be. I think."

"What is it?"

"Nate has been in touch with Carmelita. Nate and crew are off the coast about fifty miles. The Coast Guard is now out looking for them. They've got coordinates, so there shouldn't be a problem with finding them."

"Wonderful! That's good news indeed! How much more good news could we possibly have?"

"Joe's in the boat with them!"

"Oh, my God! Where did they find him?"

"I don't know. I just know he's with them. The thing is, he may be mortally wounded and the second he gets here, if they get him here alive, we are going to have to helicopter him to Portland."

"That's good! Do you want my help with that?"

"We are going to have to examine every one of them that make it back alive. I want to set up a medical triage tent out on Pilsner Hill. That's where the helicopter will land. I want you to help set it up and be the triage nurse.

"By all means, Doc. By all means! We can use the yurt that the mayor has already loaned to some of us to sleep out there."

I would say that Roy's chances are excellent for a full recovery since he awakened so soon after the event."

"Oh, I meant to tell you. We had a visitor last night who assured us he would be okay."

"Really? Who was that?"

"He said his name was Rafael."

"Never heard of him. Wasn't one of ours."

"I don't know who he was, Doc, but he was an angel to us."

"I'm glad he was right, whoever he was."

"Yes, so am I. Very glad."

"Well, let's you and I get busy. Others here can keep track of Roy while we're preparing for the boat to arrive. If Roy is okay after the tests, I've ordered that he be released. I'll have one of the volunteers take him home or wherever he wants to go."

Chapter 100

THE RETURNING PILGRIMS GREW more pensive. It was clear the boat was too small for its load and the engine was not built for the assignment it had been given.

The silence was broken by Rock, who shouted out in agony, "My God! I've lost my sight again!"

"I've lost mine, too. I can't see a thing but utter blackness," said Jeremy.

"Me too!" said Carla.

"Can anybody see?" Johnny called out.

No one answered.

"What is happening?" called out Mrs. Saugus.

"Someone ask Joe," said Nate. "Nobody can navigate in the dark."

"Joe's asleep!" said Georgia.

"Well, he's picked a fine time to sleep!" said Johnny.

"Cut the engine," said Meriwether. "Save the fuel."

Soon, the sound of the waves and the flapping of tattered sails was all that they could hear. After all they had been through and now this, Carla was thinking. She was feeling a kind of desperation now. What next? How much could they take? What is this present darkness? She hadn't ever experienced anything like this. It was so black and so deep that it seemed to be a bottomless chasm of emptiness, the essence of evil itself.

Immediately, Father Callaghan was battling all the demons he had ever encountered and fought. Little did people know that there were moments when he felt as weak and vulnerable as did they. Sometimes, he was filled with anger and cynicism. Often, he battled loneliness.

How often had he preached homilies berating the apostles for their lack of belief and their waking of Jesus in the boat! Now, here he was, irrationally resenting Joe for being sick and sleeping, when they needed his wisdom.

Georgia held Joe's hand. The darkness reminded her of her childhood, when her mother would tell her stories of her great grandparents in slavery. Their little lean-to hut had no light at all. They weren't allowed lamps. When they went to bed, everything was pitch black.

Without exception, everyone's thoughts were drawn inward to some of their darkest experiences in life, times when their love was betrayed, their hopes were dashed, or their lives were in crisis. It was as if all of the sorrow of their lives had returned and had come upon each of them as one experience.

Meriwether could feel, not only her own depression from bygone days but also, the collective sorrow of everyone aboard. It was more than she could bear.

"Oh, why do we have to go through this?" asked Daniel

No one answered.

Jeremy could feel the blows he received from high school classmates as if they were yesterday. Every Friday night, if they could find him, they would take him into the darkness behind the football field, and give him a merciless pounding.

"Faggot!" they'd say. "Faggot! Maybe this'll teach you to like girls!"

In a few moments, a breeze began to blow and then grew into a wind so powerful that it caught the imagination of even the most tattered of sails.

"Oh, my God!" said Johnny.

"Mother o' God!" called out Father.

"Now, we are not only blind, but the wind is blowing us, God knows where!" said Jeremy.

"Not even God can see into this darkness," said Mrs. Saugus.

Father remembered that Joe had told him that he was depending upon Meriwether and him to lead these good people home.

He called out, "Meriwether, can you make your way over here? I want to talk with you a moment."

"What is this?" asked Meriwether.

"I'm guessing that we've entered some kind of vortex where there is neither interior or exterior, but all is one. We can't survive in this very long. Some of us may be caught up in our own pain and throw ourselves over the side, in despair. That's why we must offer tokens of encouragement to all. We must give them hope in despair, and, when we do, we will find a remedy for our own souls, as well. We must not neither fear the darkness, nor must we reject it. We must embrace it and the holiness within it, while we wait for answers in patience and in silence."

"Yes," said Meriwether. "Wisdom sometimes comes to us in darkness, not in order that our souls be weighted down in worry, fear, or distress, but that we may learn to trust while we go through the darkness patiently, resting, and trusting in God."

By now, others were beginning to gather around this conversation.

"James says, 'If any of you lacks wisdom, he should ask God, who gives to all generously and ungrudgingly and it will be given,'" said Father Callaghan.

"I've been thinking during this time that none of you can know all the pain I've experienced from being a gay man!" said Jeremy. "I keep asking myself what I could possibly have learned from all of that fear and pain I went through as a boy."

"You mean, what wisdom have you gained?" asked Carla.

"Yes! What can I possibly learn from mean and vicious people who have beaten me up and made me lose jobs and friends just because of who I am? What wisdom is there in all of that?"

"You mean from your dark experiences," asked Johnny. "You mean bad experiences? Painful experiences? Embarrassing situations?"

"Exactly!" exclaimed Carla. "Some of us have experienced unspeakable abuse, abandonment, and loneliness."

So, being here is kinda like putting kids in detention," said Mrs. Saugus. "You make them be one place when they'd rather be elsewhere."

"Maybe. Sort of, Mrs. Saugus, said Father Frank. "Some cultures tell stories because they know that they contain the wisdom that has come to us in times of darkness. If we tell our stories to one another, it may bring us peace. Then, perhaps the light will come."

"I got no luck with women at all. Two of them have left me and the third is on her way out," said Johnny. "I don't know what it is about me that makes women like me and then drop me like a hot potato. I know I'm a drunk, but sometimes I wonder if it doesn't make it easier for them to leave because I am one. I think they'd leave me anyway. I don't know. Maybe not. It's a darkness, I tell you, not to be able to have a woman to call my own, forever."

"Think of what it was like to go to an all-white school with the surname of Chavez," said Carla. "There wasn't a day when I didn't have to go through something about my race. And being a Latino woman on top of it, didn't help at all."

"I had a love once," said Mrs. Saugus. "So deep was he in my heart, that I have never forgotten him. I think of him every day. He died when he was only twenty-three. I have often wondered why it wasn't the other way around. I should have died and he should have lived. The world would have been better with him than with me."

Daniel shared about his experiences in Iraq. Meriwether talked of her father's abandonment and her mother's sorrow. Everyone shared at least one story and most shared more than one.

Finally, after the last story was told, Georgia led them in a song.

We share our mutual woes,
our mutual burdens bear.
And often for each other flows
the sympathizing tear.

There was a deep quiet when they finished and each noticed that the pounding of their hearts had ceased. The wind slowed down now to a breeze that carried them along lightly rather than bouncing them to and fro on the waves.

They had not grown to love the darkness or even like it by any means, but they had adjusted to it and accepted it for what it was in those moments in time. Eyes were heavy but hearts were lighter as sleep overtook each person.

Chapter 101

"Oh, how I long for a drink from the fresh waters of Gemma!" a voice cried out.

It was Joe, calling for a drink of water. Almost immediately, everyone on the little boat was awake.

Nate glanced at his watch. It was three minutes after seven in the morning. What day was it?

Did they sleep the entire day? He looked again and his digital watch told him it was Sunday.

"Don't drink it too fast, Joe!" Georgia cautioned him.

"Oh, dear Georgia! Gemma water must be drunk deeply!" said Joe, who took the flask in his hands, placed it to his mouth, threw his head back, and gulped it all down in three or four large and noisy swallows.

"Everyone drink with me!" he insisted.

"We have only a limited amount of water," Carla objected. 'We don't want to run out. We can do without you but you cannot."

"The waters of Gemma never run dry!"

In order to please Joe, they all drank the water and found themselves surprisingly refreshed and awake. Nate checked the coordinates. They were right on course for Safety Harbor. He called Carmelita.

"We're so glad to hear from you. We lost touch. Is everything okay?"

"We're all suffering, I think, from a little confusion right now, but we are on our way!"

"Well, don't let us lose you again. The Coast Guard is on its way."

"Can't happen too soon, Chief! The engine is doing its best but it's no match for the weight on this boat."

"They hope to bring Joe up to the helicopter from the boat."

"Wouldn't recommend it. Joe's very sick. Right now, he's awake, but most of the time he is sleeping heavily. He's weak. I'm concerned that putting that much stress on him could make the difference between life and death."

"What do you suggest?"

"I think that the Coast Guard should tow us into the harbor, and that the medical helicopter land on Pilsner Hill. Doc can have an ambulance ready at the shore. The paramedics can slip him into the ambulance and get him up to Pilsner Hill. It'll cause the least stress on everyone, most of all, Joe."

"Your plan is a good one. We'll get that going. But, we've got to get you home first. You should be hearing the sound of helicopters very soon!"

Chapter 102

"Did we all dream the darkness?"

Mrs. Saugus was finally the one to bring up the subject of what was troubling all of them.

"Well, I know how much darkness I experienced!' said Father. "And I suspect, from what I remember of the conversations, that everyone else did, too!"

"I hope I didn't say anything embarrassing," said Johnny.

"Well, everyone here knows by now that I am gay!" said Jeremy.

"Isn't that wonderful?" exclaimed Joe, who had just awakened.

"What do you mean, Joe? It's tough to be gay! I sure wouldn't choose it!"

"It's wonderful that you are who you are!"

"Thank you, Joe!"

"It's been my mission, while I've been with you, for all of you to be yourselves, fully and completely, the you that was sent to this planet on a particular mission that only you can accomplish. It isn't so hard. What's difficult is being someone else! It's terrible pressure to keep up the image of the person others think you ought to be. You must be every part of yourselves, even the part of yourself that you don't like much. That part of you could really use a friend!"

"You mean, even the old drunk in me?"

"Yeah, that guy. Don't think you're different, Johnny, from anyone else. There's a part of all human beings that wants to kill the pain. People just have different home remedies and most of them don't work any better than yours."

"Is that what the darkness experience was all about, Joe?" asked Rock.

"Yes, Rock, you are right. The darkness gets all of us in touch with that part of us we hide from others and even from ourselves as much as we can see. It's the part of us that we don't want to escape from the dungeon in our souls where we have relegated it. But, that person is the most precious part of us. The part that made the outrageous and selfish misjudgments, is that part of us that carries most of the pain."

"So, the darkness was a gift to us!" said Father.

"I am sure it didn't feel like a gift!'

"No, it didn't, Joe!" said Carla.

There was a general laughter of recognition.

"Now, one more thing before I rest. I'm getting tired."

"Yes, what is it, Joe? Do you want to wait until later when you feel better?"

"It is necessary that I go away!"

"You've just been away, Joe," said Jeremy. "We're not even home yet! This is a bitter pill to swallow. Where will you go?"

"I have other towns and cities and villages to engage across the world, who, like you, have demonstrated that there is more of good among them than there are evil influences. I have been with you long enough now for you to be on your own. But, I will not leave you alone. In those times, when you come together, I will be among you, even though you can't see me.

"The journey to Gemma has profoundly changed you, and, when you return to Safety Harbor, you will see that those who stayed on land have had a profound journey of their own, and it has changed them in many ways. They have been waiting for you, preparing on my behalf, for your return and mine, and the new joys I have for you to experience and the new work I have for you to do. I cannot talk now. I must rest. Our rescue from the sea is close at hand."

His voice went silent. In its place, they heard the struggling of the engine as it labored to bring them home and the lapping of the sea against the little vessel, that was saving them all from the dark deep waters.

In the background, they began to hear the faint but familiar sounds of a helicopter as their safe arrival home in Safety Harbor became more assured.

Chapter 103

"THE VORTEX DIDN'T WORK. They got through it."

The Assistant was on the phone to Headquarters.

"I don't know how you guys thought it would work when Joe was in the boat. If you wanted to stop them, you should have put them through the vortex on their way to Gemma. This would never be happening, if you had, Joe would have died on the island.

"It's time to go to Plan B"

"What's Plan B?" asked The Assistant.

"Plan B is your problem."

The Assistant screamed.

"I'm the driver, for God's sake! You don't have any idea what you are doing, do you? You are just trying stuff! Give me a plan. I can work a plan that works. This wasn't my fault!"

"The Man says you need to turn this around!"

"You can count on me, as always!" Sarcasm dripped from The Assistant's lips.

He knew, when he finished the call, that he had lost it. Unless he made this work, it could be his last rodeo.

Just a few blocks away, the temporary offices combining forces of the police and the mayor's office was nearly ready.

Lou and Carmelita decided to put the word out that the helicopter that would carry Joe away to the hospital, would be landing on Pilsner Hill. They hoped that this would keep the crowd from assembling down at the harbor, which could very well slow up Joe's transportation to Pilsner Hill where the medical helicopter would be waiting.

Word had spread about the free meal available at the all-day banquet provided by Gemma, and the traffic into town was, once again, terrific. Later, *The Wave* would report that the people came to dine at Pilsner House from all the way up and down the coast, inland as far as Bend, as far south as Ashland, and as far north as Longview, Washington.

"One of them foreign cars is pulling up, Mayor," said Jens, who had arrived to inquire as to the status of his position as deputy. "I don't' recognize that it's from around here."

Emerging from the passenger side of the car, was a diminutive older blond woman, dressed expensively.

Slowly, she made her way into the bus barn, accompanied by Miguel.

"I want to introduce you all to Ms. Evita DuPont," he said. "She is the patroness of the Joe's new diner. She is very aware of your situation. She has been a friend of Joe's for many years. She, too, has come to await the outcome of the events of the day."

Sally arrived with Luke and Ginny. Buddy and Caitlin were following along happily.

"We're gonna see my Dad today!" said Buddy.

"Be quiet, Buddy! They know that!" said Caitlin.

"It's okay to be excited," said Sally.

Shirley whistled to get everyone's attention.

"Hey, folks! We're not going to be able to do our work if everyone comes here to hang out, waiting for the boat to arrive. People will see the crowd and assume this is where things are happening. Chief Biffle and Mayor Schofield strongly suggest that everyone assemble at Pilsner House, enjoy a delicious meal, and wait for our friends to arrive home! We will keep you up to date on all developments!"

Just then, Carmelita announced, "I have some news! The tugboat bringing our loved ones in from the sea is on its way to them from North Bend right now, and will escort them in safely to harbor. Our friends and families will be home soon!"

"Yea!"

It was Little Therese. There was laughter, clapping, backslapping, hugs, and tears.

Carmelita continued, "The medical helicopter people wanted to airlift Joe off the boat and get him to the hospital, but the consensus on the boat is that Joe is much too fragile for that. Nate suggested that the Coast Guard tow them in. That means they will be docking and Joe will then be transported by ambulance to Pilsner Hill. That's why everybody needs to go to Pilsner Hill to wait for Joe's and for everyone's arrival!"

"Always waiting!" said Little Therese. "Seems that we're always waiting, doesn't it?"

"Yes, it does," said Evita DuPont, who, by now, had taken to Little Therese and walked beside her on the way to Pilsner House. The two held hands as they walked. So charming were the two, that, as they made their way together, several took photos of them with their cell phones.

"Glad you're here, Reverend," said Carmelita, as Luther made joined the crowd at the bus barn. We may very well need some prayers and counseling as the day goes on. No one knows what the next few hours may bring. We expect everything to go well, but then, we don't know, do we?"

"True enough, Chief," said Luther. "We always need to plan for contingencies."

"Is that what you call them, Luther?" asked the mayor. "I have always called them God's screw-ups!"

"Lou!" called out Hope.

"Has thought been given to how we are going to transport the rest of the exiles up to Pilsner Hill once the ambulance has taken Joe up to be put on the medical helicopter?" asked Luther.

"No, we haven't," said Carmelita. "I can't believe one of us hadn't thought of that before this."

"Always Sunny has a bus," said Luther. "I could just go get it and we could load all of them at once rather than taking them up in separate cars."

"Won't your people need the bus? It's Sunday morning!"

"It's hardly ever used," said Luther, "especially on Sunday morning. They won't even miss it!"

"Are you sure you want to do this, honey?" asked Margaret. "You know Durwood."

"Somebody give me a ride and I'll go and get it, and drive it down here myself!"

"I'll give you a ride, Luther," said Liz.

"Okay, then! Let's go!"

Chapter 104

THE KEYS, LUTHER KNEW, were in the kitchen and fellowship hall area directly behind the sanctuary. He could go in through the back entrance of the fellowship hall and pick them off the wall without anyone noticing, if he was lucky. Then, he would make his getaway. That was the plan. But, the plan was not to be. The keys were not where they usually were. Gone!

Damn! The extra set was in the room right off the chancel, opposite the sacristy where the controls for the lights and speakers were located. It would be open, he thought, since the service was going on right now.

But, the side entrance was not open. Luther went into full gallop through the back yard toward the rectory to pick up his own keys to the church. But now, he remembered that his assistant, Mark, had used them last and would have placed them in Luther's desk drawer after using them. On that same key ring was the key to his office. He was locked out! It was almost as if the universe had planned for his arrival and had conspired to foil his plans.

He would not be defeated. He would make an appearance at the front entrance, he would walk up the side aisle, he would go in the control room and he would get those keys. Then he would march out! Who was going to stop him?

The entrance to Always Sunny does not go directly into the sanctuary but presents a small alcove before one turns right to go into the main sanctuary to be seated. The ushers were usually assembled there, especially during the sermon. This time he caught them playing a game of Hearts. They were obviously startled to see him walk through and up toward the front without stopping even to greet them.

Durwood followed him into the sanctuary to see where he was going. Luther didn't care. He marched up the side aisle, opened the door to the control room and snatched the keys. Then he turned around and began his victory march down the side aisle. He waved to a few of the parishioners who looked at him curiously. Some smiled and waved. Some were too stunned to do anything.

At the center aisle, he stopped and looked up at his substitute for the day, poor young Rev. Bennett, who was preaching the sincerest sermon he had delivered in his five years of service to the church. Luther smiled, waved, gave him a thumbs-up, and walked toward the alcove.

"Gentlemen!" he called out to the astonished ushers. "Good Sunday morning to you. From the looks of how the young Bennett fellow is getting wound up, you are going to have plenty of time to finish that game of Hearts!"

Then, he walked out the front door, took two steps down from the entrance, turned right across the parking lot, walked toward the bus, and fired it up. He may as well have been starting up a drag racer so high was his adrenalin and so great was the thrill. He turned the bus to the left out of the parking lot and past the front entrance where Durwood stood, stunned and with a horrified look on his face.

By the time he arrived, at the police station, he felt like a juvenile delinquent who had stolen a car and had begun to realize the eventual consequences would outweigh the thrill. Still, it was worth it and it would be worth it in the years to come. Just the memory would restore his soul again and again.

As he walked in, Hope asked, "Any problems getting the bus, Luther?"

"Nope! None at all."

Chapter 105

DOC BAILEY WOULD ALLOW family members at the boat dock to greet their loved ones. Ruth was as lukewarm with Doc's decision as she had been with his sudden release of Roy from the hospital.

"Once they've had a few minutes, though, I think they should be taken to the triage tent immediately," she said.

"No objections, Ruth."

Stewart watched from the Widow's Walk of the lighthouse, as the Always Sunny bus came into view and parked beside the ambulance that stood at the ready for Joe, when he came off the boat. Ruth was there and Doc Bailey too, to attend Joe, along with three or four other white-coated uniforms from the hospital. Carmelita's squad car was there, it's lights flashing.

He watched as crew from the tugboat unhooked the fragile vessel and guided it into harbor. Medics from the hospital made their way quickly onto the boat to remove Joe and get him in the ambulance. He heard a chopper in the distance. The medical helicopter was landing on the hill between the Pilsner Mansion and Pilsner Point. Now, the medics were moving Joe into the ambulance and backing out of the harbor area, making their way to the top of Pilsner Hill in order to meet Life Flight.

Suddenly, Stewart knew his time in the tower was over. Everyone was safe, now. He was no longer needed here. He felt a deep need to join the life that was happening below him and all around him.

He began the difficult descent from the Widow's Walk. Soon, his feet were planted firmly on the ground and he was moving with energy that he had not felt since he left the plains of Nebraska's expansive wheat fields and pastures, where a boy could run forever.

Approaching the bus, he asked, "I'm wondering, will there be room for me?"

"Why I am sure there will be," said Doc Bailey. "Why don't you just stand outside the door of the bus and help those on board who may need some assistance. And Stewart?"

"Yes?"

"Good to have you with us!"

"Good to be here!" he said.

As he walked up the church bus stairs, he looked around for a seat. Three people invited him to come and sit by them. He chose the closest seat, waving thanks to the others.

"Father, your cassock could do with a good ironing!" teased Magdalena, who had come down to see Rock and was now cuddling with him.

"A good washing, too, I would say! Mrs. McCarthy will very well take care of that, you may be assured," he said with an exaggerated rolling of the eyes. "She may not let me back in the rectory in this condition."

"Let's sing the song, Father!" said Johnny Watson. "It's what saved us on the seas!"

After getting everybody on the same note by singing a sustained "Leeeuw!" Father and Meriwether led them again in the Safety Harbor song. Tears rolled freely from many eyes as they looked around and saw the familiar streets and buildings that they called home. They were home again, in Safety Harbor.

Chapter 106

"HELLO, OLD FRIEND!" SAID Joe, his eyes twinkling in the midst of a fevered face.

"Hello to you!" said Doc. "We've been worried about you. We are so glad you are back. We're going to get you some good care and we'll get this thing turned around!"

"Yes, we will!" said Ruth. "My daughter so wants to see you. She has been dreaming of you, talking all about you!"

"Ah yes! Little Therese! I have seen her too, in my dreams and visions."

"You have a high temperature, Joe. You have no small amount of infection and we're going to have to get you to the hospital, fast."

"I understand, Doc. Thanks for all you are doing!"

The ambulance now proceeded up the hill and the bus followed.

When The Assistant saw the ambulance, he could feel the knot in his stomach tighten. It was nearly the time for the confrontation. Plan B. What he had not counted on was that the bus that followed the ambulance, kept falling further and further behind with every tenth of a mile. This would challenge his plan, but it was still possible. After the ambulance and the bus had turned into the park, the squad car joined them from the rear, all of them ascending the hill together. When they were out of sight, he started up the engine.

Then, he said to his maybe-there, maybe-not-there traveling companion, "Here we go, Bates! Keep your fingers crossed! Oh, that's right! You don't have any fingers! Wish me luck, Batesy. Oh, you don't have to, if you'd rather not. I know you probably don't feel very good toward me or anything like that. But, in the end, I did you a favor, Bates, by removing you from your miserable lonely life. You should be thanking me, Bates, but people like you never do. So, I've grown not to expect any gratitude.

"You have drawn a lottery card in life that puts you right in the middle of the whole battle between Bread from Stone Headquarters and Gemma, along with their presiding elder, one Joe Magnus. If we can kill him, we can prevent Gemma from going forward with their war of attrition, taking one city, one territory, one tiny little town like yours and claiming it for the expanding gates of light that are popping up throughout the world.

"We can't have that, Bates! Headquarters has had its way far too long. People have long forgotten what it's like to live in the light. They call dimness light, because their ability to take in the light has diminished with every generation that goes its own way.

"So, what you and I are doing today is going to be either the beginning of my ascent into glory at Headquarters or it'll be my end. Thanks for going with me, Bates. Oh, that's right! You don't have any choice, do you?"

He moved up the hill and saw that the ambulance was approaching the helicopter.

The guests gathered at Pilsner House were pressing up against the fence, straining to get a look at Joe. Some broke through but Marshall, Carmelita, and Jens held them back. They saw Joe whisper something to the paramedic and saw the attendant shake her head. Doc Bailey approached, involved himself in the situation, and Sally was not surprised to see him reverse the decision of the paramedic. A roar went through the crowd now as the ambulance attendants brought Joe close to the fence and adjusted the bed to a sitting position.

He asked to be moved even closer. Then, he raised his hands to quiet the crowd.

"You know that, when I have been with you, I have taught you to be humble and to make the last, first, and the first, last. You know that I have taught you to remember the poor, not to patronize them, but to learn from them the wisdom that comes in hardship and suffering.

"You have passed many tests and you have experienced many trials and sufferings. You will see many more sorrows and troubles in this life. Be in good spirits, always. You have become a gate of light in this world, a haven of peace, a place of blessing, where all who come here will sense, somehow, that they can do better, that they can change, that they are redeemable. Those who have been hurt by others will have their wounds healed, just by being in your presence. They will go too and be healers in the world. Keep the light shining at Joe's Fine Dine-ing!"

With that comment, he made a nod to Johnny Watson and smiled. Johnny grinned broadly through his tears and waved.

"I will see you soon, Johnny."

Then he said to all, "Keep the light shining in your hearts. I must leave you for a while now, but I will return to you; and when I do, I know that I will find you all living out your lives with humility and happiness. You are a Gate of Light. You are a Door to Heaven."

With that, he raised both hands in blessing. There was a roar of approval from the crowd, clapping and weeping, and even dancing and singing, as Joe was placed back in a reclining position in his bed and was pushed toward the helicopter he would soon board.

The moment was now, The Assistant decided.

Suddenly, there was the racing of an engine, the screeching of wheels. The crowd watched in horror as the Car of Doom made its way toward the helicopter with clear and evil intent. The Assistant began his three hundred and sixty degree clockwise and then counter clockwise turning as it moved forward toward the helicopter, making the evil transport into a moving and gyrating weapon.

Ecstasy transformed into horror as everyone present stood by, helplessly watching a potentially great tragedy in slow motion. The wheels from Hell reached the helicopter as it ascended and grazed the landing legs, knocking it into a near tailspin. But, at the last moment, it righted itself and rose inches above The Assistant and his weapon of death and began its ascent into the sky.

The crowd cheered.

The car had gained momentum and could not stop in time. It was clearly headed toward Pilsner Point. The people watched silently now, hypnotized by the spectacle.

The Assistant made a hard right. A loud gasp came from the crowd the gyrating car managed to pull itself, just in time, from the edge of the cliff, spinning its wheels and taking off with great speed, across the hill. It continued on the service road, down through the park, pursuing the helicopter.

Some followed the action, taking a short cut through the front yard and down to the edge of Pacific Coast Highway. The Assistant crossed the road and pursued the helicopter to where Joe's stood on Newman Street. He maneuvered the car directly under the helicopter and was preparing to shoot it down, when suddenly, it was filled with a flash of incredible light.

A figure appeared on the outside of the helicopter. Those who followed the action down to Joe's back yard said that, at that moment, the woman and her child appeared under the large tree in the back yard of Joes, by the side of the road. The figure on the helicopter drew a sword.

"Go back to the Devil, you son of Satan. Be gone. You shall not overcome the light. Go back to darkness where you belong!"

The Car of Doom began slowly to disappear, as if melting into the earth. At the last moment, before it began to disappear completely from view, as if from the very grave itself, a human figure came up through the earth, ejected from the car like a disturbed spirit from the grave. He was slimy and wet, as if he had been swallowed, and then vomited up by a great fish.

It was Stanley Ewing Bates.

Chapter 107

BEFORE FATHER WENT TO bed, Mrs. McCarthy made him his favorite meal of fish and chips, topped off by chocolate cake and ice cream. He hadn't had much appetite today at the banquet. It had all been a bit of a blur since they had landed in Safety Harbor.

Even with the troubles and challenges, and yes, the tragedy they had all experienced in Wendell losing his life at sea, he felt that there was meaning and purpose to it all, even in Wendell's death, and he sensed that others felt that way, too. They were all their best selves then. They not only tolerated but they laughed at one another's eccentricities that are experienced as irritations within time and space. They were vulnerable, and others respected that vulnerability.

He envied Rock and Nate who had gotten so close to the light. He thought he might have given up his temporal sight permanently, if he could just have looked into the glorious light on Gemma. Now, here he was, back in his own bed and now he wondered if it had all been real. Did it really happen? Or, was it all a dream? Is there is a place out of time and space where all is well? They had walked only on the edge of Gemma, the transition between earth and the "world to come," as the Nicene Creed would have it.

They had found Joe. What were the chances of that happening on its own without some intervention? The boat was literally driven into the island by some unseen Power and they were escorted away by some unseen Benevolence who saw them through danger and darkness. Their chances for making it home were zero without it.

He realized that he felt homesick for Gemma, even though he had only been allowed on its golden shores and no farther. Everything here seemed chaotic and random by comparison.

He was sick and tired of Mrs. McCarthy telling him what a priest should and shouldn't do. Just now, at dinner, she had told him that she thought he had no business running off on a boat at his age and with his corpulence;

and besides all that, he had work to do here in his own parish. The Deacon had provided Communion this morning, but it wasn't Mass. She droned on and on about inconsequential things that had happened in the parish that might have turned out differently, had he been here.

He longed to have an understanding wife instead of a cranky know-it-all housekeeper who couldn't keep her nose in her own business. Somewhere, he reckoned, there was a woman who was cut out to be his other half, who was either lying in bed alone, as lonely as he was, or married unsatisfactorily to someone who did not fit her at all. Of course, it was all moot to him now, as his celibacy vow was a permanent one. If he ever violated it, his next move would be a drive to the Archdiocese, where he would turn in his credentials, and go right to the Cathedral for Confession.

Sleep finally came for the priest. Mrs. McCarthy looked in on him, shut off his light, and went to her quarters. She worried about her priest. Sometimes she thought he was too kind and vulnerable to be a man of God.

Chapter 108

Nate had lingered at Pilsner House with Buddy and Caitlin, who were playing tirelessly with Little Therese and Ben, the newly acquired dog from the trip to Gemma. The kids had begged Sally to stay, and she did, against her better judgment. Ruth was relaxing with a glass of wine. Luke and Ginny Dingell excused themselves about 8:30 PM and went home, but only after Nate had thanked them profusely for looking after the kids while he was gone.

"What was Gemma like, Nate?" asked Little Therese.

"There was so much light that you could see forever. There was water there. but you never got thirsty."

"Did you miss us, Daddy?"

"I missed you, but probably not in the way that you missed me. On Gemma, you knew that all was well everywhere, even though it doesn't always seem like it. None of you seemed very far away, even though we didn't know where we were. It's kind of hard to explain."

"That's how I wish I could miss you Daddy, when we're with Mommy!" said Caitlin. "Then, I could miss you without being sad. I could miss you and know that you are okay."

"I wish that, too, for all of us," said Nate.

"Hey Dad!" said Buddy, "Maybe we'll all live with you again someday!"

"We will all be together someday, Buddy. I don't know when and I don't know how, but I know that we will. I do."

"Hey! C'mon guys!" said Little Therese. "Ben wants to play!"

They went out on the expansive lawn beyond the patio. Little Therese was on her back and Ben was bounding around the yard in circles, coming back always to Little Therese, and landing lightly on her stomach. Buddy and Caitlin pursued him while he ran.

Behind them, the sun was setting over Safety Harbor.

Chapter 109

THE NEXT DAY, JOHNNY Watson found himself walking the streets of Safety Harbor without a particular purpose. He was alone again, naturally, he thought. In order to shake off the melancholy, he decided to walk up to Harbor High, where his best memories had been left behind when he graduated in 1973. Thinking it wouldn't be likely that the front door was unlocked, he tried it anyway and found that it was indeed, open.

He walked in cautiously. He saw no one. The sounds and voices of yesteryear played themselves out in the caverns of his mind when was an athlete, when he was a favorite.

He slipped into the gymnasium. He could hear the crowd roar.

"One more basket, Johnny! That's all we need!"

He remembered how he had rescued the team at the state tournament with a three-point shot in the last two seconds. He could still hear the "swoosh" of basketball and basket as they came together. They were state champions that year, and he was the hero. He had done it here at home, too, a couple of other times. He was good at faking out the defense, and moving quickly.

Each day, when school was out, as he walked away from his life there, he felt smaller and more insignificant. Finally, when he reached his parents' home, he joined the marginalized of the town who were poor, uneducated, unnoticed, and mostly penniless.

That's why he liked school so much. He was his true self here in this building. He had never felt that again until this trip, when he went to Gemma. When he was on the island and the *Joe Boat*, there were no drunks or sober people. There were no educated or uneducated, no super religious elite who looked down on you, but only people who were honest and open.

"Johnny! That you?" It was a familiar voice. He turned and saw that it was his first love, Elaine. Everybody called her Laney. She moved to Safety Harbor when she was in Eighth Grade and for two years they were inseparable.

"Laney!" he said. "It can't be you!"

"But it is, Johnny! It is!"

"But Laney, you died in that awful automobile crash. People said you burned up. They never would let me see you again."

"I had to leave you then, but I watched over you after that for quite a while. I was proud that you did so well in high school."

"Oh, truth be told, I missed you every day after that," he said. "I'd have done a lot better with you by my side."

"Oh, we'd have probably broken up or if we'd gotten married we may have gotten divorced. I probably couldn't have put up with the bottle, Johnny."

He winced.

"No, it's better that I am a memory alive within you and we can walk together occasionally, just like old times, "she said.

"Is it better? Is it really?"

"I don't know," she said, "but it's the way it is."

"Maybe I can go with you!"

"Maybe. If I reach my hand out and you want to go. It's up to you."

"Does this mean I can be with you just like old times?"

"Yes, we'll be together, except it'll be even better."

"I don't know how that can be."

"You sort of have to be there."

"Can you take me there?"

"If you want to go."

"Yes, I want to go. I want to go and to be with you always."

She reached out her hand.

"Let's go, then," she said.

The next day, early morning walkers found Johnny on the front steps of the high school. Doc Bailey would say later that he had died of natural causes. His right arm was extended and his hand flexed, fingers open, as if he were holding the hand of another.

Chapter 110

IT WOULD TAKE A week for Safety Harbor to memorialize and to bury its dead.

A wake for Wendell was held on Tuesday night at the Parish Hall of Our Lady. Memorial Mass was celebrated in the sanctuary on Wednesday. The place was packed with overflow, outside on the lawn, in front of the church. A speaker system had to be borrowed from the City of Safety Harbor for those who were left outside. All the chairs from Always Sunny and the Country Club were placed in the front yard of Our Lady. Father Callaghan presided. The Auxiliary Bishop from Portland was in attendance to recognize the faithful service and generosity of Wendell and Irene to the Archdiocese.

Johnny Watson's service was delayed until Friday when Bates had recovered enough to perform his duties as Funeral Director. It was held at Always Sunny, with Luther presiding. People said he looked tired, strained even, as he performed the service. They would have had no idea of the tremendous battle he had fought with the powers-that-be at Always Sunny, as his nemesis, Mrs. Olmay, had said it, "in order to bring the remains of that drunk into the House of the Lord!" The funeral itself was like a wake, with laughter, tears, and song that was both planned and spontaneous. They buried Johnny in the Watson family plot overlooking the ocean, just north of Pilsner Hill.

It wasn't until Saturday that Keith's funeral was held in the Country Club. Stewart and Meriwether presided. It was a no-frills, secular affair, but it was just as Keith would have wanted it. The Harbor Barber Shop Singers and the Celtic Dancers performed. Meriwether read some of her own original poems and Stewart gave the eulogy. A small chamber orchestra she had formed, closed out the service.

"Enough death!" said Father Frank to himself after leaving Keith's service. "Enough!"

He did not go to the internment, but went back to the rectory and began to work on Sunday's homily. He wanted to do something normal. When the Church failed in everything else, there was the comfort of the cycle of the year that sustained him.

Katye had organized a visitation schedule for Joe. Father Frank and Doc Bailey went in every day to see their old friend. A week after the *Joe Boat* had landed in Safety Harbor, Doc was getting concerned that Joe was not improving enough to leave ICU.

"His infection isn't responding to the antibiotics as well as I'd like to see, and from what I can tell, his doctors in the hospital feel the same way. There is something we are missing. But, I'll be darned if I can think of one more test, one more thing to look at, Frank."

As Father was pouring over the story of the Prodigal Son for the coming Sunday homily, Mrs. McCarthy knocked on his door.

"Yes?" he called out.

She opened the door slowly.

"It's Doc Bailey, Father. He's on the rectory land line."

"Everything okay?"

"I don't think so!"

"Oh dear!"

"Frank, I've gotten a call from the hospital. They've called me in for a courtesy consultation and I'm calling to see if you want to go along."

"Of course, Doc!"

"What's going on."

"It's not good."

Upon reaching the hospital, Father was visibly alarmed at what he saw. He stole a look at Doc after he had examined him, and saw a very grim face. Joe was no longer breathing on his own and he seemed smaller. Father stood back while the physicians attending Joe spoke with Doc. He was getting impatient after about fifteen minutes, and was about to inject himself into the conversation when Doc motioned him over.

"He's not getting better, Frank. His wounds are mortal. He's not going to make it. He's not going to be with us much longer. If we took the respirator off, he would go now. I know of no family he has that can give that assent and I am inclined to allow the treatment to continue until the end."

"We never know when a miracle may occur," said Father. "I brought along the necessaries for the anointing of the sick."

Then to himself he said, "Whether we live or die . . ."

" . . . we are the Lord's, Father. We are the Lord's"

One of the nurses had overheard him and finished the verse for him. They looked at one another and nodded.

Before the anointing, he went to the chapel for a few moments of silence and centering. He was fighting back his own emotions and disbelief that this was happening. Hadn't they just rescued Joe in an adventure so amazing that very few would believe their reports? Now, he was dying. What had all of this been about, anyway? Wendell had been sacrificed, and for what? He, himself was reaching a point in his health that, to go out on such a mission, was not good judgment. It could have been he instead of Wendell. Maybe it should have been.

He was deep in meditation when a familiar voice called out to him from the chapel door.

"Why wasn't I informed of this?" It was Lou and behind him followed Hope and Liz.

"How did you hear?"

"Mrs. McCarthy told me."

"How is he, Doc?"

"Not good, Hope, not good at all. We think he'll die within the hour."

"Oh my God!" said Liz.

"I'm going back to administer the Sacrament of the Sick."

"You mean like, Last Rites?" asked Lou.

"Yes, that's what I mean."

"May I be there?"

"I don't see why not."

The room had been dim earlier, but now, as he entered again, there was a soft glow in the room.

"What right have I to anoint you, Joe? It is more fitting that you bless me!"

He looked to the opposite corner and saw Miguel. Not far from him were the woman and her child. She was in prayer while the child sat quietly and somberly at her knee.

He looked around for a moment to see if he could discern whether or not Doc or Lou saw them. He could not tell.

Suddenly, he said to Lou, "Tell your family to come in. It is fitting that they be here."

Liz drew a sharp breath when she entered the room. Father knew now that it wasn't Joe's emaciated appearance any longer that struck her. He now appeared to be living beyond his sickness, beyond his own limitations. His presence was large in the room and not that of a sick and dying man.

The crowd was growing. Little Therese and Ruth entered the room, followed by Roy and Jens. Father blinked. Could that be that Johnny Watson with a young woman he did not know, over there by the woman and her child? Stewart and Katye, Susanna and Sally. They were all there, it seemed, and right in the midst of the growing crowd, were Wendell and Irene.

Father wiped his eyes with the sleeve of his cassock. He watched in wonder as the living and the dead from Safety Harbor assembled in the room. The room was full, but it was not crowded, no matter how many people entered. It was as if the walls expanded with each new person. Father counted Jeremy, Hobe and Georgette, Georgia, Carla, and Mrs. Saugus too. Magdalena and Rock, along with others from the Unsettlement, joined the growing crowd. Ruby and three others from the Siletz Tribe came. Carmelita brought along her rosary and knelt at the foot of Joe's bed.

"Life has triumphed over death!" Mrs. Saugus shouted it out. "Death is defeated!"

Father then administered the Sacrament of the Sick to Joe. It was at that moment that the witnesses later said they saw light emanate from Joe's face, and he breathed his last.

There was an absolute and unearthly silence in the room as the woman and her child moved toward Joe's body. Weeping, she kissed Joe's forehead. Then, the child followed her example as she held him close to Joe. Finally, she pulled the sheet up over Joe's face. Not a soul moved for a full twenty minutes after the medical people had come and pronounced him dead.

Slowly, one by one and two by two, all of those who had entered the room, departed, some to their homes in Safety Harbor, and some to their eternal home.

"I will stay and make arrangements with Frank and Doc," Lou said to Hope. "You all go on home and I'll be along later."

Chapter 111

FATHER FRANK AND LOU walked Liz and Hope to the car. They were surprised, when they went back to the room, to find Joe's body was all ready gone.

"Nurse! Where is the body?" asked Doc. "We haven't even called the funeral home yet!"

"Let me check!"

After ten minutes of anxious waiting, Doc Bailey went to the nurse's station.

"If you can't tell us where Joe's body is, maybe you ought to see if the hospital morgue took it for autopsy."

"We're checking, sir." She looked nervous.

"Sounds to me as if you've checked on it already and haven't found it."

"We haven't found him yet, sir. Still looking."

"Let me talk to the hospitalist. Is he in the house?"

"I can have her paged."

"Good. Do it!"

By now, Doc was becoming more than annoyed.

"This is outrageous. A dead man doesn't just get up and walk away from his death bed!"

The nurse did not respond.

A few moments later, Lou and Father watched as Doc had an intense and serious conversation with the hospitalist. He left her abruptly and returned to Lou and Father.

"They can't find the body."

"Oh, hell and damn!" Lou exclaimed.

"Mother o' God!" shouted Father, pointing toward the corner of the room. "His hospital clothes are folded up right over there!"

Chapter 112

A WEEK HAD PASSED, and then two, since Safety Harbor had learned that Joe had died and that his body was missing. In spite of all that had happened, life was returning to its natural rhythms. So much loss had been sustained. So many hopes had been dashed. They had trusted that Joe's return would restore their town to the way it was before all of this happened, to the way that it could be once more. To think of Joe's corpse being stolen, which is what the Portland police surmised, was too much. There was something so undignified about his death and Wendell's too, with one having his body stolen before it was even cold and the other being lost in the deep ocean and swallowed up by fish.

Each day many passed by the New Joe's Fine Dine-ing, shining with a blazing glory of light. But, it was as if their eyes had been blinded and they could not see it at all.

It was a surprise, then, for the people of Safety Harbor, on Sunday morning, eight weeks into their shock and grief, to see a large *Grand Opening* sign out front of the diner. The doors were open and the smells of delicious breakfast permeated the air, all the way down to the civic center buildings.

The first to check it out were Magdalena, Rock, and Daniel. They had been passing by on their way to Portland for supplies and noticed the doors open for business. Magdalena called Sally and Susanna. The word spread until a hundred or more people were standing outside the front door which was gently barricaded with a ribbon.

"Oh, it's Joe, all right," said Rock to those who questioned the veracity of his story that Joe was back. "Take a long whiff of that food. Nobody cooks like that. Not even Georgia, if I say so myself."

Joe walked forward until all could see him. A murmur went through the crowd, then silence, and then, finally, a great rush of applause and cheers. There was a press of people against the door. Joe raised his hands as if to hold them back.

Sally was embarrassed and chagrined that she had not followed what Joe wanted her to do. She had just figured all was lost, so what's the difference? Now, she stood with the crowd in disbelief. She still wasn't sure what she was seeing.

"Ah! Who shall cut this ribbon?" he asked, with a half-smile that seemed to hold a secret about to be revealed. Once again, everyone stood in stunned silence.

"Sally, you're going to be in charge here. Come up and cut the ribbon with me!"

Tears flowed from her eyes.

"I'm sorry, Joe!" she said, and doubled over in his arms sobbing. "I am not worthy to be entrusted with such a vocation."

"Dry your tears, daughter. You have work to do."

Joe handed her the scissors and then placed his hands over hers and together they cut the ribbon.

"Children, come and eat and drink at Joe's Fine Dine-ing!" he called out. "No one is excluded. Come! It's on me today. No money? Don't need it. No one pays. The best tables are appointed for those who are small, and weak, and need protection. The strongest and most able among you will be served out back at some picnic tables. My temporary staff from Gemma will be taking care of all of your dining needs while we all share fellowship with one another.

Joe came by and had conversation with all who dined in his presence. No one was left out and no one felt cheated. Everyone had the time they needed with Joe. No one dared ask him wasn't he dead, or was he some ghost.

After they had all finished breakfast, he called them outside into the back yard, where he sat down on the top of a picnic table, and began to address them.

"I have come from far away, and yet, I am closer to you than is your nearest friend or relative. I have come to be your neighbor and to show you what it is to love your neighbor, to show you what pure love is like, to show you that even the least among you has greatness, that the most dissolute among you possesses great dignity.

"When I was among you before, I did not make a big fuss about myself. Often, you did not see me. I was too busy slinging burgers or making up some special order. A lot of you got pretty demanding!"

He smiled mischievously. At once the crowd melted and began to clap.

"My greatest hope when you came through the doors of the diner was that you would be bathed in the light of love, and that, when you left, you would take some of this love with you to share with those who live in the shadowy corners of fear and despair.

"There are few places we can find that light on this earth. When the human heart is born into this world and is never introduced to the light, the human heart grows dark and greedy. Sometimes, it takes a lifetime to come to the light and sometimes humans miss it altogether."

"Joe, can I hold your hand?" called out ever-precocious Little Therese.

"Of course you may, Little Therese. May I hold yours?"

"Oh yes, of course, Joe! Can Buddy and Caitlan come along with me?"

"Oh yes!" said Joe. "Let all the children come here at once!"

He held up a little girl and then a little boy, and he said, "When you grow weary and tired of thinking a thing through, ask a little child for wisdom. When any of you have trouble with forgiving, ask one of these little ones how they do it. After all, they are so recently arrived from the heart of the Holy One, that they have not yet have forgotten the answer."

"Stay with us forever, Joe!" a voice called out from the back of the crowd.

"I cannot stay with you for long," he said. "I have gates of light to establish throughout the world."

"How did we get to be a gate of light, Joe?" asked Hope.

"The vast majority of the world is not ready to receive the light in its fullness. In general, people are not ready to unite heaven with earth. But, there are a few people who are. We look for enough of those souls in one place, and, if we can find them, we live with them for a while to assure ourselves that what seems to be true is true."

"And what's true about us, Joe?" It was the Mayor Schofield.

"Your people are kind and good, Your Honor. At least there is more kindness and goodness about them, than not. You are humble, too. You are a little city and you are proud of who you are but you do not promote yourselves as more than you are.

"The spiritual leaders here are real. They do not live one way and tell people to do something else. They are not ambitious or lustful for power or money or position.

"When we came to you, we did not come to boast or to brag, although I could have brought from Gemma the most beautiful of building materials and built a gleaming city on a hill. Instead, I came to you running a simple and unpretentious diner where hospitality is the watchword and everyone who comes in stands on level ground."

"What is Gemma, Joe?" called out Carla

"When you talk about the beginnings of the world, you time-dwellers have your stories which came earlier in human history. Now, you have some ideas about how things may have happened according to what you call science. Both story and science are one. There is no division. They are simply different ways, human ways, of looking into the prism of mystery. However, in the vast creation and beyond, there are many things that you will never understand with the human mind.

"The intellect is limited. You must comprehend the mysteries with the human heart because the heart is wise and understands all things. It is the heart that tells and hears stories and understand what is beyond them. I will tell you a story, so that you may understand with the heart, as far as you can as mortal beings, what Gemma is.

"There was a great war in Heaven when the angel Lucifer sought to become the ruler of the celestial realm. In his great resistance to God, he came too close to the boundary between eternity and time and he fell from the heavens to this planet where, at this time, he roams at will, seeking to shore up his domain.

"Many angels followed him in that great rebellion, falling out of favor with God and choosing their fate with Lucifer. In that great battle in heaven, just as the hosts of Satan were about to fall over the precipice into the mortal realm, there was an attempt to loot heaven and take something with them.

"One such clever, thieving angel managed to loosen one of the great pearls from Heaven's gate. It proved to be too heavy and it fell from his grip and down into the oceans of earth, where it became an island, a harbinger of heaven, arriving just before the hosts of Lucifer descended upon the earth. God sent heavenly beings to populate Gemma, to protect it from becoming an outpost occupied by the forces of evil. Now, it has become a strategic island in the battle for the world between the forces of God and Satan, a moveable island, going where it is needed most in the cosmic struggle.

"The world never quite became Satan's realm, because that pearl, small in heaven, but great on the earth, has continued to be a source of heavenly eternal light on a planet that has only the sun to light it, a created light, which will slowly fade away to darkness and into the great Void.

"When I came here to Safety Harbor, I brought with me a chip of the gem of the Isle of Gemma, to leave with you in order to make you bearers of the light of heaven. From now on, the light will shine in the small huts and the humble hearts of people who are ready and willing to give their lives [and give your lives, you must] to being the light bearers in Safety Harbor and wherever you travel in this life."

A voice called out from the crowd, "How do we do this Joe? How can we be light bearers?"

"Just be yourselves, your best selves, and don't accept less. Don't try to be more than you are. Don't allow others to diminish you and make you less than you are. Don't look at someone else and envy their opportunities, or their good upbringing, or their education, or their wealth. You were sent here to be you and if you are not you, who will be?

"Now I must go!"

There was an audible groan from the crowd. Men began to cry along with women and children.

"I have to go away so that you can carry out the destinies of your lives. If I stayed here, you would all just depend upon me to do the work as Keeper of the Light. But if I go you may live as you are called to live."

"You are the light, Joe!" someone called out.

"Before you go, dear Joe, will you tell us why you left us so abruptly, without giving us any notice? We felt so abandoned, so worried, so bereft." It was Susanna.

"The dark forces of this world are in a desperate battle for the very soul of this world. The very base of operations, that has occupied this world for so many centuries, is focused on the destruction of Gemma. They don't want any more gates of light in this world, since every one that is founded establishes a foothold for heaven and hurries along the union between heaven and earth.

"I was called away from you in an emergency. The dark powers were about to attack Gemma with a great onslaught. I had only time to write the note that said, "Carry on" and hope you knew what it meant. Then, I had to head for Gemma.

"The great attack was intercepted. I was not alone. Miguel, the woman, and her child were present for the great battle. Gabriel and Ariel were there too, along with a whole host of others who came from far off spheres to defend Gemma.

"I was wounded in battle, and my friends who helped me fight, watched over me until you arrived, until they knew that I was safe in your hands. So, you see, you had a great part in this battle and you will have a great part again as you become an operable and functional Gate of Light."

"But why was it necessary for us to rescue you?" asked Nate. "Couldn't the holy beings on Gemma have come down to the shore and taken you with them?"

"Oh yes, absolutely," said Joe. "But that was not the plan. You see, human beings are meant to seek and to find. The search for me was the thing. That's why I waited for you to come for me there on the shores of Gemma. Those wounds could have been cured in an instant, but I chose to keep them so that you could come on the journey and find me. In a way, it has saved you. It was not only your finding me, but the adventure you had on the way that has cured your souls."

"Did you die, Joe?" asked Buddy.

He smiled, wistfully.

"Some say I died. It depends upon your perspective. From the point of view of this planet, I died. But from the viewpoint of Gemma and other heavenly places, you can't die, because there is no death. The last enemy that will be destroyed on this planet is death."

"Did someone steal your body, Joe?" It was another of the children who sat on his knee.

"No, no one stole my body. I, myself, stole away when no one was looking!"

"Why didn't you let us see, or somebody see you, when you went away?"

"Because, no mortal can see the fullness of that radiant light that was present in that room at that moment, and live.

"Now, I must go, children!"

"Oh, no!" said many in the crowd. "Stay just a while longer."

"I cannot," he said. "I must visit many more towns and villages and cities of the world as I seek out those who seek the light."

"We will follow you wherever you go!" called out Rock.

By now, Joe was walking across the highway and intended to go up toward the park with the great crowd following him.

He turned and called out, "Follow me right here where you are, Rock! I need Magdalena and you to establish an outpost at the Unsettlement!"

Then, he stopped again just on the other of the highway that went through town.

"Remember now, dear children, the whole thing is about love. Don't make it difficult with creeds formed in the midst of human quarrels and by establishing places of worship that make silly claims about being the only ones. Better that you meet in a diner that welcomes everyone than in a house of worship, set aside for only a few.

"It's not about right religion, my dear ones. Set your hearts at ease about that. It's about the good path. It's about the light. Many who cling to a failed past will disagree and you will be insulted and slandered and cursed because you follow me. They may even call you enemies of God. Do not be discouraged. Remember that I can see you even when you cannot see me. I am always with you. There is nothing you go through that I do not go through with you."

Realizing he was really leaving, Sally panicked. She had not even received special instructions from Joe as to how he wanted them to get started.

"Joe! Joe! How do we get started at the new diner?"

"All will be made plain to you."

Then, he turned to go. They followed him up through the park, through the great Pilsner House and onto the patio. Somehow, he had managed to slip by them. When they all reached the fence that separated Pilsner House from the Point, they watched and were amazed.

The Great Light that is Gemma, that had rested up to the north and west off the coast, came close, and began to rise and to make its way over the crest of Pilsner Point. Joe began his ascent into the light and the light descended upon him, until they had become one.

And he was received out of their sight.

Chapter 113

MOST OF THE CROWD wandered away, but some gathered back at Joe's.

"Did we really see him?" asked Mrs. Saugus.

"Here! In the kitchen!" squealed Caitlin. "Gifts for everyone!"

"Oh! Here's a note for Roy and there's one for Jens too!" exclaimed Katye.

They both opened their notes at the same time. "Look in the storage shed. Love, Joe."

The two ran like young boys as if it were Christmas morning. There, awaiting them were two gleaming motorcycles.

"Wow!" said Jens. Roy was silent.

"Don't you like yours?" asked Jens.

"Oh, yeah, I like it fine. I was just reading the note attached."

"What does it say?"

"It has been said, 'Give, and gifts will be given to you.' You were willing to give your life as I have given mine. Now, receive these gifts from me."

"Fire 'em up boys!" called out Carmelita.

"Yes!" Marshall said. "Let's see what they can do!"

Stewart, meanwhile, had intended to retreat to his place one more time in the lighthouse, in order to ponder what all of this meant, when he noticed an unfamiliar vessel harbored where the *Far from Home* had always been moored.

It was a beautiful boat, a new one. He could not resist climbing aboard and walking through it and admire it. There was a card attached to some flowers with Nate's name on it.

He called Katye immediately. "Tell Nate to get down here! The others, too!"

"What, Stewart? Where?"

"Down at the harbor."

"What is it?"

"You'll have to see it for yourselves."

"Okay. We'll be right there."

Buddy and Sally were the first to arrive with Nate not far from them!

"Look, Daddy! Look!" exclaimed Buddy. "A new boat!"

Nate's eyes were welled up with tears.

He took out the card and read it aloud to all.

"To Nate, for your heroism, for your unselfish valor in leading the search and rescue. Joe"

"I'm speechless!" he said.

"Well, you could give us permission to come aboard, Cap'n!" said Meriwether.

He beckoned a welcome. Soon, the boat was filled with laughter, chatter, and the good humor of a people who were beginning anew. He announced to all that the new boat would be christened tomorrow.

"At eleven o'clock in the morning!" called out Mrs. Saugus on her bullhorn.

"If you say so, Mrs. Saugus! If you say so!" said Nate.

That evening, a fresh wind blew over Safety Harbor. The clean smell of salt water and the pungent odor of coastal flowers and juniper berries wafted over the little inlet nestled in the crook of the wooded foothills, facing the harbor. A misty rain set in for an hour, and the smell of the good earth was added to all of the other elements of the sensuous shower of nature.

If one didn't know that Safety Harbor was in the world one could be forgiven for thinking in this moment, at this time, it was a little bit of heaven.

Chapter 114

KATYE HAD CALLED MRS. Glover, who quickly assembled what she could of the community choir for the occasion of the christening of Nate's boat. Father Callaghan wore his finest and most elaborate cassock, and sported a black broad-brimmed hat, that no one had seen him wear before. Rock and Magdalena arrived, looking forever like perfect models from another time, what with Rock's retro bell bottoms and Magdalena's black square-neck, bell-sleeved dress.

In the bright morning sun, Katye's gorgeous caramel skin adorned by a tailored dress and low heels next to Stewart in his cream-colored slacks, casual light blue shirt, and panama hat, made them both a delightful couple and a perfect contrast.

Sally smiled broadly as they walked by. She reached out and took Katye's hand. "You two look gorgeous!"

"Yes! 'Old things have passed away . . . new things have come'!" beamed Katye.

Jeremy and his new boyfriend, Samir, were there too, holding hands courageously, boldly, without shame, for all to see. Georgia came and brought her daughter and grandchildren. Ruby was there with a representative crowd from the Siletz Tribal Council, all in full celebrative dress.

Mr. Bates came, too! He had been to Confession and had agreed with Father to turn himself in to Carmelita right after the christening. Margaret was still back in Salem at the special session. Luther came, dressed casually in blue jeans and a short- sleeved summer shirt. He looked very relaxed, as if he had just made a big decision.

"Good grief! There is Clyde Beamer himself!" said Luther, who knew from first-hand experience that the neighbor next to Joe's had not been friendly toward the enterprise. "Maybe he's coming over to the other side!"

"We can hope so!" said Susanna, who had not slipped in unnoticed, in what turned out to be her mother's dress from the old island of Argostoli.

Meriwether was greeted with enthusiastic applause. Mayor Lou and Hope were escorted into the boat by Liz, where an exuberant welcome awaited them.

Nate invited all of those who were not already on the boat that had gone with him on the search for Joe to come aboard for the christening.

Mrs. Glover led the community choir in the Navy Hymn, and then, a poem by Alfred Lord Tennyson was read by Mrs. McCarthy, who shocked and dazzled them all with her oral interpretation skills.

Nate's speech came next. A man of few words, he kept it short. Afterward, he noticed his kids were close by, and he called Buddy and Caitlin up to be with him. They were not about to be separated from their friend, Little Therese, who followed them on board with Ruth.

The boat was getting crowded now, and the Mayor said that it would be best to get on with the christening.

Nate didn't know anything about christening a boat, but Hope had been through it with their boat, at Lou's insistence. She had volunteered to help Nate with the ceremony. She came forward now, and called Nate to her side. There was a silence as she raised the champagne bottle and invited Nate to place his rough hand over her small and smooth one. Would it break the first time? Everyone hoped so. Everyone wanted this to go smoothly.

Completely unable to allow Hope a solitary moment in the sun, Lou began to speak as she raised the bottle, but she raised her hand to his lips, silencing him.

"We christen thee *My Safety Harbor Home!*"

When the people heard the new name of Nate's boat, there was an immediate roar of approval. Mrs. Glover raised her baton and led them in the song that Joe had taught them to sing.

> *Sweet vision, Bless my eyes!*
> *Land upon the western skies!*
> *Constant stars, I bid you rise*
> *Over Safety Harbor.*
>
> *Home, home! At last, becalmed!*
> *Far behind us screams the storm.*
> *Tattered canvas waves like arms*
> *Greeting Safety Harbor.*
>
> *From the windows of the tower, where the beacon burns,*
> *Faithful friends at ev'ry hour watch for my return.*

Yours the calm and peace I claim
When I face the waves and rain,
When the sea road calls my name
Out from Safety Harbor

Thru the fearsome, foaming gale,
When no spirit fills my sail,
I shall see, tho' sight may fail,
lights of Safety Harbor.

Where from windows of the tower
bright the beacon burns.
Faithful friends at ev'ry hour watch for my return.

Heart's haven, mem'ry's shore,
Call me thru the tempest's roar,
Where the pilgrim sails no more,
home to Safety Harbor.
Where the pilgrim sails no more,
home to Safety Harbor.

There was clapping and cheering. After it subsided, it was followed by the sound of quiet crying, and the glistening of tears in the eyes all around.

The rest of the day was given to free rides in *My Safety Harbor Home.* Nate took anyone who wanted to sail on her, on a scenic ride around the inlet around Safety Harbor.

That night, as the last ride was coming into harbor, Lou stood, staring out through the picture window in his office, overlooking the coastline. The sun was setting into the sea and the ocean was turning to a glassy gold. He wondered if it could be the same kind of gold hue that the Gemma travelers had described. He couldn't imagine it much better than this.

Tomorrow morning, he would get up early, drive to Portland, get his radiation treatment, stop for coffee on NW 23rd, and drive on home. He did not know what his future held. But tonight, just tonight, he was home with all the good people of Safety Harbor. He thought for a moment he could hear Wendell's voice say, "Don't waste any time, Lou, not any time at all."

He looked around and no one was there. Must have been his imagination, he thought.

The carpet beneath him was getting damp. If anyone had been around, he would have said something like, "Damned allergies." But tonight, as he watched the magic of the yellow globe of fire sinking into the sea, he accepted the emotion that welled up within him, the falling tears of gratitude, the beauty of his life, the beauty of life itself, and the blessing of living in Safety Harbor.

He took one last look out the window at the glorious scene before him.

"Thanks," he said. "Thanks very much!"

Epilogue
One Year Later

It HAD BEEN AN exceptional day in Safety Harbor, with the renewal of vows for Lou and Hope on their twenty-fifth wedding anniversary. The Safety Harbor Police provided an escort from the church to Pilsner House where the reception was being held. After Lou and Hope had taken their place on the dance floor for the first dance between bride and groom, many others of varying skills and gracefulness joined them.

There would be photos at sunset on the beach below Pilsner Point. Everyone had to remain in their formal dress throughout the afternoon and into the evening. Later, the photo session seemed to go on and on, and just as they seemed they would never end, finally, photographers Jeremy and Samir said, "That's a wrap!"

Just then, a stranger, who was running along the beach, came by the group, stopped, and handed them a bottle.

"This washed up on the shore back there a few feet. I'm gonna run about another five miles. I'm wondering if you maybe could recycle this when you get back up the hill."

"Sure!" said Lou. "No problem."

He handed it off to Marshall.

"Here, hold onto this, will you?" asked Lou casually.

"Sure will, Mayor."

As they walked back up the steep incline toward Pilsner Point, Marshall caught up with him.

"Sir, something is in this bottle. It looks as if it might be a message or something."

"Let's take a look at it when we have more light."

"Sure."

When they reached the crowd, who had been watching from Pilsner Point, Lou got caught up in conversation. After half an hour, Marshall came to remind him. Father Frank and Meriwether had been standing together, taking in the last rays of the sun. Both wondered if there was Gemma-looking light coming from the ocean to the north and east again, but neither mentioned it to the other.

"Sir," said Marshall to Father, "I have this bottle that some runner gave us down there at the beach, but I can't get the Mayor's attention long enough for him to open it. It looks like one of those old-fashioned message bottles that people used to throw out to sea to see where they would end up."

"Let's see it, Deputy," said Meriwether. After inspecting it, she said, "I think you are right."

"Let's go over the patio and open it up for all to see," said Father. "It can't be less than nothing."

Those left at the party, by now, were few. Those who were still there, watched as Father struggled to open it.

"Here! Give it to me!" said Jens.

He took out a small pocketknife and pried the cork loose from the bottle and then pulled it out. He handed it back to Father who, in turn, took the small piece of paper out of the bottle.

"Here, Father! Let me read it!" said Little Therese.

"But, Little Therese," Father almost said, but held his tongue.

"You're blind, Little Therese! You can't read!" said her Uncle Roy. He got the familiar slap on the shoulder from his sister.

"But, but, she can't!" he was heard to say quietly to Ruth.

"I can read it! Sure, I can read it, Uncle Roy! I can read it because it came from that light that I could see that was once with us.

"Okay everybody! Here's what it says:

So very proud of you all!

Carry on!

Love,

Joe

There was a stunned silence. Ruth nodded to Father to look over her shoulder and confirm. He read it, afterward looking over at Ruth, wide-eyed, and nodded his head.

"And so, we shall!" said Little Therese.

"Yes," said Father. "We shall carry on, dear Joe."

All who were present on that beautiful magical summer night remember that the light from the northwest that was Gemma, shone once again brightly over Safety Harbor, as it did the night that Joe was taken up into his glory.

"I wanna say somethin' Momma," said Little Therese. "Hold me up so I can see everybody."

Then she spoke.

"In Joe's light," said Little Therese to all assembled, "I see that all of us are souls shining with beauty!"

That night, it was said that the faces of all of the people gathered there, could be seen by one another as reflections of unfathomable loveliness. And all could perceive, in that moment, in their own way, that, within every man's, every woman's, and every child's heart, lies the gate to the heavenly Isle of Gemma, a place of unspoiled and luminous mystery, wonder, awe, and delight, where there is no night, or time, or disease, or death, and the very air we breathe is Love itself.